D1141031

ALL OUR TODAYS

by the same author

ROGER MOORE
DUDLEY
THE RADIO COMPANION

ALL OUR TODAYS

Forty Years of Radio 4's 'Today' programme

Paul Donovan

JONATHAN CAPE
LONDON

617643

MORAY COUNCIL
Department of Technical
& Leisure Services

791.447

Published by Jonathan Cape 1997

2 4 6 8 10 9 7 5 3 1

Copyright © Paul Donovan 1997
Paul Donovan has asserted his right under the Copyright, Designs
and Patents Act 1988 to be identified as the author of this work

This book is sold subject to the condition that it shall not
by way of trade or otherwise, be lent, resold, hired out,
or otherwise circulated without the publisher's prior
consent in any form or binding or cover other than that
in which it is published and without a similar condition
including this condition being imposed on the
subsequent purchaser

First published in Great Britain in 1997 by
Jonathan Cape
Random House, 20 Vauxhall Bridge Road,
London SW1V 2SA

Random House Australia (Pty) Limited
20 Alfred Street, Milsons Point, Sydney,
New South Wales 2061, Australia

Random House New Zealand Limited
18 Poland Road, Glenfield,
Auckland 10, New Zealand

Random House South Africa (Pty) Limited
Endulini, 5A Jubilee Road, Parktown 2193, South Africa

Random House UK Limited Reg. No. 954009

A CIP catalogue record for this book
is available from the British Library

ISBN 0-224-04358-7

Papers used by Random House UK Limited are natural,
recyclable products made from wood grown in sustainable forests.
The manufacturing processes conform to the environmental
regulations of the country of origin.

Typeset by Deltatype Ltd, Birkenhead, Merseyside
Printed and bound in Great Britain by
Mackays of Chatham PLC

For Mary

Contents

Illustrations

Isa Benzie, the first editor of *Today*
Janet Quigley, joint midwife of the programme
An editorial meeting in the early days
Alan Skempton, the first presenter
The studio clock
Jack de Manio
Stephen Bonarjee at an editorial meeting
John Timpson and Robert Robinson
Josephine Robinson and Pat Timpson
John Timpson and Brian Redhead
Libby Purves
Peter Hobday
John Timpson, Sue MacGregor, Peter Hobday and Brian Redhead
John Humphrys and Brian Redhead
Brian Mawhinney 'smears' the *Today* team: a *Times* cartoon
James Naughtie, Sue MacGregor, Peter Hobday, Anna Ford and
  John Humphrys

The copyright in all the photographs in this book, apart from one, resides in the BBC, and the publishers wish to thank the BBC for permission to reproduce them. The exception is the picture of Alan Skempton and we are grateful to his daughter Tamsin for making it available. The cartoon by Peter Brookes is copyright © Peter Brookes/*The Times*.

Preface and Acknowledgements

The 'Today' programme, as one member of the then Cabinet described it to me when researching this book, has become a sort of organ of our constitution. As such it cannot escape scrutiny on an important occasion like its fortieth anniversary. There are different ways of looking at national institutions, and the approach taken here is not that of Margaret Thatcher (one of the programme's most avid listeners, incidentally), who according to Sir Julian Critchley was unable to see an institution without hitting it with her handbag. But neither is it fan-worship. I have sought a middle course between adulation and denigration, while the aim, quite straightforwardly, has been to trace the evolution of the programme from its days as a morning cappuccino and to sketch the main figures, events and controversies along the way. Some of that may be seen as a birthday celebration, but I have also ventilated at some length several of the sharp criticisms made of 'Today' in recent years.

The status of the book could be described as authorised, though not official. The idea for it came from me, not the BBC, and of course the BBC is not publishing it. I enjoyed complete access to the Corporation's Sound Archives at Broadcasting House, to its Written Archives Centre at Caversham and to all the programme's presenters and personnel, and considerable (though not unlimited) access to some internal papers. No restrictions of any sort were placed on what I could observe when I spent twenty-four hours with the programme earlier this year, on a day of my choice, and the only requests made not to report what I had seen or heard were in respect of a few dismissive comments made about colleagues in the building.

This co-operation, however, was not handed over on a plate: I am paying the BBC for it, and for the right to reproduce copyright material such as interviews and items that have already been broadcast on the programme. Roger Mosey, editor of the programme from 1993 to 1996, read the manuscript for factual accuracy and I am grateful to him for his eagle-eyed attention, just as I am for his co-operation over a long period; but he made no request for the withdrawal or modification of any of the more sensitive passages (presenters' pay and rivalry, for example), nor would any such request have been granted. Any errors, of course, are my sole responsibility.

I am indebted to all those in the BBC who were kind enough to give me interviews: Sir Christopher Bland, Chairman; John Birt, Director-General; Tony Hall, Chief Executive of BBC News; Roger Mosey, now Controller of Radio 5 Live; Jenny Abramsky, editor of 'Today' in 1986–7 and now Head of Continuous News; the presenters Anna Ford, John Humphrys, Sue MacGregor and James Naughtie; the sports reporter Garry Richardson; and John Allen, Executive Editor of BBC Radio News. Others in the Corporation who assisted were Colin Browne, Director of Corporate Affairs; Helen Cleary, Chief Press Officer in Corporate Affairs; Kathy Relf, the researcher on 'Today' who tracked down so many tapes; Richard Peel, Eileen Phillips, Justin Everard, Natasha Samarawickrema and Louise Brimmell in marketing and publicity; and Bobbie Mitchell of the BBC Photograph Library. At the Written Archives Centre, Jacquie Kavanagh and her deputy, Gwyniver Jones, and all their colleagues, gave me much patient and detailed assistance. So too did the librarians of Times Newspapers and the British Library Newspaper Library at Colindale.

Former programme staff and presenters who shared their recollections included Mike Chaney; Roger Gale, now an MP and chairman of the Conservative backbench media committee; Peter Hobday; Alistair Osborne; Libby Purves and Nigel Rees. I must single out for special thanks John Timpson, who also entrusted me with all his original scrapbooks covering his sixteen-year span on the programme and which contained no fewer than 1,076 pages.

This book could not have been done, either, without the generous amount of time given me by politicians. The following, with the positions they held at the time the interviews took place, were kind enough to see me: Lord Archer of Weston-super-Mare; David Blunkett, MP (Shadow Education Secretary); Virginia Bottomley, MP (National Heritage Secretary); Kenneth Clarke, MP (Chancellor of the Exchequer); Tom Clarke, MP (Shadow spokesman for disabled people's rights); Robin Cook, MP (Shadow Foreign Secretary); Donald Dewar, MP (Shadow Chief Whip); Stephen Dorrell, MP (Health Secretary); John Gummer, MP (Environment Secretary); Peter Lilley, MP (Social Security Secretary); Lord Mackay of Clashfern (Lord Chancellor); Austin Mitchell, MP; William Waldegrave, MP (Chief Secretary to the Treasury); Dafydd Wigley, MP (President of Plaid Cymru); Nicholas Winterton, MP (Chairman of the Parliamentary Media Group) and Sir George Young, MP (Transport Secretary).

I would like to thank the following people who talked to me about 'Thought for the Day': Rabbi Lionel Blue; the Rt Reverend Tom Butler, Bishop of Leicester; Charles Handy; the Rt Reverend Richard Harries, Bishop of Oxford; and the Rt Reverend Jim Thompson, Bishop of Bath and Wells. The Venerable George Austin, Archdeacon of York, and Dr Colin Morris, both provided substantial written recollections. I must also express my gratitude to the Reverend Ernest Rea, the BBC's Head of Religious Broadcasting, and to David Coomes, who, as Executive Editor of Factual Radio, Religion, is the slot's editor and producer. Anne Atkins has kindly allowed me to reproduce the whole of her controversial 'Thought for the Day' broadcast of October 1996.

There are in addition a number of people who do not fit into the above neat categories but who also provided assistance in various ways. In some cases it proved invaluable. I should like to mention Sir Robin Day; Frank Gillard; Professor Peter Hennessy; Lord Hurd, for his written insights; the Reverend Leslie Lewis, Brian Redhead's vicar at Rainow; Mary Morris of the Words agency in Acton, for her careful transcription of so many taped interviews; Abby Redhead, for giving me an interview about her late father and his time on 'Today'; Tamsin Skempton, for telling me about her late father Alan Skempton, the programme's first presenter in 1957; Professor John Taylor; and the journalist and public relations executive Eileen Wise, when she was at Conservative Central Office. I am most grateful to my agent, John Pawsey, for his encouragement, to Dan Franklin at Cape for his wise guidance and editorial polish, to Liz Cowen for her meticulous copy-editing, and above all to my wife, Hazel, without whose support this book would never have seen the light of day.

'Today' is the Trade Mark of the BBC

1

Nothing Too Long for People on the Move

So long has the 'Today' programme been with us, busily setting the agenda and dropping words in the nation's ear, that sometimes it is hard to imagine a period in which it was not there at all. And yet there was such a time: a land before Timpson, a Humphrys-free zone, a barely recognisable landscape consisting of one solitary black-and-white television channel and a grand total of three radio stations. No local radio, no commercial radio, no Radio 1, no Radio 5 Live, no ITV, no Channel 4 and certainly no cable and satellite channels. No satellite had yet left Earth.

The Third Programme was not on the air until the evening. The Light Programme (still on long-wave) opened at 6.45 am with pips and the Shipping Forecast before commencing the day with a stately offering of 'Morning Music', performed by respectable ensembles such as the BBC West of England Light Orchestra. The Home Service began at 6.25 am with a 'Market Report for Farmers'. It carried ten-minute news bulletins at 7 am and 8 am, preceded by a 'weather forecast for land areas', plus the religious homily 'Lift Up Your Hearts' at 7.50 am; but the majority of its output before 9 am was the same light music that went out on the Light Programme.

In this dim and distant past, people listened on wireless sets made with valves: no transistor radios had yet been made in Britain. The *Radio Times*, still under the giant shadow of the BBC's founding father John Reith, started its week on a Sunday rather than a Saturday, in deference to a dominant Christian faith. Unbelievable as it sounds now, there was even a ban on discussing on the air topics which might be debated in the House of Commons over the following fortnight. In this Jurassic Age of journalism there was no such thing as a colour supplement and *The Times* had not yet sunk to carrying news on the front page. Compared to today's digital communicopia, it all seems an impossibly and indeed inconceivably long time ago.

Distant as it is, however, it was not before Robin Day had joined the BBC; and in July 1955 – two months before ITV came on air – he sent the following memo to his then boss, John Green. So prophetic did this turn out to be, and so acute was its grasp of radio's fundamental advantages, that it is worth quoting verbatim:

FROM: Robin Day, Talks Department, 207 B.H.
SUBJECT: NEW MORNING TALKS PROGRAMME 7th July, 1955
TO: Chief Assistant, Talks (Mr. Green)
Copy to: Talks Organiser, Home Service, Miss Rowley Mr. Bonarjee Mr. Macdonald Miss Barker Mr. Smith Mr. Taplin

I have already discussed with Mr. Bonarjee, Mr. Macdonald and others the idea of an early morning Topical Talks programme. Mr. Bonarjee has asked me to put it forward in writing together with my reasons.

In the morning Sound Radio has the public all to itself, and listening figures for that time of day are impressive. The 8 a.m. News has an average audience of 13% [about 6.5 million]. Can we not offer this large and constant audience something intelligent and lively by way of Topical Talks, something more than the present succession of routine items, service talks and light music?

I therefore suggest a new daily morning programme under such a title as 'Morning Review'. This would be a fifteen minute Topical Talks miscellany going on the air sometime between 8 and 9 a.m. Presumably this would be on the only Service offered to listeners in the early morning, the Home Service. 'Morning Review' would give intelligent, pithy comment and description of the sort found on the feature-page of newspapers and in the more serious diary column. There would be three or four short talks (with the occasional interview). These would be conversationally linked, without scripted presentation, by a skilled broadcaster who would give the programme form and personality without intruding his own opinions.

The following are some of the things that might be included:

a) Comment on some event due to occur that day or week of the kind that, though interesting, would normally be crowded out of 'At Home and Abroad' or 'Topic'.

b) Foot-notes to the news (historical, personal, legal, humorous, etc.), similar to items in Pendennis or in the *Manchester Guardian* London letter. *Not* gossip, or tittle-tattle.

c) Comment on a notable new book published that morning.

d) Comment on last night's new play, film or other event in art or entertainment.

e) Comment on a sporting event or news item.

f) A 'Topic' on an event occurring late the previous evening or some important news released overnight and heard for the first time on the morning bulletin.

I realise that this proposal may mean radical departures from existing practice with regard to the BBC's morning output. It also raises difficult questions of staffing and organisation. But the magnitude of these obstacles is surely the measure of the opportunity open to Sound Radio at this time of day. As Television advances Sound Radio will find more and more that early morning programmes command its big audiences. These are now its big opportunity. This is shown by listening figures for the various news bulletins. In the last three years the average audience for the 7 a.m., 8 a.m. and 9 a.m. bulletins has remained constant at 10%, 13% and 9% respectively, yet for the evening bulletins over the same three years the figures have dropped from 18% to 15% (6 p.m.), 13% to 12% (7 p.m.), 10% to 7% (9 p.m.), 14% to 9% (10 p.m.). This trend will obviously be intensified. Another point is that there is a steadily increasing audience to car radios. This element must be particularly large first thing in the morning when people are motoring to work. These people cannot read while driving. Why should we not offer them comment and description that the rail or 'bus traveller can read in his newspaper?

As regards contributors, 'Morning Review' could draw on the younger journalists and broadcasters, anxious to make their names, who ought not to mind getting up for an early programme easily fitted in before their day's work. There would be a regular body of contributors like the Topic Panel. But unlike the Topic Panel their suggestions for talks and notes would be continuously invited so that the producer would be able all the time to select from ideas offered to him as well as to use his own.

I envisage 'Morning Review' as a *daily* programme (Monday to Friday). This is because its principal feature will be its up-to-date quality – overnight comment on things which people may not have

3

yet read about in their morning papers. The programme would thus have the unique advantage of giving a large number of people the *first* available comment on some late-night news item or a new book or play. As regards length, I do not see much point in doing less than a fifteen minute programme. This would mean that those responsible would have to get up early anyway and would cause the maximum dislocation of manpower for the minimum result on the air.

I think this could prove an imaginative enterprise for Sound Radio at what is now a bleak and barren time of day. If something is launched on these lines, I am sure that before long we would look back to the present morning programmes with the same incredulity with which we now regard pre-1939 days when there was nothing, not even a news bulletin, until mid-morning.

(Signed) ROBIN DAY

On the face of it there may seem little connection between today's 'Today', two-and-a-half hours long and an influential flagship programme containing daily interviews with Cabinet ministers, and Day's proposed 'Morning Review', fifteen minutes long and a lightly informative miscellany of news and features. In fact, the early 'Today' was strikingly similar to Robin Day's suggestion in that revolutionary memo. It went out Monday to Friday, as he proposed; blended news and features and contained reviews and comment, as he proposed; and the items were linked by one skilled broadcaster. Indeed, it has always blended news and features and, as time went on, has made more and more use of material gathered overnight – thus beating the newspapers, as Day proposed. Initially the pro- gramme had two editions, at 7.15 am and 8.15 am, but the second consisted largely of a repeat of the first and each one ran for approximately twenty minutes, only a little longer than Day's suggested fifteen.

In addition, his assertion – on the eve of a vast expansion of television – that radio should concentrate its fire on the morning was uncannily perceptive, as too was his awareness of the audience on wheels. This latter point was picked up two years later by Lindsay Wellington, the BBC's Director of Sound Broadcasting, when he wrote about 'the increasing number of motorists using car radios'.[1] The number did indeed increase steadily over the coming years and decades, becoming one of the key components of the audience: official figures presented to the Radio Festival in Birmingham in

1994 showed that at 8.30 am nearly a quarter of all radio listening is in the car.

However, Day was a mere pipsqueak, a temporary talks producer aged thirty-one, and his masters considered he had ideas above his station. His memo, as he explains in volume two of his entertaining memoirs *Grand Inquisitor*,[2] fell on deaf ears. So a week later he wrote again and, again, it is worth quoting in full:

FROM: Robin Day, Talks Department, 207 B.H. 14th July, 1955
SUBJECT: NEW MORNING TALKS PROGRAMME: 'MORNING REVIEW'
TO: Mr. John Green, 327 B.H. Copy to: Stephen Bonarjee, 210 B.H.

May I back up my memo outlining the suggestion for an early morning topical talks miscellany? It may help if I give two examples of the character and content that I have in mind for the programme.

As I see it the items would be linked conversationally without scripts by some skilled and experienced broadcaster such as Franklin Engelmann or Michael Brooke.

I have taken two days at random within the last fortnight. In each case the programme would have consisted of three or four items from the five possibilities shown below.

Friday, July 1st

1) Comment on Wimbledon.
2) A note on Evelyn Waugh's newly published novel 'Officers and Gentlemen'.
3) A note on the Russian oarsmen at Henley, their style etc., their lack of boat.
4) A note on the new film 'Rhapsody' starring Elizabeth Taylor.
5) A background comment on the announcement made the previous afternoon about talks on Cyprus.

Thursday, July 7th
1) Note on prospects for third Test Match beginning that morning.
2) Comment on the position in the case of Mrs Sispera.
3) A note on the Royal Agricultural Show.
4) Background comment on previous day's announcement of a round-table conference on Malta.

5) Note on the previous's announcement about prospects for colour television.

(Signed) ROBIN DAY

Day's idea was put forward at a monthly departmental meeting attended by numerous Home Service producers. It was greeted with incredulity: nobody imagined that there could be any demand for such a service, therefore there was no point in starting it. Day agreed that there was no demand, any more than there had been for a morning news bulletin in 1939, when there was nothing on national radio until the religious service at 10.15 am. But few could imagine life without the 8 am news bulletin now. It was the job of broadcasters to offer choices, he suggested. Few agreed with him. Sir Robin told me, 'They thought I was a nutcase at that meeting.'[3]

Day left the BBC a few weeks later to join the fledgling ITN as one of its first newsreaders, in time for the birth of ITV in September 1955. He does not claim to be the inventor of 'Today' but his memos do show him to have been one of its main progenitors. Indeed, as the papers at the BBC's Written Archives Centre in Caversham show, two of the people to whom he copied his first memo, Elisabeth Rowley and Stephen Bonarjee, actually went on to run the programme in the late 1950s and 1960s and found themselves refining some of the ideas he had put forward in the summer of 1955.

If Day's idea lingered in the minds of his ex-colleagues, of more direct impact in the creation of 'Today' were the conclusions of the Marriott Committee, a working party which sat between 1956 and 1957 to examine the future of sound broadcasting. It was chaired by Richard D'Arcy Marriott, Chief Assistant to the BBC's Director of Sound Broadcasting, Lindsay Wellington. Frank Gillard, the former war correspondent who had been with General Montgomery and witnessed the signing of the Armistice in 1945, was one of its members. He was head of the BBC's West region, where he created 'Any Questions?' Gillard recalls, 'It was ten years since the BBC had established the Third Programme, so it had been a decade of Light, Home and Third. In addition, ITV had started the previous year. So the BBC wanted to take stock and consider the future.'[4]

The Committee recommended that morning listeners to the Home Service be offered an alternative to the light music of the Light, and that this alternative should be topical and centre on talks. The name initially mooted for it, Gillard recalls, was 'Morning Miscellany'. But this new venture had to be built around the immovable and sacrosanct presence of the two ten-minute news bulletins, at 7 am and 8 am, each of which was followed by a five-minute trail entitled 'Programme Parade'. The idea took hold early on that the new programme should thus have two editions. The first would follow the first news bulletin, and therefore start at 7.15 am. The other would follow the second at 8.15 am. The first would have to end no later than 7.50 am before the equally sacrosanct 'Lift Up Your Hearts', and the second would have to end no later than the 9 am News.

The departmental responsibility for the new venture lay with Talks (then a department in its own right) and in particular with one of its two Chief Assistants, Janet Quigley, who had taken over from John Green. (The other person who held the title of Chief Assistant at the same time was P.H. Newby, later to become Controller of the Third Programme.) It was clear that Quigley wanted the new venture to reflect the personality of her own department with News being kept at arm's length, offering ideas on a regular basis which Talks could accept or reject as it saw fit. But there was at least a tenuous and daily relationship between the two, and that confluence was of key importance in shaping the personality of the programme as a mixture of news and features, serious and light, woe and joy, which it remains to this day.

The first meeting about the new venture was held in Room 616 at Broadcasting House at 4 pm on Wednesday 15 May 1957. It was convened by Quigley and attended by a group of her producers. The opening paragraph of the minutes (marked 'CONFIDENTIAL' and dated 17 May 1957) was a lucid summary of what the BBC had in mind:

> Miss Quigley explained that the proposed Morning Miscellany would be the Home Service alternative to almost continuous music on Light Programme between 7 and 9 a.m. It was intended to be a morning magazine containing such ingredients as the already existing practical talks (or their equivalent), an appropriate news element, e.g. Press review, morning 'topic', note on last night's first night, etc., topical O.B.s [Outside Broadcasts] and a certain amount of music S.B.'d [simultaneously broadcast] from Light.

The last paragraph of the same minutes suggests that Quigley, though herself calling the new venture 'Morning Miscellany', was open to alternatives. Among those put forward by her colleagues were 'This Morning' and 'Morning Magazine'. (Robin Day's 'Morning Review' was conspicuous by its absence: it would have been impolitic to endorse a title proposed by one who had defected to the opposition.)

There were ten people present at this meeting, of whom one was listed as 'Miss Benzie'. Without her, the subsequent history of the 'Today' programme might have been very different: it might not even have had that name. Isa Benzie is an unjustly neglected name in postwar radio history. She it was who first came up with the name 'Today', she it was who first stressed that the programme had to have a national flavour. She appears to have been the first of its immediate creators to realise the importance of Fleet Street and of television, and seems to have been the most alert to the need for a top-quality personality presenter.

Born in Glasgow, she had joined Reith's fledgling BBC after graduating from Lady Margaret Hall, Oxford, in 1926. Within ten years she had become foreign director (a long extinct post) and was one of the first two women to become a head of department at the Corporation. But in 1937, on marrying John Morley, one of the earliest television producers, she had been forced to resign because of an internal rule which forbade husband and wife both being employed by the BBC. When that ban was lifted after the Second World War she returned to Broadcasting House as a talks producer. All this was recorded in her brief obituaries in *The Times* and the *Independent* in 1988, but her role in the evolution of the 'Today' programme has never until now been acknowledged.

In a memo which stands out among the hundreds at Caversham for its informality and lack of jargon, Isa Benzie seized the initiative. A week after that departmental meeting, she wrote:

FROM: Miss Benzie
SUBJECT: 'MORNING MISCELLANY'
TO: Miss Quigley 22.5.57

I should like the job of organising this programme. I can't see how it goes on the air without an organiser. It wants lots and lots of fresh ideas, and, as you know, I feel convinced about its requiring sincere co-operation with BBC Regions and a strictly-held non-Metropolitan outlook. I also feel very strongly that this is an opportunity to be seized by those who don't believe – and never have – that there is something second-best or second-rate about taking things in by the ear . . . I am also sure that we should go all out for first-hand talks broadcasting and try really hard to grasp that person-to-person communication [she underlined the word 'communication'] can offer something which journalists talking on someone else's subject never can. The audience, to me, is typically on its feet [and she underlined 'on its feet'], dressing, making packed lunches, cooking and eating – certainly before I am. Gentlemen still able to enjoy leisurely breakfast at table may be catered for – if necessary – later on. Everything must exploit the virtues of brevity [another underlining]. Let's make this programme fairly full of things we've never done before. Let's give it character and do a splendid new service.

(Signed) I.D. BENZIE

Janet Quigley's reply to this stirring plea, remarkable for its enthusiasm and down-to-earth understanding of life in an ordinary household, is not recorded. Subsequent papers show clearly, however, that Isa Benzie got the job. By that summer she had also come up with the title. In a document dated 26 July 1957 and headed 'Morning Miscellany: Points for further consideration', Janet Quigley wrote:

We have looked upon 'Morning Miscellany' as a working title and must now find something less literary. 'Up in the morning early', 'Background to shaving', and 'Listen while you dress' have all been suggested, but I think Miss Benzie's simple 'To-day' with some such sub-title as 'A radio magazine for early listeners' is the best so far.

Quigley also emphasised the key role the presenter would have. And, demonstrating the female genius for consensus rather than conflict, outlined how the programme would benefit from News and Talks co-operating:

The more we consider the programme the more important the choice of a suitable compère becomes. Suggestions wanted urgently. A man rather than a woman I think. Money spent on the compère [whose fee, she says later in the same paper, 'could not be less than from 10 to 15 guineas per time'] will be well spent as in addition to presenting and linking the items he should broadcast some of them himself and interpose topical hints and tips . . . the sample programmes have been planned on the assumption that this is a Talks operation into which certain items provided by News Department are slotted. Ideally, however, and if this morning programme is to explore to the full the opportunities which it offers, I think it should grow out of a close liaison between the two departments.

The key word there was 'ideally'. The liaison was never very close, and the records bear witness to Isa Benzie's periodic frustration about News Division not meeting her requests for particular pieces but giving them instead to 'Radio Newsreel' on the Light Programme.

Posterity does not record what suggestions, if any, Janet Quigley received. At this stage there seems to have been no mention at all of Jack de Manio, indelibly associated with the early years of 'Today' but not in fact its presenter until 1958. Instead, by August, another name had emerged:

amongst other queries, she [Isa Benzie] has asked me to find out whether there is any possibility of Mr. Skempton being available to act as compère. He compèred the two dummy runs, and was apparently exactly right for the job. It would be splendid if he could do this as I know we are all agreed a good compère would make a lot of difference and it would be a relief to have to look no further.

Alan Skempton, a Home Service announcer, was duly hired. Today he is an almost totally forgotten figure (even Lord Briggs, the BBC's official historian, gives him only one passing reference in his Olympian five-volume *The History of Broadcasting in the United Kingdom*), but in his time he was a familiar and respected voice for hundreds of thousands of wireless listeners. Born in 1922 in Teddington, the son of a science teacher, he was of that generation for whom involvement in the Second World War was the central and defining event in their lives. This was either (as with his fellow announcers Colin Doran and Robin Holmes) from having fought in the war before joining the Corporation, or (as with Frank Gillard and Richard Dimbleby) from having worked as war correspondents for the BBC and continuing with the BBC afterwards, or (as with Robert Dougall, Wynford Vaughan-Thomas and Alvar Lidell) from having already been with the BBC in the 1930s but been released to join the armed services, or to work as a war correspondent alongside them, during 1939–45.

Skempton belonged to the first group. He joined the RAF in 1941 and trained as a fighter pilot, partly in Florida and Alabama on the Arnold Scheme with the US Army Air Corps. After the war he read English at Magdalen College, Oxford, before joining the BBC in 1949. 'As a radio announcer Alan became one of the most familiar voices of the BBC,' wrote a former wartime and BBC colleague, Eric Simms. 'There was a rounded euphony and rich colour to his speaking voice which was unmistakable.'[5] For a period Skempton was a BBC Television newsreader and liaison officer, but cancer robbed him of life at the tragically early age of forty-seven.

During the summer of 1957 memos went back and forth within Broadcasting House, trying to iron out technical matters such as studio facilities, dubbing, opt-outs and the cost of circuits. It was Benzie, again, who concentrated the minds of colleagues on a precise start date for 'Today', which until then had been left vague:

> Would you very kindly bear in mind on my behalf, that I should not wish to start later than Week 44, 28th October. That is to say I should deplore starting on a date that was already in November – it is too wintry and too much in the shadow of Christmas.
>
> And moreover we should miss some items available in Week 44 but not in Week 45, which I should like to cover. Namely and for example:- (1) The Cambridgeshire, an important event in the flat racing season ... (2) Hallowe'en: lovely games England doesn't know about and a peg for an elegant survey, in the domestic field, of the apple situation. (3) The first of the month (1st November) 'Released Today' (monthly *only*) issue of, by all gramophone companies, all non-pop music. (3a) 1st November also of course All Saints' Day.[6]

Again, her proposal was accepted. It was agreed to launch 'Today' (or 'To-Day' as she quaintly insisted on spelling it) on the first weekday of Week 44, which was Monday, 28 October.

At the beginning of October, with less than a month to go, Isa Benzie was briskly setting out her shopping list of requirements, among which – with remarkable farsightedness – was radio's brash new rival:

> I need the loan of a suitable television staff set. It is, I know, NOT

good sense – in fact, it makes no sense at all to be responsible for a topical programme if not adequately informed about the greatest domestic innovation of our time. BBC and ITV programmes, topical and documentary programmes particularly, I must become reasonably familiar with. This must be done in the evenings – reluctant homework! I prefer to think that I shall ask you to take away the set after, say, three months (one will have a firm idea of the pattern of the artists of the time and a sound existing knowledge is not difficult to keep fairly bright and shining): but in the meantime may I ask you to cause a set to come. In advance of installation I should like to discuss the size of screen and type of aerial, if I may . . .

Much the same important considerations mutatis mutandis apply to a V.H.F. receiving-set. My lack of knowledge of V.H.F. reception and studio technique in many of its branches is by now, for a programme producer, verging on the unjustifiable, even quite absurd. But of course one is not so paid so as to enable one to keep up with our technical progress! I shouldn't like to let on to the Press the day I meet them that I don't know the first thing about V.H.F. . . .'[7]

There being no subsequent mentions of either, one presumes that Isa Benzie got her television set and received instruction on Very High Frequency reception. The countdown to the opening programme had begun: some wanted to launch it with a splash, others to begin modestly. There was widespread acceptance of the need to get coverage in *Radio Times* (not always an easy matter for producers, even then) and to differentiate it from the similarly sounding television news programme 'Tonight'. Benzie thought it prudent to avoid detailed mention of shopping news and other programme ingredients in *Radio Times*, partly because 'some of them would look – to captious eyes in the press at least – frankly dull' and also because 'it does no harm to be a little mysterious'.[8]

The BBC's definitive document about the purpose and content of the programme was written the next day. Its author was H. Rooney Pelletier, the Controller, Programme Planning (Sound) and the recipient was the Director of Sound Broadcasting. Pelletier was a Canadian who had been Head of Quebec programmes for the Canadian Broadcasting Corporation in the late 1930s before becoming a CBC war reporter and joining the BBC. He set out in a detailed two-page document entitled NOTES ON 'TODAY' the details of the new venture:

'Today' goes on the air on the 28th of October in the Home Service and from then on regularly for five days in the week, that is, with the exception of Saturdays and Sundays. It will normally be broadcast between 7.15 and 7.35 a.m. and between 8.15 and 8.35 a.m.

The programme completes the first stages of a planning pattern designed to give the listener a true alternative before 9.0 a.m.: the Home Service being mainly spoken word and the Light Programme almost continuous light music plus time checks ...

'Today' is a collection of brief items, all of which can be said to have a topical interest for the average, intelligent reader of morning newspapers. It is seen as a logical 'follow-up' to the two news bulletins broadcast at 7.0 and 8.0 a.m. It will not, for the time being, embrace 'Programme Parade' (daily – 5 minutes at 7.10 and 8.10 a.m.) because it has been impossible to arrange this, so far, and still cater for the needed regional variations.

In compiling 'Today', the producer will constantly bear in mind the quickly changing audience and the fact that few people are able to concentrate for any length of time, at that time in the morning. The shifting needs of truly topical and up-to-the-minute broadcasting are self-evident.

For those reasons, Pelletier went on, items would not normally be longer than five minutes, and 'probably shorter in a majority of cases'. Some items would go out in each edition and thus be heard twice. He confirmed that Alan Skempton would present the programme each morning and that Isa Benzie would be the senior producer. She would draw her material from Talks Division, News Division ('BBC correspondents speaking from abroad are expected to be heard about three times a week'), Outside Broadcasts Department and the Regions.

He concluded by listing the items 'likely to find a place' on 'Today':

Notices of new theatrical, opera or cinema productions.
Various O.B.'s under the general heading 'Going to Work Today'.
Reviews of gramophone record releases (both serious and light).

Items about dress, fashion, cooking, shopping – and, if
    exceptional – weather.
Brief personal stories of the 'Truth to Tell' kind.
Previews of sporting events: cricket, racing, football.
Medical notes – usually suggested by items 'in the news'.
Notes on industrial developments – particularly in the
    field of consumer goods.
Foreign correspondents and material from News Talks
    Section of News Division (as noted above).
Possibly a 'daily quotation'.
Notes about significant anniversaries.

The final sentence, above his signature, was simply this:

The budget is a modest one – £200 per week.

Not a single mention, one notices, of politics. The other obvious
difference from the current 'Today' programme is the budget, which
is still a modest one – about £130,000 a week. Modest, that is,
compared with television, because that is about what it costs to make
two editions of 'Newsnight'.
    For the first year the programme followed this initial pattern,
going out in two twenty-minute editions at 7.15 and 8.15 am. The
first was followed by 'Morning Music' and 'Lift Up Your Hearts' at
7.50. The second was followed by more 'Morning Music' and, when
parliament was sitting, by 'Yesterday in Parliament' at 8.45 am. By
October 1959 each edition had grown to twenty-five minutes with a
new feature, 'Today's Papers', at 7.35 and 8.35 am. In 1963, the first
edition was extended to thirty minutes. By 1967 (by which time the
Radio Times had succumbed to secularism and was starting the week
on a Saturday), the first edition had grown to thirty-five minutes and
the second to thirty minutes. A Saturday edition of 'Today' was
added in April 1970: it was axed by Ian McIntyre, when he was
Controller of Radio 4, in 1976, but revived ten years later by Jenny
Abramsky. By October 1970, the two editions having now coalesced,
'Today' was starting at 7 am. By the time of the programme's
fifteenth birthday, in October 1972, that had moved to 6.50 am
(with Eileen Fowler's 'Keep Fit' opening the proceedings). This
changed to 6.45 am in 1973. Gradually the starting time was

becoming earlier. The present start time of 6.30 am was introduced in July 1978 and has not altered since.

Readers of the *Radio Times* had been alerted to the general outline of the new venture in September, but were not given details until the week it began. Ronald Lewin, Head of Home Service Planning, wrote an elegant little article in which he started off by stating what might seem to be the obvious – that at breakfast time there is a great deal of kerfuffle in the average household.

These early morning hours are certainly different, for most people, from all others in the day: at these times, too, many people are 'on the move' in one way or another, and have only time to listen briefly to the radio. Getting up, getting breakfast, getting off to work, getting the children off to school, getting the house straight again – this is the daily round for most of us at the times when 'Today' will be heard. And more people are quite literally 'on the move', in their cars, with the radio switched on.

A large number prefer, at this time of day, a regular service of continuous music, with news bulletins and time checks to keep them up to date and up to the minute. The Light Programme is now meeting this need. But many others, we believe, would rather listen to the sort of miscellany of views and news and interviews which will be the daily pattern of 'Today'. There will be nothing too long for 'people on the move'. The accent is on pace, on variety and informality.

Many old friends will be there, but we want to introduce you as well to new personalities and ideas. As usual, there will be tips on the best things to buy in the food markets, and if you are not feeling well enough for shopping, then the Doctor will be there to cope with such ills as Asian 'flu, rheumatism or whatever else may be bothering you. If your appetite needs stimulating you can hear from the experts how to make something different and delightful from those odds and ends in the larder ...

Last night's First Night or this morning's new book or record may be reviewed. Contributions will come in from the different regional centres of the BBC, and from our foreign correspondents throughout the world. There will of course be regular time checks as well.

From Monday to Friday, 'Today' will follow the 7 and 8 a.m. news bulletins and 'Programme Parade'. Each edition will run for some twenty minutes and, because everyone doesn't rise and get on the move at the same time, the second edition will usually contain some of the items broadcast in the first.

Lewin concluded his breakfast manifesto with a touch of the Arabian Nights:

I'm sure that all concerned with producing this new programme [was he really that sure?] have taken to heart the wise words of Omar Khayyam:

> What boots it to repeat
> How Time is slipping underneath our Feet?
> Unborn Tomorrow, and dead Yesterday,
> Why fret about them if Today be sweet?

Sadly, nothing from the first programme has been preserved in the BBC Sound Archives. Nor has a script. It must have been a strange brew, however, ranging as it did from Petula Clark to Verdi, Douglas Bader on air travel to Eamonn Andrews on boxing.

The billing in the *Radio Times* promised items on 'Briefing a pilot at London Airport', 'First Night at Liverpool: Robert Morley', 'Sale of Napoleon's letters' and 'Out Today: gramophone records' in the 7.15 am edition and 'Interview with a passenger flying to Scotland on business' (quite an undertaking in 1957) in the 8.15 am. Most of these appear to have gone out, if an internal report on the first edition written to Isa Benzie by one Anthony Thwaite is anything to go by.[9] Thwaite evidently regarded it as a classic curate's egg:

I listened to both editions, and under fairly typical conditions (i.e. the two children of the house were shrieking round the room and the coffee boiled over).

I thought the general effect was good: Alan Skempton linked the items genially and without straining (sometimes, indeed, I felt he was a little *too* relaxed and urbane), and gave the programme unity.

Thwaite's verdicts on individual items included these:

Both the pilot – and the passenger – interviews suffered from the fact that the people interviewed were not at all forthcoming, had little of interest to say, and therefore threw an immense weight on

Raymond Baxter, who had to jolly them along in the most obvious way. Perhaps a little preliminary fieldwork would find better material (more interesting people to interview) . . . The part of the Spitfire Fugue (the end, wasn't it?) was too abrupt and noisy; it didn't mix well with the equally noisy Spitfire sound-effect. It would have been better if the first 45 seconds of the Fugue had been used, as I originally suggested . . . Alan S. should have mentioned that William Walton wrote the music; he is, after all, one of the 3 leading British composers of today . . . Robt. Morley was excellent – the best thing in either edition. A pity this wasn't repeated in the 2nd edn . . .

Mary Drummond's talk was interesting, but her voice definitely soporific and/or irritating: a friend with whom I was having breakfast said, 'Good God, you'll be dead before you start if you use that kind of thing.' Brutal, but I could see what he meant . . . Both the News Talk and the Foreign Scene were interesting, and the placing of both items was right, I feel . . . The music in the programme worried me, but I don't quite know why. 'Aida' was all right . . . but the Pops seemed awkward, and not an intrinsic part of the programme. Perhaps this was just because they weren't very good (Petula Clark, in particular, was a terror: my listening-companion was unprintable about this) . . . Eamonn Andrews was good – he made people realise that boxing is (whether one likes it or not) a hard-headed commercial business, not just a sport, a fact which is too often slid round or gently ignored on the air, though not in the press.

Thus 'Today' was born. A chequered start, as media launches usually are. But its impact was felt within days, reflecting the fact that there had been simply nothing like it before. Within three weeks, ICI Paints Division had requested a copy of the script for an item on industrial films, and the National Pharmaceutical Union that of a doctor's talk which evidently provoked a spate of inquiries. The Actuality Unit at Bush House sent for the disc of a piece on Sherpa Tenzing, and the North American Service for that of an item about a Quorn huntsman (with hounds).

Other items in the first year included a report on Lord Mountbatten's presentation of the Silver Cod Trophy, awarded at the British Trawler Federation's dinner in Fishmongers Hall; sheepdog training; the advanced driving test; automation in public libraries; and the Baker Street lost-property office. Offerings from News (whose journalists then included Brian Bliss, Eric Stadlen and, a bit later, Andrew Boyle) included Barbara Hooper interviewing Spike Milligan on his reasons for going to Australia and Tom Salmon covering 'a candle-light auction of a five-acre field of cress at Chard, Somerset': frustratingly, Caversham reveals no more.

Even then, in a broadcasting era often characterised as stiff and formal, the BBC was emphasising the importance of the programme being *informal*, with items presented crisply and plainly. 'Listeners are almost certainly going about their early morning affairs with only one ear on the radio set,' wrote Rooney Pelletier to Janet Quigley in January 1958, in a two-page memo which sought to establish basic definitions and principles for future personnel. 'Clarity and total avoidance of muddle is, therefore, a prime requisite.' Shrewd, pertinent and timeless, Pelletier's advice – most of it as relevant today as it was when he set it down almost forty years ago – also included:

> Hard information – facts – are probably the most important single ingredient . . . The use of music is strongly *discouraged* with two exceptions: the notice and a review of a pop record on Monday and the 'classical' record on Friday. So far these records have been 'noticed' rather than 'reviewed'; the review or critical angle to be reinforced . . . There is nothing extraordinary about broadcasting between 7.00 and 9.00 a.m. and the 'how-early-it-is-in-the-morning' theme to be rigorously excluded . . . Spasmodic listening (probably under difficult conditions) is predicated. Presentation must be clear, friendly, straightforward, never 'olympian' and, if possible, slightly 'personalised'.

Music continued to be strongly discouraged in subsequent years, quite sensibly in view of the fact that 'Today' was designed as an alternative to music. In February 1960 Richard Marriott, by now the Assistant Director of Sound Broadcasting, wrote to Elisabeth Rowley, the senior producer on 'Today':

> I noticed in the comments of a Talks meeting special commendation of the jazz news in 'To-day'. I wonder if this is right? I had been thinking of saying to you that I thought it rather unsuitable. It is not simply that jazz is a minority subject; there are plenty of minority subjects like bird watching or postage stamps which can be made fascinating for an outsider, but jazz is one of those things that people who don't like it positively detest. It seemed to me

rather out of place, especially in the early edition – jazz fans tend to be night birds.

The need for informality evidently niggled Pelletier, for within a week of his first memo he had fired off two more mentioning the work of one particular contributor. The first one, on 22 January 1958, was critical:

I do not think Robin Boyle is yet completely at his ease. I wonder why. Perhaps I have over-estimated his ability to do this job . . . he continues to address himself to a multitude and not to the individual listener.

The second, written the very next day, was admiring:

P.S. I have now heard part of 'Today' on 23rd January. It was the second edition and I heard from the beginning of the programme to the point where Boyle was relaying advice on care of the house in cold weather. His performance up to that point almost completely invalidates what I said about him yesterday . . . For the first time that I can remember in this programme I heard the 'real' Boyle as against the performing announcer.

But if Boyle was saved, Skempton was damned. Comments evidently passed his lips that those in the curved corridors of power at Portland Place did not like. It is not known what they were, but Caversham's files contain this cryptic reply dated 1 May 1958 from Isa Benzie to a communication – from her boss, the Assistant Controller, Talks (Sound) – which has evidently got lost:

Thank you for your memorandum of today's date. John Green and I were talking about the compère the day before yesterday. He agreed that anything of much importance it was thought necessary to say to Mr. Skempton would have to be said from within his own channels of authority . . . It is not really possible to ward off in advance all the little remarks of an unscripted compère which are or are thought to be unfortunate. At the same time I was only this morning concerned by a remark he passed which I am having transcribed for Miss Quigley to consider on her return next Monday.

Skempton seemed to be on the way out. Though if his offence lay in 'unfortunate' and 'unscripted' remarks it seems quixotic, to say the least, for the BBC to have replaced him with Jack de Manio, a broadcaster whose capacity for such errors was infinitely greater. Indeed, de Manio would not be known at all were it not for one of the most notorious unscripted blunders in BBC history, when he mispronounced a talk called 'The Land of the Niger' as 'The Land of the Nigger', an offence compounded by the fact that the Queen was in Nigeria at the time.[10]

The first mention of Jack de Manio in the 'Today' files is on 18 July 1958 in a memo to Elisabeth Rowley (who by then seems to have become the acting producer-in-charge of the programme) from his boss, Andrew Timothy of Home Service Presentation:

> I have just heard from Mr. de Manio that he will be returning to London on Wednesday afternoon next, July 23rd. He has suggested that he trails the Thursday and Friday morning programmes ... I do not think there is any question about his keenness to do the programme, and I am quite sure we shall all be satisfied with the result.

That ringing endorsement may well have been tongue-in-cheek, for Timothy was on duty on the night of the 'Land of the Nigger' débâcle in January 1956 and thus had personal knowledge of the problems de Manio could unleash. He might not even have written it at all had he known how hard Jack would find it to tell the time, something of a drawback on a breakfast programme. But the die was cast. Jack de Manio, then a humble continuity announcer, would dominate the programme for the next thirteen years.

By the time the programme was one year old, in October 1958, it was already familiar with some of the perils of live broadcasting. Some editions overran, drawing this sharp rebuke of 1 August 1958 from J.C. Thornton, Assistant Controller, Talks (Sound): 'the latitude enjoyed by "To-day" is not withdrawn. What is wanted is variation on a 20-minute programme, not a more or less settled 22 or 23 or 24-minute programme.'

And Elisabeth Rowley found herself explaining why this could sometimes happen, as in this memo in which she argued against a suggestion (put forward by a member of the BBC's Board of Governors) that the contents of 'Today' be trailed at the beginning of the programme:

The contents of the programme cannot be guaranteed, even after the transmission has started. For instance, a live OB placed later in the programme may not materialise ... A speaker invited to broadcast live may, as has sometimes happened, oversleep, or arrive late. Recently a speaker who was cast for the first edition arrived in time for the second edition only ... I think the other producers would agree with me that they would not wish to be tied by an opening list of contents which would make it undesirable for them to take last minute decisions about a change of content or order. A programme of this kind must surely be one hundred per cent flexible.[11]

The programme was also becoming familiar with the efforts of *other* programmes to get mentioned on 'Today'. Pebble Mill, the BBC's Birmingham studios, sent a memo in August 1958 suggesting the programme do a piece about the 2,000th edition of 'The Archers', drawing this tactful sidestep from Rowley:

I should like to do this, but not, I think with a straight piece by Godfrey Baseley. I wonder if we could not have something original and amusing rather than informative? I myself have no bright ideas at the moment, but perhaps we could speak on the telephone, or better still, have a talk if you are to be in London some time soon.[12]

Above all, it was growing familiar with the idea of becoming part of people's lives, as they got up and went about the business of washing, shaving, dressing, breakfasting, making packed lunches, getting children off to school and going to work. This awareness was reflected in an article by Elisabeth Rowley in the *Radio Times* on the programme's first anniversary:

There is one factor common to [the two editions]: that is the steady flow of letters and telephone calls which come in from you – the listeners.
We cannot – quite rightly – put a foot wrong without being told about it almost immediately, sometimes in the middle of the broadcast itself. We cannot hit a nail smartly on the head without receiving warm congratulations (often couched in somewhat ambiguous terms!). We like both kinds of comment.
The items for 'Today' are collected from a variety of sources:

from BBC correspondents abroad; from BBC news reporters at home; from the Outside Broadcasting Department; from the Regions, and by members of Talks Department in London. The result has been a wide variety of material and this, in its turn, has stimulated many listeners to interest themselves in various subjects and activities which, they tell us, are quite new to them.

For instance, there is the listener who now reads to his wife one of T.S. Eliot's poems at breakfast each morning (after hearing Mr. Eliot reading 'La Figlia Che Piange' in 'Today'). There are the countless listeners who rush to reference books and encyclopaedia for the pure joy of providing us with bigger and better figures and more strange and unlikely facts. And there is one listener who, following one of A.R. Cooper's 'Useless Statistics', has calculated that a piece of paper 0.0013 inches thick folded 44 times would reach from the earth to the moon. We believe him of course, and although we do not propose to try it out we are grateful to him for suggesting this, which is much cheaper than launching a rocket.

More seriously, we have apparently succeeded in converting a number of listeners to do-it-yourselves – by laying their own linoleum, knocking up bookshelves, mixing their own concrete and, of course, trying out our daily menus.

How 'Today' taught its listeners to mix their own concrete is, regrettably, one of the recipes to have vanished without trace. But we do have some record of the 'daily menus', not all of which met with approval. 'Extracts from Mary Somerville's Notes on Listening – Jan. 12th–18th 1958', which reported on the views of various Women's Institute ladies, included this:

> The suggestions for dinners got a very poor hand – particularly when at least one of the dishes gave husbands nothing to *bite* into. Fish followed by baked bananas wouldn't do at all! Has anyone done a proper survey on what the British husband really likes to eat?

Perhaps not. But soon, in the Jack de Manio era, there was plenty for everyone to get their teeth into.

Before leaving the conception and birth of 'Today', it is worth making two points. First, it was a trio of females – Isa Benzie, Janet Quigley and Elisabeth Rowley – who, between them, came up with the name 'Today', brought the programme into the world, fed it, changed it, solved its teething troubles, enabled it to walk and talk and were responsible for its fresh and endearing personality. Women were thus quite capable of exerting influence in the BBC before equal opportunities and gender targets. Second, and equally clearly, the search for listener choice did not start with John Birt.

2

Jolly Jack

Celebrated for his 'rich gin-and-tonic voice'[1] and 'golf-club, bar stool manner',[2] Jack de Manio is frequently described as the first presenter of 'Today' and, although that appellation properly belongs to Alan Skempton, it was de Manio who dominated the programme for the next thirteen years, from 1958 to 1971.

'The very strong personal association between Mr. de Manio and "Today" has been in the nature of a happy miracle,' wrote Stephen Bonarjee, the programme's editor, in 1963,[3] gallantly not adding that the real miracle was that someone who could not tell the time had been hired to present a national breakfast show. 'It became a standard joke that he never got the time right,' recalls Lord Archer, 'but he was a very affable English gentleman in an age when you treated Cabinet ministers with some respect. In his time the programme was more like "Down Your Way".'[4] 'He was loved partly because he was so fallible,' said Alan Rogers, one of his producers in the 1960s and later head of BBC schools television. 'Listeners identified with him. And he had a great sense of humour. He was never too earnest.'[5]

De Manio had a truly astonishing capacity for fluffs and gaffes of all sorts, but the more he made the more his loyal audience seemed to love it. Jack's world was one of chortles and snifters, in which a telephone was a blower and no evening was complete – particularly no evening when he was getting paid for it – without popping over the road for a quick one. But he usually knew where to draw the line, something which any enduring broadcaster has to know. 'I recall one morning a producer saying after Jack had made a joke that the great thing about him was that even though you sometimes worried he was going to go over the boundary of good taste he never actually did,' says Rodney M. Bennett, a studio manager on 'Today' during the 1960s. 'He always seemed to know when to stop.'[6]

Jack de Manio was an eccentric, larger-than-life character who bestrode the BBC when such people were nearly always tolerated and sometimes indeed actually welcomed; when the culture of broadcasting was less hard, less competitive and much less obsessed with news than it is today. He was a man of his age, and eventually had to go because the age had changed and he had not. 'He was a sort of entertainment chap,' says Libby Purves, 'not a news man.'[7]

The best description I heard of Jack de Manio was from Nigel Rees, then a freelance reporter who worked frequently with him on 'Today' from 1968 to 1970. He remembered his time nostalgically:

The atmosphere on the programme was rather that of a gentleman's club and the presiding tone emanated from Jack de Manio. He was one of the great radio personalities of the transitional period between radio's great years and what we have now. He was unique, and for those who never experienced the full force of his idiosyncratic approach to broadcasting, I can but draw a parallel with Reginald Bosanquet on ITV. They both shared a somewhat raffish air of good living, fast motor cars, even faster women and plenty of champagne. Reggie was probably the cleverer of the two, though neither of them was given much chance to use his brain. Some would say that in Jack's case this was just as well. There was a shared sense of nervousness, of anticipation of some lunatic act that kept listeners agog. Would he fall out of his chair? Would he make some unforgivably reactionary remark? Such considerations became part of the de Manio legend.

On one famous occasion he wasn't even in the studio by 7.15 – he'd got stuck in the lavatory – and Tim Matthews was given his script to read, only to be stopped after a sentence or two by the sound of Jack puffing through the studio door saying he had been 'held up'. His unscripted comments also gave producers heart failure, such as his remark at the end of an interview with a Norfolk vicar who had revealed his parish's wife-swapping habits in the church magazine Cockcrow – 'I cannot wait to get my cock – er, hands on a copy of Cockcrow ... oh dear.' But of such is the kingdom of heaven.[8]

Jack de Manio was half-Polish, half-Italian and 100 per cent British. Born in London, he was sent to a public school, which he left to work in a brewery. He was evidently an early developer when it came to disasters, as he admitted on 'Desert Island Discs' on Boxing Day 1964:

> My job was to send off invoices to the publicans and stick on the stamps, and I couldn't even stick those on properly, they used to come off, and a publican rang up and sort of said, 'Barnes 'ere, Eagle, Clifton Road, I got me bill this morning – it was wrong and no stamp on it,' and of course they got a bit fed up with this, and er, they asked me to leave.

He went into the hotel business, working at the Grosvenor House in Park Lane and the Miramar restaurant in Cannes, but that too ended ignominiously: 'I poured some hot sauce down one of the King of Sweden's guests,' he told Roy Plomley. He returned to Britain, married an American, then lived for a while in New York. Called up in 1939, he fought in France and North Africa and was awarded the MC and Bar (for what, he appears never to have said, or been asked, though he was wounded in Sudan). He worked in forces radio in Palestine as an announcer and, finding that a congenial way of passing the time, did the obvious thing after the war and joined the BBC's General Overseas Service as an announcer. He was based at its then offices at 200 Oxford Street, in London's West End.

Just how much Jack liked this job, and the embarrassment he caused his bosses, can be gauged from the transcript of what he went on to tell Plomley:

> It was marvellous. *I remember that for example if one was putting on, you know, Tommy Handley and the ITMA show, you'd say how long is it and they'd say, 'Oh, about twenty-eight minutes,' and, er, you said, 'Oh, I'll be back in twenty-six,' and go straight across to the Feathers. I had all the pubs absolutely taped. I knew the timing,* one was slightly irresponsible.

That was what Jack actually said, as shown in the transcript kept at Caversham. But all that listeners heard was 'It was marvellous, one was slightly irresponsible.' All the rest of it, the italicised words, was cut before the programme went out.

From there Jack transferred to the Home Service at Broadcasting House, not too far away, where his job as a continuity announcer left him plenty of time for practical jokes. After the 'Land of the Nigger' débâcle (for which unintentional slip he apologised on air fifteen minutes later) he was suspended and sent home, but reinstated some weeks later and was working as a Home Service announcer when approached by 'Today' in 1958 to come and replace Alan Skempton. He started in July 1958 but was not billed regularly in *Radio Times* until 1959, when presumably he was confirmed as the regular presenter.

Jack's gaffes on 'Today' started early and went on throughout the 1960s. The first – the first to be documented, at least – was in July 1960 when he mentioned the television show 'The Four Just Men'. Within hours there came this acid response from Kenneth Adam, Controller of Programmes for BBC Television:

> I hope you will not think I am being over sensitive if I query the reference to 'The Four Just Men' in Today this morning. The 'Guess Whose Voice' sequence included Vittorio de Sica's and de Manio when identifying it spoke of being able to see him 'currently on television in "The Four Just Men"'. To pretend that commercial television does not exist would be absurd, but to go out of our way to publicise a programme on the other channel seems unnecessary, don't you think?

Smart executives know when to lie down, and Elisabeth Rowley did just that:

> Thank you for your memorandum of July 13th. The report is accurate and Mr de Manio tenders his apologies. The remark was unscripted and unexpected by the producer. Mr de Manio was labouring under the misapprehension that 'The Four Just Men' is a product of BBC Television and thought he was giving us a nice plug!

There was a much more serious blunder some years later, which showed just what a liability de Manio could be. It provided glaring evidence of the fact that an affable manner could not disguise a basic lack of training in either journalism or the law. This stiff letter was written by Maurice Green, Editor of the *Daily Telegraph*, to the BBC on 8 May 1967:

> Dear Sir,
> I was very surprised to learn that in this morning's programme

'Today' at 7.15 a.m., Mr. Jack de Manio said in reference to the arrest of a young man charged with a murder at Beenham that he was 'absolutely horrified to see this young man's photograph plastered all over the front page (of the *Daily Telegraph*)', and that by publishing this photograph, the *Daily Telegraph* was guilty of contempt of court.

Both these statements, being untrue, are plainly libellous. I appreciate that this part of Mr. de Manio's programme was removed from the second edition thereof at 8.15 a.m. Nevertheless, we are clearly entitled to a retraction at the earliest possible moment in the 7.15 a.m. programme. Provided that this is done, we do not propose to pursue the matter further.

I would ask that the retraction should include the withdrawal of the statement that the photograph was 'plastered all over the front page', since it was an ordinary single column block, occupying 6 sq. inches out of a total page space of 408 sq. inches. I would also ask for the withdrawal of the statement that the *Daily Telegraph* was in contempt of court. As I am sure you are aware, there is no contempt of court in publication of such a photograph unless identification is likely to be involved. Needless to say, the *Daily Telegraph* made exhaustive inquiries on this point before publishing the photograph.[9]

Faced with such a withering attack, and doubtless cursing their loose cannon of a compère, the BBC, in the person of J.A. Camacho, Head of Talks and Current Affairs (Sound), had no alternative but to surrender the very next day:

I very much regret that the words spoken by Mr. Jack de Manio in Monday morning's 7.15 am edition of TODAY should have contained a reference to the front page of that day's issue of the *Daily Telegraph* which you state were inaccurate in two important respects ... As requested, I am arranging for an appropriate retraction to be broadcast in the 7.15 am edition of Wednesday's programme ... I of course accept without question your statement that exhaustive inquiries ... had been made before you published the photograph in question.[10]

Camacho enclosed with it the text of the retraction which de Manio would be required to read out.

And the next morning, a (temporarily) crestfallen Jack did indeed read it out in the first edition of the programme:

On Monday I commented on the publication in the *Daily Telegraph* of a picture of the youth charged with the Beenham murder.

I was wrong in saying that the picture was plastered all over the front page. It was, in fact, only a small picture and before publishing it the *Daily Telegraph* – so their Editor assures me – made exhaustive inquiries to make certain that no question of contempt would arise. I'm glad to put the record straight.[11]

The happy-go-lucky atmosphere of the programme also attracted some internal venom later that year. This time it was directed at Monty Modlyn, a cockney reporter who was capable of causing apoplexy in some quarters:

I deliberately refrained from sending this memo earlier in the hope that after a day or two I might feel less urgently impelled to write it. However, I still feel as strongly that the conversation between Monty Modlyn and Sir Francis Cassell in 'Today' last Friday morning was one of the most impertinent and inept interviews ever broadcast. Although I hold no brief for Cassell as a pianist it was surely unfair and discourteous to confront him with an interviewer who may well be ideal in his own cockney world but has less than average musical understanding and good manners. Of course Cassell is of no importance as a musician but he is no Florence Fisher Jenkins [sic] and I think it would be wrong not to register some kind of formal protest even though I may well be told that it is none of my business![12]

De Manio's gut reaction to events, allied to a lack of political sophistication in a rapidly changing world, continued to be a headache for his BBC masters. In July 1968, when capital cities all over Europe erupted in riots and protests over the Vietnam War, he breezily opened the programme thus: 'Good morning – and let's start the morning by raising our hats to the London policemen, who once again have their weekends mucked up by a lot of silly hooligans.'[13]
The programme's editor Stephen Bonarjee, when responding to a complaint about this remark, acknowledged that though it might

have been ill-judged Jack probably did have public opinion on his side:

> Jack does quite frequently improvise and within reasonable limits this is regarded as part of the programme's spontaneity ... I have no doubt that he uttered words very similar to those you quote.
>
> The odd thing is that we have had to tick him off more than once for unfavourable comments on the police, mainly as to their relationships with motorists! As the police were universally praised, by the Home Secretary among others, for their restraint during the demonstrations in question it must be the reference to the demonstrators as 'silly hooligans' which your correspondent regards as offensive. The phrase was ill chosen no doubt and I will remind him again that it is not for him to make judgements of this kind, but we have had not a single written or telephone complaint ourselves, and I have to confess that I suspect on this occasion Jack represented the views of the public at large.[14]

For Gerard Mansell, Radio 4's Controller, the fact that Jack might have had the public on his side was neither here nor there. He regarded popular feeling as something to be resisted rather than embraced. That was made abundantly clear in this memo two years later, in 1970:

> I don't want to seem to be overreacting, but I think Jack de Manio's reference to 'Yoko Hama, or whatever her name is' in this morning's second edition, and his comment to the effect that he didn't care whether or not she and John Lennon went to bed together went further than we ought to allow Jack to go. Making fun of foreign names is a time-honoured pastime, but not one that's generally regarded as being in good taste, and dismissive remarks about the sex life of Mr. and Mrs. Lennon, though no doubt they will evoke wide agreement among listeners, ought not really to have a place in our broadcasting. I'm well aware that they reflect a side of Jack's personality and general outlook, and that it's part of Jack's attraction as a broadcaster that he projects a personal image of a certain kind, but there are those who are offended by it, and I think we should be careful not to allow him to go quite so far in revealing his prejudices.[15]

The cold contempt of those words reveals how some BBC

mandarins really felt about Jack, and helps to explain why he was dropped the following year (though continuing to be one of the presenters of the Saturday edition). In addition, the liberal loftiness of tone, the emphasis on restraint and the solicitous anxiety over foreign sensibilities (Mansell was born and educated in France and later became Managing Director of the BBC's External Services) says much about the spirit of the BBC.

Increasing militancy as the 1960s continued only served to show up Jack's woeful ignorance of the world, as Libby Purves recalls:

> There was a very famous story, I don't know whether it's apocryphal or not. They were talking about the civil rights marches in Northern Ireland when these were first beginning [in 1969], and he did a whole interview about it with all the questions he'd been given, but then decided to diverge and ad lib and said, 'Um, it's interesting this civil rights thing because I hadn't realised there were so many black people in Northern Ireland.' Poor old Jack, he didn't really know much about anything.[16]

Flowers as well as foreigners could find themselves on the receiving end of Jack's affable clumsiness. In 1969, for example, the Programme Correspondence department received this memo from Peter Redhouse, by now the programme's editor:

> I enclose any number of letters we have received containing four and five-leaved clovers for forwarding to Allen Kinsella, the small boy whose five-leaved clover Jack managed to destroy in the studio the other morning. Perhaps you could acknowledge these letters for us, returning all samples whether their senders wish them to be returned or not, saying that we have forwarded a cutting from a special variety of clover which regularly produces four or five leaves, that was sent in to us by a listener. Express our appreciation and thanks etc. etc.[17]

As well as the gaffes and the destruction of five-leaved clovers, there was one other problem with de Manio. He was becoming too expensive. He felt, as all freelances do, that he had to stick up for himself and there were a flat in Chelsea and a Bentley to maintain. BBC programme editors, faced with tight budgets, could hardly be blamed for preferring reliable journalists like John Timpson and

Robert Hudson – who, as members of staff, did not have to be paid – over unreliable eccentrics like de Manio, who did.

In January 1970, for example, after coming in early to do an interview with someone in Vancouver, the BBC wrote to him offering an extra £3 for his pains. Jack turned it down, on the grounds that he had an agreement that for interviews outside programme hours he would be paid not £3 but £8. In a handwritten note at the foot of Jack's letter, Bonarjee scribbled to the accountants, 'OK. Let him win! But as he seldom keeps to his contract time of 6.30am he owes us hours of work.'[18]

There was another kerfuffle over money later that year after the Saturday edition of 'Today' had been launched. A *Daily Mail* story revealing that Simon Dee had been hired to host three Saturday editions of 'Today' in August and September at £50 each caused consternation at the BBC, which had only struck the deal with his agent the previous day: no contract had even been signed. It produced an anxious memo from Clyde Logan, who as Talks Booking Manager negotiated fees (except for Dee's fees, which had been dealt with by Light Entertainment):

> I think I should make the point that Jack de Manio receives £37.10s a day and Trevor Philpott, when engaged for this programme, is paid £25 . . . there is no doubt that they will see the Simon Dee item in the papers and will quite reasonably ask for more money for their own appearances.[19]

This prediction proved spot-on, as Ian Trethowan, who had recently taken over as Managing Director of BBC Radio, was to discover:

> He [Jack] complained that he was only being offered £30 a week for the Saturday edition of 'Today', whereas Aspel was getting £40 and Simon Dee got £50. He admitted he would get extra for interviews, but claimed that the same was true for Aspel. I said that I could not possibly comment without checking the facts, but that I felt sure there was no question of us offering him worse terms than Aspel.[20]

Trethowan's irritation was clearly shared by the new editor of 'Today', Marshall Stewart. He replied to Trethowan's confidential memo with one of his own, arguing that de Manio and Aspel had complete parity. He ended on an ominous note: 'One thing that de

Manio must bear in mind is that there is no spare money available at this time: his guarantee [£2,400 for thirty-eight weeks] alone will account for 34 per cent of the Saturday budget.'[21]

Trethowan was also given chapter and verse by the accounts department, who sent him a note saying that the true figures for the various presenters' pay on the Saturday edition of 'Today' were: Joan Bakewell, £30 basic plus £7.50 per interview; Michael Aspel, £30 basic plus £7–£8 per interview; Simon Dee, £40 basic plus £7 per interview; and that de Manio wanted £30 basic plus £8.75 per interview.

Armed with this information, Ian Trethowan wrote to de Manio (he marked his letter 'Confidential', but craftily sent blind copies to three of his colleagues):

> I am glad to say that I find you are not being offered worse terms than Michael Aspel. On the contrary, in one respect – the offer of a guarantee – you are being offered something more. Any comparison with Simon Dee is irrelevant, since he was only hired for three programmes, and he was paid on a rather different basis, but in fact again you are being guaranteed no less than he was. Just to make sure that we are talking the same language, I understand that you have been offered £30 basic per programme, plus £8.75 per interview, with a guarantee of £2,400 a year, which allows for an average of three interviews per programme and works out at a guaranteed £56.25 per programme.[22]

It is worth spelling all this out in detail in order to show how pay differentials can create understandable resentment between colleagues working on the same programme, something seen later on in the Redhead–Timpson relationship and with Sue MacGregor and her male colleagues. It also shows the contrasting perspectives of artists and executives and how much behind-the-scenes paperwork this all creates.

Illness also took its toll on de Manio as the years passed. Some of it at least was gout, a traditional affliction of heavy drinkers. He missed his own farewell from the programme in 1971 because he was in hospital, but even before that it was increasingly causing a problem. In December 1970 he wrote to Ian Trethowan:

> Dear Ian,
> I hear you were a little upset about the article that appeared in

the *Sunday Express* about me not being visited in hospital by BBC bosses. I'd like to apologise to you about this; I rang the D-G [Charles Curran] on Monday morning to explain to him what actually happened, and to apologise, and I asked him if he would apologise on my behalf to you and anybody else who he thought might be concerned.

I'd like to assure you I'm not feeling at all bitter and I was completely mis-quoted, and obviously I would not make statements like that to the press which would obviously cause offence and upset my bosses. Please accept my apologies.[23]

Trethowan accepted Jack's apology, though perhaps he knew he would be having problems with him later: 'Don't give it another thought. I know enough about newspapers to guess what happened. Like everyone else in Radio 1 was distressed to hear of your accident ... I am glad you are now fit enough to be back on the programme.'[24]

The following words about de Manio were written by Patricia Brent, one of his producers on the programme, for the *Radio Times*, to mark his ten years on 'Today' in July 1968. It can hardly be bettered either as a sketch of his personality or as an assessment of what he brought to the programme:

Ten years ago, on 28th July 1958, Jack de Manio first introduced 'Today'. Before that, he was an announcer and, as he freely admits, a pretty bad one. Before that again, he was a war-time soldier and, although he refuses to admit it, a pretty brave one. He got an M.C. in France in 1940. Before the war he was a trainee chef at Grosvenor House in London and The Miramar in Cannes. Nowadays, out of working hours in Broadcasting House, his natural habitats are Chelsea, the clubs of St. James', the South of France, and the inside of his Bentley, which he drives with skill and panache. If the 'Today' Unit were ever transferred to, say, Bootle, his first reaction would probably be to blow his top and his second to make the best of it and throw the largest party the town had ever seen. Today, when so many broadcasters cultivate identical accents and attitudes, Jack remains a character from Michael Arlen rather than John Braine.

In the years that I've worked with him, as a producer on 'Today', I've become convinced that the fact that he is this sort of anachronism is the reason for his popularity. His ebullient clubman's manner, his innocent glee when he shocks the Establishment with some off the cuff comment, and his refusal to iron himself out into an impersonal 'presenter' are refreshing. Even when he gets into a muddle, it's somehow comforting at a time of day when most listeners are in a muddle themselves over the cornflakes and collar studs.

One of his favourite tipples is champagne. On special occasions, like Christmas morning, he usually takes the producer out for a champagne breakfast after the programme. July 28th is a Sunday this year, so on Monday, 29th, his official anniversary, maybe we should take him out for a change, to drink to ten exhilarating years of 'Today' with Jack de Manio.

Caversham shows that originally Patricia Brent typed 'the next ten years' before making a handwritten alteration to 'ten exhilarating years'. Maybe she had a premonition that, while the BBC had put up with dangerous off-the-cuff remarks for one decade, it was unlikely to do so for another. If so, she was absolutely right.

One area in which Jack's muddle was understandable was the regional opt-outs. Today there are none of these and there have been none for more than a decade. But in Jack's day some of the BBC's regions left the 'Today' programme to present their own local programmes for their listeners. Different areas opted out on different days. For Jack, who could hardly tell the time, this was all difficult stuff. Just how difficult can be gleaned from this note to Jack (via his editor) from Home Service Presentation in 1960:

On Wednesdays and Fridays, Scotland, Wales and part of Northern Ireland, and also North, do not take the 2nd edition of 'To-day' but perform some complicated evolutions of their own. They are becoming increasingly anxious about the form of closing announcement to 1st edition in which you normally say something like '. . . well that's all from the 1st edition of To-day, but I'll be back with the 2nd edition at 8.15.' On the two days concerned (or, better still, perhaps to save you trying to remember which day is which!) could you avoid a trail for the 2nd edition altogether. After all, the programme has now been running for some time and has become well established . . . I'd be most grateful if you could evolve some acceptable form of closing to the 1st edition which will not embarrass those regions which are listening at that point, but will not be with you for the 2nd edition.

Whether Jack understood any of that is not known. But his colleagues did, and the following form of words was drawn up: 'That's all from Today for now. I'll be back at 8.15 with a second edition for listeners in . . .'

Once, however, just after he had quite rightly got rid of Wales at 8.15 am, the 'Today' studio took a telephone call from Cardiff informing them that Wales was not in fact opting out – a decision they had made after the *Radio Times* had gone to press. From 1963, when the programme became part of Current Affairs, there were two opt-out points (one in each edition) and precise time checks became of ever growing importance. In the Timpson era, the opt-out point moved to 8.25 am and it had to be hit with pin-point accuracy. This started the tradition of using little jokes or oddities from the *Daily Telegraph* diary column, 'Peterborough', as filler material if an interview or other item had finished early and there were some spare moments to fill before 8.25 am. But all this disappeared with the growth of BBC local radio and of alternative breakfast shows going out at the same time as 'Today' on the BBC's new regional services in Wales, Scotland and Northern Ireland.

This complicated system of regional opt-outs could affect the trails too. In September 1963, for example, just before the release of the long-awaited Denning Report on the Profumo Affair (tantalisingly, there is little in the archives showing how 'Today' covered that), an internal News memo warned everyone:

On the morning of the 26th September, when we carry the extended bulletin on Denning, the cross trail from the bulletin to the Denning material in 'Today' must differ as between 7.00 a.m. and 8.00 a.m., because, while there are no regional opt-outs for the first edition of 'Today', Wales opts out for the second edition. Therefore it will be necessary to add to the trail for the 8.00 a.m. bulletin some such phrase as 'except for listeners in Wales'.

Meanwhile, behind the scenes, females were giving way to males. It was women who had created and energised 'Today' in its early years, when it was under Talks. In 1963 the programme was incorporated into Current Affairs Group whose head, in radio, was Stephen Bonarjee; and it became operationally linked with the Home Service's evening programme, 'Ten O'Clock', which he also ran. From this point on 'Today' belonged to the BBC's Current Affairs empire, which would become ever more powerful, and take an ever-increasing amount of money and attention within the Corporation. Current Affairs Group was separate from News Division, and they stayed separate, in radio, until the 1970s. In television they remained separate until combined by John Birt in 1987 to create one large bi-media directorate, BBC News and Current Affairs, which changed its name to BBC News in 1996.

Bonarjee was determined to make the 'Today' programme harder and more news-orientated and boost its audience. A four-page document he wrote for colleagues in September 1963[25] was surely one of the earliest BBC documents to call a programme a 'product' and suggest a 'sharper' edge, words that became *de rigueur* in later years. The BBC agreed to expand the programme slightly: from October 1963 the first edition was extended to thirty minutes (7.15–7.45 am) while the second stayed at twenty-five minutes (8.15–8.40 am). Bonarjee saw this as an opportunity not to be missed:

We ought, I think, to regard the extension of time as from Monday, October 7th as marking a new starting point. The 'feel' of a half-hour programme should differ in many respects ... For example ... too many 'jolly' magazine items would add up to little more than a rag-bag, and in general the programme will need rather more 'roughage' in the shape of sharper, harder material.

New professional disciplines will certainly be required to cope with the complexities of the new Regional opt-out policies, which will demand much more accurate placing of items and more exact time-keeping.

Perhaps we should now seek to re-define what the purpose of 'Today' is, or should be. We would all agree, I know, that it should invariably be a lively, polished product. To this I would add that it should have a forward-looking feel about it, should concern itself mainly with broad extrovert human interests and talking points, but should not be afraid to be serious when necessary (although hardly ever solemn) ...

We have arrested the slow decline in the audience that set in two or three years ago. We seem even to be pushing it up a bit. But 3,500,000 a day is not enough, bearing in mind there is no breakfast time television (or not yet). A daily figure topping · 4,000,000 should be well within our grasp.

Bonarjee then set out in detail the features of the new plan, and the Byzantine complexities of the regional opt-outs:

> One vital change is that Regions will be free to opt out of the last ten minutes of each edition if they wish, and we already know that West and Midland Regions propose to exercise this right. On the other hand, North Region propose to stay with us throughout both editions, but of course they are reasonably assuming that our output will include a significant proportion of material from Northern sources. Scotland, Wales and Northern Ireland will take all our first editions but will opt out in varying ways from all or the last part of the second edition on two or more days a week.
>
> This means, of course, that running orders must be most carefully thought about, and precise time checks will be essential as Regional cues just before the opt-out points at 7.35 a.m. and 8.30 a.m.

To introduce the new changes smoothly, Bonarjee wanted a new rota, a new daily editorial conference at 5.15 pm to discuss next morning's programme and the placing of items, the deputy on the 'Ten O'Clock' rota to act as an informal copytaster who would go through all incoming stories for possible use on either programme, and – very important for listeners – a time check to be given fifteen minutes into each edition prior to the regional opt-out.

There was no evidence that de Manio was concerned with these new arrangements any more than he had been with the old. While Bonarjee had been grappling with the minutiae of shift patterns and an audience fragmented by endless regional opt-outs, he was marking the programme's sixth birthday with some jocular and undemanding mathematics:

> This is the sixty-two thousand, four hundred and first minute of 'Today', and if you've been with us from the start you've been listening for forty-four days and nights. During the years we've had twenty-eight thousand contributors, twice the population of Stratford-on-Avon: head-to-tail, these contributors would reach from London to Guildford. We might try that some time – it should cause a nice old jam on the Portsmouth Road.[26]

Two worrying events in 1965 made Bonarjee think closely about the 'Today' audience. In March, the Music Programme (the daytime counterpart of the Third Programme, later to become Radio 3) started broadcasting from 7 am, creating, for the first time, a breakfast alternative for classical music lovers. In June, the West Region started opting out of the whole of the second edition – taking away thousands of West Country listeners. As a result, the 'Today' audience (the combined daily average of the two editions) fell from 4.5 million to 4.3 million between 1965 and 1967. Bonarjee's anxieties are shown in this confidential memo from May 1967:

> We must endeavour to avoid if we possibly can any more Regional defections. The decline in the second edition audience in the last two years is almost certainly the approximate size of the audience for West Region's opt-out. If ever one of the larger Regions followed suit the effect would be very serious.[27]

He also had his eye on the autumn of that year, when the BBC would launch Radio 1 and turn Light, Third and Home into Radios 2, 3 and 4:

> What we have to bear in mind . . . is the fact that from September 30 next we shall also be faced with competition from the new Popular Music Programme as well as the Light and Music Programmes. Breakfast time listeners will thus have a choice of four BBC programmes, and on the face of it increased competition will mean a harder fight to maintain the audience at its present level, let alone to set it on the path of expansion.[28]

Publicly, however, the BBC was not admitting to any anxieties as it celebrated the programme's tenth anniversary. There was a cocktail party in the Council Chamber for eighty people, including the now retired Isa Benzie. On offer were what the BBC described opaquely as 'the ordinary range of drinks as well as sandwiches and what-nots of the usual kind'.[29] The Corporation published an eight-page, black-and-white anniversary booklet about the programme, showing Jack being called on the blower at 5.30 am, Jack with two adoring Mrs Mops in the foyer of Broadcasting House, Jack eating breakfast (a proper cooked one, of course) and Jack in the studio. There were also mug shots of eight of the 'popular broadcasting personalities' frequently heard on the programme: Martin Muncaster, Brian Johnston, Robert Hudson, John Timpson, Derek Cooper, June Jay,

Monty Modlyn and Tim Matthews, some of whom stood the test of time better than others.

The brochure was a perky, upbeat affair, trumpeting that 'Today' had broadcast more than 5,000 editions and 30,000 different items and also pointing out that there was now a thirty-five-minute digest edition on Saturdays at 12.25 pm called 'All the Best from Today' (introduced the previous year, in April 1966). It explained that the programme was 'planned as a newsy miscellany, with each item designed to be interesting in its own right, and the only common thread holding everything together is the friendly personality of Jack de Manio or one of the alternate presenters'.

There was also a useful description of how 'Today' had evolved into a flexible operation able to react quickly to a big story:

> The duty producer sleeps briefly on the premises, and fresh items are prepared in the small hours if a big news story breaks. There is close liaison between the 'Today' staff and Radio Newsroom's night shift, and programme changes can be made at any time. Thus the first flash of the outbreak of war between Israel and the Arab states [June 1967] was broadcast by Jack de Manio in the first edition of 'Today' at 7.36 a.m., and by 8.15 a.m. it was possible to lead the second edition with comment from an expert on Middle East Affairs.

All that makes it sound faintly like the programme it is today, but there was also a section which points up the difference:

> 'Today' does not seek to be 'important', but it does have a remarkably shrewd ear for unusual 'goings on' all over the place, for the exceptional experiences of otherwise normal citizens, for 'character' and quirkiness, and it is this attachment to intriguing 'grass roots' stories that has endeared it to such a wide public.

The pamphlet added, correctly, that the audience was one million more than in 1962, but naturally did not mention the fact that it had also dropped by 200,000 in the previous two years.

'Today' might not have sought importance, but one can detect faint beginnings of its later notoriety for alleged political bias in the late 1960s, when Labour was in power and Harold Wilson was Prime Minister. In February 1968, for example, there was a formal complaint by a Mrs Mayer that a report from Gerald Priestland carried on the programme was a criticism of Wilson's visit to Washington: Bonarjee admitted in a memo that the piece did 'reflect the prevailing air of scepticism that was common before the visit and at the time of the P.M.'s arrival'.[30] In 1969 the BBC sent an unequivocal written apology to Percy Clark, Director of Publicity for the Labour Party, after Clark complained about an item on 'Today' concerning the bitterly contentious issue of arms for South Africa: 'speculative material in the *Sunday Telegraph*' was blamed for the error, along with an inexperienced overnight producer.[31]

Neither the Sound Archives at Broadcasting House nor the Written Archives Centre at Caversham reveal much about the content of programme in the 1960s. For example, there is no mention of how it covered President Kennedy's assassination. But there is one tantalising glimpse of its approach to another seismic event that same year, the Profumo Affair and subsequent Denning Report. A reporter was despatched to HMSO in High Holborn to interview some of the people queueing for four-and-a-half hours to get a copy of the Report. One optimistic man, who sounded Indian but said he came from Russia, said he wanted a copy in order to obtain 'Miss Keeler's telephone number'. 'Today' covered the death of Elsa the lioness and a 1961 musical on Dr Crippen ('certainly offbeat') and de Manio flew to Florida and back one weekend to see a porpoise that could jump sixteen feet.

Eventually de Manio had to go because the programme could no longer cope with 'the atmosphere of the unexpected', as the critic Gillian Reynolds once tactfully expressed it. Under him it was always in danger of becoming 'The Jack de Manio Show', rather than 'Today'. He was too expensive and too unpredictable and belonged to another age. 'In many ways he was a most disconcerting man to work with,' John Timpson said in 1971. 'He is a marvellous person but you never knew what he was going to do next.'

It is often forgotten that de Manio secured the first broadcast interview with Prince Charles, conducted on St David's Day 1969 at Buckingham Palace. The young heir to the throne, then a twenty-year-old undergraduate at Trinity College, Cambridge, spoke with apparent ease about the 'great fun' he had had sitting in a dustbin for his student revue and the show's awful 'groan jokes', which owed more than a little to his heroes the Goons. Prince Charles also recalled the incident on Stornoway, when he had found himself in a pub and asked for a cherry brandy ('I said the first thing that came into my head ... I'd had it before, cold, when I'd been out shooting'), and life at Timbertops in Australia. He described the first time he had flown solo and the Welsh nationalist protests at his coming Investiture later that year as Prince of Wales. Curiously, there is no mention at Caversham anywhere in de Manio's files of this historic interview. On the whole, Prince Charles seemed touchingly carefree, but there were hints of the concern and thoughtfulness which he displayed eighteen years later on 'Today' when he spoke to Brian Redhead in Glasgow about Business in the Community and restoration of civic pride.

The most enduring feature introduced in Jack's era was the review of the national press, introduced as 'Today's Papers' on 19 May 1959. It was a five-minute review twice each day, at 7.35 and 8.35 am. (Today it still goes out twice a day, at 6.40 and 7.40 am.)

Stuart Hood, deputy editor of BBC news, said when launching the slot that it would contain not only references to headlines and editorials, but also features, news stories and the more interesting cartoons. He pointed out that newspaper readers tended to stick to one paper and so the slot would inform them of what the others were saying. 'We are not attempting to make it unnecessary for people to go out and buy a newspaper,' he was quoted as saying, 'but to give listeners a taste of today's press and the excitement they can get from it.'[32] The BBC promised it would be neither flippant nor ponderous.

Fleet Street was interested: the BBC had never attempted such a project before on any of its domestic services (only a dry summary of the leaders which went out at dawn on the Overseas Service). Would it dent newspaper sales, or boost them? Most national newspapers, according to one trade paper,[33] preferred to wait and see how the programme worked out before committing themselves in advance. But the *Daily Herald* welcomed it as a likely boost to casual sales of papers 'with bright and interesting editorial features'.[34] Sadly for the *Daily Herald*, whatever casual sales were thus boosted, theirs were not often among them: the paper closed five years later.

On the day after the first review there was this sharp observation in the *Scarborough Evening News*, never slow to score points off its self-important national cousins:

The BBC's announcement that it was to broadcast a review of the national press each morning inspired the gloomiest forebodings. A parade of the banalities of which the national press is all too capable would not sound very well at that early hour.

On its first morning, yesterday, this review passed off reasonably unremarkably, but whereas most newspapers were mentioned nothing was said of the *Daily Mirror*. Today, for the benefit of its 13,300,000 readers, the *Mirror* devotes its entire front page to this grave omission, and this morning, of course, the BBC solemnly reported it.

How silly can you get?

The only attempt to monitor the slot to see which paper was mentioned most frequently appears to have been carried out during 1961. The *Daily Mail* headed the table in June with 58 mentions. It came top again in July, also with 58 mentions, beating the *Daily Telegraph* (49) into second place and its traditional rival the *Daily Express* (48) into third. And it came top again the following month, as this August league table (carried in the *New Daily*) shows:

1	*Daily Mail*	71
2	*Daily Telegraph*	60
3 =	*Daily Express*	58
	Daily Herald	58
5	*Daily Mirror*	46
6	*Guardian*	35
7	*The Times*	34
8	*Daily Sketch*	29
9	*Daily Worker*	11
10	*Financial Times*	8
11	*New Daily*	2

In September, however, the victorious three-month run of the *Mail* came to an end. It came third with 41 mentions, beaten by 43 for the *Express* and 44 for the *Telegraph*.

The *Mail* must have won two of the three months from October to December, however, for on 2 January 1962 it carried a short and impeccably restrained leader entitled THE TREND ON THE AIR: 'Fifty-six times in December the *Daily Mail* was quoted in the BBC's regular morning programme "From Today's Papers". For five months out of the past seven the *Daily Mail* has been the most quoted paper in that programme.' Would that still be the case today? I put it to the test. Over six weeks from December 1996 to January 1997, a period chosen at random, I monitored the two paper reviews each day, Monday to Saturday inclusive, noting down every time a title was mentioned. The results were as follows:

1	Daily Telegraph	103
2	The Times	80
3 =	Daily Mail	70
	Independent	
5	Guardian	64
6	The Express	63
7	Sun	55
8	Daily Mirror	52
9	Daily Star	20
10	Financial Times	19[35]

The paper review, which has started – very gradually – to broaden its base to include the main regional papers, is one of the most popular ingredients to this day. When I asked the BBC's Chairman, Sir Christopher Bland, whether he would make any changes to the programme, his answer was immediate: 'I wish the paper review followed the news, as it does on a Sunday morning. "Today" is my alarm clock and I listen to it for an hour from seven to eight, and forty minutes is a long time to wait until you hear the papers.'[36]

Politicians have been known to show enormous sensitivity to the slot. Jenny Abramsky, editor of the programme in 1986–7, a period which included the June 1987 General Election, recalls:

I can remember Neil Kinnock personally ringing me up in the office to explode about a paper review, because we'd quoted some things about the Labour Party and him from the Daily Express. I had just come out of the studio and suddenly there was the Leader of the Opposition on the phone. And there was this tirade from Neil, who's actually a good friend, just a tirade about the paper review. The Labour Party in those days were incredibly sensitive about the paper review, inevitably with newspapers with the political leanings they have and had, and if you go back to 1987, they were far more anti-Labour. We were very conscious of that. On the other hand, if we were going to do a proper review of the papers you had to reflect what was in the papers, whether Neil Kinnock liked it or not.[37]

The general tenor of the paper review is clearly tilted towards broadsheets rather than tabloids. John Allen, the executive in charge of the thirty-two senior broadcast journalists who take it in turns to write it, recalls: 'We once led the review by mentioning a big story in

44

the *Sun*, and Jenny Abramsky, who was editor of "Today" at the time, threw a wobbly. She said that "Today" listeners weren't interested in what was in the *Sun* but what was in *The Times* and *Telegraph*. I think our approach in the Newsroom has often been the opposite, to try and give "Today" listeners a flavour of what they would not be reading, to expose them to something they were not so likely to have seen.'[38] It looks, however, as if Abramsky's philosophy will hold sway for the foreseeable future.

3

The Man with a Chuckle in His Voice

John Timpson was brought in to co-present the programme with de Manio in his final year, having first made his mark as a stand-in presenter in the mid-1960s. Stephen Bonarjee, the editor, was particularly impressed with him. 'We all have the fullest confidence in John Timpson, and I know everyone would be happy if he could be loaned to us once again,' he wrote in August 1964. 'There seems much to be said for fostering still further the goodwill he has already created with the audience.'[1]

Originally a print journalist, a junior reporter on local papers in Wembley and Harrow before moving to Norfolk during the 1950s, Timpson transferred triumphantly to radio. He joined the staff of the BBC as a general reporter in March 1959, and covered a variety of stories at home and abroad: the *coup d'état* in Greece, the expulsion of King Freddie from Uganda, fighting in Lebanon, the declaration of UDI in Rhodesia, the Wilson–Smith talks aboard HMS *Tiger* at Gibraltar. As Deputy Court Correspondent he accompanied royal tours to Australia, New Zealand, Sudan and Ethiopia – where he was given a wooden pipe with which, years later, he tried unsuccessfully to charm Goldie, a golden eagle which had escaped from London Zoo. In 1968 he helped to launch BBC 2's 'Newsroom' and was among the first people in Britain to read the news in colour, remarking that his face seemed to be a shade of toasted beige. He stayed a BBC staffer and was keenly aware, later, that when he sat alongside Brian Redhead it was Redhead the freelance who was probably earning more money:

I've always kicked myself since for not going freelance but it was the coward in me. I preferred to cling to my patron, I preferred the comfort of being a BBC man. In those days, too, there was considerable prestige in being on the staff of the BBC. You really felt you were somebody. It was second only to the House of Commons as the best club in town, a nice feeling to be part of the establishment and I suppose I became a typical establishment figure.[2]

Many years later Dick Francis, then Managing Director of BBC Radio, encapsulated Timpson's qualities thus: 'What comes across to me with great clarity is that wherever you ply your craft, the essence of your work is a unique combination of tenacity, good journalism, and an ability to judge the right moment for the quip, such that viewers and listeners (and more particularly the latter) feel you are talking to them in their terms.'[3] Many would agree with that and the assessment of Kenneth Clarke, who described him as 'probably quite the nicest man you could have met anywhere'.[4]

The decision to bring in Timpson in 1970 started the co-presenter tradition which has lasted to this day. (Wilfred De'Ath, a contributor, had proposed in 1963[5] the creation of a 'deputy compère' who would write his own linking material, and modestly put his own name forward, but nothing became of it.) It blossomed most fully, perhaps, in the Timpson–Redhead partnership, but since 1970 'Today' has always been a two-presenter operation. Austin Mitchell, MP, put his finger on the appeal of the two-handed format:

I think a single-handed show would be awful. You may be more attached to one than to the other, but there's an interplay, a banter, between them which involves you. And they both respond as things are happening. It's the two-handed situation that is the strength of 'Today'. They're two people you can live with, not in a homosexual sense, but you feel after a time you know them, you know what their reflexes are going to be and so you can evaluate the world through their eyes. You feel the presenters are, not friends exactly, but people acting on your behalf. That atmosphere that it gives, in which the listener feels included, makes it a sort of breakfast club.[6]

(Some members of the club can recall their favourite pieces of this banter: mine was when Jim Naughtie revealed that Sue MacGregor had just slipped him a note across the table asking how cockles copulated.)

John Birt, the BBC's Director-General, also emphasises the importance of the two-handed format:

> There may have been a dominant presenter from time to time, but its success has not depended [since 1970] on a single presenter, for the very obvious reason that it doesn't have a single presenter day by day, it has a team which changes day by day. And I don't even think at the moment when you switch on that you feel a sense of disappointment if so-and-so is not doing it. The programme has a strength that goes beyond any individual presenter. The qualities which mark the programme, and therefore pretty much all its presenters, are cheerfulness, which is an important quality in the morning, humour, sharpness and political savvy.[7]

When the story broke that de Manio was to leave the programme there was a good deal of inevitable newspaper speculation, with Jack denying he had been fired. 'We've had no row,' he said. 'It's just that I'm damned tired of getting up so early in the morning. I want a change. I've been doing the programme for thirteen years.'[8] Whatever he said in public, though, Jack certainly thought he had been axed. Ian Trethowan's memo of 14 June 1971 leaves no doubt about that: 'there was some muttering about "I don't know why I have been dropped from the programme," which I simply ignored.'[9]

Jack's last weekday edition of 'Today' was due to have been on Friday 2 July 1971, and the programme had planned to mark the occasion by presenting him with a studio clock 'which he has so persistently misread over the last thirteen years', in the words of Tony Whitby, then Controller of Radio 4.[10] But, a few days before, Jack fell ill and was admitted to the King Edward VII Hospital for Officers. He had to do his farewell lying in his hospital bed. 'Rather ironically I am suffering from an acute attack of gout, not having had a drink for two weeks!' he scrawled on a postcard to Whitby.[11]

Jack continued for a short while as one of the presenters of the Saturday edition of 'Today', and in September 1971 he began his own afternoon chat show on Radio 4, 'Jack de Manio Precisely'. After seven years it was dropped, a casualty of the new broadcasting of parliament ('I can't imagine anybody wanting to listen to the cackling of those idiots,' he said).[12] At the beginning of 1981 he was living with his wife Loveday and their twelve-year-old dachshund in Chelsea and telling a journalist he wanted to get back into broadcasting: 'I would adore to be back . . . I miss it enormously.' It seemed as if he was having conversations with the fledgling commercial station Severn Sound, but clearly nothing came of them.

By 1982, Jack was broke. He was emptying slot machines in pubs to earn a few pounds a week. He told the *Sunday Express* in December 1982 that he had been forced to surrender his BBC pension of £17,000 to settle his debts, and had been to an employment exchange. He had been offered work as a cleaner and part-time gardener, and was waiting to hear if he had been accepted as a security officer. Twelve months later he and his wife were living in a council flat.

Even this miserable decline in a life which had seen such glamour did not eradicate Jack's sense of mischief and timing. He died early in the morning of Friday 28 October 1988. How many other broadcasters would have been considerate enough to arrange their passing in time for their old programme – and on the very day it celebrated its thirty-first birthday? His successors rose to the challenge, and rushed out a tribute on that morning's programme. They even managed to find a funny story from the archives, told by Jack against himself, in which he recalled having once received a letter from a listener inquiring about compensation after he crashed his car in surprise at hearing the wrong time announced on the radio.

Robert Robinson arrived in early July 1971 to co-present the programme with John Timpson. He stayed for three years, the equivalent of a wire-haired terrier succeeding an old English sheepdog. The press generally welcomed him as bringing a welcome touch of acidity to Timpson's sweet fruitiness, the wasp in the apple. If Timpson's speciality was the *bon mot*, Robinson's was the *mot juste*. Timpson always said 'A very good morning to you', while Robinson used the more ornate 'I bid you good morning'. They looked different, too: Robinson wore silk suits while Timpson sported long sideburns and had the demeanour of a rosy-cheeked farmer. Robinson liked to employ Johnsonian metaphors and Wodehousian similes; Timpson's style was the one-liner.

The Robinson–Timpson partnership drew much praise, but Robinson was always anxious that one day his television commitments would prevent him from being able to get up at 4.50 am each day. After three years that is what finished him off – lack of sleep. 'I spent three years doing it and never slept at all,' he told Roy Plomley on 'Desert Island Discs' in 1975. 'I kept waking up wondering if it was time to get up . . . there was an occasion when I had a little snooze round about tea-time, fell asleep, woke up, found it was ten to six and telephoned Mike Chaney who I think was the editor on that day and said "Mike, it's happened at last, I'm not there," and he said, "I am not too clear what you are talking about." I said the sun was streaming through the shutters and he said, "I know just what has happened" – and I said "Oh dear me, Mike, thank you very – yes I do, it's six o'clock in the evening, beg your pardon."'

Robinson had many other irons in the fire, including 'The Book Programme' and 'Call My Bluff' on BBC TV and 'Stop the Week' and 'Brain of Britain' on Radio 4. After the announcement in April 1974 of his exit (crowned by his collecting an award for Radio Personality of the Year) a succession of presenters were tried out as replacements. Among them were Michael Clayton, Nancy Wise, Desmond Lynam (whose association with the programme had started when de Manio had released mice over him as he was reading the sports news), James Burke, Malcolm Billings, Heather Summer-field and Barry Norman. Even Melvyn Bragg did a couple of presenting shifts. 'He came in wearing a white suit,' recalls Alistair Osborne, deputy editor at the time. 'He was trying to make something of the programme but what he wanted to make of it was an arts show.'[13] 'Melvyn Bragg, once described to me as Robert Robinson in paperback, came and rapidly went,' Timpson noted dryly.[14]

By the autumn of 1974, the programme had settled into a pattern of Barry Norman and Desmond Lynam alternating with Timpson (the second pairing once being lampooned in The Times as the partnership of John Trivial and Desmond Languid). Lynam left after eighteen months in the autumn of 1975 and returned to sports reporting. The impression given at the time was that he wished to restore his social life which, as an attractive thirty-two-year-old bachelor, was rather important to him. Alistair Osborne, by now the editor of the programme, remembers it rather differently: 'They [the production team] would be in despair because at 5 am he still hadn't got beyond the sports pages. He didn't have much of a clue when it came to news. So we sent him back to sport and he didn't speak to me for the next five years.'[15] Barry Norman put in nineteen months on the programme, working particularly for the Saturday edition, until he left in the spring of 1976. He too had other commitments, including his BBC-TV 'Film . . .' series, a column in the Guardian and some writing for television.

Duty editors and producers on the programme had to work unimaginably long shifts at this time. One of those involved was

Libby Purves, later a reporter and presenter on the programme but at that time a junior producer. Her first contact with 'Today' had been in 1972 when as a young trainee studio manager she had been allowed into the studio to see her heroes Robinson and Timpson, whom she remembered listening to in her bedroom at Oxford. She went to work for BBC Radio Oxford and then joined 'Today' in 1975 as a junior producer on a six-month attachment.

It seems unbelievable now, when the Corporation is plastered with Health and Safety posters about the dangers of sixteen-hour shifts, that we then did a twenty-two-hour shift. You worked from noon until ten the next morning. Two people did it, the editor and producer. The idea was that they worked that shift together while others came and went during that time, so they had continuity from the first concept of what might be on the programme until its execution.

Sometimes you got a couple of hours' sleep in the middle over in the Langham, where there were some beds for night announcers, but usually you didn't. Once or twice I went and played poker with the commissionaires because I couldn't wind down enough to sleep. Sometimes you got no time off at all because it was a busy night and foreign stories were coming in, because obviously the rest of the world was happening through the night. You worked through to the next morning and you would get this burst of adrenalin in time to put the programme on the air and do the studio production and then you would be absolutely wrecked. You would do two of these a week and that was your working week.

It was an experiment and it destroyed people and it was chopped soon afterwards to make way for full night shifts and full day shifts. But there was one guy who was running a farm in Wales and it meant he could spend a lot of time with his pigs and stuff. He used to bring in eggs and sell them in the office.[16]

Tony Hall, then a young producer like Purves and now Chief Executive of BBC News – in charge of the BBC's entire news and current affairs output and all its hundreds of journalists – had to work twenty-hour shifts during his six-month spell on 'Today' in 1975. He does not remember pigs, but ghosts:

You began at two in the afternoon and there were four or five hours in the middle of the night when you could go over and have a kip in a room which the 'Today' programme had over in the Langham, when the Langham was part of the BBC. It was full of weird rooms, one of which was a bedroom. You couldn't sleep because the building was extremely noisy at night, even though it was deserted. There was a legend that there was a ghost that haunted that floor of the Langham. It was probably the fourth or fifth floor as I recall. You went up in a clanky lift and down these echoing corridors, nobody there at all, into this little room not on the front of the building. Somebody, way back when, on the 'Today' programme had actually woken up and seen a face looking at them, a face of a made-up variety artist. So not only was it noisy, you dropped off to sleep and you'd suddenly wake up and have this man from variety looking at you, so I must confess I remember sleeping with the lights on. In the end I think I just gave up on the idea of going over there at all. You couldn't sleep or relax.[17]

Hall said he personally had never encountered the phantom vaudevillian, but went on, 'People said that it walked along the corridor with the bottom bit of the leg missing. The ghost of the Langham was much talked about by producers in those days. But the worst thing about the shift was that it was completely and utterly knackering.'[18]

There were also, thankfully, jollier moments too:

There was a group of insomniacs who would go out and have a meal late at night. You'd go out about midnight down to Soho, to Lee Ho Fook or one of those restaurants and have a meal until about two or three o'clock and then come back and do the programme. That was the alternative to the spooky bedroom and it often used to happen on a Friday evening. It got you through the night. And you'd come back and sort through the various tapes, listen to things, sort out the running order. It was quite relaxed. But it was a bizarre feeling at the end of the programme because bottles were produced. You know, it's the end of the shift, the end of the day, so you have a drink. But this was nine o'clock in the morning! It was a strange feeling leaving the building afterwards and seeing all these other people coming in to work, and you knew you were a bit smelly, and wanted to get to bed and you'd had a glass or two. It was a great programme.[19]

Timpson, incidentally, says he never had any ghostly encounters: 'I think the room allocated to me was too bleak and unwelcoming for any ghost!' he recalled.[20]

Marshall Stewart, who became editor of 'Today' in the year that Timpson joined as co-presenter, was a sure hand at the tiller, guiding the programme through the choppy waters of presenter changes and commercial competition. But no one is infallible. On 22 December 1970, for example, 'Today' carried an interview with Peter Sellers, whose new comedy *There's a Girl in My Soup* was opening in the cinema that night. Sellers told the interviewer, Malcolm Billings, that his co-star Goldie Hawn was such a joy to work with that often they had 'just pissed ourselves with laughter'. The Director-General, Charles Curran, choked over his cornflakes when he heard that, and told Ian Trethowan to rap the knuckles of those concerned. Trethowan duly did so, and reported back to the D-G in contrite vein:

> You asked before Christmas about the Peter Sellers interview in the 'Today' programme. Why was not one offensive phrase edited? The answer, I am afraid, is an error of judgement by someone who is normally very reliable. The editor of the programme, Marshall Stewart, had already picked up the point, and it has been emphasised that what is permissible on Radio 3 at 8 o'clock at night is not necessarily acceptable on Radio 4 at 8 o'clock in the morning.[21]

Britain's entry into Europe meant increasing foreign assignments: Timpson's first Euro visit was to Brussels in 1971; he went to Luxembourg the following month, covered the Queen's state visit to Paris in May 1972 and later that summer went to Belfast to report on the troubles in Northern Ireland. 'We stayed at the Europa Hotel, a charmed place with a cosseted atmosphere. Both sides knew the press were there and wanted to keep on the right side of them, so they didn't blow it up too much.'[22] He was in the United States for the November 1972 election when Richard Nixon won, travelled to Dublin, Oslo and Brussels in 1974, was back in America at the end of that year for the mid-term elections and in Dublin the following year for the EEC Summit.

Commercial competition began when the BBC finally lost its fifty-one-year radio monopoly with the birth of LBC at 6 am on 8 October 1973. Marshall Stewart had been preparing for this moment for many months. In March that year he had written to the Controller of Radio 4, Tony Whitby, arguing that 'Today' needed a punchier, and earlier, start to put it ahead of the competition:

> A permanent opening time of 0645 for the Morning Sequence would also give the programme a cleaner start with a more natural junction on the quarter hour. It would enable the programme to exhibit its natural personality at a much earlier stage; at the present time Robinson and Timpson in their conventional roles do not appear until 0710 approx. A programme beginning with news headlines, followed by a short hard news interview and developing public service information would, it seems, be likely to have a greater pulling power.[23]

Stewart returned to the attack in August, only two months before the competition was due to start:

> It may be interesting to know that, as a professional, he [David Chipp, Managing Editor of the Press Association], switches on to Radio 4 at 0625 to hear the early summary and promptly switches off afterwards until 0650 when 'Today' begins in a fairly light-hearted vein. As you know, London Broadcasting are proposing to begin transmissions at 0600, and it seems to me that it is imperative that 'Today' has the benefit of a 0645 start from the earliest possible date.[24]

He won his campaign, as Whitby announced the following month:

> I have M.D.R.'s [Managing Director, Radio] agreement to open up Radio 4 five minutes earlier (Monday to Friday) in order to enable the TODAY programme to begin with a bang at 0645 rather than with a whimper at 0650 ... The first five minutes of the programme from 0645–0650 will be self-contained, will include the main presenters Robinson/Timpson and will meet a firm junction as at present at 0650.[25]

Whitby was very flattering about 'Today' a few weeks after LBC had started: 'Listening to the "Today" programme in the first weeks of commercial competition has been a real pleasure. It's like choosing between a seat in the Leeds United stand and the terraces at Brentford.'[26]

Third division LBC may have been, but it could still offer handsome transfer fees. Marshall Stewart defected there in early 1974, taking 'Today' presenter Douglas Cameron ('dependable old Dobbin', according to one piece of BBC audience research) with him. He was succeeded by his deputy, Alistair Osborne, to whom fell the task of organising the programme's coverage of Nixon's resignation in August 1974 – without Timpson, who was on holiday. Marshall did, however, return to the company of his ex-BBC colleagues to collect yet another award from the Radio Industries Club, which made 'Today' the radio programme of the year for 1971, 1972, 1973 and 1974.

Osborne was the person most closely involved in the search for Robinson's successor. He recalls that it was he, among others, who brought in Brian Redhead in 1975 to fill that slot.

> I had been brought up on 'The World at One' under William Hardcastle, a former editor of the *Daily Mail*, so we were aware of the value of former editors. Redhead didn't get the editorship of the *Guardian* and a few months later walked out of the group in disgust. It took a lot of talking, but eventually we persuaded him to become a presenter of 'Today'. I started on the phone and later went up to Manchester to see him. My intention was to get someone to be number two to Timpson, but of course we didn't put it like that. Presenters can often be told that they are going to be the senior ones. It's what you say to them for their morale.[27]

Osborne also proposed that Eileen Fowler's long-standing physical fitness spot be axed. His 1974 memo about this to his boss, with a copy to the Controller of Radio 4, shows how disingenuous the BBC can be when getting rid of people – and the importance of audience reaction:

> The daily Keep Fit item will disappear. Eileen Fowler has been told that we intend resting [one of the favourite words in the BBC's lexicon] this item for at least one quarter although it is our intention that it should be for longer. Any undue reaction on the part of the listeners, however, could change our minds in this.[28]

He also proposed shortening the main 7 am and 8 am news bulletins to ten minutes (they had been creeping up to nearly twelve), extending the summary on the half-hour to two minutes, introducing a weekly letters' slot to be presented by Timpson, starting shorter and more factual news packages, reducing national travel information to the role of filler material, and pressed for a yet earlier start time ('at least 6.30 but 6.00 would probably be more appropriate'). There was also one very welcome change in January 1975: the birth of Radio Ulster meant the disappearance of the notorious 8.25 am opt-out 'which has bedevilled our producers for so long'.

4

'This Perfect and Unbeatable Duo'

The carousel of presenters finally stopped turning with the arrival of Brian Redhead in 1975. A loquacious and boisterous Geordie, he was already well known to Radio 4 listeners from 'A Word in Edgeways', which he had chaired for nine years in Manchester. It was in the Athens of the north, as he always liked to think of his adopted city, where he had made his name; as Northern Editor of the *Guardian* from 1965 to 1969 and then Editor of its sister paper, the *Manchester Evening News*, from 1969 to August 1975. (He claimed he was sacked: others believed he left in a fit of pique after failing to win the editorship of the *Guardian*.)

To someone on the margins of British society, Redhead and Timpson might have seemed cut from the same branch. Both of them were white, middle-class, middle-aged men who sent their children to fee-paying schools. Even their home towns had a similar ring: Cheadle Hulme and Chorleywood. But they felt they had little in common and did not, at first, get on. Even today, Timpson says that the one thing they had in common was that they 'both enjoyed showing off'.[1] Despite what the press quoted them as saying at the time, Timpson concedes now that they never became great friends. They never did much socialising and they never visited one another's homes in all their years together. The first and only time Timpson saw Redhead's home was at his funeral.

But the professional association they – eventually – enjoyed in the studio was as powerful as the personal gulf that stretched between them, and they grew into one of the greatest and best-loved partnerships in the history of broadcasting. It was that partnership which, as Peter Hobday so rightly said when Redhead died, earned the programme 'its special place in the nation's affairs'.[2]

It was not simply that, to a nation with a ready ear for the nuances of class and district, they represented north and south, tenor and baritone, town and country; though certainly they played on those differences in their ping-pong verbal exchanges. It was more fundamental than that: they had different senses of humour, different senses of what was important on and off the programme, different approaches to life. Away from work, Redhead liked to *do* things; Timpson liked to do very little except eat, sleep and potter about. Redhead was a serious man who saw public activity, and thus the public acts of politicians and the polls which elected them, as vital to the nation's health. Timpson was profoundly bored by politics and politicians and much preferred to entertain with a quip or a joke, chuckling over innocent little advertisements such as 'Eight thick sausages – Irish recipe', or 'Insulation – Britain lags behind', or unfortunate headlines like 'Crash Course for Learner Drivers'. 'He wasn't Jack de Manio, but he was half-way back to Jack de Manio,' says Libby Purves, who described Timpson and Redhead as 'chalk and cheese'.[3]

Timpson was one of two children, with a sister, Joy, who became a music teacher. His family was keen on amateur music and dramatics. Redhead was a classic only child, vain and (literally) self-interested, proud of being an infant prodigy, of having played the clarinet on 'Children's Hour' at the age of eleven, of having won a place at Newcastle's Royal Grammar School and gone on to Downing College, Cambridge, where he took a First in Part One of his History Tripos (but only a Second in Part Two, which of course he did not mention). Timpson, by contrast, had found academic work formidably hard, and at the age of sixteen left Merchant Taylors' by mutual consent. He recalls:

The big difference as far as I was concerned was that Brian had risen to far dizzier heights in journalism than I had. I had never risen above the position of reporter, and never particularly wanted to. But Brian, as he never stopped reminding us, had been Editor of the *Manchester Evening News*. He had also done a lot of television very well and he was a much more intellectual chap than I was. He had gone to university, which I hadn't, and I was slightly overawed when I first worked with him, I must say. I thought, my word, here's one of the great men of journalism and I'm put up here beside him. But that wore off after a bit. He was just another chap and one got through life.

I always felt he would look most at home sitting with a fishing rod beside a garden pond with a little curly hat with a pom-pom on top. He was everybody's idea of a lovable garden gnome. But he didn't like me saying that, so I shouldn't say it.

He felt deeply about politics, not so much party politics, but because he felt politicians were responsible for the lives of millions of others. I could never take politics seriously at all, but to keep the thing balanced I insisted on doing as many political interviews as he did, although most of the time I wasn't too clear what I was talking about.[4]

Their initial rivalry was so great that Libby Purves remembers occasions when the two of them would count up the live interviews allotted to them by the production team:

There was a phase early on when they were real rivals and wanted to make sure that neither had more lives [live interviews, the most exciting ingredient for presenters] than the other. Both of them reacted the same way with me. If there were five lives, they wanted to be very certain that they had three and I had two. I thought it was absolutely hysterical, the way they minded.

They didn't get on at all well at first, but they grew into each other, and this is the important thing. John is from the lawn-mowing classes, an old BBC chap, apolitical, who had a rather old-fashioned, rather courtly sort of humour, ha-ha, ho-ho, hurrumph-hurrumph, and a timing for those sort of jokes. Brian was a chippy Geordie, up from the people and, God didn't he know it, ex-newspaper editor. He used to go round saying he was the only real journalist here. He was verbally extremely acute, and mannered, and bumptious. He loved the networking, the conferences, the big meetings, he liked being on the inside track. John didn't give a stuff about being on the inside track.

We used to collect Brianisms. There was a famous one when he was in Rhodesia and some kind of row had suddenly blown up overnight about sanctions busting and he came on and said on the programme, 'Yes, I told Peter Carrington [Lord Carrington, Foreign Secretary from 1979 to 1982] about it this morning and he was as shocked as I was . . .' We all used to fall about. 'I was speaking to a lady the other day, the Queen actually . . .,' that was the apocryphal one.

But because they represented rather different extremes of the way you could approach a programme like 'Today', they were complementary. For the first two years they worked together only on Wednesdays, because I partnered Brian on Mondays and Tuesdays and John on Thursdays and Fridays. After I took my shifts down they obviously had to start doing more days together and that was when they started to grow into one another. They became one of the great double acts.

Something happens when you sit next to somebody in the studio. It's a live programme, it's quite tense, while one of you is doing an interview the other might be getting briefed for the next one – about a coup in Grenada, or a fire, and you know sod all about it – and you look down and you see an appalling misprint on his cue, like 'now' for 'not', or they tell you that a problem is coming up for him. You slip a note across, you help, you pick things up, you catch each other's balls before they hit the ground, as it were, all the time on a busy morning. So their real rivalry became friendly rivalry, because they needed each other, and I think John was as shattered as all of us when Brian died so young.[5]

Shortly after Redhead arrived, a new editor, Mike Chaney, also joined the programme. His appointment at the beginning of 1976 was announced by a most unusual BBC press release. It said, 'Mike Chaney is married and lives in Dulwich. They have twelve children, three from his previous marriage, four by his wife and another five by his wife's previous marriage.' Nigel Rees remembers him as 'a hearty, bearded cove . . . a popular newspaper man at heart'.[6] He moved over from Radio 1's 'Newsbeat', which he had been editing since he created it two years before. He had been in charge of its pacy coverage of the two 1974 elections ('Newsbeat' was the first Radio 1 programme to put a Prime Minister on the air in the shape of Edward Heath) and the Patty Hearst saga. Chaney brought with him from 'Newsbeat' as one of his duty editors Roger Gale, who worked mostly on future planning but also did some producing. Gale, who later became a Tory MP, started out as a pirate radio DJ on Radio Caroline North, Radio Caroline South, Radio Scotland and Radio 270 in the mid-1960s before turning legitimate and joining BBC Radio London, moving from there to become one of the founding production team of 'Newsbeat'.

Taking up the reins of the 'Today' programme, Chaney decided to move it out of London and have it co-presented from Manchester. The spirit of devolution was afoot. 'They were very keen on getting out and about,' remembers Purves, who, having recovered from her twenty-two-hour shifts in 1975, joined the programme in 1976 as a contract reporter, doing three shifts a week at £25 a go and building up to five a week within two years.

They used to send reporters off to 'beat up a region'. You went to somewhere like Wisbech and found four or five Lincolnshire stories and brought them back for the programme. They were very keen on outside reporting, on vox pops, on taped features, on getting real people's voices, and that has fallen away rather. Of course, there were far fewer local radio stations then.[7]

It was also a much more cavalier age, as Libby Purves recalls:

I was kind of festering in the reporters' room and Mike Chaney came in and said, 'Look, this business of kids beating their teachers up and violence against schoolteachers [this was twenty years ago, educational Jeremiahs should note], we've got Norman St John-Stevas [then opposition spokesman for Education] but I'm not just having talking heads. Go out and find some kids that beat up their teachers, Libby.' I said, 'It's seven o'clock at night, fair dos, where am I going to find children that beat up their teachers?' He said, 'You're a reporter, I fucking well pay you to report, get on out there,' and so I went out into the rain with my Uher [tape recorder] and found an adventure playground I had once been to before in south London which was full of kids prepared to tell doughty tales of classroom violence.[8]

Two of the first victims of Chaney's new régime were Gillian Reynolds, who was co-presenting 'Today' on Mondays and Fridays, and Barry Norman, who hosted it on Saturdays. 'As far as Gillian was concerned, she did have some fine qualities,' Chaney recalls. 'She was a woman, which was hugely important. She was North Country. She was intelligent, in a questioning sense. But I thought she had a bad broadcasting voice, certainly for the morning. There was a sort of querulousness about her and a tremulousness about her voice which didn't sound right for the morning.'[9] Timpson described her in his scrapbook as 'The First Casualty'. He wrote, 'By February, Gillian Reynolds had gone.'

Barry Norman, recalls Chaney, was a very busy man, 'and didn't like coming in to do interviews on a Friday. I was able to replace him with Paul Barnes.'[10] He is as open about these events ('I fired two excellent journalists, Barry Norman and Gillian Reynolds') as he is about his own overthrow two years later.

Chaney claims that it was his own decision to get the 'Today' programme presented from both London and Manchester. It was all part of getting out and about, and, he says, an effort to lighten the programme:

> All the news programmes, including 'Newsbeat', 'Today', and 'The World at One', had become heavily politicised. My feeling was that 'Today' had lost touch with its listeners from the de Manio period. He had been immensely popular, as shown in the fact that he had his own effigy in Madame Tussaud's. The well-built package was in danger of losing its place on the programme. That is why I brought in skilful, witty reporters like Paul Heiney, and Libby, and Ed Boyle, to balance the programme.
>
> It was said at the time that Radio 4 was listened to almost entirely by people over forty living south of a line from the Wash to the Bristol Channel. Certainly it was not listened to greatly in the north. It was my idea to start co-presenting the programme from Manchester and really it was a conspiracy between Brian Redhead, David Hatch [then running the Manchester end of BBC Radio], Colin Adams [then Chaney's deputy] and me.[11]

Senior BBC executives have often expressed similar views: for example, John Birt, Director-General, once said that Radio 4 was 'skewed far too much in its concerns and its appeal towards the Southern middle classes'.[12]

But Chaney's predecessor, Alistair Osborne, remembers it all quite differently:

> It was not Chaney's idea at all, but that of Martin Wallace, who was Head of Current Affairs Group, Radio. He'd been brought from Northern Ireland by Ian Trethowan, who had been very impressed with him there. They wanted more days out of Redhead, but Redhead didn't have a pad in London then, so he was reluctant. The only alternative was to get him to do it from Manchester. I said it wasn't a goer so I got shunted off to 'The World Tonight' and Chaney was brought in with that instruction.[13]

Whether acting under orders or executing his own idea, Chaney introduced the split presentation on 'Today' on Monday 5 April 1976. Timpson stayed put to present it from the London end, and Redhead – increasing his number of days on the programme from three to five – moved to Manchester, along with six members of the twenty-strong production team. The BBC's publicists gave it a clever nickname, 'the new inter-city style of presentation'. The new arrangements were also able to make use of the BBC's new £7 million studio complex in Manchester, but the Saturday edition stayed in London.

The new system did not meet with wide approval: it did not sound very good and also led to the near disappearance of the weather forecast. Timpson's increasing irritation with what he calls the 'ridiculous idea'[14] of having it co-presented from London and Manchester meant he was in a receptive mood when Christopher Capron, editor of BBC1's 'Tonight', asked him if he was interested in moving into television to alternate as presenter with Denis Tuohy. Flattered, Timpson accepted the invitation, and in September 1976 started on the programme as successor to Sue Lawley, who had left to have a baby. But he had a rude awakening. He discovered all too soon, as did BBC TV, that it was his voice and not his face that was his fortune.

> It was sheer conceit that I went. Chris Capron had been an editor on 'Today' and assured me that 'Tonight' was going to be very similar, but would have the additional glory of television surrounding it. I didn't always see eye to eye with Mike Chaney so I thought I'd give it a try. It was an unmitigated disaster from my point of view. I didn't enjoy working late at night. Everyone said how dreadful it must be to get up so early in the morning, but in fact it's a jolly sight better to get up early and do the job and get it finished with than have to worry about it all day. One gets into the office at ten in the morning and has to try and occupy oneself until half-past ten at night and then actually start the real work. I was generally on the brink of going to bed rather than going into the studio by the time it all began, so I can't say I was at my best.
>
> I never really got used to the television world. You were just a sort of little automaton with this thing stuck in your ear telling you when to start, when to stop, which way to look, when to get up, when to sit down. I found it all terribly restricting and worrying and hence I wasn't terribly good at it, I'm afraid. There

was a great argument over why did I always have such a schoolboy haircut. I remember getting criticised in one of the papers and my masters took this immediately to heart and insisted I had to go and have fancy haircuts and blow-waves, much to my wife's fury!

We worked down at Lime Grove, a weird little world cut off from the real world completely. Nobody dared go out because you got mugged. It was a sinister area. So everyone spent their entire lives crouched in the club or canteen talking about each other. I found it absolutely appalling, I'm afraid. I think they were as relieved as I was when I went back to 'Today'. I was absolutely delirious. It was when Ken Goudie took over as editor in 1978. He was rejigging the programme and rang me up at home. I can remember the day now. My wife was out in the garden and he said, rather diffidently because I don't think he realised what problems I'd been having, how would I feel about coming back to the 'Today' programme? I said I would be delighted, I'll just go and check with my wife. I said what do you think about me going back to the 'Today' programme? She said, marvellous, start tomorrow! I'm jolly glad I did go back. It saved my sanity.[15]

For the first two months of his ill-fated television period, Timpson hosted 'Tonight' once a week and 'Today' four days a week, becoming full-time on 'Tonight' in November 1976. At that point he was replaced as the London presenter on the 'Today' programme by Nigel Rees, who now became, at the age of thirty-two, the youngest regular presenter of 'Today' up to that time (Libby Purves was twenty-eight when she became a presenter two years later).

Timpson's defection may have spelled disaster for him at Lime Grove, but he left behind an even bigger disaster at Broadcasting House. Ian McIntyre had become Controller of Radio 4 in the autumn of 1976, just about the time Timpson moved into television. In actions which gained him the inevitable nickname 'Mac the Knife', he proceeded to cut 'Today' in half – with a 25-minute edition at 7.10 and a 35-minute one at 8.10 am. ('A good time not to be around,' Timpson noted in his scrapbook, which was something of an understatement.) In between, and under separate editorial control, was a new programme called 'Up to the Hour', a 25-minute ragbag of lighter material broadcast at 6.35 and 7.35 am. Peter Dacre in the *Sunday Express* called it 'a chaotic hotchpotch' and many other newspaper commentators were equally scathing.

Chaney spoke for many when he said:

Up to the Hour was absolute crap, the floor-sweepings. There was enormous reaction against it within Broadcasting House and Peter Donaldson, the announcer, was almost sacked when he called himself Donald Peterson on Radio 4 one morning and made a disparaging remark about it. It was a brave thing to do, mutiny on the air. If McIntyre had had his way he would have been hung by the bollocks outside Broadcasting House.[16]

The background to McIntyre's decision was that he felt the previous Controller of Radio 4, Tony Whitby (who had died in 1975), had introduced a great many speech and news programmes which were freezing out general programming. McIntyre was determined to reverse this, and did so. He scrapped 'Newsdesk', cut the broadcasting hours of both 'Today' and 'PM' and got rid of the Saturday edition of 'Today' as well.

Libby Purves, too, remembers how grim it was:

It was desperately demoralising. We had all this material coming out of our ears, the whole world to report on, stories to tell, and we hungered and thirsted for the 'Today' programme to be a proper 'Today' programme. It was a kind of physical pain to have to stop for 'Up to the Hour' each day with its dreadful bits of old Victor Borge records and junk like that.[17]

It was hardly a happy occasion, therefore, when on 28 October 1977 the programme celebrated its twentieth birthday. Jack de Manio (still working on Radio 4, just), John Timpson (visiting from television) and Nigel Rees mingled with Director-General Ian Trethowan, BBC Radio Managing Director Howard Newby, and 'Mac the Knife' himself. Brian Redhead was away, visiting his son in Cambridge: perhaps he wanted to avoid champagne with a sour taste. But the programme still tried to put a brave face on things and the anniversary edition contained this song written and sung by Richard Stilgoe:

In 1957 when 'Today' was young and green
It went out in two editions with a vicar in between
Who gave thanks for the first one and offered up a prayer
They'd get it right the second time the show went on the air

It wasn't so much news as a sort of topical 'Down Your Way'
That was the day before yesterday is today.

The ditty was played on the thirtieth birthday programme as well.
Eventually the BBC saw sense. Aubrey Singer took over as
Managing Director of BBC Radio in 1978 and axed the hated 'Up to
the Hour'. (He also tried to import Sue MacGregor from 'Woman's
Hour': she eventually joined on Mondays in September 1984 when
Timpson took over the chairmanship of 'Any Questions?' and
reduced his number of days on the programme to three a week.)
Nigel Rees quit, to be replaced by John Sergeant, and Libby Purves
was invited to join as a presenter, too. 'I was down interviewing
some Druids at Stonehenge and I phoned in and they said will you
present the programme for a week with Sergeant. Then Ken Goudie,
who had just taken over as editor, said would I do it as a permanent
thing. And I said no, they had been getting through so many
presenters it would be like marrying Henry VIII. I said I would do it
on a shift basis.'[18] For six months she did it day by day, then
eventually signed a year's contract.

Timpson turned fifty on the weekend the news broke that he was
returning to radio after his embarrassing twenty-two month flirtation
with television. He returned to a programme that was being
relaunched. The date of the relaunch was Monday 3 July 1978 and it
took place under the new editor, Ken Goudie. Chaney explains how
he was pushed out and Goudie given his job:

There was a good deal of rivalry between News Division and
Current Affairs and I, part of Current Affairs, got pushed out. It
was a News putsch. In 1978 I was presented with an ultimatum.
News and Current Affairs were going to be more closely
integrated and as part of this internal reorganisation I was invited
to apply for my own job as editor of 'Today'. Ken Goudie had
been groomed to take over and he got the job because he was a
senior person in News.

I was the only one of the sequence editors [senior journalists in
overall charge of Radio 4's daily news and current affairs
programmes] who was fired. I was forty-nine, not in a position to
take early retirement, and I did consult a solicitor. But in the end
they offered me a nice quiet job in local radio. [He set up and
became manager of BBC Radio Norfolk in 1980, the first BBC
local radio station to broadcast in stereo and one of the first to

cover a county rather than a city or town.] There I complained bitterly about under-resourcing and lack of money. Eventually I left when Aubrey Singer sent me a two-word message, the second word of which was 'off'.[19]

He retired from the BBC in April 1982 after twenty-three years' service, going on to become director of communications for Southampton University and then Dorset County Council.

The July 1978 relaunch took place as soon as McIntyre was pushed out of Radio 4 to become Controller of Radio 3. 'The Monday after he went, "Today" went back to being a two-hour programme – and in fact became a two-and-a-half hour programme,' Chaney said.[20] The relaunch, under Goudie, was ambitious: as well as the abolition of 'Up to the Hour', the programme now ran from 6.30 to 8.35 am when parliament was sitting, and 8.45 am during the parliamentary recess. Full news bulletins continued to go out at 7 am and 8 am, but summaries were now introduced on the half-hour and headlines on the quarter-hour, rather like LBC. The new format embraced both 'Prayer for the Day' at 6.45 am and 'Thought for the Day' an hour later.

Broadly speaking that format has continued ever since, though there was one subsequent change of importance. 'Prayer for the Day' was moved out of the programme and 'Yesterday in Parliament' moved into it, an indication of the way politicians now took priority over priests. 'Prayer' was exiled to 6.25 am, so that it now immediately precedes the programme of which it was once a part.

Brian Redhead moved to London from Manchester, co-presenting with John Timpson one day a week and with Libby Purves two days a week. She remembers the infectious enthusiasm of the period:

There is absolutely nothing like that feeling that you're first up in the morning and, 'Wake up everybody, things have happened in the night and we're going to tell you.' You're bringing the nation to itself first thing in the morning and that is the big buzz. It's that adrenalin thing. Sometimes Brian used to get incredibly high on a developing story and if it was a grim story I used to kick him under the table and say, 'Brian, people are dead you know, this is serious,' and Brian would always respond by saying, 'You're quite right, you're quite right.' His problem was sounding too gleeful, but that glee is entirely understandable. It is a fun job to do.[21]

Redhead did not disguise how much he loved the job. In one much quoted (and frequently broadcast) remark he said, 'It's a marvellous job. I think it fits me like a glove. I say that not meaning that I think I do it well or anything, but I'm happy doing it. I sit there gurgling with happiness, and thinking, "Right, I will now tell the nation what I think about the Budget."'[22]

'At this stage they were mostly very civil about all of us – the exception was the girl who *didn't* get the job,' Timpson noted in his scrapbook, referring to a piece by Gillian Reynolds in which she remarked that 'it can't be much fun working on the "Today" programme these days'.

There was champagne after the first edition of the relaunched 'Today', provided by Goudie, and Redhead was quoted as saying – probably for the first time – 'If you want to drop a word in the ear of the nation, then this is the programme in which to do it.'[23] He was quoted as saying it again when breakfast television began in 1983: 'Anyone who is anybody tends to listen to the "Today" programme. If you want to drop a word in the ear of the nation, you go on "Today". If you want to whistle in the wind, you appear on breakfast TV.'[24]

Redhead's move south was greatly welcomed by David Wade in *The Times*: 'Up north he always sounded as if he were talking to himself (and apart from the microphone he probably was), but his chairing of "A Word in Edgeways" leaves no doubt that he is a man who likes a bit of company in the studio; having got it he is now filling the loudspeaker with the same confident energy as Timpson.'[25] Jilly Cooper wrote that he 'seems to have turned into some Regional Bosanquet, "yer knowing" all over the place and calling everyone "love". And Libby Purves sounds exactly like a Katie who's abandoned Oxo and gone back to Oxford.'[26] That criticism was echoed by another spry writer who said that she 'sounds for all the world like the captain of the first lacrosse eleven taking a recalcitrant Lower Third for prep'.[27]

All three presenters carried out foreign assignments. Timpson seems to have had the lion's share, which included papal trips to Ireland and Britain and the Queen's visit to Jordan in 1984, an occasion also marked by a Muslim 'Thought for the Day' (years before a regular Muslim speaker for that slot was discovered). In between there were jobs in Salisbury, Detroit, New York (for the presidential election in which Ronald Reagan was elected), Jerusalem, Ottawa and San Francisco. But there was also one memorable assignment in China, which went to Libby Purves:

Aubrey Singer was responsible for sending me. He was one of two people, the other being Ian Trethowan, who stood up for me enormously. Not Monica Sims, the Controller of Radio 4, who was really quite hostile. She thought I was too juvenile and bouncy and would have liked me off the programme. But Aubrey was always very supportive.

It was a magical thing to have done, the absolute cherry on the cake really. This massive ancient land of China was suddenly flowering and opening up to the rest of the world. For years it had been in the grip of Maoism and now it was wanting to be accessible. Aubrey was thrilled by the romance of it all and I was sent out for a fortnight, Steve Rose the producer and I collecting material, going round doing interviews through our interpreters. There were Chinese doctors who wept talking to us saying that we simply could not imagine their joy in at last being able to write to colleagues in the West to find out what had been happening in medicine.

For fifteen years they had not been allowed to know what developments there were. They had only heard of the scanner. We used to walk down the street and women would beg to look at my bra because they had never seen a bra. We went to a commune and had it explained to us how a rich family was one with a pig and a bicycle. We got led off to a nursery school where a little boy sang a song called 'I Grow Up in a Communist Garden' and so on.

Two or three programmes resulted from this, which I presented live from Peking. I think it was the first programme to be broadcast live from China by satellite. There was a real feeling of bliss was it in that dawn to be alive. But years later when Tiananmen Square blew up [1989] I burst into tears because I suddenly realised that those students who were being shot down by the soldiers were the little children who had been singing 'I Grow Up in a Communist Garden'.

I remember when I got back and Brian suddenly turned to me on the programme when we were on the air and asked me, 'Libby, you're back from China this morning, how does it actually feel to be back, what strikes you about this country?' You never knew when he was going to ask you something. And I said, and it was straight from the heart, 'How rich we are and how much meat we all eat.' And of course I got an indignant letter saying, 'Do you realise what the old-age pension of a retired Brigadier is? We're not all rich, you know.' And I thought, Oh God, I'm back in bloody England again![28]

Other big stories in that period were John Lennon's murder in Manhattan in December 1980 ('one of the editors was so distressed he spent the whole morning playing "Imagine" down the telephone to his wife at home and talking about their early days together', recalls Libby) and the Brighton bombing of 1984, when Timpson was one of the first on the scene and gave his eye-witness account as the programme began at 6.30 am.

Under the editorship of Julian Holland, who succeeded Goudie in 1981, the programme became more weighty and attracted a succession of serious national figures. Enoch Powell talked about repatriation as a way of avoiding civil war in July 1981. The traindrivers' leader Ray Buckton dropped his words in the nation's ear, as did other union leaders. Margaret Thatcher appeared in 1982 to discuss the prayer she had chosen for an anthology of famous people's poetry and prose in aid of Action for Dysphasic Adults. (It was the seventeenth-century 'The Nun's Prayer', which included the appropriate lines, 'Teach me the glorious lesson that occasionally it is possible I may be mistaken . . . make me thoughtful but not moody, helpful but not bossy.') All of this helped to get the programme written about and noticed – and listeners noticed the silver jubilee even if the Corporation did not. A London couple sent in a card adorned with primroses and butterflies and the rhyme:

> BBC is sixty
> 'Today' is twenty-five
> When 'Today' is sixty
> Here's hoping it's still live.

The coverage of the royal wedding on 29 July 1981 underlined the programme's growing reputation. John Timpson was with David McNeil (then the BBC Diplomatic and Court Correspondent) aboard an Outside Broadcast vehicle outside Buckingham Palace, which at 7.30 am led a media convoy along the processional route to St Paul's Cathedral; Robert Hudson and Robert Fox were at St Paul's; Hugh Sykes was at Wellington Barracks; Andy Price reported from Trafalgar Square; and Brian Redhead anchored it all in the studio.

Prince William's arrival in June 1982 served to focus attention on breakfast broadcasting as a whole. Margaret Forwood in the *Sun* captured the mood well:

> I have not been enthusiastic about the idea of Breakfast TV. I have yet to be convinced that there will be enough people free to watch it at that hour in the morning or with television sets in the right place in the house.
>
> But lying in bed on Tuesday morning, listening to all the excitement about the royal baby on Radio 4's always excellent 'Today' programme, I began to wish I could see it as well.
>
> In fact, I popped downstairs just to check whether either side had, by some remote chance, mounted a special breakfast TV show to mark the occasion.
>
> Of course, they had not.
>
> But I think I could become a convert.[29]

The job of fighting off the competition from breakfast television fell to the highly respected Julian Holland, who had arrived after Goudie switched to 'The World Tonight' in October 1981. Libby Purves left at about this time and, in a move which stunned Fleet Street, later became editor of *Tatler* for three months before succeeding Henry Kelly on Radio 4's 'Midweek' in 1983. She explains her departure thus:

> John was very avuncular and he used to say to me, 'Your trouble, young lady, is that you've peaked twenty years too early,' and quite possibly he was right, bless his heart. But I was only thirty-one and afraid that I would sit there becoming a lovable bloody national institution like the Albert Memorial. I wanted to write more, I had a lot of other things to do. The Falklands War broke out the year after I left and everyone said don't you wish you were back in there and I said no, I've had enough, I've done that kind of news. I wouldn't have wanted to sit there asking Christopher Lee how Harrier jump jets work.[30]

One of Holland's first moves was to appoint Peter Hobday as her successor. He was to stay fourteen years, one of the longest-serving presenters in the history of the programme. The two men had worked together on 'The World at One', Holland as editor and

Hobday as a stand-in presenter for Robin Day, though Hobday's journalistic credentials went back a lot further.

A Midlander, born in 1937, Hobday read modern languages at Leicester University College, though he failed to get a degree after failing a classics component in his first year. He then did his National Service at NATO headquarters in Paris, where he met the woman who became his first wife. A Parisienne, she was the daughter of Russian emigrés, and through her and through living in France Peter became bilingual. He also acquired a working knowledge of Russian. Returning to Britain, he worked for three weeks as a song-plugger, moving back to the Midlands as showbusiness editor of the *Wolverhampton Chronicle*, then coming to London to work in public relations for GEC, as a journalist for business magazines and as a freelance for the World Service. From there he moved to Radio 4's 'The Financial World Tonight' (British radio's first daily business programme), 'Money Box', and BBC2's 'Newsnight', where he worked alongside Peter Snow, Charles Wheeler and John Tusa. Peter's late brother, John, his senior by eight years, had trodden a much more venerable BBC path, working first as an actor (he played the first policeman to appear in 'The Archers') before becoming an announcer at Broadcasting House.

Hobday recalls:

When I joined 'Today' in 1982 my wife was battling against cancer. She died in 1984. So for the first two years I was rather distracted. But Julian Holland was a wonderful editor, the best I ever had, and the last old-fashioned editor the 'Today' programme had. He bollocked all of us every day, Brian and John and me, and quite rightly too. He worried and nagged and pushed, every day. We all loved him. For him the programme came first. The programme was all. When Jenny Abramsky took over in 1986, the emphasis changed. For her, a career in the BBC was more important than that particular job. That also applied to her successors [Philip Harding and Roger Mosey] and there was a growing tendency to do what their masters wanted and listen to the marketing men. The desire to make programmes took second place to the desire for a BBC career. The sooner they could get off the journalism, the better.[31]

Holland, who had joined the BBC from the *Daily Mail* after it became a tabloid in 1971, decided to fight breakfast television by making the most of his three extremely skilled presenters and continuing to emphasise the programme's identity as a serious and wide-ranging newspaper of the airwaves. He was determined that it should remain indispensable for the middle-class, middle-aged, decision-making audience. However, he also decided to introduce a listeners' letters slot and a signature tune called 'One for Today', composed by John Dankworth, which made its début a few days before breakfast television came on air. Dankworth said he had tried to compose something that would suit all situations and was not too jaunty. It was not a success and listeners rose in uproar, but it took four months before the BBC bowed to public opinion and scrapped it. Monica Sims, Controller of Radio 4, said she received protest letters 'by every post' and that she would 'talk again to Julian in the near future'.[32] Gillian Reynolds summarised the general horror in her *Daily Telegraph* column:

> Letters from all over the country this week reassure me I am not alone in feeling irritated by Radio 4's 'Today' programme jingles.
> Heartfelt testaments of annoyance were reinforced by an American friend's inquiry as to whether little tunes without lyrics could actually be called jingles, as the term presupposes rhyming words. The same friend suggested the word 'jangles' for the 'Today' tunes and, judging by the groundswell of irritation at their intrusion into the programme, I think the term neatly appropriate. They are superfluous, inappropriate, unsettling.[33]

Holland defended the tune on 'Feedback' by asserting that actually some people did like it, including the Chancellor of the Exchequer and Ken Livingstone, and that it was easily identifiable. Even as he was saying this, however, he knew the way the wind was blowing. He sent a memo to all staff, saying:

> I have decided to discontinue the use of the signature tune and the stings [short musical phrases taken from it] as from now . . . this means that there will be no signature tune nor stings in the programme tomorrow morning. No reference should be made within the programme to this change.
> Inevitably, there will be telephone calls. Would anyone taking a call asking why the change, please answer with a formula response to the effect that 'It was clearly annoying a number of our listeners

so we decided to discontinue the experiment.' Please refer any press queries directly to me.[34]

Holland was to have more success in the battle against breakfast television. BBC1's 'Breakfast Time' began on 17 January 1983, hosted by Frank Bough, Selina Scott and Nick Ross. Its commercial rival, TV-am, followed a fortnight later with the so-called 'Famous Five' of David Frost, Anna Ford, Michael Parkinson, Angela Rippon and Robert Kee. Both services suffered an uncertain start and, even before they began, Redhead put his finger on the difficulties they would encounter:

Where are the people who are going to be watching and listening to breakfast TV? People whose time is short can cope with the radio, but they won't have time to cope with television. And if it's only middle-aged women running around in leotards, who cares about that?[35]

A little later, a leader in the *Guardian* suggested that TV-am's new team just did not strike the right note:

There are Day People and Night People. Brian Redhead and John Timpson are day creatures: breezy, unbleary, as smooth and rich as a pint of gold top chinking on a 6.30 a.m. doorstep. But commercial television's morning stars seems nocturnal transplants. Kee, lined and pensive: thoughtful of an evening but merely shattered of a morning. Anna Ford, the moonbeam balcony lady with the Black Magic box. Parkinson, as crinkly as an old leather armchair. And Frost himself, best taken after two strong scotches and a quick thrash at Annabel's.[36]

And, for politicians, trade union leaders and celebrities, radio continued to have distinct advantages – as the writer and MP Gerald Kaufman explained pithily:

You do not have to take any trouble with your appearance. If you are interviewed in the radio car, you can conduct the whole operation in your dressing gown and pyjamas. Even if you go to Broadcasting House, you can simply tumble unshaved into a jersey and slacks; no one there will mind or even notice, since they all look pretty much the same themselves, if not worse. On television you have to look your best.[37]

The lacklustre performance of breakfast television was of great interest to Fleet Street, as was the continuing success of radio's pear-shaped men in suits over the women in leotards on television. Under the clever headline 'The Odd Couple who outshine the Famous Five', one leading feature writer, Garth Pearce, called Redhead and Timpson the 'undisputed stars of the early morning ratings war . . . Their programme, presented entirely without flamboyance and sensation, has captured a daily audience of more than four million. That is twice the viewing figures of TV-am and BBC's "Breakfast Time" combined, with none of the publicity or hype.'[38] When, later, Peter Jay was forced out of TV-am the same paper said in a leader, 'In those British homes where breakfast is taken at all, there is little time or patience with David or Frank, Anna or Selina. The most that is needed to sustain us over the toast is an informative bit of chat on the radio. And, of course, a good newspaper.'[39] *The Times* said that TV-am 'was not to know that the consumers of breakfast broadcasting preferred cardiganed, comfortable middle-age to self-regarding, tinselled celebrities, though the wit and sharpness of Mr Brian Redhead and Mr John Timpson on "Today" showed that the wearing of pullovers is not a stigma of stodginess'.[40]

David Wade, radio critic of *The Times*, gave the clearest answer as to why the eyes did not have it and breakfast television had failed to poach the radio audience: 'Getting up, preparing breakfast and attending to the business of the day are not, at least in my family, processes which lend themselves even to a casual communion with the television set – and I have a job imagining the households in which they might.'[41]

Wade may have been spot on in that judgement, but it is still possible that radio would have lost ground had it not been in such capable hands. 'Under Redhead and his various changing partners "Today" effortlessly went on setting the nation's political agenda while the best efforts of glamorous presenters on both BBC TV and TV-am merely succeeded in rustling a few cornflakes,' *The Times* recalled more than a decade later.[42] 'It was not solely his achievement. "Today" has always been a tightly edited programme and much of the credit for its success belonged – even under Redhead – to its production team.'

On Thursday 15 July 1982 Brian's youngest son was killed in a road accident in France. William, 'a golden youth' as his father described him,[43] was eighteen years old. He had just left Cheadle Hulme School, was going up to Cambridge the following October, and had his whole life before him. He and two friends decided to go on holiday to France in his car. One was going up to Cambridge and the other had a place at Oxford. The accident, which involved a collision with another vehicle in the small hours of the morning, happened near Moncy-le-Preux, outside Lille. William and the other occupant in the front, James Nelson, who was seventeen, were both killed. The third boy, Nick Robinson (now a BBC political correspondent, and frequently heard on the 'Today' programme), was in the back and was severely burned before he kicked his way out of the back window. A producer from 'Today' had to wait outside Brian's flat in the Barbican all evening until he returned, and then had to break the news to him. Only the previous day he and his wife, Jenni, had been at a garden party at Buckingham Palace.

Only one or two papers reported the fatal accident, and then only in one or two paragraphs, but it was announced on the programme the following morning. The funeral was held at the family's parish church, Holy Trinity, in Rainow, outside Macclesfield, and Brian said later that he had received 2,000 letters of sympathy from listeners.

Brian Redhead once told me that he took comfort from knowing that the world was a different place from what it would have been had William never been born, and that therefore every person born into the world does actually change it for ever, irrespective of how long they live. 'The world is altered by the arrival of a person which their death doesn't take away,' he said.[44] He very rarely spoke about the accident, perhaps, his daughter (and William's twin) Abby believes, because William may have been partly to blame.

Brian was much comforted by his faith and, more particularly, by his local vicar in Rainow, the Reverend Leslie Lewis. 'When Will died he said he had never really stopped to think about anything,' said Lewis. 'So we started to have talks, and this led to him being confirmed the following year.'[45] The confirmation service was conducted by the Bishop of Stockport on 24 February 1983. 'It was a Thursday and the BBC were not very happy about it because they wanted him to cover an important by-election in Bermondsey,' Lewis recalled, 'but Brian would not alter his plans.'

The two men got on well: both had inquiring minds and down-to-earth characters. The Bishop of Oxford recalled that Brian had told him how much of a comfort and stimulus Lewis had been. 'He used to talk to me about the person who had helped him, his vicar at home, who was marvellous. He had really helped Brian and had brought him into the Church and got him confirmed. He was a real kindred spirit.'[46]

Nicholas Winterton, MP for Macclesfield and a friend of both the Robinson and Redhead families, said of Lewis, 'Clearly he did assist Brian a lot. He was able to talk and help him through it. Maybe it was that which re-lit Brian's interest in religion. I personally don't think he ever seriously intended to get ordained, though he saw that he might take up the challenge of preaching.'[47]

'Many of us felt he was stronger as a layman,' said Jim Thompson, Bishop of Bath and Wells. 'He was an irritant and stimulator of the Church. He couldn't bear the holy huddle.'[48] Richard Harries, Bishop of Oxford, agreed: 'He was seriously thinking of being ordained and very nearly did, but, probably rightly, decided not to.'[49] Harries pointed out that Brian had always been receptive to religious impulses, even in the late 1970s when he, Harries, frequently did 'Prayer for the Day' in its old slot at 6.50 am: 'He had a slightly mischievous side to him. When I used to come to the actual tiny prayer at the end, he used to go like this [the Bishop inclined his head and put his hands together in prayer]. You know, slightly mocking himself, but also at the same time at least half of him taking it seriously.'

Bishop Thompson was a particular kindred spirit. One of the causes they shared was women's ordination, which Thompson told me they were both 'keen supporters' of: he also says that Brian was the person who coined the nicknames 'Bishop Jim' and 'Big Jim'. Thompson recalled that the death of his son led Brian to search himself spiritually:

He wasn't the sort of person for whom his suffering and the loss of his son would close down faith. There's an old saying about man's extremity being God's opportunity. I don't think he'd follow that as a philosophy because he had far too strong a sense of God being just and God being love to see God as going round deliberately creating extremity. But I think he felt that somehow this crushing blow was an opportunity for God to get through to him in a way that it had not before, and we did talk about that ... To me he was symbolic, in a way, of the fact that somehow one comes close to God in the midst of suffering.[50]

According to Frances Gumley, one of the producers of BBC Radio's religious programmes, the death of his son prompted Redhead to 'read the Bible from cover to cover', an immersion which led him to suggest a radio series 'devoid of virtuous churchspeak'. This became the 'The Good Book', which Brian presented and she produced. It was broadcast in twelve parts on Radio 4 in 1986 and repeated on the BBC World Service. When it came out in book form in 1987, Brian gave a copy to his vicar in Rainow with the inscription 'To Leslie, who showed me the Way'. The significance of the capital W was not missed.

The death of William, Timpson recalls, seemed to deepen Brian and bring out a gentle side to his character:

> When he put aside his bluff exterior and all the intellectual stuff, he was a very sensitive chap, and this came out so much after his boy got killed, which was a terrible period. There wasn't a flicker from Brian for some time. He did his job, he did it extremely well, but the banter stopped. I don't think he got over it, but he put it behind him. He was very good at the gentle interviews. And he was marvellous with children, marvellous with people who had gone through some bereavement or disaster or something and needed treating gently, he was awfully good at that. It happened more than once and it is why, quite honestly, I wasn't too surprised when it came out that he was thinking of going into the Church. I thought what a marvellous priest he would be, quite honestly.[51]

Abby Redhead has similar recollections of the way her father's approach to others changed slightly following his son's death: 'When he was interviewing other parents who had just [been bereaved], I suspect he understood them and sympathised with them far more. He certainly understood the pain they were going through.'[52]

Timpson and Redhead went on to enjoy their finest period in the mid-1980s, with Hobday as third man in the background. 'Theirs is an alliance which takes the nation gently by its early-morning ear and urges it to consciousness with incisive interviews and amiable urbanities,' said one writer.[53] For Paul Gambaccini, Timpson was 'the closest thing Britain has to Walter Cronkite, the television newsreader who is uncle to all America' and managed 'to convey both warmth and authority'.[54]

The BBC's own research demonstrated the consistent popularity of the best double act in the business:

> Brian Redhead's ability to ad-lib and his informal, yet probing style of interviewing endeared him to many listeners ('for me Brian Redhead is the "Today" programme') and helped him to achieve a high personal rating. Although the figures indicate that Peter Hobday and Michael Stewart were also well regarded, the loyalty of regular listeners towards the long-established team of Timpson and Redhead led them to concentrate their remarks on what one sample member described as 'this perfect and unbeatable duo'.[55]

Two attempts to analyse their magic stood out. Charles Nevin put it like this:

> [They are] known to their audience as 'Me' and 'Him' . . . 'Me' is Redhead, ex-newspaper editor, talker, thinker, a man not given to ostentatious self-doubt. 'Him' is Timpson, an avuncular Auntie man, with the stolid looks of a cricket umpire and a voice like policemen used to have.
>
> Redhead and Timpson, as they say in the trade, 'work together'. They have 'chemistry', they 'bounce off' one another. Redhead is the irritant, Timpson the emollient. Four million listeners can't be wrong.[56]

And David Wade commented:

> Without wishing to undervalue Peter Hobday, who is sounding more and more at ease as the latest third presenter, I must say that the programme's jollity, style, wit and many other appetising qualities are at their best on the three mornings each week when his two longstanding colleagues are in tandem. Each sparks the other off, each sounds immensely interested in what he is doing and possesses that rare ability in a broadcaster to address his listeners as if there were no microphone. It is part of the attraction of any good thing that one fears its loss: so we may wonder nervously what will happen to 'Today' if Timpson and/or Redhead should get fed up and withdraw.[57]

Years later, Peter Hobday said simply: 'They were the partnership which gave this programme its special tone, its special place in the nation's affairs.'[58]

The two of them were also well remembered, and appreciated, by Kenneth Clarke:

> Timpson was very good, a good interviewer, but Redhead was better. Redhead had a very interesting personality. It was a very distinctive style of interviewing and he stamped a personality on the programme. Timpson was a good foil . . . Redhead was rather a dominant personality. He and I got on very well together, in that banter before and around the programme. We used to just enjoy being interviewer and interviewee.[59]

One example of the wit praised by Wade came when a listener wrote a letter protesting at their tendency to abbreviate sentences by omitting verbs. 'Point well made,' said Redhead, after reading the letter out on air. 'Complaint duly noted.' But success brought satire as well as praise and prizes: *Private Eye* lampooned them as Brian Bargs and John Targs in a spoof entitled *RADIO BORE*.

The two of them never tried to analyse their partnership too deeply, on the grounds that it might make the magic go away. Their utter professionalism was certainly part of it. Timpson says:

> I think we felt we could rely on each other, that was the great thing. If one of us had any problems, the other one would pick it up. I always felt very happy that I was sitting beside him, knowing that if you did fluff or forgot something or got carried away or anything disastrous happened, then Brian would pull things together, and I hope I would have done the same for him. It rarely happened that way but it was a comforting feeling.[60]

But, even though Redhead and Timpson saw more of one another than many married couples, they were different people and they did like different things. Timpson was much in demand as an after-dinner and luncheon club speaker, which he called 'gigs' and did for a fee. He spoke again and again and again, all over the country, never tiring of delivering forty-five minutes of polished anecdotes.

In the studio it was, of course, the jokes which appealed to Timpson the most. One light-hearted poem he read out in 1983 drew a substantial number of requests from listeners for a repeat broadcast, perhaps because of its obvious appeal to all the forgetful over-fifties in the audience. Timpson preserved it in one of his scrapbooks:

> Just a line to say I'm living
> That I'm not among the dead
> Though I'm getting more forgetful
> And mixed up in my head.
> Sometimes I can't remember
> At the bottom of the stair
> If I must go up for something
> Or if I've just come down from there.
> I'm before the fridge so often
> And my mind is full of doubt
> Have I just put food away
> Or come to take it out?
> And there are times when it is dark
> With my nightcap on my head
> Could I be retiring
> Or getting out of bed?
> If it's my turn to write to you
> There's no need of getting sore
> For I may think I've written
> And I don't want to be a bore.
> Just remember I do love you
> I wish that you were here
> Now it's nearly mail time
> I must sign off, my dear.
> I'm standing at the mail box
> With a face that's near beet red
> For instead of posting my letter
> I've opened it instead!

He loved the lighter side of the programme and wrote a book called exactly that – *The Lighter Side of Today*.[61] When he stepped in to do something more serious, such as chairing seminars organised by the British Association of Industrial Editors, he found it heavy going. But that was exactly the sort of outside work that appealed to Brian: chairing discussions and making presentations for companies and in-house videos for staff.

Both Timpson and Redhead developed parallel, and lucrative,

careers training executives and public figures to deal with the likes of them:

> They were business people, mostly, who wanted to know how to go about it if they were ever invited on to a programme. I don't think anyone ever objected. Nearly everyone was doing it in the BBC as far as I could see. The king of them [of the media trainers] was Cliff Michelmore and another one was Michael Barratt. Malcolm Billings had a much more modest set-up and I did quite a lot with him. We used to do various companies. Their spokesmen were taught how to answer questions, to slip in what they wanted to say, instead of what they were asked. It could have been argued that it made for a better programme if the chap you were talking to had some idea how to handle himself in front of the microphone and didn't ruin the programme by stumbling and floundering. But it's resulted in politicians being so well trained that they now know all the tricks of the trade, and the poor devil of a presenter has got to turn nasty at times to get any sense out of them at all.[62]

As the early 1980s became the mid-1980s, Timpson was beginning to get increasingly tired of the party conferences, the travel and the grind of getting up at four in the morning. He was approaching fifty-eight and not getting any younger. Leaving 'Today' would not mean leaving Radio 4, because he also presented 'Any Questions?' and its sister programme 'Any Answers?'. Most irksome for him was the growing seriousness and, in his view, humourlessness of the programme, which stemmed partly from the nastiness of party politics and the growing hostility between the BBC and the Thatcher government, and partly from the end of the opt-out:

> The programme did get a bit more solemn, which was one reason that I was not only not sorry to leave, but decided to leave. It wasn't the fun it used to be. One of the key changes was when we lost the regional opt-out at twenty-five past eight. I sometimes said that Northern Ireland had left us at twenty-five past eight and I made myself unpopular when I said that we were often asked by the Northern Ireland minister how on earth we had managed to achieve this.
> If a tape finished early or if your interview ran out you had to fill up this gap before the opt-out and that's when the fun started

because those were the moments we [Brian and he] had time to have a go at each other, or slip in a ho-ho or a quote from 'Peterborough' to fill it up. It was a very useful little safety valve, I always thought, though Brian thought it was a waste of time. He felt the airtime would be better employed talking to a politician – or him talking, more to the point.[63]

Julian Holland retired at the BBC's compulsory age of sixty on Good Friday, 28 March 1986. He was succeeded by Jenny Abramsky, editor of 'The World at One' for the previous five years. She took over on 1 April – the day that Timpson had joined 'Today' in 1970 – after beating three male applicants. Her appointment confirmed to Timpson that the seriousness and relentless emphasis on politics would continue.

He told Abramsky early on that he wished to retire at the end of the year and, in a comment released to the press, said that he thought it was time he and his wife Pat 'enjoyed a rather more peaceful life'. Absolution from the 3.50 am alarm was almost upon him. His final programme, the last of nearly 3,000, was on Christmas Eve 1986, with his colleagues taking him for a slap-up breakfast in Smithfield afterwards (the official wake had been held the night before in the Council Chamber of Broadcasting House).

The loss of Timpson and what John Gaskell in the *Sunday Telegraph* called his 'Bath Oliver of a voice'[64] was a considerable blow to the programme. Timpson had timing, good manners and a wry, self-deprecating humour sprinkled just occasionally with a caustic touch. The phrase 'end of an era' is one of the most over-used in the language, but for all those hundreds of thousands who cherished him as one half of a warm and welcoming national institution that description certainly fitted. William Russell in the *Glasgow Herald* identified the essence of their partnership:

Like all great double acts they are cast in the classic mould – one large, stately, and ever so slightly lugubrious, the other short, dapper, more aggressive, and, for all one can tell (they are, after all, a radio double act) with short, fat, hairy legs as well. Timpson is the big one, the Eric to Redhead's Ernie ... Each man has, of course, worked with other presenters ... but it is the Timpson--Redhead combination which produced the mysterious chemistry.[65]

Timpson's departure was widely and sincerely regretted. Sir Martin Gilliat, Private Secretary to the Queen Mother, could have been speaking for many when he wrote: 'It was with a heavy heart that I listened to all those poignant farewell and thank-you tributes today. You will be enormously missed not only by your millions of listening afficionados but also by all your "Today" team. On behalf of the Queen Mother and all your friends at Clarence House a very big "thank you" for all you have done for us over the years.'[66]

Timpson not only left 'Today' but also, after twenty-seven years, retired from the BBC staff. As a freelance, he continued to chair 'Any Questions?' and 'Any Answers?' until July 1987. He and Pat moved back to rural Norfolk, where he rejoined his old paper, the *Eastern Daily Press*, as a weekly columnist, and also began a semi-autobiographical novel about cub reporters in Norfolk in the 1950s.

Part of Julian Holland's legacy was the programme's Man and Woman of the Year Award, which he initiated in 1982. It always threw up strange anomalies: Mrs Thatcher won almost every year – eight years out of nine to be precise – which seemed to suggest a right-wing audience. Yet in that same period the male winners fluctuated wildly: from CND General Secretary Bruce Kent (1983) to Tory icon Michael Heseltine (1990), from Pope John Paul II (1982) to Arthur Scargill (1984). In the year Bruce Kent won, Eddie Shah (creator of the now extinct newspaper also called *Today*) came second, Heseltine eighth and the Bishop of Oxford tenth; Margaret Thatcher won the female poll for the second year running, but her runner-up was CND chairman Joan Ruddock. There was a suggestion of cheating even then, with one newspaper reporting that 'the BBC refused to give details behind the CND's apparent success in the poll . . .'[67]

The oddities in the poll were again manifest in 1989, when the winners were Margaret Thatcher and Mikhail Gorbachev (the same winning pair as the previous year). Their runners up could hardly have been more different, and the margins of victory were enormous. Thatcher received 1,515 votes and Kate Adie, who came second, only 305. The Russian President got 1,635 votes while his runner-up, Sir Anthony Meyer, the Tory MP who challenged Thatcher for the party leadership, collected 499. Gorbachev and Thatcher each polled more votes than all their rivals put together.

Oddity turned to farce the following year when both leading contenders were disqualified on the grounds that orchestrated campaigns from their supporters were responsible for the high

(*Above left*) Isa Benzie, the first editor of *Today*, as a young woman. (*Above right*) Janet Quigley, joint midwife of the *Today* programme with Isa Benzie. (*Below*) An editorial meeting in the early de Manio days. On either side of the window are Elisabeth Rowley, the editor, and Jack de Manio.

(*Left*) Alan Skempton, the first presenter. (*Below*) The studio clock in the days before Broadcasting House became a smoke-free zone.

Jack de Manio in October 1967, just after the Home Service became Radio 4.

Stephen Bonarjee (with cigarette) steered *Today* into a new era in the 1960s.

(*Above*) John Timpson and Robert Robinson, the programme's first presentational partnership, and (*below*) their wives, Josephine Robinson and Pat Timpson.

Chalk and cheese: John Timpson
(*above left and below left*) and
Brian Redhead, one of the greatest
double-acts in radio history.

Libby Purves, presenter 1978-81.   Peter Hobday, presenter 1981-96.

The team in 1986, the year John Timpson left and just before Sue MacGregor joined full-time. *Left to right*: Timpson, MacGregor, Hobday, Redhead.

John Humphrys (*left*) and Brian Redhead.

The day after Brian Mawhinney's outburst on *Today* about its presenters asking 'smeary' questions came this cartoon in *The Times* by Peter Brookes. It harks back to an incident where the Tory Party Chairman had paint thrown at him outside the House of Commons.

The *Today* team in 1994: (*left to right*) James Naughtie, Sue MacGregor, Peter Hobday, Anna Ford, John Humphrys.

number of votes they polled, and that this was not in keeping with the spirit of the poll. The BBC conceded that Lal Krishan Advani, leader of the Bharatiya Janata Party in India, had received the greatest number of votes, but claimed that many of them were identically worded and had been posted at a small number of post offices in Bradford and Birmingham. There was some anger about this in India, as the 'Today' programme itself reported in a despatch from Mark Tully. The woman who gained the highest number of postcards was a Jenny Coates, a playgroup leader from Wiltshire, and she too was disqualified after a similar letter-writing campaign from her locality. 1990's winners were, instead, much more predictable – Michael Heseltine and Margaret Thatcher, a tiny consolation for the latter for her overthrow as Tory leader the previous month.

After this débâcle it was hardly surprising that Philip Harding (editor of 'Today' from 1987 to 1993) decided to drop the poll in 1991 to avoid any more embarrassing charges of ballot rigging. Had it been held, the male prize would surely have gone to Terry Waite, released that autumn after five years of captivity in Beirut, though there was no obvious candidate for the female one. Sue MacGregor was strongly supportive of the BBC's decision to drop the poll. 'It's grown beyond its useful life and was rather predictable,' she said, 'although there were sometimes winners who caught the heart such as Gordon Wilson in 1987, who prayed for the Enniskillen bombers who killed his daughter.'[68]

The poll would probably have ended for good had there not been a change of editor. As it was, its absence lasted for only three years (1991–3) before it was resurrected by Harding's successor, Roger Mosey, in 1994. This time the programme resorted to what it hoped was advanced electronics to prevent any jiggery-pokery. Counting postcards was a thing of the past: instead, listeners had to write in with one nomination for a gender-neutral 'Personality of the Year'. The six people who received the most nominations were each given an 0891 number and the lines kept open for twenty-seven hours. To ensure that the voting could not be rigged by people simply staying up all night and pressing the memory recall button over and over again, thus voting for the same person hundreds if not thousands of times, the programme arranged with BT for each vote to be registered at one of eight exchanges (in Manchester, Birmingham, Bristol, London, Guildford, Cambridge, Leeds and Glasgow, the last being also where the Ulster votes were recorded) so any fluctuations would show up immediately.

The results were announced on Boxing Day. The entertainer Roy Castle, in a posthumous tribute to his courage in fighting cancer, gained 36,936 votes, beating John Major (27,838), Nelson Mandela (23,738), Tony Blair (16,067), Teresa Gorman (13,185) and John Hume (12,796).

In 1995 this method was used again, but the lines were kept open for only five hours, not twenty-seven. The BBC said this was to prevent any orchestrated campaign, though there had been no evidence of that in 1994. John Major was beaten into second place by Philip Lawrence, the headmaster stabbed to death outside his school.

The greatest furore in the history of the poll, which seems to have become more and more tarnished as the years go by, came in 1996. On 12 December, three days after the poll opened, the BBC suddenly issued the following statement:

Early this morning the BBC discovered that an organised attempt had been made to distort the annual vote for the 'Today' programme Personality of the Year in favour of Tony Blair. We deeply deprecate any attempt to interfere with what is intended to be a spontaneous opportunity for the programme's listeners to express their point of view.

The BBC suspended voting immediately, fourteen hours early. It publicly apologised to listeners who had intended to vote at the last minute and said that the top six nominated (who did not, in any case, include Blair) would go forward to the telephone poll.

The rest of the media went crazy: for 'News at Ten' it was the second most important story of the day. Camera crews door-stepped Blair in Dublin, who immediately condemned the attempt to rig the poll. Both *The Times* and the *Sun* splashed on it the following morning. With other newspapers, they carried the same basic details: that a letter from a hitherto unknown part of the Labour Party's campaign headquarters at Millbank, the 'Audience Participation Unit', had been leaked to the BBC. In that letter a woman with the curious name of Jules Hurry (later identified as a civil servant on unpaid leave from the Ministry of Agriculture) had urged fellow Labour members to write in and also find others and tell them to write in with nominations, so that Blair would defeat Major in the annual competition. It added: 'Alternatively they can be faxed (though preferably NOT on fax machines which identify the sender as the Labour Party!).' For Labour, that was probably the most damaging sentence in the whole affair, for it made clear the clandestine nature of the operation. The Tory Chairman, Dr Brian Mawhinney, said that Labour had been 'caught red-handed trying to cheat'.

For many people, even the Shadow Foreign Secretary Robin Cook, one of Labour's most senior figures, it was news that Labour *had* such a unit. I asked him if he had ever heard of the 'Audience Participation Unit' and he said:

> No, no. [But] I wasn't surprised that there was such a unit because there are a lot of programmes that require audiences and indeed it is quite a long-standing practice of 'Question Time' to invite political parties to send some people to the audience and that is entirely healthy because there should be a representation from all the political parties. There are a lot of phone-in programmes and letters pages round the country and it is both legitimate and common practice in political parties to make sure that their views are represented in these programmes and letters pages.[69]

Cook stressed that he was not condoning what had happened: 'The exercise was illegitimate and, I'm informed, was unauthorised. It was wrong, there's no two ways about it. It was condemned by Tony as soon as he knew about it.'[70]

Of the eventual shortlist that emerged five were women. The only man was John Major. A good point was made about this in a leader in the *Sunday Times* on 22 December 1996:

> John Major is the only politician to reach the finals. The others are all women made famous by their own courage, be it the bravery of Lisa Potts in facing a machete-wielding madman in her nursery school, or the call for a crusade against violence by Frances Lawrence, widow of the murdered headmaster.

It was the solitary male, however, who won – but only after yet more skulduggery. This time it was the Tories who stood accused of cheating. Sue MacGregor, announcing the results on Boxing Day, revealed that 4,000 votes for the Prime Minister had been disqualified because of 'evidence of multiple voting', though the BBC refused to say what that evidence was, or throw any light on how the telephone votes were recorded, or even to say what the precise number of disqualified votes was. Major still won by a clear majority, however, with 32,769 votes. Potts was runner-up (29,940), the Burmese opposition leader Aung San Suu Kyi third (24,463), 'Thought for the Day' speaker Anne Atkins fourth (17,425) and Dunblane campaigner Anne Pearston (16,352) fifth. Frances Lawrence, rather surprisingly, came sixth (14,527).

Other scandals surrounding media polls also erupted around this time. In particular, members of the gun lobby admitted to an organised attempt (on the Internet) to alter phone-in polls on Radio 5 Live and Sky News about Prince Philip's views on handguns. It was hard to disagree with a leader in the *Guardian* which said the BBC ought to be ashamed of itself for perpetuating the poll after years of attempted rigging, or with a leader in the *Independent* which described it as an 'annual farce'.

Robin Cook made a good point when he said:

When somebody like Philip Lawrence succeeds in getting it, that is worthwhile in that it enables the public to express their admiration and respect for somebody who is not holding a great office in public life but has undoubtedly made an immense sacrifice, which has made a big impact on public consciousness. But all such phone-in, write-in polls are undoubtedly subject to the fact that they are self-selecting. One should not be misled that this is a random test of representative opinion.[71]

As this book is being written it thus seems extremely doubtful that the BBC will wish to perpetuate a poll stained by so much scandal – and which, even at its best, could never choose anyone who is more than a Personality of the Headlines.

John Birt, though not committing himself, also seemed doubtful about its future:

I don't think anybody would ever have made any high claims for it. It's not remotely going to be a representative sample of the country at large. It may not even be a representative sample of 'Today' listeners. It has had value none the less. But if others are going to go to extraordinary lengths to have an impact on the poll, than we have to think about that. I've asked people to look at that. I wouldn't offer a view myself about what we should do, but we certainly have to consider the consequences of events at the turn of the year, and people will come forward with a suggestion about how we handle it in future – whether we have one at all and, if we do, what we will do about it.[72]

Let the last word go to the radio critic Edward Wickham. 'Frankly,' he said, 'if the producers really want a more scientific, less corruptible system of voting, they might as well try the clapometer.'[73]

5

Storms in the Studio

Short, active and lively could describe not only Jenny Abramsky personally but also her period as editor of 'Today'. It ran for only nineteen months, but in that time she brought in John Humphrys and elevated Sue MacGregor, restored the Saturday edition after a nine-year break, reduced 'Thought for the Day' from four-and-a-half minutes to three, slotted in an important interview at 7.33 am and had the fun of coping with Norman Tebbit during the 1987 election.

Abramsky's general approach to the job was to build on Holland's success:

> Julian Holland is one of the greatest editors I've ever known. He had given the programme a very clear focus and made it far tougher. So I was following someone who had started to turn the 'Today' programme into what we know it as today, and I thought my job was actually to move it to where I think it is today. I believed it had to be 'Today', not 'Yesterday', and that to do a programme that just reflected what had happened rather than took everything forward would be wrong. Our job was to set the agenda. As you woke up in the morning you almost made the newspapers redundant because we'd taken it on from the newspapers. Having edited 'The World at One' I had spent most of my time trying to show that we had a better judgement than 'Today' and to out-do them in terms of the big issues. When I arrived at 'Today' I said 'Right, we're now going to make life almost impossible for "World at One".' There is great rivalry between the two programmes.[1]

When she arrived the line-up of presenters consisted of John

Timpson, Brian Redhead, Peter Hobday, Sue MacGregor and Chris Lowe.

> I decided I didn't want Chris Lowe [she thought he lacked personality] and I brought Jenni Murray across from 'Newsnight'. Sue was still presenting 'Woman's Hour', as well as doing two days a week on 'Today'. Then Jenni started doing some 'Woman's Hour' programmes too. Michael Green [Controller of Radio 4] and I got together and I said, 'This is crazy. This is utterly ridiculous. One of them should do "Woman's Hour" and the other one should do "Today".' It was important to have real clarity as to who the presenters were.
> I think Jenni was half-hoping she would end up with 'Today', but in the end we gave Sue the choice. She chose 'Today', which meant that Jenni therefore had 'Woman's Hour'. Each of them probably ended up in the right place.[2]

Sue recalls, 'Jenny said, "I can't have you on a part-time basis, I need you full-time. I can't have you with divided loyalties." By then I'd been on "Woman's Hour" for fifteen years and, sorry as I was to leave, I severed that cord.'[3]

Sue MacGregor's arrival on 'Today' meant that breakfast listeners would now be able to savour the voice once described as the one you would like to hear on the loudspeakers shepherding you to higher ground if ever the Thames Barrier broke down. Of Scots descent, and raised and schooled in South Africa, she worked for five years (1962–7) for the state-controlled South African Broadcasting Corporation before coming back to Britain in the flower-power era to work as a reporter on 'PM', 'The World This Weekend' and 'The World at One' (then in its highly influential period under founding editor Andrew Boyle) before moving to 'Woman's Hour' in 1972. Cool, restrained and possessed of impeccable grammar and diction, she is quintessential Radio 4 in its best Home Service tradition. 'Compared to others, who shall be nameless, her career has progressed on the work done as opposed to the column inches written about her,' Brian Wenham, a former Managing Director of BBC Radio, once said. 'That's the classic Radio 4 persona, not putting yourself forward, and the better people don't.'[4]

Some years before Abramsky hired her on a full-time basis, there was another, abortive, attempt to get her on to the programme, as she recalls:

It was in the early 1980s and Aubrey Singer, who was the great panjandrum of radio then, and Peter Woon, who was in charge of correspondents or something, apparently wanted me to join the 'Today' team. By then I'd been at 'Woman's Hour' for about ten years. They didn't want to let me go and there was a great fight between 'Woman's Hour' and Aubrey Singer. Theresa McGonagle [editor of 'Woman's Hour'], a BBC lady of the old school, was summoned into Singer's office and he was saying, 'Why won't you let this woman go?' I had no idea at the time that this was happening. It was all going on behind my back. I hadn't even been approached. And Theresa said, 'We're not letting her go because we want to hang on to her and she certainly can't do "Today" part-time and "Woman's Hour" part-time, it has to be one or the other.' And apparently Singer said to somebody, 'I'm going to knock that fucking woman's block off,' and this echoed round the corridors of the BBC and we all shrieked with laughter down at 'Woman's Hour' when we heard about this.

Typical of the BBC, of course, that the person involved hears about these things last. Eventually, about three years later, it did come about. Julian Holland asked me if I would join part-time. There was a new régime on 'Woman's Hour' and they were more flexible so I started doing 'Today' on Mondays and Fridays with Hobday, as well as 'Woman's Hour' three days a week, before I joined 'Today' full-time in 1987.[5]

She is thought never to have lost her temper on the 'Today' programme and did so only once before that, when she was hosting an 'It's Your World' phone-in, a joint venture between Radio 4 and the World Service in which listeners in every continent could put questions to world leaders:

Pik Botha, then the South African Foreign Minister, was the guest and I remember he made some terribly patronising remark along the lines of, 'Of course if you knew South Africa, Miss MacGregor, you wouldn't say that,' and I suddenly said, 'Well, actually it's a country I know extremely well, I was brought up there,' and afterwards I thought aaagh! I don't normally reveal anything about myself and I was cross with myself. That's the only time I've actually made any sort of outburst. I suppose I could be considered rather over-cool at times, but that's just the way I am.[6]

MacGregor, the first woman to become a regular presenter of 'Today' since Libby Purves left in 1981, has had up and down relationships with her male colleagues. Humphrys she described to me with a slight touch of frost as 'oozing testosterone',[7] but recalls that he was the kindest of her colleagues when she went into hospital for a hysterectomy in 1988. Redhead, she says, showed an interest in her family far away in Cape Town, but she also had to put up with belittling gestures such as the time when, not long after she had started on the programme, he scrawled 'FOOL' on a piece of paper and pushed it across the table to her in the studio.

Indeed, Brian does not always seem to have been particularly pleasant to his new female colleague, as his daughter Abby recalled:

> He always used to be very rude about Sue MacGregor. I used to wind him up, because I never listened to the programme. I used to say, 'Oh, MacGregor was awful,' 'Wasn't she fucking atrocious?' Sue's *forte* always has been South Africa and [on that] she was always brilliant, but there were times when she wasn't very clever. I think possibly she hadn't done her homework. Brian always used to do his homework. He listened to every single news bulletin imaginable.[8]

Jenny Abramsky also had to find another presenter – to succeed Timpson who, soon after she took over, took her aside to say that he wished to retire at Christmas.

> A friend of mine who worked in television said that John Humphrys was not happy co-presenting the 'Nine O'Clock News' with Julia Somerville. So I rang him up and asked whether he'd come and have a chat with me and Jolyon Monson, my deputy, whom John knew very well. The two of us took him out. And then I rang Ron Neil, who was editor of television news, and said would he object if John Humphrys came and joined 'Today' as a presenter? It was a very risky thing, because we couldn't try him out. I just had to take the gamble and say, 'All right, John, you've got a contract.' John made the right judgement. A lot of his television colleagues thought he was bonkers. They just didn't realise the power of the 'Today' programme, but John did.[9]

Humphrys readily agrees that the approach could not have come at a better time:

I hated co-presenting the 'Nine O'Clock News'. I'd done it by myself for years and I think it was Michael Grade who wanted a bit of glamour. Well, more than glamour, Julia's a very attractive, very competent presenter, a proper journalist. But I didn't want to do it and regretted that I'd agreed to. It was a mistake. So when Jolyon rang up and said, 'Do you want to come, Timpson's going, it hasn't been announced, he's leaving, do you want to do it?' I said yes, instantly. I didn't even say 'How much?' Radio was a poor relation but the 'Today' programme, even then, was not.[10]

His arrival on 'Today' brought Humphrys back to the world of radio, which he had left for television many years before. Born in Splott, a working-class area of Cardiff, in 1943, he left school at fifteen and trained as a cub reporter on a tiny paper called the *Penarth Times* before widening his newspaper experience on the *Cardiff and District News*, *Merthyr Express* and *Western Mail*. He joined the BBC in 1965 as a reporter in Liverpool, covering the north-west and doing both radio and television jobs.

That is why I'm so small these days [he is actually 5ft 9in], from carrying a tape recorder on one shoulder and a huge, acid twelve-volt battery that weighed about four tons on the other shoulder for the cameraman, and carrying a huge wooden tripod in one hand. I would do a report from a strike at Liverpool docks, a piece to camera standing on the dockside, then rush to a telephone and talk to Bill Hardcastle to do a two-way for 'World at One' down the line. This idea that bi-medialism is new is nonsense.[11]

Talented and driven, Humphrys (whose boss, Tony Hall, describes him as 'workaholic') rose swiftly through the ranks in the 1970s and 1980s. He was the Northern Industrial Correspondent, then BBC TV's first full-time correspondent in the United States, its first full-time correspondent in South Africa, the Diplomatic Correspondent and finally presenter of BBC 1's 'Nine O'Clock News'.

Switching from evenings to breakfast was one obvious change; swapping television for radio was another.

It was a completely different culture. In television you have God knows how many people around and you just sort of sauntered into the studio and you would know that on the desk your scripts would be neatly laid out for you and there would be a floor manager with an assistant to pour you a glass of water and a make-up lady to straighten your tie and there would be somebody else to make sure that your microphone was properly attached and each time a news story came in they'd come and put it in your pack and make sure it had the right number. It was all done for you.

The first time I ever did the 'Today' programme I sauntered in, trembling a bit, sat down, sort of looked around, no scripts, and Brian was my co-presenter, and I said, 'Where's the scripts then?' and he gave me a very old-fashioned look and said, 'You get your own scripts here, lad.' So I had to get up and find them. It was only a tiny detail but it was saying, it's different over here, you know.[12]

Humphrys's arrival changed the delicate ecology of egos yet again, as Hobday recalls:

The general view when I joined [in 1982] was that all the presenters were equal, though listeners obviously had their favourites. Then Brian began to streak ahead in many respects and become the voice of the programme. Somehow one took one's pace from him. He was the equivalent of the first violin in a string quartet. Then after Sue came in [1987], Brian often presented with John, and Sue with me. People began to see us as two teams. Sue was keen to establish herself as one woman among three men. When John came, he was obviously a very competitive journalist and he tended to push harder.[13]

The critic Peter Barnard also acknowledged Redhead's dominance when commenting on 'Today' some years ago, and made a good point: 'Redhead helped to make the programme what it is, but he was no more and no less than the emblem of its standards and its accessibility.'[14]

Accusations of anti-Tory bias had started at the end of Holland's era, with Norman Tebbit, having returned from convalescence after the Brighton bomb, complaining the BBC was anti-capitalist when he clashed with the equally forceful Redhead over unemployment figures in early 1985. The attacks on 'Today' cannot be seen in isolation: they were part of a wider breakdown in relationships in the 1980s between the BBC and the government, a mutual hostility fuelled by bitter rows over the coverage of the Falklands War in

1982, the 1984 'Panorama' programme 'Maggie's Militant Tendency' (which resulted in two Tory MPs winning libel damages from the BBC), Kate Adie's reporting of the bombing of Libya in 1986, the suppression of Ian Curteis's patriotic drama 'The Falklands Play' and the Special Branch raid on the Glasgow headquarters of BBC Scotland over a spy satellite edition of BBC TV's 'Secret Society' in 1987.

The first suggestions of the Thatcher administration's antagonism to 'Today' were hints in early 1985 in the *Daily Telegraph*, a reliable barometer of Tory opinion: 'Mrs Thatcher listens to that every morning. Not impressed. Increasingly irritated, one gathers, by what she perceives as a dangerous Leftist bias.' There were rumours that she interpreted Redhead's jovial references to motorway repairs and hold-ups as criticism of government transport policy. Nigel Lawson, then Chancellor of the Exchequer, described 'Today' in the first half of 1985 as 'an opposition programme'. Holland said in response, 'I think you get sideswipes when you are putting questions to a government which is not having the easiest of times. And it's irritating to them.'[15] Austin Mitchell saw things the same way: 'The response from the politician in difficulties is always to kill the messenger, and "Today" is the first messenger to arrive in the household.'[16] Norman Tebbit once showed his irritation, when he pulled a duster out of his pocket as he arrived for an interview and proceeded to wave it in front of Holland's face – just to dust off the bias and clean up the BBC, he quipped.

Even Timpson, much less political than Redhead, found himself caught up in the rancour of the political climate in 1986. He was interviewing Norman Tebbit and the Tory Chairman decided he would simply steamroller on. Jenny Abramsky recalls:

Tebbit just wouldn't let him ask a question, and in the end John was just brilliant. He suddenly sat back and Tebbit went on and on and on. John just literally sat back in the chair and then Tebbit stopped. And then John leant forward and said, 'Can I ask a question now, Mr Tebbit?' It completely threw him.[17]

It was a brave move on Timpson's part and this was his reasoning:

Interrupting isn't so bad if the other chap stops talking. But when you interrupt and the other chap is determined to carry on and you're determined to carry on with your interruption and you've got two people talking simultaneously so that you can't hear either of them, I think that's bad radio. If they're obviously determined to go on I think you've got to stop and get at them when there's a decent gap.[18]

Sitting next to Timpson that morning was Peter Hobday:

He just paused at the end of Tebbit's tirade, for what seemed like an age but was probably about two seconds, and then he said, 'Have you finished, Mr Tebbit? May I, er, possibly ask a question?' And he did it in that port-stained, slightly affected, faintly aristocratic stutter he could put on. 'May I, er, er, possibly ask a question now?' It was quite devastating, but of course in terms of urbanity and good manners he simply could not be faulted.[19]

But the Tories' real target, according to Ian Aitken in the *Guardian* in the summer of 1986, was definitely Redhead:

His jokes about the M6 are sometimes precisely what the Tories are complaining about. One typical off-the-cuff jest which has been solemnly taken down for use in evidence concerned the fact that the notorious motorway [the M6] was not only bunged up again, but that the emergency telephones were also out of order. Mr Redhead, in his dangerous revolutionary way, apparently suggested a possible link with the privatisation of British Telecom.

So is the Tory Party now hoping to persuade the BBC to get rid of the hugely popular and vastly professional Mr Redhead? Well, no, actually. Not even the hardest men at Central Office entertain illusions about the extent of their influence. But the BBC, if not Mr Redhead, can expect to face sustained pressure. The calculation is that a steady drip, drip, drip of criticism will, like the Chinese water torture, eventually bring results.[20]

The complaints intensified with the arrival of Abramsky and John Timpson's departure in 1986. There was now no one to balance, or counter, Redhead's mischievously partisan remarks, which the other presenters never challenged. On one Boat Race day in the mid-1980s he said, 'There was a time when such an important occasion divided the nation – now we leave that to the Tory Party.' In 1990 he linked one item on strife in Russia to another on government policy on

Hong Kong with the words, 'Well, let us now come home and turn to the civil war inside the Conservative Party.'

It was that same impish sense of humour that the Archdeacon of York, George Austin, recalls. He had travelled down to London to deliver 'Thought for the Day' in August 1991, on the day after the Russian coup attempt had collapsed and nine months after Margaret Thatcher had been deposed:

John Major had decided to come into the studio rather than be interviewed at Number 10. Brian Redhead came into the hospitality room to run through the general pattern of the interview. With that wicked gleam which sometimes came into his eyes, Brian said, 'Now, you've just been involved in a coup against Mrs Thatcher. I'm going to end by asking what you did right that the plotters in Moscow did wrong.' And he did.[21]

This tendency of Redhead's to give his *own* opinions, and to exploit the fact that in practice he could usually have the last word, was what infuriated many Tories. It was on the face of it a breach of BBC impartiality, though this never bothered the robust Kenneth Clarke:

Redhead liked projecting his own personality, his own opinions. So you had to try and project your personality and opinions back in response. He did have a bad habit at one stage of putting a rider on the end of the interview when you'd no longer got any possibility of answering. He would come out with some remark. I once complained to him – not formally, I never have complained formally about the programme – after I'd been interviewed by Timpson and audibly over the air he made a remark about 'getting away with murder there'. Redhead was not only questioning and arguing the case, but trying to get over his own opinions, in a very persuasive, charming, boisterous way. And you had to try and do the same back.[22]

Exactly the same point was made in Redhead's lifetime by the feature writer George Hill: 'It is not so much his politics that rankle, as his inability to resist those one-liners, cheekily getting in the last word.'[23]

Sometimes people portrayed Redhead and Timpson not only as north and south, town and country, but also left and right. It looks now as if this was not the case at all. As far as voting is concerned, it may have been the wrong way round completely. When I asked Redhead if he considered himself to be on the left, he replied, 'Yes, but not in an aggressive way. I'm more like a Tory wet than anything else. I find myself agreeing with John Biffen and Ian Gilmour. They say the kind of things I think.'[24] Nicholas Winterton, Redhead's Tory MP in Macclesfield, says that Brian told him in 1987 that he had voted for him:

It was a few days after the tussle with Lawson and we were attending an opening of a facility at my local hospital. The publicity that had resulted from that tussle was the topic of conversation and he made it known that he'd voted for me and that it had been a personal vote. He had written on the ballot paper, 'This is a personal vote, not for the Conservative Party.'[25]

Winterton says this was not a spoiled vote because the voter had not identified himself and he and the other candidates, together with the Returning Officer, had all accepted it. 'I remember the wording, it was drawn to the attention of all the candidates at that election. It was a personal vote because Brian and I got to know each other extremely well.'[26]

Abby Redhead doubts this story. She says it cannot be true because Brian did not vote. This was because he was on the electoral register in Macclesfield, where he lived, but never there on polling day because he was in London preparing for the all-night election coverage on Radio 4 and did not have a postal vote. She said, 'He voted in 1992 because that's the only year he was certainly at home on the morning of the election. The last time he voted [before 1992] he voted for Mike Winstanley, who was Liberal. I'm assuming in 1992 he voted for Nick [Winterton], purely because he was a good constituency MP, but to be truthful I honestly don't know.'[27]

Timpson's recollections make the situation even more opaque.

I think he [Brian] always assumed that I was Conservative and I vaguely assumed he was Labour. Both assumptions were wrong, probably. I haven't voted Conservative for years, but don't tell them that round here, they all think I am. I'm a Liberal, basically. It's fair to say that every time I finished a Conservative conference I was a confirmed Labour man and every time I got to the end of a Labour conference I was a confirmed Conservative. But as far as interviews were concerned one played devil's advocate, and that was what one was paid to do.[28]

Lord Archer, Deputy Chairman of the Conservative Party from 1985 to 1986, is quite open about why he and his colleagues attacked Redhead and the programme at that time. It was simply an easy way, he now admits, of stirring up the Tory faithful – because the party faithful were quite sure Redhead was a leftie, as were most people in the BBC.

If I'm half-way through a speech and I need a bit of cheering and shouting and screaming, then I will say something like, 'Did you hear the "Today" programme last week, what a bunch of leftie communists,' they will all cheer and shout and scream and I don't believe it, I don't believe it for a moment. I had a line which couldn't fail in Party conferences. I always used to say 'Well, there's one thing that you can be certain of, we'll never have on the "Today" programme someone called Brian Bluehead!' It never failed. Never failed. In my speech at the Party conference two or three years ago, you only had to throw in one semi-witty line – 'We have our problems with the Labour Party, but it's nothing compared with the BBC' – and it's guaranteed.

You've got to know your audience. All serious hard-working politicians on the ground [Archer means grassroots Tory activists] are prejudiced. They don't see the programme dispassionately and long may that be so. So the man in the audience is sitting there saying, 'How *dare* you speak to Ken Clarke like that?' but when he [the interviewer] says to John Prescott, 'You second-rate little trog from Hull, how could you ever be Prime Minister?' the Conservatives say, 'Quite right, quite right.' And you've got to be intelligent enough to realise that and laugh at it.[29]

In terms of Redhead's leanings, as opposed to his voting, it seems fairly clear that he was very broadly on the left on most issues, if not all. He was not often attacked by people on the left. In what I think was an subconsciously revealing remark, Austin Mitchell gave the likely explanation for this: 'Perhaps I never noticed Brian Redhead's predilections because I shared most of them myself, so I just took them for granted.'[30] Peter Lilley told me[31] that in private conversations Brian had 'never made any bones about which side of the political spectrum he was on', had accused the Tories of falsifying economic figures and had frequently spoken to Christian socialist groups (Abby Redhead denies this).

Nicholas Winterton, a friend for over twenty years, said, 'I would say he lay one point to the left of centre. Not dramatic. He was nowhere near as radical as often my colleagues would have you believe.'[32]

Brian's own published writings[33] offer conflicting evidence. He dismissed the notion of widespread social security fraud, accused fee-paying schools of encouraging snobbery (forgetting to explain why in that case he sent his own children to one) and attacked the Social Services Secretary for 'whimpering about the cost of pensions'. Yet he also defended the tapping of terrorists' telephones and was an ardent supporter of Britain's constitutional monarchy, arguing that it ensured political stability and prevented power from falling into the hands of the military. 'He was interested in economics and in politics in the Athenian sense,' says John Humphrys. 'Had he been born a few thousand years earlier he would have wanted to join in their conversations round the table – him and Socrates.'[34]

Many of Redhead's passions, it should be pointed out, were non-political or cross-party. He would have banned opinion polls during election campaigns, believed all governments were characterised by muddle and incompetence, and was passionate about the north of England, National Parks, better industrial management and hospices. 'Brian was a great supporter of the hospice movement,' says Virginia Bottomley, 'and one of the reasons we changed a lot of the rules to give much more money to hospices was because of the advocacy of people like him.'[35]

Given his belief in state intervention, his *Guardian* background and his pungent anti-government barbs at a time when a Tory government was in power, it would not have been surprising if he was slightly to the left. Though it is interesting to discover that Lord Mackay of Clashfern, a professional lawyer and a man who has spent a lifetime studying verbal nuances and leading questions, did not notice any bias at all: 'I thought he was very good at his job. He had a good way of getting to the heart of matters, without appearing other than a fairly impartial kind of investigator. I just felt, on the things that I was interested in particularly, that he was well informed and he gave me the impression of being pretty impartial. I admired him very much.'[36]

The question of Redhead's politics first came to listeners' attention when he famously clashed on air with Nigel Lawson, the then

Chancellor, on 18 March 1987, the morning after the Budget. Since this is one of the most celebrated episodes in the history of the 'Today' programme, it is worth recording verbatim:

REDHEAD: Now, what are we to make of the Budget? It appeared to be a Budget rather like the housemaid's baby – only a little one and Prudence, they say, is her name. Well, the father of the child is in our radio car. Mr Lawson, good morning.

LAWSON: Good morning.

REDHEAD: It didn't seem like one of your Budgets – for a moment I thought you weren't really the father – you usually go for something a bit more dramatic.

LAWSON: Well, I don't know about that. Last year I was able to cut a penny off the income tax, this year I was able to cut twopence off income tax, so that was twice as much. And at the same time there was a dramatic cut in the government's borrowing, down to the lowest level it's been for goodness knows how many years.

REDHEAD: But in that way aren't you getting the worst of both worlds – that you haven't enough money, as it were, in the public purse to have the right amount of public investment to create jobs, but you're not putting enough in the private purse to have enough private investment to create new industry.

LAWSON: No, nothing could be further from the truth. Investment, first of all, is at an all-time record level and I expect it to rise by a further 4 per cent this coming year. As for the public sector, we do things of course in two parts in this country, as I think you well know, Brian. We announce our public expenditure decisions in November and the tax decisions in March, and in November I announced increases in public expenditure on key priority areas like the National Health Service and education by something over £4,500 million. But, you know, I think the main point to keep your eye on is not the Budget but the economy. That's what matters. That's what matters to the country, that's what matters to ordinary people, and the economy is stronger than it's been at any time since the war and this Budget will ensure that it keeps on.

REDHEAD: But an economy that carries three million-plus unemployed is not an economy one would want to see continue in that shape.

LAWSON: But it's not continuing in that shape. Unemployment is falling. Unemployment over the past six months has fallen far further than it's fallen at any time since 1973 and, as I said in the Budget speech, I expect unemployment to go on falling as a result of the policies we are pursuing and as a result of the strength of the economy. Unemployment will go on falling throughout the course of this year.

REDHEAD: But much of that fall is in the creation of special measures. You may have heard Mr Hattersley talking about young people being invited to job clubs to play games under the supervision of nursery school teachers. Creation of two-thirds of the new jobs are low paid, part-time jobs. These aren't real jobs that you used to talk about way back in 1979 and 1980.

LAWSON: Well, you've been a supporter of the Labour Party all your life, Brian, so I expect you to say something like that. But you really shouldn't sneer at these job clubs, which are giving real hope to the long-term unemployed, getting them out of their depressed state of mind many of them are in and they are going on to get real jobs.

REDHEAD: Do you think we should have a one-minute silence now in this interview, one for you to apologise for daring to suggest that you know how I vote, and secondly perhaps in memory of monetarism, which you've now discarded?

LAWSON: I see no cause for a one-minute silence. Monetarism, as you call it, is not discarded. What has happened is that we have liberated the financial markets to a tremendous extent and this has happened in some other countries, in the United States as well, and as a result of that, the behaviour of the monetary aggregates has changed and I decided that the interpretation, which has been evolving all the time, of financial conditions, should evolve with the evolution of the financial markets. Now that's only common sense.

REDHEAD: So you've abandoned all the M3s and things?

LAWSON: No, we've not abandoned looking at monetary aggregates. I've decided to have only one explicit target, for narrow money – M nought, but of course broad money we will continue to look at. But the main point is this, and I think this is what matters to people, is that we will maintain a proper financial discipline and everybody knows that no business can flourish and no country's economy can flourish unless there is a degree of financial discipline. And that is why we've succeeded in getting inflation down to the lowest level for twenty years.

Jenny Abramsky, editing that morning, was watching Brian from the cubicle. 'I can remember dropping my pencil when Brian said "Let's have a minute's silence." We all thought he was going to go completely silent! You could hear the tension. Brian was angry. He was very angry. But it was controlled anger and it was polite anger, I think.'[37]

By the time he telephoned his daughter a short while later – according to Abby, he telephoned her without fail after every programme – any anger Brian may have felt had been replaced by regret:

> He was quite upset. He was probably a little taken aback at the response from Lawson. He said Lawson had got a bit agitated with him or something but he said [that of the calls that had come in from listeners] 85 per cent were in his favour, and that made him feel better. I think he thought he might have been offensive and he always said that when you were interviewing somebody there was no need to be rude to them. He would have been genuinely upset if he thought he'd offended anybody. He wasn't a nasty person. He really wasn't nasty, he was nice.[38]

It was, all in all, a rather mild exchange, compared with another one almost exactly four years later. The date was 7 March 1991 and the interviewee Peter Lilley, then Secretary of State for Trade:

REDHEAD: Is one of the problems, Mr Lilley, that there have been too many changes of Secretary of State and what we need is one chap in the job for a long time?
LILLEY: Well, I have a vested interest in agreeing with the committee on that point. (Both laugh)
REDHEAD: I bet. But are you committed to the, I mean, we used to be number two in the league of prosperous industrial nations in the world, we're now number nineteen. When Spain overtake us this year, we'll be number twenty. That is silly.
LILLEY: Well, it's a silly point because it won't happen –
REDHEAD: It's an important point, it's just –
LILLEY: . . . it's nonsense, Brian. Spain isn't going to overtake us this year –
REDHEAD: But you said, well you didn't, your predecessor said that about Italy –
LILLEY: Please may I answer or do you want to monopolise this?

REDHEAD: No, you answer.

LILLEY: During the sixties and seventies we fell behind, in growth terms and in manufacturing productivity, every other major country. During the 1980s our manufacturing productivity grew faster than any other industrial country including Japan. We're on the path to industrial recovery and regaining the ground we lost under the party you support, Brian.

REDHEAD: Don't you say that. You have no idea how I choose to exercise my vote and it is entirely my business.

LILLEY: You're better at handing out criticism than receiving it, Brian.

REDHEAD: I will just reflect upon your policies.

Recalling that bitter exchange more than five years later, Lilley said:

His [Redhead's] approach was to preface his question with a tendentious preamble, which always puts the interviewee in a dilemma. Either you can try and rebut the false assertions in the preamble, and appear to be avoiding the question, or you can answer the question and appear to be accepting the assertions in the preamble. His preamble that day said that Britain was in decline and was set to have a GDP falling behind Spain. It was an absurd statement but I didn't want to get sidetracked. So I just said that may have been true when the party he supported was in power. I wasn't particularly referring to his voting record, but he chose to interpret it that way. Later that day he said it was quite untrue that he had voted Labour, he voted for Nicholas Winterton. One of my colleagues said that was even worse.[39]

Lilley claimed that taking this 'robust line' with Brian had produced a welcome dividend:

I was frozen out for a while, but then they decided this was a bit petulant and let me back in. I wasn't invited on for a while. They don't have to have you on. But after a while I was invited back and various grand men in the BBC walked backwards down the corridor saying, 'Thank you very much Mr Lilley, it's extremely kind of you to come in again, would you like any questions in advance,' and they seemed to think I was doing them an honour going back on, and since then I've got on rather well with them.[40]

Lilley admitted that nobody in the BBC had actually said that the reason why they stopped inviting him to appear was because he had hit back at Redhead on the air. But, he went on, 'It was quite clear, it was because I had duffed them up.'

Tony Hall seemed genuinely puzzled when I told him what Lilley had claimed. He said, 'I have no memory of that whatsoever. None. I don't believe he was frozen out, though I suppose it's possible. I've met Peter Lilley on numerous occasions, but I've never walked backwards in front of him and neither would I, so it sounds to me as if he's having a bit of fun at our expense.'[41]

Sue MacGregor was also sceptical about Lilley's claims. 'I don't recall anybody on the editorial side of "Today" saying, "We won't have Lilley for a while," I really don't. I think he's making a great deal more of it than it was . . . I think the answer may be that he's now a more confident performer than he was and is misinterpreting what's happened.'[42]

The growing importance of the programme was shown by the fact that in 1988 Mrs Thatcher telephoned it live from Downing Street on the morning she learned (from Radio 4) that the Soviet leader Mikhail Gorbachev had cancelled his trip to Britain because of the terrible Armenian earthquake. The date was Thursday 8 December and the event was unprecedented. As Humphrys said at the time, 'a Prime Minister at the end of a crackling phone line is literally unheard of'.[43] Thatcher had started her day, as usual, at 6 am with 'News Briefing', from which she learned that Gorbachev had flown home straight from New York because of the disaster. Then, at 6.33 and by now listening to 'Today', she heard Humphrys interviewing Gennady Gerasimov, the Soviet foreign affairs spokesman, at his New York hotel. Gerasimov was telling Humphrys that Thatcher had not yet been told that Gorbachev was no longer coming to Britain. Hearing this was what prompted the Prime Minister, via a duty press officer, to ring the programme. 'It took me a few minutes to get through because they thought it was a hoax,' she recalled years later.[44]

Humphrys had thirty-five seconds' warning that he was going to be talking to the Prime Minister. 'I heard it [the news that Gorbachev was no longer coming to Britain] on your "News Briefing",' a slightly husky-sounding Mrs Thatcher told Humphrys and a million listeners at home. 'It was the first indication we had. Then I heard later that you didn't know if I knew, so I thought I'd better phone . . . when there's trouble like that, home is the place to be . . . we offer our deepest sympathies to the Soviet people and the bereaved.' The words were in keeping with the scale of the tragedy: 25,000 people had lost their lives.

This remarkable event obviously proved that the Prime Minister listened to 'News Briefing' and to at least part of the 'Today' programme. And both the Bishop of Oxford and the Bishop of Bath and Wells have good reason for believing she was a frequent listener to 'Thought for the Day' (see Chapter 7). But whether she tuned in as much as some have suggested, and was as obsessed with the output as much as legend has it, is not at all clear. Bernard Ingham, for so long her Downing Street Press Secretary, referred to the programme's 'ill-considered output' in his memoirs.[45] On the other hand, she did not hesitate to record a warm tribute to Brian Redhead when he died, an honour bestowed on few. And her comment to me about the programme four years ago was, to quote it verbatim, 'I still listen and enjoy it very much. It's an excellent review of news and current affairs.'[46]

Kenneth Clarke is pretty sure there was a difference between the two Prime Ministers he had served under: 'Margaret Thatcher listened to it and John Major doesn't. She would occasionally mention it. She'd obviously heard it. As far as I'm aware, John Major doesn't listen to the programme. He's not a listener. I think he's told me he doesn't listen to it.'[47] Major's relative lack of interest was confirmed to me by his wife, Norma, when I interviewed her just before she made her début on Radio 2. Referring to their constituency home in Huntingdon, she said:

We have a radio next to the Teasmade in the bedroom. We always used to switch on 'Today' when we woke up and had our tea. But I almost couldn't bear it after John became Prime Minister. Hearing him on the radio and then hearing someone bash him – I couldn't cope with it. It depressed me . . . In addition, neither of us is particularly fond of all that endless news commentary. What we listen to and read about doesn't always match up to what we know to be the case. I can safely say John doesn't listen, at least not when I'm around.[48]

The clergyman Richard Chartres, then also a radio critic and now Bishop of London, confessed to 'great sympathy' at this: 'although the programme is a daily marvel of editing and presentation, its breathlessness and the multiplicity of themes do not make for a contemplative start to the day,' he wrote.[49]

Stephen Dorrell, who worked for Thatcher in the 1980s as a government whip, has some doubts as to her supposed zeal for the programme:

> She always was said to listen to it. I'm not sure. She also had a voracious appetite for reading papers, so whether she listened to it as assiduously as she was alleged to, I don't know. I'm filled with admiration for these people who can read all the contents of their box and listen to a two-and-a-half-hour radio programme.[50]

Nobody, including Brian Redhead himself, realised just how ill he was in his final years. He suffered considerable pain in his leg (always joking that he leaned to the left orthopaedically, not politically), but nobody would ever have known from listening to him. His voice never gave it away and he was too brave, and too professional, ever to complain. In the autumn of 1993 his health seemed to be failing: he limped more on the way to the studio, and there were mornings when he looked (though he did not sound) tired and drawn. He was well enough to cover the Tory Party Conference in Blackpool in October 1993, having a jolly fish and chips supper at Harry Ramsden's afterwards with his editor, Roger Mosey, and making time to visit a hospice with Virginia Bottomley. Mosey remembers him as being particularly benign to interviewees in this period; Abby recalls him as having been much more tetchy. Both could have been true: he may have given vent to his discomfort only when he was away from the BBC.

The 'Today' programme which went out on 7 December 1993 was destined to be Brian's last, though nobody knew that at the time. After the programme, which he partnered with Hobday, he went straight home to Macclesfield, intending to have an operation before returning to the programme after Christmas. He never saw London again. Abby says:

> He was grey and in agony and within twenty-four hours he was in hospital. He should have gone into hospital six months before he did. He had become very irritable, which was part and parcel of the toxins in his body resulting from the appendix leaking into his bloodstream.[51]

There was no suggestion, during the first fortnight, that Brian's life was nearing its end. Roger's recollection, which he put into this simple and very moving public statement, was as follows:

I last spoke to him by phone on the afternoon of December 22. He was the same old Brian – amused by a get well card from Virginia Bottomley, frustrated with the boredom and indignities of hospital life, itching to be back on the programme. That evening he was operated on, and the following morning we were warned that his chances of surviving the next twenty-four hours were no better than 50:50. Over the following days there were some grounds for hope. Brian regained consciousness and for a few hours he was moved out of intensive care. But he then had to face successive battles: against a threatened liver failure, a weak heartbeat, respiratory problems and finally kidney failure. It's a sign of his raw courage that he withstood the onslaught for so long, and his family told us that towards the end of his life he seemed to achieve an inner calm which comforted them in their most difficult hours. What we'll miss about him is his sheer vitality and the sense of fun he brought to those around him. It was a privilege to know him, and we'll miss him more than words can say.[52]

Nobody visited Brian in hospital apart from his family. But one of the last people to see him in public was his friend and MP, Nicholas Winterton:

It was at the beginning of December 1993. He came to launch something that was very close to his heart, the endowment fund appeal for the East Cheshire Hospice [of which he was Vice-President: his widow Jenni is now]. It was held at Capesthorne Hall by courtesy of Billy Bromley-Davenport, who is now Lord Lieutenant of Cheshire. Brian arrived about four minutes before the function was due to commence and he looked grey. We were walking up the hall and he turned to me and said, 'Nick, you know I'm having my left hip replaced when I retire next March – well my right hip is now beginning to play up and I'm suffering a lot of discomfort.' Of course it wasn't his hip at all. It was a perforated appendix.
His appendix wasn't where it would normally lie, it was slightly displaced and tucked up at the back as a result of which, of course, it was jettisoning poison, which ultimately formed a huge abscess

in his back, close to his spine. When they finally discovered what it was, they drained over a pint of poisonous fluid and mucus from his body. It was the combination of the damage that the poison had done to his body and the drugs he had to take for his diabetes that brought about the collapse of the vital organs, which six weeks later led to his death.

At Capesthorne I had no idea that he was actually probably already dying. [Later] he was rushed into hospital. Initially he went into a private hospital, into the Regency Hospital in Macclesfield, and I don't know what they thought it was but they didn't give him the appropriate treatment and he got worse and worse and it wasn't until he was taken into the District General Hospital next door and had a scan that of course they realised what was the problem. By which time, tragically, although we hoped for the best, it was I think too late. They drained all this off and the surgeon did everything he could for him, but unfortunately on the 23rd of January 1994 he died.[53]

Abby does not herself blame the Regency. She said, 'He had the same doctors in the NHS hospital as in the Regency.'[54] Whatever the rights and wrongs of the treatment, Brian himself might well have pondered the irony of such a staunch defender of the National Health Service choosing private medical care when it came to his own treatment.

Brian died on a Sunday. Three days before, Abby had alerted Roger Mosey to the sad news that her father was not expected to survive the weekend. Roger was galvanised into the sort of action which all journalists have to take from time to time, whatever their emotions. He organised the immediate production of an obituary programme, and of material to be broadcast on 'Today' itself. He asked Lady Thatcher if she would be willing to say anything, and she immediately accepted, recording a personal tribute on the Friday. Michael Green, Controller of Radio 4, agreed to change his schedules and broadcast the obituary programme as soon as possible after notification of Brian's death.

That notification came when Abby rang Roger from the hospital to say that Brian's suffering was finally over. The BBC's machinery swung into action and the network for which Brian had worked so long hastily rejigged its evening schedules to insert its by now completed tribute programme. For something assembled so hurriedly, it was remarkably fair, balanced and polished. John Humphrys, the presenter, struck an affectionate though far from unctuous tone: the programme quoted Brian's own description of himself as 'a bighead' and pointed out that he always liked to have the last word. Humphrys himself admitted on the programme that he had often wanted to throttle Brian because he had been so 'excessively opinionated'.

While that was going out, next morning's edition of 'Today' was being prepared, much of it devoted to Brian's life and career and the reaction to his death at the early age of sixty-four. There was some criticism later that this coverage went well over the top in both quantity and tone, although those carpings did not surface on the day itself.

All three co-presenters were heard saying nice things on the programme, but their reaction was subtly different. Peter Hobday was openly emotional: his voice breaking at times, he recalled how Brian had never let him down and what it had been like in the studio on that last programme in December. Brian had looked so ill and grey that 'we wondered if he'd get through it'. He added, and it was the most raw and piercing moment of the programme, 'I loved the man.' Sue MacGregor, more evenly, described him as 'a lovely man'. John Humphrys played safe and described him as 'a brilliant broadcaster'. Lady Thatcher, who had been interviewed by Redhead on 'Today' about her memoirs only three months before, acknowledged the 'breadth and depth' of his knowledge, which she described as 'quite remarkable'. With what sounded like genuine admiration, she said to John, 'He was true to his faith and true to himself.'

Ernie Rea, the BBC's Head of Religious Broadcasting, speaking in the same Manchester studios which Brian had so often filled with his presence, himself did 'Thought for the Day'. Paying tribute to Brian's 'insatiable curiosity', he said, 'Whether he was interviewing the Prime Minister in Maastricht or a medieval historian on Hildegard of Bingen or a schoolboy on the GCSE results, his interest and his commitment to finding out were self-evident . . . if the measure of a man is the extent to which he loves and is loved in return, then Brian Redhead stood tall.'

National reaction was loss and shock and typical was the listener from Stoke-on-Trent who sent a message saying she felt Brian had been 'a friend, brother and teacher for eighteen years'. There was a palpable sense of loss for a man who had so much still to offer. The Archbishop of Canterbury, Dr George Carey, wrote to Roger Mosey:

The loss of such a brilliant and warm personality must leave you all feeling bereft and very sad, and I do share in this feeling along with millions of other people who valued him so much ... I am very conscious that he was only a front man who represented the commitment, flair and hard work of all the others working on the 'Today' programme. The tributes flowing in for Brian should make you all feel some pride, as well as sadness, and it matters very much to me, as to millions of others, that the splendid traditions of the programme should continue to play an honoured part in our national life.[55]

In a leader, *The Times* argued that Redhead gave great benefit not just to the programme but also radio as a whole:

Redhead's encounters with politicians were not always peaceful. Yet such spats did nothing to dissuade ambitious politicians from seeking the imprimatur of an intelligent feature on the programme – especially in the precious minutes either side of the 8 o'clock news. Redhead made 'Today' a programme that no member of the political class could afford to miss. It was a reflection of its importance under Redhead that it attracted so much controversy and that so many Britons tuned into it for early guidance to the day's major issues.

The beneficiary was not a single programme but the very medium of radio. Forty years after the invention of colour television, middle-class Britons will still turn to radio for intelligent news broadcasting in the same way that they invest more emotion in 'The Archers' than in any television soap opera ... Redhead was one of the most compelling figures in the glorious firmament of postwar radio.[56]

More than a thousand people attended the memorial service at St Paul's Cathedral. The less savoury aspects of his character – his vanity, his pugilism, his capacity for inventing self-glorifying fantasies for himself, his alleged attempts to take the credit for what others had done – were discussed in a controversial episode of the biographical Radio 4 series 'Radio Lives', broadcast on 7 November 1996. Produced by Bob Carter and presented by Michael Bywater, this particular life of Brian interviewed an impressive collection of former colleagues and friends, but it was a warts-and-all portrait whose emphasis was very much on the warts. Mosey thought that 'it looked for the negative aspects of Brian's character'[57] and the critic

Sue Gaisford chose exactly the right word when she described it as 'lop-sided'.[58] Gillian Reynolds made it a contender for her worst programme of the year award. There was a good deal of genuine anger and the *Daily Telegraph* even devoted a leader to the programme, which it described as 'cowardly'.[59]

While Redhead may have dominated the period of Abramsky and Harding's editorships, several other matters of interest also arose. Harding felt the programme was rather London-orientated when he took over, a trend which he tried to counter. He was also one of a number of BBC radio executives over the years to have gone for the youth market, with items about how Carnaby Street was selling neo-Nazi goods and Pepsi's sponsorship of a Michael Jackson tour. There was the saga of Charles and Diana's decaying marriage, which showed the problem 'Today', and to a wider extent the BBC, has often had with royal stories. 'We were totally wrong,' recalled Harding later. 'It was one of the most important stories of the decade and we got it wrong. I remember John Humphrys giving Andrew Morton a really hard time. How do you know this? and so on. We were very sceptical about the Morton book.'[60]

Sue MacGregor was awarded the OBE in 1992, a probable reflection not only on her long and distinguished service with Radio 4 but also a willingness to take on unpaid jobs with a civic flavour: she is a Marshall Aid Commemoration Commissioner, guides media studies students at the London College of Printing and Nottingham Trent University and sits on the Royal College of Physicians' Committee on Ethical Matters in Medicine.

> There were certain colleagues whom I won't name who felt this was something I should not have accepted because journalists shouldn't accept gongs for doing their job, and I understand that point of view. But they all said nice things and if they couldn't bring themselves to say congratulations at least they said something like, 'It will have pleased your family very much.' One of the reasons I accepted it was because I knew my mum in Cape Town would be bursting with delight, and indeed she was. Towards the end of her life [she died in 1994] she was an invalid and I was just very glad that this happened while she was still alive because she was of that generation to whom it meant a lot. She followed my career from the very beginning, as proud mums do. So I was really pleased that that had happened.

I got the impression from the Queen that she was a listener to the 'Today' programme. You have a very brief time when you get your gong. She says something and you curtsey and go up and then you walk backwards hoping you're not going to fall over, and curtsey, and disappear. You can buy a video of yourself getting this thing and I looked at the video afterwards and I realised that the poor Queen didn't get a word in edgeways because I was jabbering at her. But she did indicate she was a listener. She said something like, 'I'm very pleased to give you this', and I asked her if she listened and there was a sort of regal inclination of the head to suggest that she knew the programme.[61]

Another development of the period was the consolidation of Garry Richardson's position as sports reporter. He started doing three appearances a week in the mid-1980s, succeeding Charles Colville when he moved to Sky, and still does three a week today. (Steve May and Brian Alexander do it on the other days.) Richardson's soft Berkshire accent, touches of humour, occasional one-liners and 'Morning to you' greeting have endeared him to many listeners, even if they are not sports fanatics. He decides on the content of the sports package, produces, edits and presents it: it is his own mini-empire within the programme. He brings with him a black stopwatch and presses a green, rectangular button when he starts his four-minute bulletin: some listeners claim they can hear the little ping when he does so. It is a good moment on the programme, partly because it is light relief and partly because it is useful for people like Kenneth Clarke: 'I usually listen to the sport, because I never have time to read the sports pages. So I suppose I pick up the midweek sports news from the radio.'[62]

Richardson, brought up on the Shaw council estate in Newbury, left school at seventeen in the early 1970s and started work as a clerk at the Written Archives Centre in Caversham, outside Reading, though his burning passion to break into radio was such that he was prepared to take £1.50 for four hours' work helping out at BBC Radio Oxford every Saturday morning, eventually becoming a full-time station assistant (embracing a variety of technical jobs and reading bulletins) there in 1978. He came to Broadcasting House on attachment to the sports section of the Newsroom in 1980 and succeeded Derek Thompson, after he moved to Channel 4, as one of the sports correspondents. In that year he became one of eight people who took it in turns to present the sports bulletin on 'Today', guided by experienced hands like Brian Butler. Julian Holland was in favour of a regular person and gradually Richardson and Charles Colville emerged as the frontrunners.

'It was very daunting the first time I did it,' he recalls. Brian Redhead was on and he said, 'The time is 7.25 and here now for the first time in his life is Garry Richardson.' On another occasion he said, 'It's 7.25 and here with the sports news is Mr Garry Richardson wearing a bright yellow jumper.' You never knew what he was going to say.

Ninety times out of a hundred the sports report is light relief. That's why I sometimes put in little jokes like saying that Mike Atherton [England cricket captain on the disastrous 1996 tour of Zimbabwe] had been banned from a pub in Zimbabwe because they wouldn't accept him in the happy hour. Someone who heard that contacted the *Mail on Sunday*, which actually got their man out there to try and find the pub.[63]

He has to work very hard to get his interviewees, he says. Politicians will walk over broken glass to appear on the programme, but sports people are not quite as keen. It is not as important for them. We've never had Alex Ferguson of Manchester United or Ruud Gullit of Chelsea, for example. But Jack Rowell will always come on to talk about Rugby Union and Tim Henman has been excellent.[64]

One of the jolliest aspects of the sports section, whoever is presenting it, consists of the two racing tips. These have acquired a reputation for being hit and miss. The selections are made by Cornelius Lycett, BBC Radio's racing reporter, but in the world of the turf they do not enjoy a scintillating reputation. Charles Colville once gave the rationale for this. 'Our listeners don't tend to be avid sports fans,' he said. 'They like John's jokily disparaging remarks about our racing tips and Brian's references to his hero, whom he calls Sir Geoffrey Boycott.'[65] Lord Archer was as dismissive as he could be: 'I don't gamble, but I'm told [that the programme's] record on horses is second to none for being awful. If you can pick a three-legged racehorse with one ear that can't find the winning post, you seem to manage it most mornings.'[66]

Robin Cook made by far the most penetrating comments about the racing selections, as befits a man who for five years wrote a weekly racing column himself.

I don't know how they do them, but I do notice that they

overwhelmingly tend to focus on favourites. It's very rare for it not
to be a favourite. They are in a slightly different business from the
tipsters on the morning papers, because if you're doing it for the
morning papers, as I do myself for the *Herald* in Glasgow, you
have to complete it by six o'clock the previous night, which means
you can do it by the form book, but you can't do it by looking at
what everybody else is saying because you don't know. When the
'Today' programme do their tips at 7.30 a.m. they have presumably seen the *Sporting Life* and *Racing Post*, which have tables
setting out everybody's tipping, and it's the easiest thing in the
world to establish which entry has the most tips. I'm not saying
that's how they do it, but I'm left slightly suspicious by the fact
that the tips are almost invariably the favourite.[67]

Such an approach is ultra-cautious, says Cook:

The problem with tipping favourites is that you certainly have a
higher probability of winning, statistically 38 per cent of all
favourites win, but you don't actually make much money when
they come in. To make betting pay, which is a very challenging
undertaking, what you are looking for is not the favourite that is
going to win, but the horse that is better than other people
suspect.[68]

6

Hirings, Firings, Status and Journalism

Roger Mosey took over as editor in March 1993 at the early age of thirty-five. He succeeded Philip Harding, who left to organise an inquiry into the state of FM as part of the BBC's preparations for setting up a radio news network (which led to the creation of Radio 5 Live). Mosey, son of a sub-postmaster from Yorkshire, had shown his ambition early by writing to Austin Mitchell while still a teenager:

> He wrote to me when he was a kid at Bradford Grammar School and was interested in the media, both Yorkshire Television and Pennine Radio, where I was then a director and also a presenter. He used to come along and help with programmes at Pennine, before he went to university. I put him in touch with Dorothy Box, who was then presenting a morning session at Pennine and he used to come along and help behind the scenes. He got his first experience of radio at Pennine.[1]

Mosey read history and languages at Oxford and, after returning to Pennine for one year, joined the BBC in 1980 as a reporter with Radio Lincolnshire. His rise was swift: two years later he went to Radio Northampton as a producer and then joined Radio 4 as a producer on 'The Week in Westminster', moving to a producer's job on 'Today' (when Holland was editor) before becoming a duty editor under Abramsky. He edited 'PM' before becoming editor of 'The World at One' in 1989. His era at 'Today' was eventful: he hired both James Naughtie and Anna Ford, fired Peter Hobday, made the journalism more rigorous, took a more sceptical line towards pressure groups, handled a lot of political flak and maintained the programme's audience figures against mounting competition – including that of 5 Live, which began in March 1994.

Under him, also, the programme hired its first publicist, Justin Everard, who in 1994 answered an advertisement for the job in the *Guardian* (the BBC's favourite recruitment vehicle) after spells with Conservative Central Office, Saatchi & Saatchi and a City public relations firm. 'Today' thus became the first BBC radio programme to have a press and publicity officer for its exclusive use, though Everard's brief subsequently took in its sister programmes 'The World at One', 'PM' and 'The World Tonight'. (Mosey regarded this appointment as of great importance: he wrote[2] in his job application, under 'immediate priorities', that in his view 'Today' had to 'generate more publicity'.)

When he applied for the job, in February 1993, Mosey knew that Redhead would be leaving in a year's time. With that in mind, he also wrote in his strategy paper – which he submitted to the appointments board as the basis of his application – 'John Humphrys should be The Voice of Today'. It was the fifth item he listed.[3] Humphrys, knowing Mosey was such a fan, therefore had every reason to think he was going to be *primus inter pares* after Brian's departure. As the year went on, the press speculated as to who would come in and replace Redhead and Radio 4's entertaining little series 'The Radio Programme' (later axed to make way for 'Mediumwave') opened a book on who would get the job. James Naughtie was always the favourite, but Humphrys, quite naturally, thought that the mantle of senior presenter would settle on him after Brian went.

Naughtie, a close friend of Mosey's from their days on 'The World at One' – close enough for Roger to be godfather to his youngest child, Flora, born in 1991 – was appointed. Born in Aberdeen in 1951, he had spent seven years on the *Scotsman* and five on the *Guardian* (latterly as chief political correspondent) before going to 'The World at One' in 1988, where he was the first of its presenters to have a regional accent since it began in 1965. He started at 'Today' on 28 February 1994, Nick Clarke succeeding him on the lunchtime programme.

The relationship between Naughtie, Humphrys and MacGregor was finally settled in March 1996 when Mosey announced that they constituted an even troika. Formal parity was established, with Mosey announcing that each of them had committed themselves to doing 184 'Today' programmes a year and the programme was committed to giving each of them the same 184 a year (the 'guarantee', in BBC jargon). As this book is being completed, contracts are being renegotiated and it is possible that Humphrys will take his days down from four to three a week, which means, obviously, that others will have to do more.

Theoretically, there is no pecking order among the presenters. Theoretically, they are the Portland Place equivalent of the Holy Trinity, three equal persons. 'Our basic policy is that there is an equivalence between them all,' Tony Hall, Chief Executive of BBC News, told me.[4] In that case, I asked him, why do the two men get paid more than Sue MacGregor? There was a nine-second pause – this is quite a long time when you are talking to someone, try it out some time – while Hall sat with knitted brow. 'Let me think about that and I'll give you an answer,' he said. When, after my prompting, he finally replied, he said, 'You know that the principle is that we don't discuss the contracts of individuals but – to answer your question as far as possible – it would not be unusual for anomalies to arise over a period of years. This would in no way make any difference to the "status" of presenters.'[5]

The imbalance between the presenters is manifest not merely in pay (my understanding is that MacGregor receives about £100,000 a year, Naughtie and Humphrys about £120,000), but also in how frequently each of them does the 8.10 interview, which MacGregor described as 'the fulcrum of the programme'[6] and John Humphrys calls 'the prestigious slot'.[7] Hall said that he would be 'genuinely surprised' if it were the case that Humphrys usually does the 8.10 interview if he is on the programme, and that he was 'never aware' of that.[8] In which case, Hall is going to be genuinely surprised – but regular listeners may not be – by these figures, which I discovered by going through all the 'PasBs' (Programmes as Broadcast documents) for the calendar year 1996.

Humphrys did the 8.10 interview on 67.04 per cent of the days on which he presented the programme; Naughtie did it on 47.8 per cent of the days he was there; but MacGregor did it on only 29.65 per cent of her appearances. Roughly speaking, therefore, Humphrys does the big set-piece interview on two out of every three programmes he does, Naughtie does it on almost half of his but MacGregor does it on less than a third of hers. (There were some days, of course, when there was no 8.10 interview, others when it was split, others when someone else did it – John Sergeant, for example, with the Prime Minister – and a few occasions for which the PasB has got lost. All these days have been discounted. The percentages are correct to two decimal places.)

When I spoke to MacGregor, she confirmed she felt her own position on the programme had slipped:

> I'm aware that a lot of the top political stories go to John or Jim. They're both brilliant at doing them, but I think that perhaps the balance has shifted a little too much in their direction. I have [made representations] but it's very difficult . . . I get there shortly after 4.15 am and you're presented with the running order and your briefs and that's it. It's all been decided, probably around midnight or earlier, and it's a result of the interplay between the editor and the night editor the night before. There's nothing I can do. If John has got the 8.10 interview and it's with Heseltine or the Chancellor, I can't say, I think it's about time I did an 8.10 interview. Well, I can say, but it wouldn't make a blind bit of difference.
>
> I don't want to appear to be a whingeing woman. It's a great programme to be on and it's not something I whinge about on a regular basis, but I think every now and then it has to be pointed out that this is the case.[9]

It was interesting that Sue used the word 'whinge' about herself, because it was the same word the Chancellor of the Exchequer used in describing her:

> Sue is a first-class, straightforward interviewer. But I don't think she's as good as the others. There's nothing particular about her interviews. And at times she's just waspish and she whinges a bit. And can get a bit testy. The others are deeply political animals. I don't think she is. She's interested in a wider range of things. And I happen to have had some very good interviews with Sue MacGregor. I don't go in there thinking this is arm-to-arm combat and I've never come away personally annoyed. I think she's a first-class interviewer. But it doesn't always have the bounce and the oomph that, on their best, the others can produce. I'm probably damning Sue MacGregor with faint praise, but not intending to. She won't speak to me again.[10]

Other leading politicians have also observed a disparity between the presenters, as Robin Cook remarks: 'One cannot but notice the way in which it is farmed out that John Humphrys does the tough interviews and Sue MacGregor is given the relatively softer approach stories which perhaps lend themselves less to interruption.'[11] These other stories did, however, include a memorable interview with the Duchess of York, in which she nearly came away with an admission of adultery: 'Q: "Were you unfaithful to Andrew?" A: "Mmm, I think . . . Have I admitted that? Where did I admit that? I haven't admitted it. I don't think that's relevant to this interview."'

Sue also said:

I did say that 'Today' was sometimes a very macho programme to work on. It is less so than it was. When I first joined under Julian [Holland] there were few women in positions of authority, and now that's changed. There are some mornings when I walk in and the office is almost entirely female. Brian was a very sort of bluff, typical northern male in many ways. John is oozing testosterone. Jim's more of a new man. There are still some mornings, I guess, when I feel that I have to assert myself quietly in order to be listened to in any way. I think I can detect in some male politicians a slight irritation when I ask them a toughish question, rather than John or Jim. My antennae are still out there for those manifesta-tions of M.C. Piggery. Just as black people can detect the subtlest of racial slurs, and Jewish people can detect the tiniest grains of anti-semitism, I think women still detect chauvinism. Maybe our antennae sometimes are over-sensitive.[12]

After this evidence of the marginalisation of MacGregor it was heartening to hear the Director-General say this about the First Lady of 'Today':

Sue strikes me as being beloved of the audience. I always notice when Sue comes to any BBC social occasion, which she often does, that people almost want to curtsey when they see her. She is hugely respected. She has so much dignity as an individual and people have so much affection for her, that her warmth and qualities as an individual come through.[13]

Anna Ford is the fourth member of the team, hired for fifty days a year compared with an annual 184 for each of the other three. As the woman who will be remembered forever for throwing a glass of wine over Jonathan Aitken while at TV-am in 1983, she is the only one of the 'Today' presenters to have had experience of both breakfast radio and breakfast television, and thus possesses a unique perspective on the snap, crackle and pop of early-morning broadcasting:

> They [TV-am and 'Today'] are completely different, as different as chalk and cheese. I don't think [at TV-am] that we gave ourselves enough time to let it take off. If you look at the history of the American stations like CBS, it took them fifteen years to capture the public imagination and to be really successful. And our own Chairman, Peter Jay, was rubbishing us practically before we'd got on air. So there were problems of numerous sorts. But [radio] is a very different kettle of fish, and the 'Today' programme is unique in what it does, which it does extremely well, I think.[14]

Roger Mosey, with Tony Hall's backing, invited Anna to come and present some editions of the programme in 1993. Her charisma naturally attracted him, as well as the fact that she was believed to be receptive to a change. As she recalls, she had reached an age (she turned fifty in October 1993) when people do not always branch out into new directions:

> Roger Mosey said would I like to have a go at the 'Today' programme. I was doing the 'Six O'Clock News' three days a week, and I've always liked the radio. I knew that Brian was going and there was all this stuff in the newspapers about them looking for a replacement for Brian. Well, there was never going to be a replacement for Brian, that was not the point. What they wanted to do at the time was try out a number of people, and I know they approached some people who said, not on your nelly. And they approached other, braver, folk, like me who said, yes, I'll have a go.
> If you do something entirely new at my age, you're slightly putting your neck on the line. It was taking a risk, but I think it's good to take risks. It's good to be frightened. The only way you learn in life is to push out the boundaries. I do believe people should be allowed to try new things and spread their wings a bit.[15]

The new things were indeed very new, and at first they did cause problems:

> I wasn't used to doing it. It was like learning to ride a bike. I'd

never done this sort of programme before and it was quite frightening, nerve-racking. You've got to remember all the things the programme cares about, like telling the time at the right time and talking to people at the right time. There is a grammar to the programme so you're carrying that framework in your head as well as being asked to do five or six interviews, sometimes eight. And these interviews sometimes get changed, so they might send John out of the room and suddenly say, 'Take over his interview with those two people sitting in front of you.' So you've got to carry the briefing for quite a large number of topics across a wide range of things. And you've got to be able to do those interviews incisively.[16]

Roger, who patiently and skilfully helped her through the early period, despite occasional bursts of understandable impatience from one or two members of the production team, explains what was different:

In television you start talking when the light comes on, in radio when the light goes off. A television news bulletin can just go to another picture when you move to another story, but in radio things have to be signposted and one has to say, 'That was Roger Harrabin and the time is now nineteen minutes to eight and we go over to ...' or words to that effect. It was very different from anything she'd done before. In addition, there was enormous press interest in her and anything she did was immediately picked up and magnified, such as when she said to David Sheppard, the Bishop of Liverpool, that she was 'a single mother too', when all she meant was that she was raising her daughters singlehanded.[17]

Anna recalls the difficulties of the period: 'It was like going to work on a conveyor belt in a factory [she once worked packing fruit in Israel, so does actually know about conveyor belts] with several million people watching you, saying, 'Oh, you didn't do that one very well, you didn't throw that one out, you didn't put the submarine in that packet of cornflakes.'[18]

David Blunkett is one of many who considers that she has made a most impressive improvement. 'Anna Ford is now learning the job well,' he said. 'When she first started she was very wooden, and obviously extremely nervous. I think she's come on a lot.'[19]

Anna explained:

The wooden is to do with the fact that your brain is separating itself in about four different parts. You're thinking, am I going to tell the time next? Have I got to do that? And then you're speaking and somebody's talking down your earpiece at the same time. So you sound less than relaxed. But then you begin to throw all that away and you think, what the hell, this is a programme where relaxation and enjoyment is part of the fun of it and what people want is presenters who are relaxed with each other and to feel some sort of friendly relationship in the studio and also, I think, they want to know you're completely equal to your interviewees. Inevitably I'm more confident [than when I started], yes.[20]

Her new confidence showed itself in what became by far her most controversial moment on the programme, an acrimonious interview with Kenneth Clarke. It was also a vivid example of what can sometimes go wrong when the interviewee is in the radio car and has no eye contact with the person interviewing him, making it difficult for each of them to know when the other one has stopped speaking. Clarke was in the radio car in Westminster, having just unveiled a new Tory campaign poster. Since this episode prompted an official (and therefore rare) Conservative Party complaint, and a formal BBC admission of the interview's shortcomings, it is worth quoting the entire exchange full and unexpurgated:

FORD: For decades the Conservatives have derided the Labour Party for not loosening its links with the trades unions and for not abandoning socialism, but in the past weeks allies of the Labour leader, Tony Blair, have shown publicly that they are willing to contemplate both courses of action which must, in the approach to a General Election, put the wind up the Tories. In fact, it's now looking as if the three main parties are engaged in a fierce battle for the middle ground of politics. Tony Blair will take the argument a stage further tonight with a keynote address in the traditional Tory stronghold of the City of London. You might think that the Tories would welcome the apparent conversion of Labour, but today they renew their campaign about the dangers of New Labour. The Chancellor of the Exchequer, Kenneth Clarke, is on the line now. Good morning.
CHANCELLOR: Good morning.
FORD: You're a very reasonable man and you're seen to be one of those people who generally behave in a reasonable and adult way

– don't you feel rather silly being made to go and stand in front of these posters continually?

CHANCELLOR: The posters point to the increased living standards which good economic policy has brought us since the last election, and campaigning involves advertising your achievements. The average family, which Labour always use when they comment on economic policy, has £700 a year more to spend now than they had at the time of the last election.

FORD: Well of course they don't agree with that. They say that taxes have gone up by £2,000, but just, just –

CHANCELLOR: I'm sorry you put that in. That is the silliness of politics, when you say they don't agree with that, I'd like them to explain why they don't agree with that, because on top of taxes, on top of inflation, the genuine figure, the best figure you can calculate, is £700 a year, and the campaigning I'm going in for is firstly, of course, to say good economic policy will deliver an ever bigger figure if we keep UK Ltd on the course it is now, but secondly that they have already announced policies which would damage that with new taxation, with the so-called windfall tax, with the way in which they'd let council tax for example go up –

FORD (testily): Yes yes yes –

CHANCELLOR: . . . with the way in which they will take Child Benefit, well you say, you know –

FORD: No, I say yes yes yes.

CHANCELLOR: You say, it's all rather demeaning. I think it's very reasonable to say this government has been an economic success –

FORD: But, but, Mr Clarke –

CHANCELLOR: . . . and the Labour Party should answer questions about things that change it.

FORD: But Mr Clarke, aren't you pleased that Labour has changed?

CHANCELLOR: I'm pleased that Labour is not such a threat as it was –

FORD: Oh good –

CHANCELLOR: . . . to national interests, well of course. When we used to have, for instance, Michael Foot leading the Party, when there was a sort of Marxist-Leninist element inside the Party, he wasn't a Marxist-Leninist but a lot of his followers were, it was a very, very serious threat to this country.

FORD: So you're saying they're really less of a threat now.

CHANCELLOR: But that isn't the answer, you see. It's no good just saying, well New Labour isn't the kind of party we had in 1983. New Labour is still advocating increased taxation. It's still committing itself –

FORD: But they're severing their ties with the unions, they're looking at new policies, they're even contemplating, some of them, people very close to Tony Blair, even contemplating dropping the word socialism. They're so close to the centre now they're almost indistinguishable from parts of the Tory Party.

CHANCELLOR: The junior spokesman who suggested there was a plan to get rid of the trade union links was instantly denounced, and as far as I can see they have not got rid of the block vote and they are taking money from the trade unions and they're not severing the link, but that isn't the *key point*. The *key point* is, because of those links and other links, the Labour Party, it's New Labour, but it's still advocating new taxes. It's still in favour of regulating the labour market, the so-called Social Chapter.

FORD: But on the point of taxes – :

CHANCELLOR: No, well –

FORD: . . . you are the party who said you weren't going to put up taxes and you put up VAT twenty-two times. The fact is that you've failed, haven't you, to catch the mood of the electorate at the moment, who are well aware of the important issues in this election of health, of education, certainly of taxes, but of not behaving in the puerile way that the majority of the electorate now seem to think that political parties are behaving.

CHANCELLOR: With great respect, the twenty-two changes to VAT is a fairly puerile point made by the Labour Party, which you've adopted. They included tidying up loopholes like putting VAT on gold dust –

FORD: I haven't adopted the Labour Party –

CHANCELLOR: . . . well, the twenty-two changes to VAT is a straight Labour Party slogan and includes, just to give you an example –

FORD: . . . you deny –

CHANCELLOR: . . . putting VAT on gold dust, because people were using that as a way of evading VAT –

FORD: That's an example you always give –

CHANCELLOR: But what matters in this country is that we're becoming a modern, successful industrial economy. We have growth, we have falling unemployment, we have rising living

standards, we're competing successfully with our competitors in Western Europe and the world and it is that which matters –
FORD: But the –
CHANCELLOR: But there has to be a political debate about how to keep it going. Just to have a PR campaign saying you're New Labour is no substitute at all for sensible economic policies –
FORD: So you –
CHANCELLOR: ... and they will not answer questions and all the campaigns I associate myself with, when I talk about new taxes, I want Central Office to show me why are we saying they're doing this, who said it –
FORD: I'm afraid I'm going to –
CHANCELLOR: ... where, what document and all of them are authenticated by Labour speeches and documents.
FORD: So you're not going to elevate the debate. [Silence, apart from slight rustling of paper.] Thank you Mr Clarke.

What happened at the end was that Clarke had got cut off in error. Either the studio pulled the plug on the radio car or the other way round: each blames the other. So he did not hear her parting shot about elevating the debate.

Anna Ford remembers:

Roger shouted over my headphones, 'Ask him why he isn't going to elevate the debate' and I think I made a mistake in saying it. By which time they'd switched off his equipment, so he [Clarke] didn't hear it. I listened, thinking, did he hear the question, is he upset, what's happened, and I said thank you and that was it. And then the Labour Party that morning said, 'Oh that's a useful point for us, he's admitted that Labour *have* changed, we'll campaign on it,' at which point Brian Mawhinney hit the roof and said, 'No, no this was all the fault of Anna Ford and this interview, she was extremely rude, she interrupted him too often,' at which point there was an investigation and the BBC decided to apologise. [I was] somewhat irritated, but nothing more than that. I think it was less than grand behaviour. He invited me to drinks at Number 11 but unfortunately I couldn't go, but I have no reason to suppose that Ken Clarke and I are any less friendly than we've always been. I find him delightful. I suspect he was irritated by Brian Mawhinney's intervention.[21]

Those suspicions turned out to be accurate. Clarke confirmed to me that, yes, he *had* been irritated at Mawhinney's intervention. Significantly, he also revealed that he had asked Central Office *not* to complain:

I'd asked somebody from Central Office not to when somebody told me they were going off to complain. My feeling was they should not. Perhaps it didn't reach Brian, I don't know. Anyway, Central Office complained and blew the whole thing up into a newspaper story, and I'm not sure what good that did. I only complain to journalists or broadcasters if something outrageously defamatory is being said. Anna Ford's was just a combative interview that went off the rails and it didn't do either of us any good.[22]

Mawhinney either did not get Clarke's request or decided to put it in the bin – he would not tell me which. For him, the crucial point was the glaring contrast between Anna's mauling of Clarke at 7.33 am and Jim Naughtie's polite handling of Tony Blair ('kid gloves', Mawhinney called it) at 8.10. He complained, in writing, to John Birt. So did fourteen other listeners, though twice that number wrote in to defend Anna's interviewing. The complaint was upheld:

While noting the success of 'Today' in testing all political viewpoints and achieving balance over time, the Director-General acknowledged that Mr Clarke had been subject to too much interruption, and that not enough thought had been given to ensuring a consistency of approach to the two interviews.[23]

For the Chancellor, clearly, the whole episode had been a messy and rather pointless scrap – caused by the lack of eye-contact:

What had gone wrong was what can go wrong when you're not in the studio. I was sitting in a freezing cold radio car about two miles away, somewhere in Westminster, having just unveiled a poster. We weren't in the same place and the whole interview got off on the wrong footing. After a bit we were just shouting at each other into disembodied microphones. Then a sort of pause came. Some of the press said I put the telephone down. I didn't put the telephone down. Some boffin somewhere disconnected us. She thought I was still there and a silence ensued. Only afterwards did people tell me the silence was audible on the air.[24]

Clearly, the incident strengthened his determination always to go into the studio, if at all possible:

I don't like using the radio car. When I do [interviews with 'Today'] from Nottingham or Brussels, two of my slots I do sometimes, I only do it because it happens to be the right day and I have to do it. It's always more difficult, Nottingham because they can never get the kit to work, and Brussels because you're slightly out of touch with what's actually going on in London. My approach has always been to go into the studio. I always say I want to go in and see the red of their eyes.[25]

Virginia Bottomley, one of many listeners that day, commented later:

If you have a programme which is fast moving and sharp it's a bit like going round a speedtrack on a motorbike. Every so often, people will lose their balance and fall off. It was not, I think, an acceptable standard of interviewing. On the other hand, the idea that Ken Clarke needs protecting makes me chuckle. Most of the people who are on frequently are going to come back time and again so there's time to make good the damage. But it was good for the BBC to make it clear that they get it wrong sometimes. The programme is too significant and strong for the BBC to feel they must always defend everything they do in it. You do that with a fragile plant.[26]

Mosey, too, wished to put the episode into perspective: 'Our approach to political interviews is consistent – even if very occasionally there are outcomes which fall below our usual standards. When that happens, we acknowledge it; but it doesn't dent our pride in what we achieve in fourteen-and-a-half hours of live broadcasting each week.'[27]

More of a free spirit than the others, as many startled listeners realised when she called Simon Pemberton, the heartless landlord of 'The Archers', 'rather a shit',[28] Anna is an idiosyncratic broadcaster whose distinctiveness arises partly because, alone of the presenters, she has not had a conventional reporting background. Her left-of-centre idealism, and reluctance to be muzzled by the BBC, manifested itself in a stinging letter she wrote to the *Guardian* in September 1995 chiding Jack Straw, Shadow Home Secretary, for his robust new approach to beggars:

> He's always seemed a decent enough chap, and I was wondering if he'll ever be reduced to sitting on a cold bench in a dirty street drinking Brasso or aftershave? ... I wondered if the trials and tribulations of political life might ever lead him to a nervous breakdown, or his being told he's schizophrenic, then losing his job, home and family? I wonder if he's ever walked over Waterloo Bridge to the land behind St John's Church or sauntered down The Cut, and spoken to some of the beggars, drunks and mentally ill ('symbols of social decay') he so wants to rid us of?'

The BBC reminded her that presenters are not supposed to give opinions on matters of public controversy. Mark Damazer, editor of BBC TV news (and her boss, as she works primarily for television), tracked her down to Ecuador, where she was on holiday, to rap her knuckles over the telephone. Anna clearly found this irksome:

> I do have strong feelings about all sorts of things and my letter to the *Guardian* was to do with the humanitarian aspects of people who are down and out. I knew about this very well because my father was Vicar of [St John's] Waterloo, and had many winos outside his front door permanently and in his parish, so that was a letter based purely on humanitarian concerns. The fact that the BBC didn't see it as such was their problem, not mine.[29]

Asked if she resented the BBC's response, she said:

> I think the BBC is a bit too uptight occasionally. They have to accept that if they employ people to do the sort of jobs that we do, they must expect people of character, with views. Certainly in France this would be so. Newscasters write books about the political situation. They're extremely bright, they're considered to be part of the cultural scene, therefore they're considered naturally to have opinions on things. The BBC has got a little bit uptight about all that, I think.[30]

Almost as soon as she had said that, however, Anna went on to give a very reasoned defence of the BBC tradition of impartiality:

I've been asked to write columns for newspapers [the one she mentioned was the *Daily Express*] and because they want opinionated columns it's impossible to do while I'm a broadcaster and an interviewer. Because if I wrote an opinionated column about the millennium, prison reform, health, education – things I might feel strongly about as a parent or an individual – and the next day I was interviewing the Secretary of State for that particular department, they would say we don't want to be interviewed by Anna Ford because she's made her views expressly known in such-a-such a newspaper yesterday. And they're quite right – you can't do it.[31]

John Humphrys is the presenter most often mentioned by the famous in connection with the programme. 'Brian was the big one, then Humphrys took over and Humphrys has really taken the top spot now,' said Archer. 'I think Jim Naughtie is very conscious of the battle between him and Humphrys.'[32]

Naughtie was phlegmatic about this:

Well, that's just his view. There's no battle. Competitiveness, professional competitiveness, of course. We're both trying to do a job very well. What we're not trying to do is do each other down. You know as well as I do that the programme works because of a kind of chemistry. If there was a battle it would be obvious to the listeners and it would undermine the programme and secondly, it just wouldn't work. We've got more things to worry about than having a battle with each other.[33]

Naughtie also dismissed any notion of a pecking order:

There is no pecking order between John and me. The position is quite simple. When Brian was going to retire, the announcement was made that I was joining the 'Today' team to replace Brian. Brian and John and I posed for a picture outside Broadcasting House. There we were. John and I have both done long interviews with the Prime Minister over the last six months. John did Gordon Brown today on top people's pay, I did Gordon last week on tax. Over the course of a month it evens out. John and I are a team.

We've got to be. If we weren't it wouldn't work . . . I understand that people are fascinated by our relationship but it's not a relationship, it's coming in and doing a job . . . And it's a two-presenter show every morning, it's not a one-presenter show.[34]

David Blunkett thought Humphrys was 'very good because he does inform himself and he does his homework, maybe he's even a little bit laidback'.[35] Bottomley said, 'I often go and take my jacket off and say, "Right, who's going to give the first punch?" Both my best and worst interviews have probably been with John Humphrys, so he's more extreme, but I am essentially a fan.'[36] Kenneth Clarke was also a fan: 'Humphrys is more aggressive than Redhead, sometimes more hectoring. But he's cheerily interested in politics, it's a good interview and if you hold your own, it's very enjoyable. He and I are just people who like a good argument, so that's OK.'[37] William Waldegrave thought Humphrys could

be aggressive and is sometimes unwilling to go off the prepared list of questions that he's thought of and he interrupts too much, but I don't find him unfair. It's a difficult balance: if you just let politicians talk they will ramble on and say what they want to say. It's perfectly fair for the interviewer to try and bring them back to what he thinks are fair questions, even if John does sometimes get rather carried away.[38]

Clearly, however, Humphrys is not to everyone's taste. Nicholas Winterton, for example, felt that he 'lays it on a bit heavy, compared with the sparkling touch and rapier thrust of Brian Redhead'.[39] And John Timpson was not taken by a Humphrys newspaper article[40] after the BBC had upheld Mawhinney's complaint about the Kenneth Clarke interview, in which he wrote that the day he was told to back off was the day he quit.

I came so close to writing to the Editor. I thought it was insufferably pompous of the man, this business of 'I'm going to carry on until I get my way, I don't care what anyone else says, I shall carry on even if they tell me not to,' and so on. There was a letter in the *Telegraph* soon afterwards, very short. 'Mr Humphrys said he will carry on until someone tells him to back off. Mr Humphrys, back off!'[41]

Some people think nothing will ever be as good as Timpson–Redhead, just as there were those in that era who thought Jack de Manio represented the golden age. Some people think the present set-up is the best yet. 'Redhead didn't do much for me,' says Sir Christopher Bland, Chairman of the BBC, 'I like it now with its ensemble team.'[42] 'Both Humphrys and Naughtie are, in my view, better interviewers than Redhead,' says Austin Mitchell. 'Brian could be fobbed off with an easy answer. An answer to which he was sympathetic would satisfy him, whereas he should have questioned it. Humphrys is more persistent and so is Naughtie, and they can do it without alienating people. They are the best interviewers around. They don't do hectoring, "Come off it" kind of interviews of the Paxman variety.'[43] Tony Hall felt something similar: 'Humphrys is more acerbic, clearly, but I think they can both engage the audience extremely well.'[44] Stephen Dorrell said he had always felt that with Naughtie and MacGregor one could have 'a civilised conversation of the kind you might have over the breakfast table', but that Humphrys was 'famously assertive'.[45] Donald Dewar echoed that:

I know Jim Naughtie quite well, I knew him way back on the *Scotsman*, so I possibly find him slightly easier. I think John Humphrys is a more persistent questioner. He does tend to concentrate on a narrow area and push you and push you and push you. If you've been at the wrong end of this you come out saying he's obsessive, but if you're listening in and it's one of the people you don't particularly like you think it's very effective. It's like all these things, it depends on what point you're viewing it from.[46]

It was clear that Humphrys has admirers in high places in the BBC, too. John Birt told me that after his lecture in Dublin in 1995 in which he criticised some aspects of modern media, including belligerent interviewers, he had sent Humphrys a handwritten note 'of warm reassurance that whatever the papers may have said he was the last person on my mind and that the remarks I'd made in Dublin definitely did not apply to him. It was a billet-doux.'[47]
Birt also praised Humphrys's skills:

I'm glad he is persistent. I think he's a very, very effective interviewer. I think we've seen him emerge into his full maturity as an interviewer in the last five years. He's extremely well informed on the whole range of issues, and ever more skilled in how he conducts interviews. And he is very rigorous. He's a tough person to be interviewed by. You've got to be pretty good to go up against him.[48]

Some politicians thought that what Naughtie lacked in aggression he made up for in subtlety and cunning. Kenneth Clarke said:

Jim is the pleasant, reasonable, friendly, soft-spoken Scot. If you get into difficulties with Jim, it's because he's lulled you into a sense of false security. You can get into more trouble with a friendly interviewer than with a combative one. And he's bright. His questions have a point. So the fact that he appears to be less boisterous, less combative, less interrupting, doesn't make him any less effective.[49]

Birt agreed with this: 'There are many ways of skinning the cat as a broadcast interviewer. And I think Jim does have those different qualities. But never does he depart essentially from a firm line of questioning.'[50]

Clarke's Treasury colleague, William Waldegrave, pointed out that Naughtie had the sort of detailed political knowledge which was invaluable on what had now become such a political programme:

Jim Naughtie is an extremely shrewd operator. I do think in those programmes where there's little time to prepare, it's very important to have people with a really deep background of political journalism. When you're dealing with politicians, it's as well to have a long memory, and that's why people like Robin Day and David Dimbleby are so good. Jim on another programme ['The World at One'] is the only journalist I have ever known who voluntarily, without my complaining, corrected something he said the next day, and that's very high standards, I think.

They both have a good sense of humour. I actually made John laugh once over an absurd fracas I was involved in where I said that there must be some extreme circumstances such as wartime when it's right not to tell the truth. And he said to me, 'Well, that was a silly thing to say, wasn't it? Of course it's true what you said, but you shouldn't have given that answer.' So I said, 'What, you mean I shouldn't have told the truth?' And he laughed.[51]

Humphrys jibbed at Dorrell's description of him as 'famously assertive':

It's not my job to be assertive. You assert a point. I truly believe that I do not in interviews express opinions. That is not my job. Whether I am interviewing a Tory, a Labour politician or a Liberal Democrat, I will put exactly opposite points to each of them, so I can hardly believe in all those things, obviously. 'Persistent' I would absolutely agree with and would hope that I am. Virginia Bottomley did once whisper in my ear in the studio, 'I have to keep reminding myself how very beastly you can be,' but she did smile as she said it.[52]

Humphrys it was who extracted from John Prescott, son of a railwayman, grandson of a miner, and Deputy Leader of the Labour Party, an admission that he was now 'middle class'. This statement sent the press into such a lather of excitement that the programme hit upon a brilliant stroke – returning to the topic the next day but this time interviewing Prescott's staunchly working-class father, aged eighty-five, as well as his more ambiguously statused son. Day one of this diverting saga was on Friday 12 April 1996, the day after Labour's victory in the Staffordshire South-East by-election, which had inflicted on the government their thirty-fifth successive by-election defeat. The conversation went like this:

PRESCOTT: . . . We clearly are the really one-nation Party and the only alternative.
HUMPHRYS: You say the alternative, but a lot of people say you've just become another middle-class party and haven't you done terribly well because you keep making reassuring noises to the middle class. No one knows what you'd actually do in government and a lot of your backbenchers are very uneasy about it. Can I just play you a clip of one of your backbenchers, Chris Mullin . . .
PRESCOTT: Why are you disparaging about the middle class? You're middle class, I'm middle class and we welcome votes from wherever they come.
HUMPHRYS: I thought you were working class, but there we are.
PRESCOTT: Well, I was once, but by being a Member of Parliament I can tell you I'm pretty middle class.
HUMPHRYS: I'm not sure whether that's allowed but still, let's play you what Chris Mullin said, one of your backbench MPs. He says

you should not be appealing, and I quote, to the greed of the middle classes: 'I know we need the votes of the middle classes, but frankly most middle-class people did rather well out of the Thatcher decade. The social fabric is crumbling and I think most sensible people realise that and I don't think we should pretend that it can all be put right either overnight or without somebody somewhere contributing, and the people best fitted to contribute if there have to be tax increases of any sort are those who have done best out of the Thatcher decade.' Well there you are, you see, that's the point isn't it? What you're saying to everybody in Britain at the moment is nobody is going to have to suffer. Jam for everybody.

PRESCOTT: Well, we don't say that at all and I must say to Chris, I don't know whether he was happy with the votes that we got in the last four elections, but it was not enough to win. You have to appeal to all parts of the community and be fair in your approach to them and I think we've been doing precisely that, and that's the case we're putting across and I must say it does seem to be really recognised and accepted and that's what we intend to keep on doing.

HUMPHRYS: Even if you've got to sell your soul to do it?

PRESCOTT: We're not selling our soul . . .

Humphrys was on again the following morning for this memorable sequel featuring Prescott *père et fils*, both called John:

HUMPHRYS: The papers have gone to town this morning. *The Times* called his father, who seemed a bit surprised to say the least. Well, father and son are on the phone. Mr Prescott Senior, good morning. What was your reaction?

JPS: Well, I was a little surprised at the word middle class, because I've always assumed myself and my family have been working class and I call a man working class who works for his living such as quarrymen, milkmen, roadmen, which I was.

HUMPHRYS: Politicians?

JPS: Well, it's very difficult with politicians, because some say they don't work. But I believe they do.

HUMPHRYS: So they're still working class then?

JPS: Yes, except they have a middle-class style, possibly.

HUMPHRYS: There you are then, John Prescott Junior, you're still working-class even though you have a middle class style.

JPJ: This is amazing. I think in that programme I said to you, why are people so disparaging about the middle class? When I was a seaman and a catering person, I was working class by definition, on the census. Once I became a Member of Parliament they defined me as middle class. I'm a working-class man with working-class values and roots that I'm proud of, living a middle-class sort of style of life.

HUMPHRYS: But you didn't say that. You said you were middle class. That's what made everybody's eyebrows shoot up.

JPJ: But I'm defined as middle class. My heart is always the same, I'm working class, I come from the roots of working class and my party represents both middle class and working class and we want to do something about making a fairer Britain. I mean, John Major, when he was a bus conductor, was he working class or was he middle class?

HUMPHRYS: Well what is he now, that's the point, I mean some people would say . . .

JPJ: He's middle class now. It's amazing how the British press treat it in such a way, but that's life and I'm proud of that working class. I come from Hull, which is largely working class, but many of them are middle class, we're not disparaging about them, but we want to do something about it.

HUMPHRYS: So it's 'them' now. The middle class is 'them' now, is it?

JPJ: I live that style of being middle class with working-class friends and I think my father defined it – it's what you do for your work and your living in a way and it's also about your style and values. My values, make no mistake, are working-class values about fairness and middle-class people share it and if you look at the history of the Labour Party it was brought about by many middle class and working class getting together.

HUMPHRYS: So Mr Prescott Senior then, has he redeemed himself now? He says he is really working class now after all. Is that all right?

JPS: Oh it's all right, because it does appear now that our horizons have merged, you see, and the Labour Party as he rightly says are proud to represent working class and middle class, if there is such a section of people.

HUMPHRYS: Both of you, thanks very much indeed.

This is more satisfying as entertainment than elucidation – there is

no attempt to define terms, apart from JPS's at the very beginning –
but it demonstrates Britain's obsession with class, Prescott's scorn for
the press and Humphrys's speed of mind. Who else would have
instantly picked up Prescott's giveaway use of 'them' to describe the
bourgeoisie? He is the least well educated, formally, of all the
presenters, but the one who is fastest on his feet.

Humphrys's confidence in his own dominating position on the
programme emerged most clearly in the fact that, of all four
presenters, he was the most generous about his colleagues:

> Sue is an absolutely consummate broadcaster, the most professio-
> nal broadcaster of all of us in terms of the skills, microphone
> technique, delivery, studio craft and so on. Literally I don't know
> a better one. She comes across as this super-cool, quite refined,
> slightly posh Englishwoman but when you've listened for a bit you
> realise that there's a really feisty woman in there, who enjoys the
> chase and whose personality does come across. Every so often
> you'll get a real little buzz. Somebody will say something thinking
> that Sue's a kind of pushover and she'll snap back, and sometimes
> she'll do the headmistress thing and be cross with somebody and
> she's a great, great strength on the programme. Peter was more
> laidback. He had a great sense of humour and a very easy natural
> style that the audience liked. Jim is more discursive [than me] and
> is absolutely fascinated by the business of politics, by the House of
> Commons. For Jim, politics is almost a kind of art form and he
> appreciates it almost like an artist.[53]

He was very realistic, too, about Hobday's enforced departure:

> I was sorry when he left. He was a good bloke to work with. But I
> think of every contract as potentially the last. We all have to go at
> some time. We're all going to die. All editors want to move
> presenters around. There are very few ways in which an editor can
> make a mark on a programme and the easiest way is to change the
> presenters, bring in a new one, or get rid of one who's been around
> a long time.[54]

In April 1995 Mosey had to deal with the Social Market
Foundation report which accused 'Today' of an uncritical attitude
towards those spokesmen – for lobby groups and charities, for
example – who thought that the solution to all social problems was

simply to spend more money. The charge was therefore that the programme was not impartial and devoted more airtime to those who wanted to increase public expenditure than to those who wished to reduce it. It was a charge echoed by the Conservative Party Chairman, Dr Brian Mawhinney, when he addressed his party conference in Blackpool in October that year.

Mosey thought the methodology in the report was seriously flawed and rebutted it with vigour:

> The Social Market Foundation estimated the cost of the spending commitments demanded by interviewees on 'Today' at £780 billion per annum; by September the analysts at Conservative Central Office had revised the figure downwards to a mere £412 billion. At the current rate of reduction we should be able to push the trade figures into the black by the middle of next year.[55]

He did add, however, 'I wouldn't argue that every item on "Today" throughout history has been a model of fiscal probity. But I'm convinced that special pleading has been drastically reduced over the years.'[56]

However, Tony Hall now admits that the report was listened to and did play a part in changing the tone of the programme:

> We took the criticism seriously and we listened to it. It is right that we listened to those who say we give the Opposition an easier ride on some occasions when we should have been asking them tougher questions about where the money was going to come from. Given that impartiality is number one in what we do, it's the number one value, it's proper that we ask tough questions of everybody. To that extent the report was pushing at an opening door. You learn about how you can do things better and I think we did that . . . It's right that there has been some change.[57]

Peter Lilley also noticed this change:

> It was an influential pamphlet in showing how the 'Today' programme was effectively becoming a voice for public-sector spending bids every morning. It was an institutional, rather than a Party, bias. It unthinkingly adopted every cause that put up a claim for more money. It didn't occur to them there could be arguments for anyone spending *less* money. Since that report

they've been a little more cautious. They don't automatically side so much and so frequently with the spenders and spending arguments. They're now more likely to say, 'What are you doing to curb the budget?' rather than 'Shouldn't you be spending a billion more on such-and-such?'[58]

His Cabinet colleague William Waldegrave also noticed a difference:

I think you hear them more often than they used to put the question to the lobby group, 'Well, this is going to be very expensive, isn't it?' There are a lot of increasingly powerful lobby groups in society and they have to report them to some extent, and lobbies are generally asking for more money. But the 'Today' programme is better than most at remembering that there is also a wider common good which is called not creating inflation. I think they're conscious of the issue.[59]

Kenneth Clarke accepted that the pamphlet had made a difference, but as one of a number of factors:

It was a joke I'd often made that if you listened to 'Today' and agreed with all these compelling lobbyists, you could get through a few billion every morning. And there was a style of questioning, which has died out now, which suggested to each lobbyist who came on that the problem was funding. The line of questioning was always about under-funding and the shortage of resources and so on. It hadn't occurred to me that it was the Social Market Foundation report that stopped it. It might [have helped]. I rather thought it was because big spending has gone out of fashion on both sides of the political divide.[60]

What Mosey tactfully did not say in his *Standard* rebuttal was that he had already started to cut down the amount of time given to pressure groups, and that, specifically, he had seen to it that the 6.50 am slot became less of a propaganda slot for lobbyists. Mosey also got Niall Dickson to do a three-part series on social security, which went out in September 1995 and was sympathetic to the notion (by then accepted by all main parties) that welfare spending had increased, was increasing and ought to be reduced. Roger Harrabin also did a report about an unmarried mother who had six children by four different fathers, which was followed up by several national newspapers. Mosey, shrewdly and significantly, declined to allow on to 'Today' a charity's claim that some British children were living 'in Dickensian conditions', though it did make some other programmes (on Radio 1 and Radio 5 Live) not edited with the same intellectual rigour. 'I had little time for what I regarded as spurious surveys,' he said.[61]

The least pleasant task he had was not renewing Peter Hobday's contract in 1996. Mosey underestimated the widespread hostility this would arouse, which was perhaps one of the two serious misjudgements he made as editor (the other being his enthusiastic resurrection of the tarnished Personality of the Year poll). *The Times* launched a Save Hobday Campaign and Hobday was accused of fomenting it, partly because of comments he made to Geoffrey Levy in the *Daily Mail*. He had no need to do this, however, because the campaign was quite genuine. 'Out in listener land they like his jokes, they like him, they even like his frequent bulletins on the health of the camellias in the garden of his Kensington home,' Hugo Gurdon wrote in the *Daily Telegraph*.[62] Hobday was also not above making jokes about his girth. Nor were his colleagues: once, after a travel item about an abnormal load going down the A40, Timpson remarked that it must have been Peter Hobday.

No official explanation was given by the BBC for its action. Even when Mosey wrote to *The Times*[63] denying that it was connected with 'age, class or accent', he failed to say what it was connected with. Hobday did have many other commitments, but he argued that he had to take them on because he was never used nearly as much as the others: indeed in 1995 he was hired for only fifty programmes.

The truth was that Hobday had always been a third man – that is how he had started in the Timpson–Redhead era – and the BBC wanted its 'Today' presenters to have higher profiles. Perhaps they were irked that, unlike the other presenters, he never made it into *Who's Who*. More particularly, there were grumbles about his commitment to the programme and the extent to which he would ignore briefing documents written for him by the production team. When I raised the question of Hobday with his ex-editor Jenny Abramsky, she said:

There are a number of presenters who are actually a nightmare for editors. They don't do enough work. They don't take a brief well enough [i.e. concentrate on and learn their instructions about the

questions to ask, and the background to an interviewee]. Therefore they ask questions that reveal ignorance, or they completely
miss an opportunity. And people who have been working all night
preparing a brief which isn't done justice to get very upset.

But as I've got more mature I started to understand other things.
On various programmes I've been responsible for I've gradually
learned that if you look at what the audience feels, very often the
person you cannot stand working with is the person the audience
enjoyed most. For some reason the audience have not seen through
his ignorance of this or that. I'm not saying this about Peter, who
is highly intelligent and a lovely, lovely man. But I think Peter's
interviews perhaps are not as sharp in some ways as the team
might have wanted and therefore they felt frustrated with it. The
audience, however, felt he was a warm person who represented
them.

I think the point at which Roger made the decision [to axe
Hobday] was the right one. The programme needed to move on. I
didn't make that decision in 1986–7 because I still felt that Peter
had something to offer the team that in those days was useful.
That's not to say I didn't find it from time to time extremely
frustrating. Particularly when you come from a background on
'The World at One' where you've been trained by Andrew Boyle
and Julian Holland and where you knew that every question had
to count and therefore if you didn't ask the right question you'd
wasted some airtime.[64]

Tony Hall commented, 'If you asked me to rank the five of them
[Ford, Hobday, Humphrys, MacGregor, Naughtie] I would put Peter
at the bottom and that's the way it is. You're picking and choosing,
trying to work out the winning team.'[65]

Apart from being an uncharacteristically cruel remark, this seemed
to let the cat out of the bag about the reality of the ranking order.
When I asked what the rest of his ranking would be, Hall replied, 'I
wouldn't make any difference between them, you know bloody well I
wouldn't. I'm not going to fall into that one, life's too short.'[66]

Hall also said:

I thought Hobday was a very good broadcaster. You're right
about the listeners liking him. He's a workaholic, as is Humphrys
actually. But he spread himself around a lot, got a huge amount of
work and the 'Today' programme was only one part of that

portfolio. In the end I felt strongly that to get real identity on the programme we needed to narrow down the range of presenters that we had and to get to where we've got now.[67]

Timpson, who worked with Hobday for nearly five years, has another explanation for the sacking, which clearly left him disgusted:

I think Peter Hobday was the most underrated person who ever worked on the 'Today' programme. Always charming, always good-humoured, toiling away and doing the same dreadful hours and the same sort of interviews and everything else. The reason he fell out with them [Abramsky, Harding, Mosey and Hall] is because he is not part of the new aggressive knock 'em down and kick 'em brigade, isn't it? I don't think he could do that any more than I could. He was the last breath of sanity.[68]

Timpson's view may well have had much truth in it, as Hobday himself conceded with self-deprecating grace:

A fat, middle-aged hack like me didn't really square with the lean, mean interview machine. Nobody ever said to me, 'You're crap.' But when people say my interviewing wasn't as 'sharp' as it could be, perhaps what they mean is that it wasn't invasive and I didn't feel the need to scream and shout. I always felt you could undermine an illogical argument with a good question, and you could always ask questions with a smile in your voice. As Brian did, incidentally. I had the same approach on 'Newsnight' and some people said then that I wasn't 'tough' because I avoided the confrontational manner.[69]

On Hobday's last programme, in March 1996, there was not a single mention of his departure. Afterwards there was no party, no final handshake, no gold watch, nothing. It was very different from when John Timpson left nearly ten years before.

I have had no letter of thanks from anyone in authority, no farewell lunch or dinner, nothing. I walked out of Broadcasting House on that Saturday morning after the programme. It was the end of twenty-five years with BBC News and Current Affairs and there was nothing to mark it. I never did anything to let them down and there was nothing, not even a phone call. That's the only bitterness I really feel.[70]

The Mosey era also witnessed the growth of new technology and the birth of the Internet. He himself started to communicate with the programme each evening from his house in Richmond, using his laptop computer on which he could inspect the running order and read cues. One example of the new technology, and the way it provided a story of the sort that can make radio so diverting – and of the sort that 'Today' has always liked, because of its origins forty years ago as a blend of both news and features – came in 1996 when Tom Feilden did a telephone interview with an American mathematician 5,000 miles away. Naughtie introduced the item, which went like this:

NAUGHTIE: Stop all the clocks, cut off the telephone. The world has a new prime number. I won't bore you with all the digits – if I did, we'd still be here at nine o'clock reading them out. Suffice it to say it's the biggest prime number ever discovered and as a result the computer scientists at Cray Research at Chippewa Falls, Wisconsin, are feeling rather pleased with themselves. David Slowinsky in Wisconsin explained the significance of the find by first reminding our long-suffering reporter Tom Feilden what a prime number was:

BOFFIN: Just exactly as you learned in school – a number, an integer, that has no factors. So for example six is not prime. It's two times three. Seven is a prime.

REPORTER: Because it's only divisible by seven and one?

BOFFIN: Exactly.

REPORTER: So what's the number you've come up with, then?

BOFFIN: It's really big. It's the biggest ever found. Two to the power of 1257787 minus one.

REPORTER: So the minus one is important then, is it?

BOFFIN: Oh yes, yes.

REPORTER: What happens if you forget about the minus one?

BOFFIN: Then it's not prime. It would have more than one million factors of two.

REPORTER: Uh huh. So what's the significance of finding this number? What do we have now that we didn't have yesterday?

BOFFIN: Well, before yesterday we had billions and billions of prime numbers and it's interesting that we have the biggest one, but even more interesting is that this is related to the thirty-fourth known perfect number.

REPORTER: What's a perfect number?

BOFFIN: A perfect number is equal to the sum of its factors. Six is a perfect number because it's equal to one plus two plus three, which are its factors. Twenty-eight is the next one, equal to one plus two plus four plus seven plus fourteen. These are, I don't know, sort of mystical. There are only thirty-four known perfect numbers in the world.

REPORTER: Mathematicians have been fascinated by prime numbers [he means perfect numbers] really for centuries, haven't they? Even the Greeks were very intrigued by prime numbers. What's so special about them?

BOFFIN: Well, even the ancient Egyptians, I understand, knew about perfect numbers, so it's been a fascination, as you say, for thousands of years.

REPORTER: Is that it then? Have we found all the prime numbers now or are there more discoveries you'll be unearthing with your Cray computer?

BOFFIN: I'm sure there are more prime numbers, but we don't know for sure that there's another perfect number.

REPORTER: Are you going to be looking for that now?

BOFFIN: We'll look. We hope to be the record holder for a while but many, many people are looking, even as we speak.

REPORTER: What's the point of it? What benefit is mankind going to accrue from knowing this number?

BOFFIN: I don't know. Right now it's a curiosity. But numbers in the past that were large and a curiosity at the time have proven to be useful for fields like cryptography.

REPORTER: That's, er, encoding information?

BOFFIN: Sure, to make secret codes and crack secret codes.

REPORTER: But for now, your number is just a number?

BOFFIN: For now our number is just a curiosity, just the record holder.

MACGREGOR (co-presenter): That was David Slowinsky. Don't tell the people who govern our telephone numbers, for goodness sake – they'll put it on top of all the new numbers we're getting next year, or whenever it is. The time now, very simple, it's twenty to eight . . .

David Gibson, a senior producer who was night editing that night, explains how they tracked David Slowinsky down:

The story came through on AP [Associated Press] in the middle of the night – a big computer company had revealed that they had found this number. All we had was this little piece of copy and it seemed ideal. We're always on the lookout for a good light story. We went through Directory Inquiries but couldn't get the number for the actual individual, so to help Tom [night reporter that night] I started to search various Web sites. It was a computer story, so it was more than likely to be in there somewhere. They would have made sure it went on to a Web site.

I suppose there must be three or four of us on the programme now who can surf the Net, of whom I am one. Eventually we found the company's press release on the Internet, and later the full name and address of the actual mathematician, and his phone number. That was how we were able to ring him up and do that interview. We've used the Internet on some other occasions as well, for example getting background information on gun groups.[71]

Mosey was widely held to be a brilliant editor, acute in his political and journalistic judgement, outstanding at handling the press and massaging presenters' egos. He also polished up the reporting, making use of fine reporters such as Mark Coles and Winifred Robinson. He developed the internal structure to put more emphasis on forward planning – an integral part of any news programme and any newspaper, which keeps a detailed diary of future events, plans their coverage and liaises with spokespeople. In 1994 he appointed as assistant editor for forward planning a senior producer called Richard Clark. He became the key figure on 'Today', after the editor. Most of the programme's twelve reporters, wherever they happen to be in the world, work to him. He also runs a small team of two researchers and two producers who organise long-term 'bids' (interview requests), liaise with spin-doctors, corporate affairs people and correspondents throughout the world, and plan stories up to several weeks in advance.

While keeping the macho politics at the key times Mosey also maintained the first half-hour (6.30–7 am) as a useful, non-confrontational period in which presenters talk over big issues and stories with the BBC's correspondents in a sort of extended briefing. He and

Richard Clark choreographed some impressive pieces of reporting and inquiry, including three stories about alleged Nazi war criminals in Britain for which the reporter, Jon Silverman, won the Radio Journalist of the Year prize in the 1996 Sony Awards. He also got the presenters out and about more: MacGregor went to South Africa, Naughtie to Dunblane, the United States and France, and John Humphrys to the United States and to South Africa, for the first free elections in 1994.

'One of the most moving bits of reporting on the "Today" programme in the last five years has been Humphrys in the queue in Soweto,' says Tony Hall. 'I was [driving] in the car and it brought tears to my eyes. It was the elderly and infirm who could vote forty-eight hours before everyone else could and they went down there and just talked to people about what it was like to vote and it was really uplifting and very, very moving and brilliantly done by John.'[72]

At the end of November 1996 Roger Mosey was promoted to Controller of Radio 5 Live. It was the third occasion he had, seemingly, stepped into the shoes of Jenny Abramsky. She was editor of 'The World at One' from 1981 to 1986 and he was from 1989 to 1993. She edited 'Today' from 1986 to 1987, as he did from 1993 to 1996. Now he followed her immediately as head of the news-and-sport network, following her elevation to the BBC's new post of Head of Continuous News.

Internal candidates to succeed Mosey included Anne Koch, editor of 'The World Tonight', Jonathan Baker, executive editor of Radio 5 Live, and Rod Liddle, deputy editor on 'Today'. Hall chaired the appointment board (as he had when Mosey was appointed) and another member was James Boyle, the new Controller of Radio 4. Things happened behind the scenes. Jon Barton, editor of BBC 1's 'One O'Clock News' (since 1994) and also of its 'Six O'Clock News' (since the summer of 1996), and formerly a journalist on 'The Money Programme', 'Breakfast Time' and 'Newsnight', was told to apply because he had an excellent chance of getting the job. He had not intended to apply, having only just taken over the 'Six O'Clock News' and being immersed in the intricate process of combining its resources with those of the lunchtime programme. But the hint was so broad he could not ignore it. He had three days in which to write his 1,000-word paper for the appointments panel, did so, and was duly appointed.

Like his predecessor, Barton is a Yorkshireman (born in Huddersfield) but, by contrast, started life as a teacher. He taught English at a

British comprehensive school and in Tanzania before switching careers and joining BBC Radio Derby in 1980 at the age of thirty.

Barton is less marinated in politics (both of Westminster and the BBC) than Mosey and is a family man with children, not a bachelor. He has a noticeably idealistic streak (two of his greatest heroes are Tom Paine and Uganda's Yoweri Museveni), slightly wider interests and as editor of the 1 pm News on BBC 1 made it his practice never to start a political story with a picture of the Houses of Parliament. Given that he was approached for the job, it seems likely that the BBC wants this slightly less political approach, plus his detailed knowledge of television, for 'Today' in the future. The 'Today' programme is moving in late 1998 to a bi-media environment in the BBC's Television Centre in Wood Lane.

Hall told me that after the May 1997 General Election he and colleagues would see if 'Today' could provide a slightly wider range of items, including more on education and science, both of which he regarded as having been 'undercooked'. It seems as if the programme will shift, slightly, and become less obsessed with Westminster argy-bargy, and try to appeal more to listeners under forty. But John Birt warned against the likelihood of major change:

> It doesn't do any programme, including 'Today', any harm to say that, however successful we are, we take a look at ourselves and work out how we can do better, [but] I would be very surprised if we're not talking about incremental developments rather than major change when we're dealing with programmes as manifestly successful as this. I would regard 'Today' as one of the most successful programmes on the BBC in recent years. This is a programme with style, character and personality that is beloved of its audience.[73]

7

The Breakfast Pulpit

Like the programme which enfolds it, and like anything to do with religion, 'Thought for the Day' arouses strong passions. It is hard to think of any three minutes in the whole of British broadcasting which is more sensitive. Humanists, who have been waging a forty-year campaign on the subject, object to the fact that it is reserved for believers in a deity; religious absolutists object to what they see as its imposition of soggy liberal propaganda peddling a line that all religions are ultimately the same; and political activists, both socialist and Tory, have been protesting vociferously about bias and censorship ever since it began in 1970. 'Thought for the Day' was controversial years before anyone had ever heard of Anne Atkins, though the way in which it transformed her overnight from unknown vicar's wife in Fulham to a front-page celebrity is the clearest possible evidence of the phenomenal impact which Radio 4 exerts on the nation at breakfast time.

The Home Service has had a religious slot at this time for nearly sixty years, beginning with 'Lift Up Your Hearts' in 1939. It originated in Scotland and was intended by the BBC's Scottish Director, Melville Dinwiddie, to be a comforting and uplifting Christian homily in the early morning.[1] The title 'Lift Up Your Hearts' – as perfect a title as has ever been, perhaps – was itself lifted from the Holy Communion service of 1662. Like so much of the Book of Common Prayer, the words hold a transcendent beauty, but, being specifically Anglican, were hardly appropriate for introducing speakers of other faiths. Which is why, in the mid-1960s, when religious policy began to open up, the glorious language of Cranmer was discarded in favour of the grimly prosaic, but neutral, 'Ten to

Eight'. This in turn changed in 1970 to the much better 'Thought for the Day'.

BBC religious policy at the time, as summarised in its evidence to the Annan Committee in 1977 (originally set up in 1970, but not reporting until 1977) was 'to reflect the worship, thought and action of the principal religious traditions represented in Britain'. Speakers continued, however, to be mainly Christian: the first Muslim, for example, did not appear on 'Thought for the Day' until 1992, when a 51-year-old South African called Umar Hegedus made his debut in the middle of Ramadan.

When the 'Today' programme began in 1957, it went out in two halves because in the middle lay 'Lift Up Your Hearts' and the 8 am news. Today, renamed and multi-faith in character, that same religious enclave is still there, its speakers uninterrupted and unchallenged. It is a protected, and protective, oasis of spirituality, a reminder of a day beyond today, of the next world in the middle of this; a moment for looking into the soul rather than out to the world.

That very sacrosanctity, allied to what some saw as an endless procession of waffling clerics, has however always tended to divide the audience. 'Rather a large proportion didn't like "Thought", considering it unnecessary or limited ("Don't non-Christians think?"),' wrote Julian Holland, the then editor, in an internal fact sheet about the audience in June 1982. Later that year, it had become even more unpopular. '"Thought" was liked by just under half – others found it dull, irritating, sanctimonious, an irrelevant waste of time, and many of the speakers were labelled dull and didactic,' reported Jolyon Monson in a staff memo dated 16 November 1982. Four years later, when Jenny Abramsky took over and cut the slot from four-and-a-half minutes to three, she did her own research, finding that 'Thought' was more popular than sport or business. Another four years on and it still was, as the BBC's Head of Religious Broadcasting, the Reverend Ernest Rea, recorded at the time:

> Earlier this year some research was commissioned by the BBC which was expected to prove that there was growing resistance to a religious 'Thought' in the middle of a secular programme of news and current affairs. The results showed that, quite the contrary, 'Thought for the Day' exceeded in the popularity stakes such tried and tested favourites as sport, the business news and 'Yesterday in Parliament'. What is presumably a largely secular

audience seems to enjoy the different perspective which 'Thought for the Day' brings to current events. That is why, if I was asked to name the most important contribution that religious broadcasting makes to the BBC schedules, TFTD would come high up the list.[2]

Further audience research in April 1994, into the 7.30–8 am segment of the programme, showed that, though still popular, it was also something which nearly 20 per cent of the audience did *not* want to hear. Today, it still divides the audience and Lord Archer, for example, says he reaches for the off switch: 'I find it often supercilious and condescending and not a lot to do with what's happening in the real world. I find very good human beings on it trying not to prove they're very good. It doesn't catch the level I want it to catch in this modern world. I turn it off.'[3]

Almost as disparaging, rather surprisingly, was the Chairman of the BBC himself, Sir Christopher Bland, 'I think it has been let down by the tendency of some speakers to enter the political area. It's as if they want to be presenters of "Today", not "Thought for the Day". I think it should stay philosophical and religious, not be political.'[4]

Labour's Robin Cook had the sharpest barb: 'My problem with "Thought for the Day" is that it very rarely makes me think.'[5] William Waldegrave was also dismissive: 'I'm not a great listener to "Thought for the Day", I'm afraid, partly because the speakers from my Church [the Church of England] always irritate so much.'[6] Virginia Bottomley, by contrast, is definitely a fan: 'It's a good moment. To me it's a kind of reminder that in a busy world there is still space for a spiritual life.'[7]

Some others are ambivalent, as displayed in this rather odd exchange I had with the then Chancellor of the Exchequer, Kenneth Clarke:

AUTHOR: And what about 'Thought for the Day', which seems to divide the audience, including your colleagues and people in general. Do you listen to 'Thought for the Day'?
CLARKE: Well, it tends to be there, yes.
AUTHOR: Yes, I know it's there, but do you listen –?
CLARKE: I regard it as one of those bizarre BBC traditions, like 'Down Your Way', if that's still on, or something of that kind. I was actually a fan of Rabbi Lionel Blue. He, I suppose, summed up 'Thought for the Day'. People seem to either hate Lionel Blue and throw things at the radio when he's on, or be rather amused

by him. And I'm of the second category. I used to listen to Rabbi Lionel Blue. I'm not sure he's still on.

AUTHOR: He was on this morning.

CLARKE: Was he? My radio has packed up, because the battery went flat and it now wants to know its code before it'll work again.[8]

The brief to today's 'Thought for the Day' contributors is that they should 'reflect on the events of the day from the perspective of religious faith'.[9] This means that the contributors have to be both journalists and broadcasters, as well as theologians, able to cope with last-minute rewrites and to articulate instinctive national reactions at times of shock and sorrow. Speakers also need 'the sensitivity to know the fine line that separates genuine theological reflection from party political comment'.[10] The Bishop of Oxford, Dr Richard Harries, who, before he was dropped (he has since been reinstated), did several hundred over the course of thirteen years and ten years of 'Prayer for the Day' before that, describes some of the rigours:

It is a very, very difficult slot to do. It's a real challenge. You may not spend a lot of time actually writing it but you can burn up a lot of nervous energy trying to work out what on earth can I say that is going to engage this audience at that time of morning. For the Friday talk which I often did, as soon as I woke up on a Thursday I would begin to listen to the news and try to get ideas. I would always try to write it as late as possible on Thursday and read it through to the producer on the Thursday night. But as I say, it's not the time, it's getting an idea which is interesting to *you* first of all, and then making it accessible to a very wide audience at that time in the morning, and relating it to the news without being political, without being too overt or oppressive, but seeing that it does have a spiritual dimension. It's a very difficult assignment.[11]

The Archdeacon of York, George Austin, who delivered ninety-six 'Thoughts' before he (like the Bishop) was 'rested' in 1996, agrees:

You need to be a broadcaster of some experience to be able to cope with 'Thought' and the 'Today' programme, which is, after all, the flagship news programme of the BBC. I always appreciated the help which the many 'Thought' producers gave me over the years, and I learned more about communicating a message from them than I ever learned from the Church.[12]

For most of the 1980s the pattern was that Rabbi Lionel Blue (someone, like Harries, whose experience of broadcasting dates back a quarter of a century) appeared on Mondays and Harries on Fridays, with a third speaker – whoever it might be – doing Tuesday, Wednesday and Thursday. 'Mondays was a time you had to help people get up and out, you had to give them some help to face the week, and that I liked very much,' says the Rabbi.[13] 'People always used to associate me with Fridays and with good news because a weekend was coming up, and that was a great privilege,' says the Bishop.[14] Both men became nationally famous for their appearances and both released anthologies of their most memorable scripts. Their approaches, however, were quite different. Rabbi Blue ('Well, good morning Sue, good morning John, and good morning all of you') seemed to use his broadcasts as thinly disguised psychotherapy, while Bishop Harries chose gems of Western poetry and prose to illustrate his theology. In Lionel Blue's broadcasts, there was – and still is – a sense of a vulnerable, rather damaged soul trying to reach out to others:

> I want to give people a thought, one thought for the day, you can't give them more. You want to leave one thought in them which can help them feel better and happier and to be constructive or creative about what life slings at them. How you can keep your morale up in a dole queue, how to give up things gracefully. Failure's not the end of the world, and it's the way you learn pity and compassion.[15]

Blue also never shrunk from sharing with listeners his own inner turmoil: his mental breakdown, his homosexuality, his years in therapy, the deep arguments with his mother, their reconciliation late in life and the way, as a Jew, that he had actively considered Christianity while an undergraduate at Balliol. Almost uniquely among presenters, he stressed his isolation:

> Being gay and having depression and also nearly becoming a Christian made me an outsider. The outsider part of my life, which I had been trying to cover up a bit, took on a new importance when I started to talk about it on 'Thought for the Day', because it

was that part which was the most convincing and important, so therefore it was important to admit being an epileptic and being gay. Most of the letters [I received] and people [I met] gave me a sense of being given a great deal of affection, and that affection made me blossom. It gave me a feeling that there was a lot of love around and it did something spiritually for me, too. It made me realise that revelation doesn't come down from above, it seeps out of people's lives.[16]

The Bishop of Oxford, by contrast, was and is an insider, an archetypal Establishment figure. Son of a brigadier, he was educated at Wellington and Cambridge, and is a former Dean of King's College, London. Not being gay, epileptic, or depressive, he had no need to fill his slots with self-exploring melancholia. Instead, his approach was to borrow the insights of great poets to illustrate meticulously crafted little essays. His broadcasts were just as distinctive as Blue's, though in a totally different way. Where the occasion warranted it, however, he too could be personal:

When I talked about the death of my father, that brought in a huge response. My father had died the week before and I talked about that and how he had been very much at peace at the end. Very often people remember that and say, 'Oh yes, I remember that script you did about your father.' If you talk about human suffering you always get a response, because there are always people whose husband or wife died that week or who have gone through some tragedy and that is when people are receptive.

In terms of people responding to me, it's not necessarily any one script, but they have liked my particular approach, which has been to try to use some poetry or literature and to give people a theological dimension. Frankly the main constraint of 'Thought for the Day' as opposed to 'Prayer for the Day' is this tremendous pressure to relate it to the news in a very direct kind of way. Lionel Blue was never under any kind of pressure – he used to talk about his mother or transvestites in Amsterdam or whatever, he could get away with anything – but the rest of us were expected to conform to the news of the day. My general approach was trying to give people a bit of poetry and some hidden theology as well. Not moral exhortation. I really don't think 'Thought for the Day' is a place for moral exhortation.[17]

Rabbi Blue was keen to stress what he personally had gained, and learned, from his 'Thought for the Day' broadcasts:

It's made me much more conscious of being a human being and much less of being a Reform Jew. It forces you to make your religion relevant to daily life and not stick out like a sore thumb but fit into the rest of the programme . . . What I learned is that radio is a very intimate medium and it works providing you say what's really in your mind and not what other people think ought to be in your mind or what you think other people think ought to be in your mind.[18]

That had always been his approach, he said, but it had got stronger over the years:

As long as you were yourself it worked. People are listening to you in the bathroom, in the loo, in bed, in a traffic jam, so it's a very intimate situation. It's not like a sermon. You're quite fragile, it's early in the morning, you've got the problem of getting out of bed, you've heard some horrors on the news and you need a little bit of affection. The ones who can do it with affection are the ones who grasp me.[19]

Rabbi Blue was also clear what he did not like, as a listener:

[I don't like] the ones who think they've got to be minor prophets and unload a lot of anger on to me, even if I quite sympathise with the cause. Sometimes I feel attacked, as if I'm made to feel guilty about things I can't deal with. If there's a famine, or a war, or dreadful things are happening far away and someone says, 'Isn't this dreadful of human beings?' But I'm a human being too, so what the hell do I do about it? I'd like to know how I can start dealing with this mass of guilt I feel afterwards.[20]

The other part of Rabbi Blue's approach is his jokes – leading *Private Eye* to call him Rabbi Bluejoke, a nickname which Blue said rather amused him:

Jokes contain the distilled essence of whatever wisdom Judaism has, although I don't regard my talks as PR work for Judaism, and they're also the way people cope with problems they can't solve.

And since most problems in life can't be solved, they have a very important function. Since starting 'Thought for the Day' I've had to acquire an awful lot of jokes.[21]

The most terrifying aspect of 'Thought for the Day' is the ever-present possibility of having to do something else at the last minute, and hence the need for experience. Dr Kenneth Slack, former Free Church Moderator, was due to give 'Thought' on the morning after the Brighton bombing in 1984 and did so, but rewrote his talk in the taxi on the way to Broadcasting House, adjusting it to incorporate the horrors of violence and murder.

The Bishop of Bath and Wells, Jim Thompson (who has been doing 'Thought for the Day' since 1978) was another speaker forced to re-write his talk in a moving vehicle. It was in 1994 and he was trying to collect his thoughts in response to the sinking of the Scandinavian ferry the *Estonia*, in which 838 people drowned:

I heard about it as we were driving to Bristol [the nearest BBC studio to his home in the Bishop's Palace in Wells] and I wrote it in half an hour in the car [he was being chauffeur-driven, one of the privileges of diocesan bishops]. I did the last full stop just as John Humphrys said, 'And in our Bristol studio is the Bishop of Bath and Wells.'

I had been listening to all the eye-witness reports and it raises the thought, always does raise it, what is God doing in all this? It's almost like having to justify God in the face of what a lot of people will be feeling. So I concentrated on human life and its risks, the ambiguity of creation. The water, the wind and the storm are the dangerous side of something that makes human life possible. Without water, without wind, without the energies in the universe, we wouldn't exist, and we certainly wouldn't exist as the creatures that we are. So human experience is, from the moment of birth to the moment of death, a long series of terrible risks. And because we are so keen on controlling our lives, it comes as something of a shock to us that the forces of creation are so enormous that sometimes we are just flotsam.[22]

This summary of the talk he had given two years previously was given to me completely extempore and seemed to capture the right sort of tone for national disasters: sympathetic, reflective, adequate to the sense of numb hopelessness many listeners would be feeling, consolation without sentimentality. The question of tone was also stressed by another Anglican bishop, Richard Harries, who also had to rise to the occasion after a ferry disaster – in his case, the loss of the *Herald of Free Enterprise* at Zeebrugge in 1987:

> When there's a national tragedy, it's crucial that you get the tone absolutely right. That's almost what you're paid to do. You don't have to say anything very startling. What you have to do is try and capture in a sensitive way the mood of the audience and express that. One person who has done that very well is Charles Handy, a superb broadcaster. I remember hearing him once after a major disaster. He didn't really say anything, but he just caught the feeling of sorrow and sympathy.
>
> In the case of Zeebrugge, I got rung up in the middle of the night and of course I had to do a totally new script. Luckily some literature came to mind, Gerard Manley Hopkins's *The Wreck of the Deutschland*, which I was able to use the next morning. You're trying to draw in people's feelings of shock and sorrow and sadness and highlight the tragic dimensions. The last thing you want to do is try and give a simplistic answer as to why this has happened. That is what you don't want to do. The point of bringing in something like *The Wreck of the Deutschland* is that there are some very powerful verses there when the nuns are drowning and how they call on God. 'Thou mastering me, God.' You can bring in a powerful religious message in an oblique way. Those nuns felt that even as they were drowning somehow God was there in that darkness with them. People can take it or leave it, because it's a quotation from poetry.[23]

Charles Handy, the broadcaster mentioned by Harries and much admired by him and others, is an Irish national (his father was an Archdeacon in the Church of Ireland) who made his name as a professor at the London Business School from 1978 onwards, after a successful career as an economist and marketing and management executive, mainly with Shell. He has been doing TFTD since 1982, having been approached when he was running the St George's House study centre at Windsor Castle.

> It had long been one of my ambitions to pontificate to the nation at breakfast time, but the producer who gave me most help was Robert Foxcroft, who was very tough and on occasion tore up my

scripts in front of me. His advice was to let my thoughts come to the surface as near to the deadline as possible. He used to say that you're dropping in on people at breakfast time, and they don't want to be preached at. You're just trying to leave them with a thought that will go rumbling round in them for the rest of the day. It's not the wisdom of a lifetime. And you've got to remember that people are listening to you half-naked, in the bath, in the loo, having breakfast. You can't kid yourself that they're all going to be very attentive. So your first two sentences are very important, because they can make people stop and listen.[24]

His most famous broadcast – the one Richard Harries referred to – was made a few hours after the San Francisco earthquake of 1989, which claimed the lives of 273 people. Handy, having cleared with his producer a 'fairly anodyne' script about unemployment, then went to a silver wedding party.

I came back at two o'clock in the morning, rather the worse for wear. The BBC woke me up at half-past five to tell me about the earthquake. They said the lines were down, so they couldn't get through, but they knew it was pretty bad. I had no idea what God thinks about earthquakes. I try not to mention God and I'm not even sure that I'm a Christian, though I do believe there are forces greater than us. So I just reflected on the fact that I was in fact due to go to San Francisco in two months' time. I sort of talked to the friends I had there. I said I hoped they were still alive. It was all I could do. It was quite personal. A lot of people did ring in and at that year's Religious Broadcasting Christmas party Colin Morris came up and said congratulations. I told him that for the first time in my life I understood what the Holy Spirit meant. He said, 'We call it blind panic.'[25]

Lionel Blue recalled that he too had had to change his script, in his case after a terrorist bomb in Northern Ireland. Unlike the bishops, who as national leaders always wanted to encapsulate national emotions, the only important thing for him was to try to be true to his *own* emotions: 'You've got to let the listeners into your own problem. What I've done is say, look, I had a nice sort of thought for the day all ready for you and then this happens, and one's got to start thinking about what happens when a lump of tragedy comes into your life. The more open you are about your situation, the easier it is for everybody.'[26]

The Bishop of Leicester, Tom Butler, found himself doing TFTD the day after Robert Maxwell disappeared off his yacht:

The news had come through in the daytime that Maxwell had disappeared, so it was obvious that would be the topic and I had written it at about ten o'clock in the evening and cleared it with the producer. It didn't leap to any conclusions. Round about midnight they rang up to tell me a body had been found in the water, so I did another script. Then at about six the next morning the news came through that the body had been identified as Robert Maxwell's. So once again I amended my script and I just tried to make the point that he had died in the manner in which he had lived – larger than life.[27]

Butler also did TFTD the day after Laurence Olivier died, in July 1989, when he was Bishop of Willesden:

I remember sitting outside Broadcasting House and writing another script. I couldn't check it with the producer in time so I broke all the rules and delivered a script which the producer had not seen or vetted. The producer [John Newbury] was absolutely furious. 'I couldn't believe you'd do such a thing!' he said. There were some very positive responses to my talk but he told me I was never to do it again. As you know, what the speaker says is completely unchallenged and they are very aware of the dangers of misusing the slot.[28]

There have been other crises, too. Blue recalls the day when he found that page two of his two-page script simply wasn't there:

I read the first page then turned over and found that what I was looking at was a carbon copy of the first page. I had two copies of page one instead of a page one and a page two. I had just forgotten to bring page two. It was like diving into a swimming pool where they've forgotten to put in the water. I remember feeling, 'Thank God I'm leaving for Canada today.' So I gave what I thought was a précis of what I had written and I went off to Canada. When I came back a few weeks later there were a lot of interesting letters. Somebody said he had always been convinced these programmes were pre-recorded and he was pleased to discover they weren't. Somebody pussyfooted about what he was trying to say which is that Jews were too clever by half, so he was pleased that I muffed it, which was fine. One woman wrote, 'Because you make mistakes it's easier for me to admit to mine,' which was a very good point.

From then on I did quite a lot of thoughts which stemmed from that, mainly about coping with failures in one's life. I found from the correspondence that lots of people were weighed down with the idea of being successful. It was a burden on them. So this was a way I could help them, helping them be free of the feeling that you've got to be a success.[29]

The Archdeacon of York also had moments of panic: 'I preferred to go to the studio when I could, rather than do it down the line from York, where crises abounded. Once I could not raise them to let me in and had to call the "Today" office for them to call York – and a very crestfallen youth eventually came down to open the door.'[30]

Barely a year after the slot changed to what it is now came the furore of Colin Morris's 'Thought', broadcast on 1 March 1971. It was a Monday morning and it was also, of course, St David's Day. Morris remembers:

The government [Edward Heath's] had just published a draft Immigration Bill which proposed to classify British residents as either 'patrials' or 'non-patrials' – the latter being without a father or grandfather born in Britain and therefore without any absolute right to stay here. In somewhat skittish mood I pointed out that St David, having been born in France, would have been denied entry to Britain had the proposed Immigration Act been in force; that St George, if a historical character at all, was a Libyan and hence a non-patrial; St Andrew had been born in Palestine, etc. etc. I then named a number of prominent people of mixed parentage who would have to be listed in a new reference book Who's Half-Who. After a parody on 'Ten Little Nigger Boys', I ended with an appeal in the name of the greatest non-patrial, Jesus of Nazareth, for the government to think again. I suspect I compounded my offence by not simply opposing the measure but ridiculing it as well.[31]

A huge row ensued. The government protested to the BBC, Colin Morris was dropped for a while, and more than seventy Labour and

Liberal MPs signed an early-day motion deploring this BBC 'surrender' to government pressure:

The BBC didn't formally ban me; nothing so crude as that – these were the laid-back old days when top management could cut out your heart without spilling a drop of your blood. After having done 'Thought' live on Mondays for a long time, I was simply not asked to do it again for years. I finally assumed I'd been forgiven when I was invited to become Head of Religious Broadcasting in 1978.

The 'Thought for the Day' producer, Roy Trevivian, a wayward genius if ever there was one, was lumbered with the responsibility for having allowed me to do the broadcast and got the full blame. He left the BBC shortly after ... the broadcast sparked the inevitable debate about the permissible limits of 'Thought for the Day' which has broken out periodically ever since. It also taught me the power of self-censorship – in the end it is the recognition that the producer will pay the price for foolish speech that keeps the speaker on the rails when broadcasting live, though Roy Trevivian stood by his judgement through thick and thin that the script was within the permissible limits by a whisker.[32]

Apart from that, the 1970s appears to have been a quiet decade, and the Corporation could note in an official booklet: 'Religious broadcasting for millions of Britons is "Thought for the Day" on Radio 4 every morning at a quarter to eight. This five-minute treatment of an inspirational theme, often related to the current scene, attracts an audience of up to three million listeners every week-day. It has made such broadcasters as Dr Colin Morris, C.A. Joyce and Claude Muncaster household names.'[33]

By the time Abramsky took over eleven years later, however, it had become four-and-a-half minutes and she cut it down further to three:

I had a long discussion with David Winter [then the BBC's Head of Religious Programmes, Radio] and said that much of the research I'd done showed it was too rambling and people were switching off or switching over. It was a lump that didn't fit into the programme. I said in my view it shouldn't be longer than three minutes, which meant that if you took away the cue it came down to two minutes fifty seconds. And I think if someone can't say something in two minutes fifty seconds they've got nothing to say.

It would have been a great mistake to have lost it. Sport and business were both less popular in the research I did, they came bottom, and I wouldn't have done a 'Today' programme without them. So there was no question of 'Thought' going, it just had to fight its way in terms of the quality of what it did. David was very sympathetic, and agreed. I believe the new shorter length made it a lot sharper.[34]

The contributors appeared not to mind. 'You can say as much in a three-minute 'Thought for the Day' as you can in a twelve-minute sermon,' says the Bishop of Oxford. 'I frankly enjoy the discipline of having a short period of time and I think four minutes now would seem too long.'[35]

The slot sometimes came under attack during the Thatcher years, just as the whole of the 'Today' programme did. Margaret Thatcher evidently listened and had her views. The Bishop of Oxford – a defender of government policy on nuclear deterrence, 'moderately supportive'[36] of the Falklands War, but often a fierce critic of Tory social policies – remembers being introduced to the Prime Minister with other bishops at a rather tense and uneasy meeting at Chequers: 'Ah yes, the Bishop of Oxford,' she said. 'I hear you on the radio. Sometimes I agree with you and sometimes you make me mad!'[37] Harries says he was pleased about this equivocation: 'It's important not to use "Thought for the Day" to be too political. Anyway, I would never put an unequivocal point of view. One would always do a bit of wrestling with people.'[38]

Bishop Thompson felt her antipathy to the views he often expressed on 'Thought for the Day' cost him, or rather delayed him, a job:

> She never expressed a comment to me [on his broadcasts] but she must have developed a view about me because of what happened in relation to the Birmingham appointment. I was chosen to be Bishop of Birmingham by the Church's part of the system and she overruled it. So she obviously thought, whatever she'd heard me say or whatever she'd been told about me, that I wasn't 'one of us'.[39]

Eventually he was given Bath and Wells – but, as he quickly pointed out, only after Mrs Thatcher had left Downing Street: 'I was one of Mr Major's first appointments.'[40]

One of his closest colleagues, Bishop Butler of Leicester, said: 'I think it's true to say that neither Jim Thompson nor myself were her favourite presenters, but we were London bishops and had first-hand experience of schools and hospitals in some of the most difficult areas of the country, so we felt we had a duty to describe what we saw.'[41]

Another contributor who expresses similar urban angst, and incurs the same sort of Tory wrath, has been Gabrielle Cox of the United People's Church in Manchester. Dr Brian Mawhinney complained that her talk of 6 August 1996 about the International Monetary Fund was 'not so much spiritual guidance as anti-government propaganda'. The BBC upheld this as follows:

The brief of the series is not to offer spiritual guidance but to reflect, from a religious and ethical viewpoint, on a topic arising from the affairs of the day, and it had been quite in order for the speaker to touch on politically contentious matters. However, she did so in terms which could be interpreted as having a party political application, and this was not consistent with the BBC's duty of impartiality as it applies in such contexts.[42]

Complaints have not only come from the right, however. Several socialist contributors have also attacked the BBC over the years. Canon Eric James, director of Christian Action and a chaplain to the Queen, angrily resigned from the breakfast pulpit in September 1990 after refusing to accept the BBC's changes – censorship, he called it – to his outspoken scripts, which had included a spirited defence of that year's rioting poll tax protesters. He had had several acrimonious telephone 'battles'[43] with Beverley McAinsh, the then editor of 'Thought'. The final straw came when he had submitted a script about a radical Wapping priest, Father John Groser (1890–1962). He was ordered to cut approving references to 'the spiritual value of revolt' and Groser's opposition to fascist marching through the East End. He refused, and was replaced by the Methodist minister Dr Leslie Griffiths (who himself left rather suddenly six years later).

The BBC's Head of Religious Broadcasting pointed out that the talk would have gone out on the opening day of the Labour Party Conference, and 'to allow Canon James to deliver a panegyric on a parish priest who "was a socialist because he was a Christian" would have left the religious broadcasting department open to the charge of political partiality. We would have had little defence.'[44] After three years in the wilderness, however, Eric James rejoined the rota of speakers.

The year in which the slot came in for the closest scrutiny was 1996, following the BBC's decision to purge – or 'rest', as it always says on these occasions – a number of long-standing contributors. This was a messy and undignified business, clumsily handled by the producer and editor of 'Thought', David Coomes, who sent out a number of near-identical letters and was then surprised when these bolts from the blue started leaking. *The Times* broke the story (on 24 April), identifying the Venerable George Austin, Archdeacon of York, Canon Philip Crowe, former Principal of Salisbury and Wells Theological College, and the Methodist minister Dr Leslie Griffiths, former president of the Methodist Conference, as three who had been dropped. I revealed in the *Sunday Times* that the Bishop of Oxford was the fourth victim (5 May). Then John Humphrys announced on the 'Today' programme itself (8 May) that a Roman Catholic parish priest from Notting Hill, Father Oliver McTernan, was the fifth. Finally, I supplied the last two names as Dr Donald English, former chairman of the World Methodist Council, and John Newbury, the former producer of 'Thought' and now at the World Council of Churches (14 July). The severed seven were all male, white, ordained Christian ministers.

The way in which these people were cast into what John Humphrys called 'spiritual limbo' prompted this savage denunciation from the Reverend Richard Thomas, Diocesan Communications Officer for Oxford:

> One of the most obvious rules of personal relationships, let alone public relations, is that if you have something difficult to say to someone, it has to be said confidentially and in person. Letters are the worst possible way of communicating difficult news. To compound the insult by treating some of the nation's most senior religious leaders as if they were third-rate actors who had outlived their sell-by date has caused intense anger, not just amongst Christians but across the whole religious community . . . My own view is that the BBC, recently more and more uncomfortable with those who have a definite Christian viewpoint, has taken one more step towards a sponge-rubber view of religion that sees all faiths as essentially the same.[45]

There was a similar response from Dr Sheridan Gilley of Durham

University's theology department: 'The programme sedulously shuns the real differences which exist within and between religions by operating on the liberal dogma that all religions are the same.'[46]
The Bishop of Oxford recalled:

We all got this standard letter and it was rather irritating. You thought it was a letter just to you and then you find other people quoting from it, so it was clearly a standard letter. What they were doing was talking about bringing in new people and I totally approve of that. They need to bring in more women, more people of other faiths. My objection was that there wasn't anybody else doing what I was trying to do, using literature and a bit of theology, with one exception – Angela Tilby, and they don't seem to use her that often.[47]

Bishop Harries was talking eight months after he was dropped and it was remarkable to discover that he had still not received any explanation:

Nobody has given me any explanation. My guess is that if they wanted to broaden the constituency, and they've already got a number of Anglican bishops doing it, someone would have to be dropped. I imagine they wanted to bring Bill Westwood back because he's retired and a very good broadcaster. Jim Thompson is a very good broadcaster. Tom Butler I imagine they would want because he has a regional accent and does it from the regions. So one of this group has got to go for the time being, and Harries has done it for a long time and he's south-east and all that. That would be my guess, and I can understand that reasoning. I don't feel resentful about it, but nobody gave me any reason.[48]

The Archdeacon of York, who had been doing it for thirteen years when the axe fell, was also wry and phlegmatic:

I had already told David Coomes that I wanted to retire gracefully after I had completed a hundred scripts (I made it to ninety-six), rather than be 'rested' which is BBC-speak for 'sacked'. He told me there was to be a look at contributors but there was no intention of resting me – and promptly forgot my request.[49]

Paul Johnson thought it meant the BBC was trying to make 'more room for up-to-date secular figures including academics and journalists such as Gabrielle Cox of the Low Pay Unit and Indajit Singh of the *Sikh Messenger*.[50] Philip Crowe, at the other end of the political spectrum, thought the opposite: 'An election is near, and party chairmen and others are notoriously volatile, particularly on the "Today" programme. It would not surprise me in the least to learn that the editor of "Thought" . . . has been under pressure to clear out any provocative or controversial contributors.'[51]

The real truth was that Coomes and Rea thought all seven had become dull. They were after fresh blood. Among those who came in were the Roman Catholic commentator Cristina Odone, the Open University physics professor Russell Stannard, and the novelist Anne Atkins. Another speaker who began to appear more often was James Jones, Bishop of Hull, a friend of Ernie Rea's from the days when they both worked in Bristol during the 1980s.

John Gummer, a member of the General Synod for more than ten years but who subsequently converted to Roman Catholicism, was unhappy about the BBC's decision to drop the Bishop of Oxford:

> I found that a very, very curious decision. I think he has done some ['Thought'] which are particularly valuable, particularly when he is sharply Christian and doesn't get led on to any of his hobby horses. And George Austin does have a very remarkable way of bringing a sharply Christian focus to bear not only on controversial matters but also some of the Christian challenges. He is another person I miss. The word 'rested' is very odd because if ever there was someone who was restless and able always to make the kind of pithy, worthwhile three-minute interjection, it's him.[52]

The biggest ever furore erupted on 10 October 1996 when Anne Atkins delivered her now famous talk about the Church and homosexuality. It prompted about 1,000 letters and calls, the majority supportive of the stance she had taken. If ever there was a case of overnight fame it was this: one day Anne Atkins was unknown and the next, and the next, and the next, she was on the front pages, and on radio, and on television. Within a month she was the agony aunt of the *Daily Telegraph*. As one writer, Luke Harding, observed a few weeks later: 'Mrs Atkins now occupies a decent stalls seat in the theatre of British public life. She has risen without trace, from the obscurity of a West London parsonage to the inside pages of Britain's bestselling broadsheet.'[53]

Anne Atkins's script, reproduced here word-for-word, was as follows:

Good morning. An all-day celebration has been planned in Southwark Cathedral to mark the twentieth anniversary of the Lesbian and Gay Christian Movement. Various churches have expressed concern but the celebration will go ahead.

I want to make one thing clear. Homophobia is reprehensible. Discriminating against people on the grounds of their sexual orientation, which they may or may not have chosen, is indefensible. It is shocking that the armed forces can dismiss an employee, not just because of what he has done, but what he might do; not because of his behaviour, but his feelings. This is like court-martialling a man, not for desertion, but for being frightened before battle.

But what we do with our feelings is another matter. Nobody is condemning the Bishop of Argyll for his feelings. He didn't break his vows when he fell in love. It was what he did afterwards that caused the rumpus. One's sexual desire and one's practice have always to stay separate.

We don't have, on record, any conversation between Jesus and a sexually active homosexual. But we know what he said to the woman caught in adultery, so we can imagine a similar scene: a group of rather self-righteous, macho people bring a gay man to our Lord. He should be stoned, they say. He was caught having sex with another man. Jesus looks at the pious mob. Fair enough, he replies: anyone who's never committed a sin can throw the first stone. They shuffle their feet, look embarrassed, move off. Now, Jesus says to the accused: go and sin no more.

One of the truest clichés of all time is that God loves the sinner but hates his sin. It's the Church's duty to love and welcome everybody, because Jesus's message is for everyone. But it's also the Church's duty to condemn sin. It's this that we're failing to do. Soon, no doubt, we'll have an Adulterers' Christian Fellowship or a Sex Before Marriage Christian Fellowship. I see no reason why the list should ever end, unless and until the Church comes back to God's standards of morality. Not that we reject those who don't keep them. But that we know, and say, what they are.

Yesterday, a report was publicised called 'Numbers in Ministry', which said that candidates for ordination in the Church of England are steadily going down. Surprise surprise. In an age in which bishops are supporting a cathedral event celebrating twenty years of gay sex, we should hardly expect anything else. If the trumpet sounds an uncertain note, who will prepare for battle? Sadly, the note from the Church of England today is so uncertain, you'd think it was a cracked penny whistle.

The Reverend Eric Shegog, Director of Communications for the Church of England, fired off an angry complaint to both Ernie Rea and Roger Mosey, accusing Atkins of making a 'preposterous' claim that the decline in ordinands was attributable to the Church of England's position on homosexuality, and demanding an apology. The complaint was put out to the media and the story was all over the front pages the following morning. 'Church rages at BBC attack on gays', was the headline in the *Daily Mail*; 'Church attack on BBC's anti-gay Thought for Day', said *The Times*. The *Evening Standard* followed it up with 'Traditionalists join battle with BBC over gays', with the first report of the messages of support Atkins had received, a stream that soon became a torrent. The 'Today' programme did the obvious thing, journalistically, and invited Atkins into the studio the following morning to debate the issue with Richard Kirker, main spokesman for the Lesbian and Gay Christian Movement: they had a relatively civilised and surprisingly even-tempered discussion. But the story had now engaged the attention of the weekend newspapers and commentators, too. Photographers and reporters beat a path to Atkins's vicarage home in Parson's Green. Instinctively, everyone now knew that the debate was not just about 'Thought for the Day'. It was about saying the unsayable, about the growing but largely unspoken unease about homosexuality, about the nature of sin and the role of the Church. The avalanche of letters showed a perception that, *at last*, the liberals who ran the BBC had allowed someone to express feelings in accordance with the majority of the population. 'I was pleased to hear her piece,' said the Bishop of Roborough, Edwin Barnes. 'It seemed to me to redress the balance.'[54]

Both sides, inevitably, were misrepresented. The misrepresentation of Shegog's position was that it disregarded the extent to which his objections rested on factual inaccuracy, and the fact that speakers on 'Thought for the Day' do enjoy the privilege of going completely unchallenged. Shegog said, 'Mrs Atkins gave the impression that the whole cathedral is being given over to a gay jamboree. In fact, the cathedral will have just one service for the Lesbian and Gay Christian Movement. For the rest of the day, it will go about its normal business.'[55] In a letter to *The Times* on the same day, he wrote, 'Our major concern was the use of a platform to attack the Church of England, which did not have an immediate right of reply.'

Strong support for his stand came from the Bishop of Oxford:

> It is simply not true that the decline in ordinands in the Church of England has to do with the fact that the Church of England is too liberal on the gay issue. She suggested that in the last paragraph and it is patently absurd. But she clearly is a compelling broadcaster, she has a very good broadcasting style and as a novelist is vivid in her imagery. And she does represent a very vocal constituency in the Church.[56]

However, other clerics *did* think there was a connection: 'Mrs Atkins has correctly discerned the causal relationship between laissez-faire doctrine and the appalling numerical decline of the Church of England,' the Reverend David Dale of Ryde, Isle of Wight, said in a letter in *The Times* on 12 October 1996.

The misrepresentation of Anne Atkins's position was that it accused her of homophobia: she was described in the *Evening Standard* as the 'Daily Telegraph's new homophobic agony aunt'[57]; John Mortimer wrote that her '"thought for the day" consisted of calling down the wrath of God on homosexuals'[58] and one critic, Robert Hanks, remarked that her 'sole claim to fame is that she once spent two minutes on the "Today" programme slagging off homosexuals'.[59] In fact, the very first thing she had done in her broadcast was to condemn homophobia and attack the Ministry of Defence, which nobody seemed to take any notice of at all, and she did not even mention the traditional Christian denunciation of homosexual acts as sinful.

The affair precipitated a heartfelt debate about the Church's attitude to sin, and the *Daily Mail* hit the nail on the head in its first story on the affair: 'There was unease in the Church of England itself that leaders who stayed silent when the programme axed Christian contributors earlier this year should complain loudly only when it criticised the homosexual lobby.'[60] The point was neatly echoed by the columnist Taki, when he criticised the Church of England for 'having demonstrated ... that its tolerance extends to everyone except those who adhere to scripture'.[61] It is quite important to realise that Atkins certainly had scripture on her side, for Christ did say to the woman taken in adultery: 'Go, and sin no more' (John 8:

11), even though He refrained from condemning her. And the traditionalist point of view was also expressed by Colin Hart, director of the research group the Christian Institute:

> According to independent studies some 70 per cent of the population believe that homosexuality is morally wrong. For once, Radio 4 allowed a contributor to state the traditional Christian view. I hope Radio 4 will not cave in to the gay pressure groups, and continue to allow Mrs Atkins to broadcast. It is an outrage that the Church has demanded an apology from Radio 4 for allowing Mrs Atkins's broadcast.[62]

The BBC's view was that it had an obligation to air different points of view on contentious matters. Rea, who fully backed David Coomes's decision to broadcast the talk, pointed out: 'Mrs Atkins's absolutist view of scripture may be a minority view among British Christians, but she is by no means alone and she has just as much right to be heard as those other contributors who have expressed the contrary view on "Thought for the Day".'[63]

Opinions were expressed with vigour, but at least the debate was now out in the open. Gavin Ashenden, Chaplain at Sussex University, said that 'what was so offensive about Mrs Atkins's contribution to "Thought for the Day" was that by its tone and content it came across as more of a "Polemic for the Day"',[64] and Terry Sanderson of Ealing commented: 'People shouldn't get the idea that vast numbers of gay people are banging on church doors begging to be let in. Like most of the rest of the population, the majority of gay men and lesbians are indifferent to religion and the unpleasant people it seems to attract.'[65]

John Gummer said:

> It's not a statement I would have chosen to make, nor a statement I would have chosen to use my three minutes on, but she did. The Christian gospel challenges us all in different ways. That was the thought she wanted to communicate. She thought it was something of considerable importance which people ought to be shocked about and told about. For the Church of England, which has no views on anything very much, to tell her that was one view which she shouldn't make, or the BBC shouldn't have allowed, seemed to me to be a very peculiar position to uphold. Mr Shegog, that pretty self-opinionated spokesman on behalf of the Church of

England, said that it was outrageous and made a complaint. I found the idea that she should be gagged really very unacceptable.[66]

Rabbi Blue had a different perspective. He said, 'What I wanted to ask her [Atkins] was do you know many homosexual people and do you know their lives and how they try to make steady relationships with very little encouragement? That's what I wanted to ask her.'[67]

As is often the case, the funniest comment came from *Private Eye*, whose lampoons on the programme have included renaming the presenters as John Humbug and Sue MacGhastly. In the issue of 18 October it ran the following:

SODOM ATTACK
by our Biblical Staff, Sodom Hussein and John Selwyn-Gomorrah

Tuesday, 1000BC

Gay rights organisations throughout the ancient world have launched the strongest possible protest at an 'unprovoked homophobic assault on the popular cities of the plain known as Sodom and Gomorrah'.

The two cities were reportedly completely wiped out by a massive dawn bombardment of fire and brimstone leaving everyone dead.

Said a spokesman for the progressive Gay and Lesbian Pre-Christian Movement: 'This is typical of the reactionary Old Testament approach that we have come to expect from Jehovah.'

As long ago as 1949 Lord Astor was campaigning for 'Lift Up Your Hearts' to admit Christian Scientists. In the mid-1950s the Rationalist Press Association and Humanist Council were asking that their speakers be allowed access to it; again the BBC said no, and on the same grounds – that the slot was more of an act of worship than a talk.[68] In recent years both the British Humanist Association and the National Secular Society have waged a campaign to be allowed access to the slot. The BBC no longer deploys the same argument (that the slot is more liturgy than talk) but the ban has remained. When Rea was revealed to be deliberating on the matter the *Church Times* wrote in a leader:[69]

There is no reason to resist the change . . . It is a thought, not a prayer. The present speakers are most effective when they stick to moral and ethical points, most unconvincing when they slip into unsubstantiated piety. Believers have no monopoly of the illumination needed on dark mornings.

Mosey, then editor of 'Today', was cautiously favourable about the possibility of non-believers being heard in the slot:

I would give it a qualified welcome. The base of speakers should be as wide as possible, to reflect society. The slot should be about the human condition and the human spirit, and I don't think it should be used as a platform for militancy of any kind. To put it at its crudest, one wouldn't want someone to say, 'There's been a terrible disaster. There is no God. What a shame.'[70]

However, Rea decided early in 1995 to maintain the policy whereby the slot was reserved for believers: '"Thought for the Day" constitutes the only three minutes in the whole of the "Today" programme that is devoted to a non-secular perspective. If you dilute that, and turn it into a general ethical talk, it will lose its *raison d'être* and its distinctiveness [and] I fear that allowing atheists to present it would turn it into an exercise in God-bashing.'[71] The atheists' campaign is thus unlikely to succeed as long as Rea remains Head of Religious Broadcasting, but the campaigners press on. For example, Roy Saich, Secretary of Coventry and Warwickshire Humanists, said in 1996, 'We have been trying unsuccessfully for years to persuade the BBC to adopt a more open approach for this daily item in a current affairs and news programme.'[72]

All the evidence suggests that 'Thought for the Day' will continue to be a very important part of 'Today' into the new millennium. This is not just because it is patronised by the great and good, with the then Archbishop of Canterbury presenting it on the opening day of the Gulf War in January 1991 and the Prince of Wales (a frequent listener, according to a BBC statement) on VE Day in May 1995, when he offered royal reflections on the 'gossamer-thin line' between civilisation and barbarity. It is because there is now a consensus within the BBC as to its intrinsic value, which has not always been the case.

John Birt, who came to the BBC in 1987 as Deputy Director-General and in charge of all its journalism, admitted:

I was a bit sceptical when I first came. As somebody coming out of a journalistic tradition, I just found it too abrupt a change in the programme, suddenly to go to something completely different. I can remember querying it at the time [and asking] was it good broadcasting? I was told rather sharply that it was.

My scepticism has disappeared over the years although I know it's odd, for some, to suddenly tip out of the mêlée of the political agenda. I saw the value of it as a continuing tradition and my sense is that it has got more effective at choosing people. The people who appear on it choose subjects and speak in a tone which is more harmonious with the programme than it used to be.

I think it works extremely well. It's a sort of pause for reflection, a different quality of thought. It's harmonious with the programme in the sort of subjects that are chosen. But the perspectives are very different from those you get from most people who comment on public life. And I find it engaging and enjoyable.[73]

8

Discos and Doughnuts

Room 4058, Broadcasting House
10.15 am, Wednesday 15 January 1997

On the window ledge are the remains of breakfast – a messy sprawl
of slices of toast under silver foil, cartons of milk, packets of white
sugar, some half-full jugs of tea and coffee, catering-size sachets of
marmalade, raspberry conserve, honey, Flora margarine and Anchor
butter and one small carton, of the sort that children like so much, of
All Bran. This is where the great and the good are invited to fortify
themselves before dropping their messages into the nation's ears from
Studio 4A a few yards away.

The rest of Room 4058 (sometimes known as the programme's
Green Room), on the fourth floor of Broadcasting House and
overlooking Portland Place, is nondescript and functional. It is about
twenty feet by ten. There are two cabinets of twenty-four lockers
each, whose chipped, royal blue doors each have a different surname
on them – HUMPHRYS, MACGREGOR, COLES and so forth. A few tired-
looking pot plants. Two grey-cloth sofas, with no arms, consisting of
three seats each. Three swivel seats. A coatstand with some coats on
it. A coffee table about thirty inches square with the day's morning
papers dumped on it. The only interest is to be found on the cream
walls: framed certificates of Sony Radio Award prizes, an original
Barry Fantoni cartoon from 1986, photographs of Brian Redhead
and some of the other presenters.

In this dull room are sown the seeds for Britain's most influential
programme. This is where 'Today' holds its editorial meetings. The
first of them, the morning planning meeting, is held among the debris
of breakfast just after ten each morning. Usually there are about

seven people present but the 'flu has taken its toll and today there are only four: the editor, Jon Barton; his deputy, Rod Liddle; a senior producer, Cathy Packe; and a man from forward planning, John Rigby. They are more casually dressed than their equivalents at an editorial conference in a national newspaper would be – none of the men is wearing a tie, for example – and the atmosphere seems a good deal less hierarchical and more relaxed. They do not seem to sit in any particular place. Each is clutching a scarlet, A4-size hardbound exercise book, a bit like a desk diary, in which all sorts of things are noted and jotted and underlined.

Barton speaks first. He is a quietly spoken, enviably slim man of forty-six with the sort of ruddy, healthy looks which you get if you spend a lot of time in the open air. He is wearing casual blue trousers and moccasin-type shoes. The unemployment figures are coming out later today. The weekly Cabinet meeting is tomorrow. Kenneth Clarke, the Chancellor of the Exchequer, is the 'likely lead', i.e. the person they would like for the prime 8.10 am interview slot, but they feel he might do 'The World at One' today instead. Discussion moves to Princess Diana in Angola: the morning's big story has been the attack by an unnamed government minister on the Princess for supporting a worldwide ban on anti-personnel mines. Would there be anything left in this by tomorrow morning? Nobody seems to think so.

Barton mentions a bishops' conference in the north of England. It raises the question of whether the Church should be speaking with one voice. He concedes that the programme has done bishops and politics a lot. Someone adds that the Bishop of Edinburgh had declined to give them an interview to expand on his trenchant piece in the *Church Times* on why he would be voting Labour. Barton suggests that next day's programme could perhaps do a piece about committed clerics. He speaks animatedly about the vicar of his own church (in Oxfordshire) who used to be leader of the Labour group on Oxford City Council and a forklift driver, and was now a semi-retired vicar. For the first time in the meeting one hears the word 'disco', BBC journalists' slang for 'discussion'.

This morning's discussion moves on to Labour councils setting their council tax levels for the forthcoming financial year. Frank Dobson was said to be getting worried lest some councils imposed such cripplingly high rates that the Tories would be able to use this to bash Labour-run authorities. Does anyone know of any councils which were going to set very high rates? Lambeth and Southwark, someone says.

Barton moves the meeting on to Labour's new campaign, just unveiled, warning supporters against complacency and pointing out that the Conservatives could still get in. 'There's an assumption they could win,' he says. 'Based on what?' someone asks. 'Based on the fact that they've won before,' says Liddle, who used to write speeches for Labour frontbenchers in the 1980s. There is a general feeling that something on the rival party strategies would make a good piece for next day's programme, but a package would be better than a disco.

The conversation moves back to the landmines. The assumption at the meeting, shared by everyone that morning, is that the unnamed minister was Nicholas Soames at Defence. Having rubbished Princess Diana on television immediately after the famous 'Panorama' interview with her, he is obviously the prime suspect. Barton thinks this is now 'a Soames story', but shrewdly points out that by taking her to Angola the Red Cross has achieved what it set out to do – draw attention to the appalling devastation caused to innocent civilians by millions of landmines left in Third World countries. Is this the first time she's got involved in politics, he inquires vaguely? No, says Liddle, there was a previous occasion, on homelessness, when she defended Jack Straw. There is still no enthusiasm for doing anything on it the next day. It would seem 'day two-ish'. They decide to leave it to 'PM'.

At this point Rod Liddle, a wiry, curly-haired man in an open shirt who sports a ring in his left ear, gets off his chair and sits on the floor, where he remains for the rest of the meeting. Nobody bats an eyelid, so presumably this is his normal practice. He says he has approached Sir Edward Heath, who some say has been libelled by the Referendum Party in its newspaper, which has accused him of telling lies, and also in its advertisements, which have accused him of taking Britain into a federal Europe by deceit and deliberately misleading the British people. Heath keeps putting them off and they fear he may prefer to do the Frost programme on BBC1 if he does decide to talk. Tom Feilden is in northern Cyprus and will be filing later. The axe is hanging over Ford's plant at Halewood. There are fears that hundreds may lose their jobs; management is saying nothing, though it may do at about 9.30 am, which will mean the story will break in time for 'The World at One'. How can 'Today' take it further the following morning? There is some murmuring about the Mondeo no longer being made in Britain. Steve Evans, one of the BBC's industrial correspondents, is in Merseyside covering the story closely. Barton says he may do a 'doughnut', and there is some talk as to how good this would sound. A doughnut, it transpires, is the broadcast of a conversation between a reporter and several people standing around him, the journalist being the jam in the middle. Or perhaps the hole.

Discussion shifts to Szymon Serafinowicz, facing Britain's first war crimes trial, and then to the volatile situation in South Korea, where the government's new anti-union laws have provoked violent and internationally publicised opposition. On to Nicola 'Superwoman' Horlick, the Deutsche Morgan Grenfell fund manager who has apparently been sacked from her £1 million-a-year City job. There is a general feeling that the programme ought to do an item on business ethics. Ideas continue to be knocked back and forth, but without enormous enthusiasm. There are brief mentions of a conference on teaching morality which is just about to open, and Virginia Bottomley's stance on National Lottery money going to transsexuals. Apparently she was on 'The World at One' (WATO as BBC journalists always call it) the previous day.

Barton brings things to life by referring to the Duchess of York's much-trailed appearance for Weight Watchers in America that day. Her fee is said to be £1 million, or $1 million. He has an excellent idea. If you're given a million quid, he says, can you stay thin? Could you *promise* never to eat cake again? There is a suggestion that Dawn French could be contacted on this. The name of Andrea Dworkin, the American feminist, also comes up, but there is a consensus that Dawn French would be funnier. Cathy offers to find out if Dawn will be interviewed.

John Rigby, the forward planning man, mentions the Israeli Cabinet meeting later in the day. The programme should do something on Israel because the situation in Hebron is still volatile. Cathy suddenly says it is the fortieth birthday of the Cavern Club in Liverpool, the place where the Beatles started, and is this a story? This makes me feel very old, but no one else seems particularly interested. At this point a handsome young man enters and sits down. He is Andy Tighe, the day reporter who is arriving for his shift. He says he didn't know the meeting would still be in progress.

Barton says he is fascinated by the solo American balloonist Steve Fossett who, after Richard Branson's spectacular débâcle, is still going strong. He likens him to Phileas Fogg and seems to think that when Fossett goes to the loo it involves tipping it over the side of his 'gondola thingy'. The meeting seems drawn to what seems the appealing, low-tech simplicity of the venture, but no one is actually ordered to do anything. Barton mentions Washington, where President Clinton's $30 million inauguration is due to take place the following Monday but which may also be the nastiest city in the United States. A bit sheepishly, because he admits it is 'élitist', he refers to the correspondence in *The Times* about the extent to which Oxbridge admissions tutors still take students from independent as opposed to state schools. Someone says the Lord Chief Justice is about to back a Liberal Democrat amendment in the Lords. Someone else mentions a report in the *Financial Times* that the Indian software industry has expanded by 60 per cent in the last year. The ideas float in the air, a bit like Fossett's balloon. At about 11 am the meeting breaks up, and Liddle and the others go off. Liddle is the day editor today, so it will be his job – in the light of the feelings expressed at the planning meeting – to try to line up interviews and build a skeleton of the programme before handing over to the night editor at 8 pm. Broadly speaking, about twenty items are needed for each day's programme, in addition to all those which come from other departments and are slotted in. There are more of these than most people think, including the news bulletins at 7 and 8 am; the summaries at 6.30, 7.30 and 8.30 am; the paper reviews at 6.40 am and 7.40 am; the sports reports at 7.25 and 8.25 am; the weather (which always comes from the duty meteorologist in the BBC TV Centre in Wood Lane) at 7.55 and 8.55 am, and 'Thought for the Day' (which may come from Broadcasting House or one of the BBC local radio stations, depending on where the speaker is) at 7.50 am.

Room 4058, Broadcasting House
4.15 pm, Wednesday 15 January 1997

The second meeting of the day takes place soon after 4 pm. It is always attended by a journalist from the BBC Radio Newsroom, which produces the bulletins and summaries heard on all five of the BBC's radio networks. The 7 am and 8 am bulletins on the 'Today' programme are not under the editorial control of 'Today' but of the Newsroom, and this has always been the case. (The summaries on the half-hour are a grey area: officially the responsibility of the Newsroom, they have sometimes, in practice, been subject to tinkering by 'Today'.) But the fact that they are sacrosanct does not obviate the need for liaison between the Newsroom and the programme: it would sound very strange if the stories on 'Today' bore no relation to what listeners were hearing in the bulletins.

Barton wants to know how strong a story Korea is. Liddle says it is a respectable one. He has arranged an interview with the South Korean Ambassador and earmarked it for 7.10 am. Someone asks a very sensible question. Does he speak good enough English? Nobody is quite sure. There is general consent that Halewood is shaping up as a big story: the job losses, not yet confirmed, will obviously have a major impact on a city where unemployment is already high. The question arises as to whether the Ford Escort is ceasing to be made in Britain. They have arranged for Labour's Robin Cook and Warwick University politics professor David Clark to talk about semiotics and Labour's new campaign warning its supporters against complacency. They have also fixed up for an Irish-Nigerian woman geneticist to talk about genetic screening: the peg for this is the opening of a conference in London.

John Rigby says he spoke to the Treasury twenty minutes before. The Chancellor was still ensconced with Eddie George, Governor of the Bank of England, but was considering the programme's request ('bid', as broadcast journalists always call it) to be interviewed at 8.10. Andy Tighe has finished making his report on corporate head-hunting, spawned by the Nicola Horlick saga, and has gone shopping. Barton is still keen on the politically committed clerics. Can they get Canon Eric James? Or George Austin, the Archdeacon of York? Other names mentioned are Donald Reeve of St James's, Piccadilly, and Tony Higton. Someone is not sure who Higton is. 'He's the one who wants to set fire to homosexuals,' says Liddle, sitting on the floor as usual. Everyone laughs: I think we all realise that this is what is known as hyperbole.

Two embargoed stories are mentioned, one about 'killer bugs' and the other on an international literacy survey in which Britain, surprise, surprise, came bottom. There is a general feeling that it has been a hard, unrewarding day in which most of the stories the team have pursued have fallen down. 'I feel quite guilty about going home,' says Barton, though he has already put in a ten-hour day and will be working from home, in touch with the night team via his laptop. There is no mention of Diana and Angola, even though the government minister has now been identified as Earl Howe, not Nicholas Soames (the *Evening Standard* has this on the front page). Too 'day-twoish', as Barton said.

Room 4058, Broadcasting House
8 pm, Wednesday 15 January 1997

The handover from the day team to the night team takes place at 8
pm. Liddle's day has ended. He now passes responsibility to Hilary
O'Neill, who is night editing tonight. He has prepared for her, as the
day editor always does, a ten-page document marked 'Prospects', an
up-to-date summary of the progress made on each story, or, as is
often the case, the lack of it. A copy is given to each of the seven
people present. It has copious notes on the state of play on all
inquiries and telephone numbers for interviewees and go-betweens.
Liddle, looking more like a gipsy than ever, is sitting on the floor
with his feet on the coffee table.

Dawn French has said no to an interview about Fergie and Weight
Watchers. Michael Portillo has said no to an interview on landmines
and an apparent change of policy on the Gurkhas. However, Clarke
has definitely agreed to come in so that is the first item listed. He
wants to concentrate on the economy rather than Europe, but will
take questions on Europe, says John Rigby's note. Clarke will be live
in the studio at 8.10 am and the name of the press officer who will be
accompanying him is also listed. The overnight contact on the story
is listed too – the duty press officer at the Treasury. Robin Cook has
agreed to be on the programme and will need a car to collect him
from the Edinburgh sleeper at Euston at 7.20 am and bring him to
Broadcasting House. Dafydd Wigley, leader of Plaid Cymru, has
accepted an invitation to come in and be interviewed at 6.50 am
about the terms under which he and his fellow Welsh nationalists
would support a minority Labour government. There is more on
politics: Labour is launching yet another campaign on the Thursday,
and item five on the document (wittily entitled 'New Day, New
Slogan') summarises the work done so far on a piece about the
politicians' choice of words and phrases, what they mean and how
effective they are. 'To DISCO we have Prof Terry Hawkes, Prof of
English at the Univ of Wales, Cardiff, and an expert on semiotics . . .
from the more practical, marketing, end will be Roger Heywood,
former chairman of the Chartered Inst of Marketing . . . we also have
archive of Mawhinney and Blair spouting slogans,' says 'Prospects'.
Victoria Whaley, a researcher, has arranged for Heywood to come
into the studio and for Hawkes to be interviewed at the end of a
telephone line: telephone numbers are given for each. She has put the
sound clips of Mawhinney and Blair in a safe place for the night team

to find. There is some excited chatter about Hawkes, who is said to be a 'post-structuralist': Liddle says he will be on the programme's panel of pundits during the election campaign, along with a woman pop singer who appeared on the programme a few days earlier in a head-to-head debate with Lady Olga Maitland over cocaine possession and the police's lenient treatment of Liam Gallagher.

Canon Eric James, a friend of the programme and a long-serving 'Thought for the Day' speaker, has agreed to participate in a disco about the wisdom of the Church's involvement in politics and will be interviewed by telephone. However, despite having spent much of the day on this, Victoria has been unable to find anyone else to take part. She has tried numerous bishops, none of whom will talk. Her briefing note on page 4 of 'Prospects' ends: 'Having problems finding other side of disco – need RABIDLY political vicar or one who thinks Church should stay well clear.' One knows the feeling.

Steve Evans is doing interviews with Ford workers likely to be affected by the following day's announcement of the loss of a third of the workforce. To discuss the demise of the Ford Escort, Rod has arranged for Denis Gregory to be interviewed. Gregory is now a lecturer at Ruskin College, Oxford and an adviser to the TGWU. He and Rod Liddle, it turns out, used to be speechwriters for members of Neil Kinnock's frontbench team in the 1980s. Gregory has agreed to go into BBC Radio Oxford to do a live interview 'down the line'. Cathy Packe, meanwhile, has arranged for Hilton Holloway, news editor of *Car* magazine, to be in the studio at 8 am to explain why the Escort is not selling sufficiently well. The precise details are given as to when the night team needs to send a car to pick him up from his home in south London.

The South Korean Ambassador, however, does not need a car. He wants to come to Broadcasting House at 7.30 am under his own steam. His name is Choi Dong Jin and he will be defending his government's controversial anti-union legislation. But there is a delicate problem with Mr Choi. One of the studio producers, Tom Heap, ascertains by means of a very precise and intelligent question that his English, though comprehensible, is hesitant. This is important information. Hilary, the night editor thinks pre-recording him would thus be wiser than interviewing him live, as Rod blithely suggests: ums and ers and hesitations can always be edited out, a process known as 'de-umming'. It is her decision now, for she is in charge. Rod, getting up from the floor, is going home.

The 'Prospects' document lists the presenters (James Naughtie and

Alex Brodie, formerly the BBC's Middle East Correspondent and now an occasional presenter for both 'Today' and the BBC World Service). It also names the announcer who will sit alongside them at the U-shaped table in Studio 4A to read the bulletins and summaries – it will be Andrew Crawford who, like all the BBC announcers, has a mellifluous voice with perfect diction. It also names the sports reporter (Steve May), the business reporter (Nigel Cassidy), the weather forecaster (Isabelle Lang) and the three studio managers (John Whalley, Rod Farquhar and Peter Roach) who will start and stop tapes, operate the controls and run the telephone links in the cubicle next to 4A the following morning. Finally, the arrangements for 'Thought for the Day' are listed. The speaker will be Anne Atkins and there is a sentence to the effect that she will be talking about cryonics and returning to life. She requires a wake-up call at 6.25 on a given number and a taxi at 6.45 from her home in Parson's Green. Plus a return car at 8 am, after her broadcast. The bookings have already been made.

Room 4059, Broadcasting House
12.30 am, Thursday 16 January 1997

The overnight team consists of Hilary, two producers and a night reporter. Having inherited the stories from the day team, her job is to distribute them among the fixed points of the bulletins, summaries, 'Thought', sport, papers and weather – as well as listen to the tapes that have been left for her and cut them where she feels appropriate. It will also be her responsibility to follow up anything of importance which appears in the first editions of the daily papers. These are biked round by their respective publishers in Wapping, Docklands, Farringdon Road and so on at about 11 pm.

Things have moved on a little since the handover meeting. The Labour press office has rung to suggest that Alistair Darling appear on the programme rather than Robin Cook. This is because Darling is a Shadow Treasury Minister while Cook handles foreign affairs, and Labour has claimed that the Tories might put VAT on food, which the Tories have promptly called a lie. The story has therefore changed its emphasis. Hilary had accepted the suggestion, so Darling will be coming in instead, at 7 am. The cab for Euston is cancelled. The first editions of nearly all the papers have big stories about Diane Abbott, Labour MP for Hackney North and Stoke Newington, returning to one of her favourite topics – black nurses. She was widely condemned the previous November for having a go at 'blue-eyed Finns'. Now she has written an article in *Nursing Times*, alleging black nurses are often discriminated against. Hilary is trying to get her on the programme but holds out little hope: she declined the last time. They have also invited a senior official from the main hospital in her constituency to discuss her claims, and are much more hopeful about this.

The top of the front page of the *Independent* has a huge exclusive claiming there are confidential Franco-German plans to impose a single tax rate across the EU after the single currency is in place. Bill Cash, the Eurosceptic Tory MP, has already been on the telephone about this. It is clearly first-class ammunition for him. But the programme has not invited him on or made plans to follow up the *Independent* claims, which do not appear to be substantiated.

Tom Heap wheels to his desk a tape machine supported by four metal legs on castors. He proceeds to play each tape aloud, partly for Hilary's editorial judgement, partly to time its duration. He also reads aloud the 'cues' – the few sentences of introductory material which the reporters have written as suggested links for the presenters. There is Andy Tighe's piece on corporate headhunting, as well as the second part of Andy Bell's three-part report on Islam in what used to be Russia, and the authorities' forcible suppression of Islamic fundamentalism. This piece is centred on Tashkent. Obviously it must run, because it is an integral part of a series.

Tom Feilden has filed his report from northern Cyprus and Stephen Evans has sent his from Halewood. Both these 'packages' – a blend of analysis, facts, quotes and evocative sound effects to make the pictures more vivid in your mind – are now being mixed in one of the studios, on another floor of Broadcasting House, by Tim Ashburner, a senior audio supervisor. Hilary has told him the length she wants them to run at. The rest of the night is spent eating food from the twenty-four-hour canteen on the eighth floor, adjusting the running order, deciding which presenter should conduct which interviews and introduce which items, checking the timings to ensure everything can be fitted in properly, and trying as best she can to ensure that each of the five half-hours (6.30–7 am, 7–7.30 am, 7.30–8 am, 8–8.30 am and 8.30–9 am) has an internal balance of light and shade, political and non-political, which on some days is extremely hard to arrange. But it is important to try: most people listen for only half an hour or an hour, so each half-hour segment should ideally contain more than one mood. It is a quiet night and there are no crises.

Room 4059, Broadcasting House
4.30 am, Thursday 16 January 1997

This is when the presenters usually arrive. Messrs Naughtie and Brodie are more formally attired than the production team and are already dressed in jacket, collar and tie. Presenters have been known to arrive unshaved, but these two look as if they've certainly managed that. They sit at a bank of desks in the middle of the long room which has Room 4058 at one end and Barton's office at the other. They switch on their screens and find the running order, so they can see which items are being carried, who is introducing what and who is doing which interview. It is important to realise that the presenters are presented with a *fait accompli* each morning. They have no control over the content of the programme or who does what. That has all been decided by the night team. What they have to do is write their own cues in as sharp, informative and entertaining a manner as possible, and digest the briefing notes so that they will be able to ask sensible and pertinent questions. Naughtie, who will be interviewing Kenneth Clarke at 8.10 am, has been given three pages of notes on the Chancellor and VAT, including significant comments Clarke has made on the subject in the past. He is expected to master this material thoroughly: presenters are most fiercely criticised inside the BBC when they have not read, or acted upon, their written briefs. Someone may have toiled over a brief for hours, collating the background information from newspaper cuttings, electronic data-bases, speeches, press releases and official documents. Brodie and Naughtie work away quietly. Naughtie, preparing his cue for the Chancellor, asks who was it that said death and taxes are the only two things we can be sure of? No one seems to know. He gets up and consults a book of quotations on the shelf. It turns out, surprisingly, to be Benjamin Franklin, and he puts it into his script.

The only moment of excitement comes when the presenters see that 'Thought for the Day' is going to be presented by Anne Atkins. 'That bigot!' explodes Naughtie, who seems personally affronted. It is as if he thinks she has been put in just to annoy him. He seems very angry and goes on murmuring and growling. 'What a bigot,' agrees Brodie, who echoes Naughtie's feelings. Nobody dissents. They calm down a bit after a few seconds but it is a heartfelt outburst. Gay rights are part of the culture of today's BBC, where Atkins's views, though obviously commanding much support in the country, are widely reviled as 'homophobic'. The topic is also, perhaps, of particular sensitivity on the 'Today' programme. One of its former reporters, Nigel Wrench, now a presenter on 'PM', is the host of Radio 5 Live's gay and lesbian series 'Out This Week' and announced at a Sony Radio Awards lunch a year or two back that he is HIV-positive. Another colleague, a producer on 'Today', is the partner (to use the BBC-preferred word) of Labour's election candidate in Exeter, the openly homosexual Ben Bradshaw, who works for 'The World at One'.

Three weeks later, over breakfast, I asked Naughtie why he thought Atkins was a bigot. He had been in full verbal flow until then, but for some reason his loquacity suddenly deserted him and he concentrated on dissecting his kipper. 'Office badinage is office badinage,' he said finally, 'and that's it.' He declined to say what he thought of her views: 'I don't think my views about a particular "Thought for the Day" are really of any relevance and I wouldn't comment on her one any more than I would comment on a Lionel Blue joke or a Lavinia Byrne attitude struck in the course of a "Thought for the Day".' (He had, however, already commented on Sister Byrne's attitudes, by contributing a glowing foreword to her latest book which included the words, 'Lavinia Byrne has a voice of her own, full of character and good sense.')

Studio 4A, Broadcasting House
6.25 am, Thursday 16 January 1997

Five minutes before they go on air Naughtie and Brodie pick up their papers and walk the twenty yards from Room 4059 to Studio 4A on the same floor. They sit side by side at the straight end of the U-shaped table and put on their headphones, looking businesslike but relaxed. In the middle of the table is a sprouting arrangement of microphones, each one a different colour, and around the table are several chairs. The production team are in a cubicle next door, separated from the studio by a thick wall of glass.

Bang on 6.30, after the handover from Radio 4 Continuity on the floor below, Naughtie offers a cheery 'Good morning' to the programme's one million listeners – double what it is at 6 am, but which will double again by 7.30. The programme opens with its quite leisurely, informative half-hour in which correspondents set the

scene for what is going to happen today. Naughtie talks to Jeremy
Vine, one of the political correspondents, about Labour's launch
later in the day of the advertising campaign suggesting that the
government might impose VAT on food. Brodie talks to Steve Evans
on Merseyside about the meeting to be held at Halewood, and the
widespread forebodings of Ford workers about what the company's
'restructuring' would mean for them. Naughtie interviews Richard
Hannaford, one of the BBC health correspondents, about the
government's position on transplants involving organs from pigs.
Then it is 6.40 and time for the first of the two paper reviews. It lasts
two minutes and fifty-five seconds and is read, immaculately, by
Andrew Crawford, who sits a few feet round the table from
Naughtie. That is followed by a package about the start of
campaigning in the Wirral South by-election: it includes reportage
from Jon Pienaar, another of the BBC's political correspondents, the
voices of some South Wirral golfers, actuality from the Tory
campaign headquarters, the sound of a dog barking and children
playing, and short comments from the prospective Conservative,
Labour and Liberal Democrat candidates.

Twenty seconds of news headlines are delivered by Brodie,
followed by four minutes and ten seconds of financial and commercial news compiled and delivered by Nigel Cassidy, the business
presenter. And then comes the first of the live studio interviews with
a politician: Dafydd Wigley, president of Plaid Cymru, who talks to
Brodie about the possible position of the Welsh nationalists under a
future Labour government. That leads into Isabelle Lang's all-
important two-minute weather forecast, Peter Jefferson's Radio 4
programme trails, a nineteen-second travel update from Naughtie
and the pips that tell the world that it is exactly 7 am.

In the next half-hour the audience will climb, sharply, to 1.8
million. Everything moves up a notch, with noticeably starrier
interviewees and more foreign affairs. The first item after the nine-
minute news bulletin is acknowledged to be one of the key moments
in the programme, along with the 7.33 interview and the plum one at
8.10. Alistair Darling has come in to defend Labour's latest salvo in
the battle of the posters, which shows a hand breaking an egg and
the slogan: 'Next Tory tax? £10.50 a week VAT on food. Enough is
enough.' Labour is claiming that the Tories do have such plans, and
have come up with a figure based on a calculation of the increase to
the average weekly food bill were VAT to be imposed on foodstuffs.
Brodie gives Darling a hard time, suggesting there is no evidence for

this claim and that it amounts to little more than a smear. Darling stands his ground. A purposeful, unsmiling exchange.

The second of today's packages comes from Tom Feilden in Cyprus, and is being broadcast to mark the fact that today is the day President Clinton's envoy flies back to Washington. He has been engaged in a frantic round of shuttle diplomacy designed to prevent further fighting between Greece and Turkey, against a backdrop of the Greeks' wish to instal anti-aircraft missiles in their section of the divided island. Feilden's four-minute report is an evocative mix of a café, bustling streets, the voices and views of Turkish Cypriots, a British army base commander and the Greek Orthodox Metropolitan of Kyrenia. Back from the Mediterranean, the focus turns to Hackney and Ms Abbott's stated opinion that hospitals cannot recruit enough black nurses because institutional racism is forcing them out. She has turned down the programme's invitation to be interviewed. Instead Nancy Hallett, Director of Nursing at the MP's local hospital, the Homerton, is in the studio. She steers a middle course in her conversation with Brodie, denying any suggestion of racism at the Homerton, but avoiding complacency about the situation more generally.

The radio car now makes its first appearance: the programme's Manchester-based car has driven over to Newcastle where the Reverend David Holloway, a prominent conservative evangelical, has agreed to be interviewed about the extent to which the Church should become involved in politics. He is there to put the argument that it should stay out. The other side of the debate is represented by Canon James, veteran socialist and director of Christian Action. He is on the telephone. Naughtie talks to them both. As an active member of the kirk session (congregation) at the Church of Scotland church where he worships in Covent Garden, he probably has his own views on this. You would not know what they were from his interviewing, which is characteristically even-handed. Steve May quietly enters the studio to deliver his sports news; there's a four-second 'ident' in which Brodie tells listeners they're listening to 'Today'; then it's 7.30 and time for the news summary.

The programme is now attracting its biggest audience, which is also the biggest audience for the network as a whole. Between 7.30 and 8 am, the average audience is 2,057,000 (compared with 1,924,000 from 8 am to 8.30). It is in fact the only time in the entire week that the Radio 4 audience tops 2,000,000. This crucial half-hour is opened by the second of no fewer than three items this morning on the gloom enveloping Halewood, where Ford workers are expected to learn within a few hours that a third of them will lose their jobs. Steve Evans's package incorporates remarks from several people involved: the man who runs the Citizens' Advice Bureau near the plant, a metalwork teacher in a local school, an economics fellow at Liverpool University, and Canon Nicholas Frayling, Rector of Liverpool. It has been mixed with a clip of bagpipes playing at a twinning ceremony to link Halewood with Dublin.

That is followed by quite a highbrow item on political language. In his cue Naughtie refers to the paragraph having given way to the slogan, and points out that the coming election will be fought using the labels the parties have invented for themselves. New Labour, New Danger, New Britain, Euro Danger and so on. Much money is expended on finding just the right word. Naughtie interviews Roger Heywood, former chair of the Institute of Marketing, who is in the studio, and Terry Hawkes, Professor of English at the University of Wales, on the telephone. Andrew Crawford reads the second of the paper reviews – quite different from the earlier one an hour ago, but exactly the same length – before Andy Tighe's report on executive poaching. Like so many things on the 'Today' programme, it is less than three-and-a-half minutes in length but has a great deal packed into it, including the thoughts of Oliver Wells, managing director of a London-based firm of corporate headhunters; Geoffrey King, boss of a recruitment company; Helen Barrett, editor of a guide called *Executive Grapevine* and Fiona Lafferty, a columnist on *Sunday Business*.

Hunting of heads turns to freezing of heads, for it is 7.50 and time for 'Thought for the Day'. Time for Anne Atkins to ruminate on immortality. She has crept quietly into the studio and taken her space at the table, laying out the two pages of her script in front of her. Very early on in her talk she uses a line which I had heard used the day before by Brian Barron on another Radio 4 programme, on how appropriate it was that one of the leading cryogenics companies was based in Phoenix. (Ho-ho, as John Timpson might have said.) Anne's conclusions are broadly that freezing corpses in liquid nitrogen offers false hope, and that real immortality is provided only by Christianity. I notice that Naughtie does not once look at her. He keeps his eyes down, apparently studying his running order and briefing notes.

Those in the cubicle have been ensuring that the next guest, Professor Brian Pentecost, is coming over loud and clear from the Midlands studios of Radio WM. He is put through to Brodie as

Atkins tiptoes out, and Brodie starts interviewing him about the possibilities, and ethics, of transplanting animal organs into humans. The peg for this item is the belief that the Department of Health will, later in the day, pronounce with great caution on the question of xenotransplantation. Another time-check follows, then another weather forecast from the other side of the capital, the repeat of the programme trails, a quick travel update, another 'ident'; then the 8 am bulletin. This is usually the longest or the second longest item on the programme. Today, it is the second longest, lasting nine minutes and thirty-two seconds. It is long enough for the main presenter to leave the studio, walk down the corridor into the Green Room to greet the main guest and have a quick chat before the interview. Sometimes the politician wants to be reassured that the presenter is definitely going to ask him, or her, a particular question, for which he has a prepared and newsworthy answer and which the party officials, and the programme, have previously agreed is the reason for his appearance. Today, Clarke comes in while Andrew Crawford is reading the bulletin. He takes his jacket off, hangs it on the back of a chair, and sits down directly opposite Naughtie on the other side of the table. The interview is brisk, no-nonsense, more friendly than hostile, with the Chancellor interrupting Naughtie more than the other way round; Naughtie tries to get words in, but his half-formed sentences seem to get snapped off by the Chancellor before he can complete them. As the conversation continues there is some murmuring in the cubicle that Naughtie has not put to Clarke a previous statement Clarke made which appeared to encompass the possibility of VAT on food. Eventually, he does manage to put the direct question, 'Will you put VAT on food?', and gets the answer, 'No, and I can't imagine any Chancellor who would,' and one knows immediately that that is the quote which will run. That is the crux of the matter. That is the only bit of the whole interview which really counts, but in 'Today' terms the whole interview is probably worth it because of that one clear commitment, that unequivocal promise from the Chancellor of the Exchequer.

The interview with Clarke has lasted nine minutes and forty-one seconds, longer than most. It is followed by the last of the three Halewood items, with Brodie doing a telephone interview with union adviser Denis Gregory of Ruskin College, Oxford, and talking in the studio to the wonderfully named Hilton Holloway of *Car* magazine about Ford's model range. That is succeeded by a brief telephone interview Naughtie does with geneticist Dr Elizabeth Anionwu, who is involved with a new 'Genetic Choices' exhibition opening the next day at the Science Museum in London, Steve May's second sports package, a weather summary and the 8.30 news.

In this last half-hour of the programme, the average audience will be 1,503,000, about 500,000 fewer than an hour ago. Given the number who have to leave for work and be out of the house by 8.30, the drop is not surprising. The rhythm of the programme naturally changes and the pace slackens: the last half-hour is not the place you would seize on to drop your word in the nation's ear and almost half of it is occupied by 'Yesterday in Parliament' (when parliament is sitting: during the recess the slot is used for a reading). The items tend to be worthy and solid but sometimes rather dull. Today there is the second part, centred on Tashkent, of Andy Bell's three-part series about Islam in the former USSR, and then Brodie's interview – recorded in a neighbouring studio while the programme has been on the air, and quickly edited – with the South Korean Ambassador, Choi Dong Jin, on his country's controversial new law making it easier to sack people. That is the last item in the programme, which finishes, as usual, a few seconds before 8.58. Another day about to begin, another 'Today' has ended.

Room 4058, Broadcasting House
9 am, Thursday 16 January 1997

An inquest on each day's programme is always held within a few minutes of it ending. (During those few minutes the Radio 4 audience drops by 600,000, the equivalent of six Wembley Stadiums suddenly emptying.) The two presenters are there, plus the members of the production team from the cubicle and the editor, Jon Barton. At once Barton raises an interesting point: should minders be allowed into the studio with their masters? He asks this because Clarke's press officer, who accompanied him into Broadcasting House, also accompanied him into the studio: she sat a few feet away from him while the interview was taking place. Barton says he has never worked on a programme where that has taken place and seems perturbed by it. (Nobody mentions that the BBC always insists that a minder be present if one of its own broadcasters or executives is interviewed.) Someone promises to look into the matter. Brodie is praised for pushing Alistair Darling hard. Naughtie is praised for prising from the Chancellor the categorical pledge that the Tories would not put VAT on food. Hilary points out that this statement is already leading

PA. Once again 'Today' is setting the agenda. Barton doesn't think the disco on political language worked very well, but otherwise seems satisfied enough.

It was not the most exciting programme in the history of 'Today', or the most eventful twenty-four hours. No coups, crashes, assassinations, resignations, volcanic eruptions, tidal waves, amazing leaks or red-hot revelations. But there are many more days like this than ones when Pan-Am airliners fall from the sky over Lockerbie and the running order is torn up and Humphrys is on the first plane to Glasgow. It is a normal programme made by a group of normal journalists reflecting a normal day, and a salutary experience for anyone who thinks the programme is constantly assailed by spin-doctors and that no Cabinet minister ever turns down the chance to appear on it.

9

Morning Miscellany to Morning Macho

Just as it was in 1957, the 'Today' programme is still aimed at busy people on the move. But it has moved on several light years from the days when it happily gave airtime to the chap who played 'Rule Britannia' by hitting himself on the head with a nine-inch spanner. No more can presenters ruminate, as Timpson once did, on what is the longest palindrome in the English language (deified, apparently). Nigel Rees recalls the day the programme carried a story about a man whose hobby was raising a type of poultry called bantam Orpingtons: he had married somewhat late in life and taken his new bride on honeymoon to, yes, Orpington. Subsequently he had been interviewed by a 'Today' reporter and so had his wife. At one point she was asked, 'And when you were on your honeymoon, did he show you his Orpingtons?' Gems like that are of the past. The 'Today' programme still carries lighter items but eccentrics are long gone.

Whether it is 800 feet below the frozen surface of Siberia with striking miners, reporting from the only brewery in Eritrea, investigating abattoirs at home or interviewing the Home Secretary about miscarriages of justice, 'Today' has become the one national noticeboard that nobody can afford to miss – even though 96 per cent of the adult population do miss it. It is the indispensable alarm clock of the élite, a three-line whip for the ears of all those interested or involved in public life.

It was on the 'Today' programme that Kenneth Baker, the former Home Secretary, made his unforgettable comment about James Bulger's murder ('a crime from the heart of darkness'), when he was being interviewed about juvenile crime; where Gillian Shephard first embraced the cane; where John Prescott came out as a member of the middle classes; where Gordon Brown made his famous pledge that Labour would not raise income tax; where Malcolm Rifkind admitted that the government was on balance 'hostile' towards the idea of a single European currency; and where the BBC itself chose to tell the world of the death of 'Mastermind', by giving the programme the story and enabling it to do its own exclusive interview with Magnus Magnusson, which was followed up by every national newspaper in the land.

It is taped at 10 Downing Street, in party headquarters, and by the London *Evening Standard*, so that the paper can get the quotes on a big interview word-for-word and not waste valuable time waiting for a transcript. When, at 8.30 am, the Cabinet's sub-committee on policy presentation, once chaired by Michael Heseltine and now by Peter Mandelson, sits down, it has the 'Today' running order in front of it. Labour used to have a 9 am press conference at its offices on Millbank and, says Donald Dewar who usually attended it, 'it is extraordinary the amount of time spent on what came up on the "Today" programme'.

How therefore does 'Today' actually 'set the agenda' and what does this mean?

Peter Lilley was one of many people who were absolutely clear about the programme's importance:

> It's become a sort of organ of our constitution in that it's now used increasingly to announce, or set the scene for announcements, and consequently it becomes agenda-setting for the media for the next twenty-four hours. That's something politicians connive in. We allow it to do that rather than have it forced upon us. If one is making an announcement in parliament, it's not uncommon now to be interviewed ahead of that announcement on the morning and set the scene for it. You don't give the details in full, that's the privilege of parliament, but you can convey a sense of what is forthcoming and put your own spin on it.[1]

His Cabinet colleague John Gummer said much the same: 'If you are concerned to launch a new initiative about air quality, for example, or trying to get some understanding of a difficult decision, the "Today" programme will be absolutely crucial.'[2] William Walde-grave points out that a snappy sentence on 'Today' can run for the rest of the day: 'If you can say your piece on the "Today" programme you're quite likely to get it on to the *other* BBC programmes for a considerable part of the rest of the day. They will take it because it's available to them and it's their company.'[3]

Donald Dewar made the same point:

> If there is an exchange of some political significance, it's going to be a story that will be picked up by lunchtime and may, if it has legs, run right through the day. It's very important, you know, to get that right. You can start any hare running on 'Today'. There is no point in thinking you can do a casual interview and if you make a slip-up it won't be noticed. If you do it on the day it *will* be noticed.
>
> If we've got to launch a policy statement or campaign, then obviously one of the first things you want to do is get on to the programme, because that gives it something of an imprimatur as a news item. You can be sure that almost all the serious journalists will be listening in.[4]

William Waldegrave also identified a further way in which the programme occupies a vital role for politicians, lobbyists, spin-doctors and opinion formers:

> It's an important way of judging whether a story which may be in the papers is going to run, because it's the first time you see whether *other* serious editors and journalists feel the story is a big one. Some things fly, some things don't. If something that is in the morning papers hasn't flown on the 'Today' programme, it's quite likely that that's an indication that other journalists think, 'Oh well, we know that,' or, 'It's not really a story,' or something like that. It's the first independent commentary on the morning press.[5]

Robin Cook explained in detail how politicians use the programme to carry their propaganda, and how it has almost completely supplanted traditional press conferences:

> It has been very noticeable in recent times that the 'Today' programme has an obvious way of focusing on the stories that are going to break that day, and anticipating them. Now that is quite attractive to politicians, because if you're going to have a press conference to release a document, a policy, a news story, an initiative, then you want to get on the 'Today' programme beforehand, that morning, to get it up and running. And the

Standard, which has a symbiotic relationship with 'Today', will then run your comments in the early edition so they in turn will be read by people on all the daily newspapers, even if they didn't hear you on the 'Today' programme in the first place, and then it all rolls forward.

There was a time about ten years ago, when I was doing Health, when I would find myself in a little bit of difficulty if invited to appear on the 'Today' programme on the morning of a press conference, because to me the press conference was the main event and what you were keeping your punchlines for. So there would be some sense of drama, surprise, novelty when you unveiled your package, and you would want that to carry forward into the lunchtime broadcasting media and hopefully into the next day's broadsheets.

That has comprehensively gone now. Nowadays you put as much as you can of the story into the 'Today' programme, recognising that if you can get the story across in the 'Today' programme and on 'Breakfast News' on BBC1, then you have got it very strongly up and running. These days a press conference is the peg on which you hang a bid for all the breakfast programmes, and the press conference itself, by contrast, can be, not exactly an anti-climax, but what Bagehot might describe as the dignified part of the exercise rather than the functional part of the exercise.

For instance, the initiative when Tony [Blair] went to Oxford to give a speech on a new initiative in our state schools policy. That ran very big on the 'Today' programme with interviews with a Labour spokesperson, Estelle Morris, and from then on the news content went downhill and by the time you got to the next day's papers, it was buried on page four or five. Whereas, ten years ago, one would have been aiming all that at the front page of the papers with only a small hint of it on the 'Today' programme.[6]

This is not only a vivid account of how the programme now operates and helps 'set the agenda', but revealing in its evidence of how the emphasis of journalism has shifted from reporting to speculation. Anybody looking for a plain report the next day on what the Leader of the Opposition actually said – what had actually *happened* as opposed to what his colleagues had trumpeted in advance was *going* to happen – would, as Cook points out, have been looking largely in vain. Broadcasters, print journalists and politicians, as he says, are now actively engaged in whipping up interest and publicity before an announcement, rather than carefully pondering the details afterwards. 'Newspapers now don't want to report what happened yesterday,' says Cook, 'they want to report what Kenneth Clarke or Michael Heseltine are scheming to do tomorrow.'[7] Some people believe that this is one of the most worrying aspects of modern journalism; one such is Douglas Hurd, former Home Secretary and Foreign Secretary:

> The modern media are far less competent in the routine reporting of ordinary events, of what is actually said and done. Television is confined by the soundbite. The written press, at least in Britain, has deteriorated in quality perhaps faster and further than any other institution. We are confronted each day with acres of comment and gossip, but a dearth of actual reporting of what has occurred.[8]

Because of the programme's vital role in providing a springboard for politicians' initiatives, and allowing them to speak to the most influential audience enjoyed by any programme in the land, it is regularly on the receiving end of calls from ministers' special assistants, government press officers, personal press secretaries or those who work in the PR departments of the various Party headquarters. (Very few politicians make direct contact, preferring to let their underlings do so, though the hi-tech Paddy Ashdown has often sent e-mails to 'Today' and, using his laptop computer and cellphone, once sent one from the garden of his holiday home in France.)

It is this that has given rise to the myth that spin-doctors lay siege to the programme with a permanent barrage of suggestions and requests. In fact, requests *from* the programme to interview leading politicians outnumber the supplications *to* it, as is the case with all programmes and publications.

In practice, spin-doctors are often as much help to the programme as to their own masters. A good example concerns Gordon Brown, when he made his famous promise on the 'Today' programme that Labour would not increase either the standard or the higher rate of income tax – the first time Labour had made this pledge. On the previous Friday, after the interview had been set up, Brown's economic adviser Ed Balls telephoned Jon Barton, editor of 'Today' and told him that Brown would have something of major national importance to disclose, adding that another conversation on Sunday might be helpful to both sides. On Sunday, therefore, Charlie Whelan, Brown's press secretary, rang James Naughtie (who had been told he would be doing the interview) at his home in Clapham and suggested he ask the Shadow Chancellor about tax. It was a strong hint that could not be ignored. Just after 8 am the following morning, when Brown and Naughtie were chatting in the Green Room a few minutes before the interview, Brown reminded Naughtie of what he had come in for. 'You will ask me about tax, won't you?' he said. Naughtie duly obliged, though not until half-way through the interview, and Brown duly came out with his carefully prepared pledge. Brown's office had meanwhile briefed both the Press Association and the London *Evening Standard* that Brown would be delivering a bombshell on the programme, so within minutes of the interview going out Brown's words were appearing, via PA, on the screens of every newspaper and news programme in Britain.

So Virginia Bottomley is not being excessively lyrical perhaps when she says this about the programme's impact:

It has an extraordinary influence in national life. I'm only really off-duty if I leave the country and can't hear the 'Today' programme. If I'm within earshot I'll tune in and feel involved. To be truly switched off from my work I know that basically I have to be out of its footprint. It sets the agenda. It has a unique influence on setting the agenda for politicians and the media generally.[9]

Bottomley has a special reason to feel admiration:

When I did the Health job [Minister of State, 1989–92, Secretary of State, 1992–5], there was a particularly able reporter in Niall Dickson [Glasgow-born former teacher who went on to become editor of the *Nursing Times*, joining the BBC as its Health Correspondent in 1988, becoming Chief Social Affairs Correspondent in 1989 and Social Affairs Editor in 1995]. Goodness knows where he got the information from but he always seemed to have a better briefing than I had myself in the box overnight.[10]

It is not only politicians who become obsessed with 'Today', tycoons can too, as Sir Christopher Bland admits:

I started listening in the late 1960s when I lived in a £6-a-week flat in Fulham and I've listened ever since. I've had three periods of infidelity: when I was at the IBA in 1973 and we launched LBC; when my wife was a non-executive director of TV-am when it began in 1983; and when Greg Dyke and I started GMTV to wrest the franchise away from TV-am. But on each occasion my infidelity lasted only a fortnight and I came back to 'Today'.[11]

David Blunkett provided an admirably cogent explanation of why exactly 'Today' is so influential:

There are two ways [in which it influences public affairs]. One is very straightforward and that is that other politicians, and opinion formers such as leader writers, listen. So it does make a difference to people's perception of one's competence and visibility, though constant appearances can reduce your gravitas and people's willingness to listen to what you're saying.

The second element is that the editorial people on television and other radio channels do pick things up from 'Today'. If you want a soundbite running through the morning on Radio 4, Radio 2 and Radio 5 you really need to have got something on to the 'Today' programme. The television people tend to contact politicians' offices after they've heard something interesting on 'Today' and between nine and ten in the morning they'll have their morning conference and they'll say, we heard that, that sounds a good line, and they'll run with it. In addition, the 'Today' programme is well placed in terms of something that might take off in parliament. We pick things up from the 'Today' programme that would be usable during the afternoon question sessions.

So it's established itself as something that's worth being on, a) to talk to opinion formers, b) to get a message across to other people interested or involved in politics and, c) to actually affect that agenda.[12]

From the other side of the political divide, Lord Archer agrees:

It's a very important programme and it does set the agenda. I cannot arrive in the House of Lords and have people say to me one after another what did I think about the Prime Minister on 'Today' this morning, or have the press ringing me asking for my comments, if I haven't heard it. I may be asked to appear on radio or television at a moment's notice and I can't not have heard it. I've got no choice.

I find that when I appear on 'Today' and 'Newsnight' I get more comments than if I appear on any other programme. That's because they're considered serious. So if I'm going on the 'Today' show I take it seriously, I prepare sentences, I'll work at it. People hear you on Radio 5, they hear you somewhere else, they say that's fine, that's Jeffrey doing his bit for the Party. But with these two programmes they make a judgement. Were you good or were you bad? Did you beat John Humphrys or did he beat you?[13]

But 'Today' does not just set the agenda. Sometimes it follows it as well. It is not immune from media-feeding frenzy. For those not acquainted with how stories can build up into a mish-mash of misunderstanding, so that eventually nobody knows who actually said what or to whom, the following experience of Austin Mitchell is illuminating:

I wrote an article for the *New Statesman* about Labour's document *The Road to the Manifesto*. It tried to explain to Party members, plenty of whom were dissatisfied with that document because they felt they weren't being consulted, why things were as they were. It basically argued that we had to feel beyond Party members, we couldn't frighten people, we couldn't impose a radical manifesto because it would be taken down and used against us.

I did quote in it a Party member, whom I didn't name, who asked me jokingly what was the difference between our policy processes and those of Kim Il Sung. It was just a remark made at a Party meeting. Well, the magazine appeared on the Wednesday night. 'Today' had rung up and invited me on a discussion the next day about *The Road to the Manifesto* and they said they wanted a wide range of views. It was to be with Robin Cook who would of course, as usual, much prefer to be on his own, but it was still a chance to put the same lines of argument that I put in the *New Statesman*, so I said yes and they arranged to send a car round for me the following morning.

Late at night they rang and cancelled that and I assumed it was one of those cases where as a backbencher you are disposable because it's more important to get Robin Cook. I wasn't bothered. Then they rang again and said would I come on the programme after all? They said it was a mistake that they'd cancelled me. It turned out that the *Independent* had got hold of the *New*

Statesman article and put it on the front page as an attack on Blair, which it wasn't, and the 'Today' programme was reacting to this. They were reacting not to *my* views but to the distortion of those views in the *Independent*. I did a phone interview with John Humphrys the following morning and it seemed to baffle him that what I had written was in fact very supportive of the leadership.

When asked what I wanted to get out of it, I said 'a job'. I went back to bed but having put the phone down it suddenly became red hot because all the other media are listening to 'Today', and they'd either heard this or seen the front page of the *Independent*. I think probably they were responding to 'Today'. Sky News, BBC, ITN, Radio Humberside all rang, all wanting to do interviews. While I got up and prepared to sally out Heseltine was brought on to the 'Today' programme and chortled away, 'Kim Il Sung, Kim Il Sung', he kept going on, 'I say that's a bit rich, nobody has ever called John Major Kim Il Sung . . .' Robin Cook was asked his opinion and he said well, Austin Mitchell is a serial maverick. Major even referred to it in his Conference speech, if you remember, about how some people had called him [Blair] Kim Il Sung.

Ever since then people have been writing me letters and abusing me saying, 'What the hell did you call Tony Blair Kim Il Sung for? I left the Party in 1982 to get away from wreckers like you.' I was asked by the Party's press officer, Jo Moore, not to give any more interviews on the grounds that it would give the story legs and keep it alive. I wasn't therefore able to point out that I had *never* called Tony Blair Kim Il Sung. I hadn't even mentioned them in the same sentence or the same paragraph. I think this demonstrates the infuriating power of the 'Today' programme. Here I am, my career ruined, my future in the Labour Party wrecked, and all because of the 'Today' programme.[14]

Although he made that last comment with a smile on his face, Mitchell's annoyance was clear; and what his story does is show the following things. First, he will always be remembered for something he never did – likening Tony Blair to the dictator of North Korea. (He was accused of it yet again by John Major at Prime Minister's Question Time on 25 February 1997, to much uproarious Commons laughter.) Second, newspapers and programmes are desperate to out-do one another in taking stories 'further', and much less interested in looking at what was *actually* said and analysing that. Third, inaccurate front pages can perpetuate myths which radio and television programmes further perpetuate by repeating them. Fourth, that everybody listens to 'Today'.

As far as bias is concerned, I found nobody who thought that was now a serious problem, and there was general recognition that in recent years, post-Redhead, the programme had become more even-handed in the tone of its coverage of public spending arguments. Sir George Young said, 'There may sometimes be problems with individual interviews, but I do not believe there is any systematic bias in the programme at all.'[15] Stephen Dorrell agreed, 'It's biased only to the extent that it challenges authority and seeks to call powerful people to account, and that's what journalism is there for, partly.'[16] Dafydd Wigley, MP for Caernarfon and leader of the Welsh nationalists, put it pithily: 'Their job is to bowl, ours to bat.'[17] William Waldegrave said, 'I would resist strongly the idea that they have any systematic party political bias. I think all political programmes have an inherent sort of fifth-estate-assumed, constitutional idea that they have to question the government. Governments get a harder time than oppositions in all programmes.'[18]

Those further on the right, like many grassroots Tory activists, have in the past been suspicious of the programme, just as they have been about the BBC in general. There is less antagonism now, with both the Tory leadership and a BBC culture less partisan and more consensual in approach. But there have been some famous recent attacks, notably that of the abrasive Brian Mawhinney when he accused 'Today' presenters of asking 'smeary' questions. It happened on 17 April 1996, on the day the Tories launched their manifesto for the local elections in England. The interview with Sue MacGregor went as follows:

MAWHINNEY: I grant you that these local elections will be a challenge, because we are defending seats which we won four years ago in the immediate aftermath of the General Election victory, when we were running, if my memory serves me right, about 10 per cent ahead of the Labour Party so, yes, they will be a challenge.

MACGREGOR: Now you're behind the Lib Dems. In 1990 you did something dramatic, you got rid of the poll tax, you also got rid of Mrs Thatcher – aren't you going to have to do something as dramatic as that not to lose a lot more seats?

MAWHINNEY: Oh come on, Sue, let's stay in the real world, can we?

MACGREGOR: Well, I hope I'm talking about the real world.

MAWHINNEY: What you have just suggested to me, in front of the nation, is that we should dump the Prime Minister. Don't be ridiculous, Sue, that isn't even worthy of an answer.

MACGREGOR: I wasn't suggesting you should dump the Prime Minister, I was saying dramatic gestures sometimes work.

MAWHINNEY: On the contrary, you drew the parallel with Mrs Thatcher and that is a ludicrous and indefensible question and if you think I'm annoyed with you it is because that is the kind of smeary question by 'Today' programme presenters which so annoys people who listen to this programme up and down the country.

MACGREGOR: Dr Mawhinney, thank you.

I found nobody who was prepared to agree with Mawhinney's accusation, either on or off the record. Most regarded it as a bilious outburst from an Ulsterman with a notoriously short fuse. For the *Independent*, it 'confirmed his reputation as a short-tempered bruiser'.[19] Lilley made a comment which spoke for itself, 'You throw your audience away the minute you start getting angry with your interviewer.'[20] Stephen Dorrell also administered what seemed like a clear rebuke when he said:

Certainly politicians are sometimes asked questions that have a spin on them, but they should be quite capable of looking after themselves and replying with a spin on their answers ... People don't like being challenged and having their judgement questioned, but I think it's actually part of being a democratic politician.[21]

The closest I heard in support of the possible ideas *behind* Mawhinney's anger came from Lilley:

The real way to tell what people think is not to ask them what they think, but see what their questions and statements presuppose, what they assume without thinking. I would think that their general presuppositions and unspoken assumptions tend to be politically correct and left of centre and that's a general BBC view. For example, if you took most people in the BBC and ask what they think about hanging, the vast majority would be against it. It so happens I'm against it too, but neither they nor I would be at all typical of the world outside. Outside, three-quarters would favour it. So they have certain in-house views that would not necessarily be the average of the population as a whole, or represent the spectrum of views of the population as a whole, but [which are] politically correct. To the extent they are aware of that, they'll try and compensate. Particularly Naughtie, you can hear Naughtie trying to make his questions even-handed, which sometimes makes them too long.[22]

Naughtie gracefully acknowledged this:

They're certainly sometimes too long. I think that's an accurate assessment which editors would agree with. Trying to be even-handed? Trying to be fair, but not to the point where the thing becomes exaggeratedly on-the-one-hand-on-the-other, because then you lose the thread or the edge of the interview. I think I'm quite conscious of wanting to be in a position afterwards where nobody can say, 'That was an unfair, inconsistent position you adopted; you weren't actually trying to find anything out, you were playing games.'[23]

Responding to Lilley's comments, Tony Hall, Chief Executive of BBC News, eventually conceded that 'most' people in the BBC would be against capital punishment. He also said:

It's the old shot, which is 'You all read the *Guardian*, you're all pinkos,' which we've heard for ten or more years from some parts of the Conservative Party. It's not true ... he's looking at it [attitudes within the BBC] from the mindset of a person in government who, *because* he is in government, is having his every action scrutinised by the press and broadcasters and is probably wondering, 'Why is it these people are always asking me these questions about what I'm doing, why don't they give an equally rough time to the Opposition or to pressure groups?'[24]

Lilley didn't think, however, that what he saw as the vaguely leftish personality of the programme was a cause for concern:

One can't complain too much about these things. Probably it

would be true to say that under Jack de Manio it was slightly Tory orientated. You have a period one way and then a period the other. Basically it's foolish for politicians to get too worked up about the media. As Enoch Powell said, that's like a ship's captain complaining about the sea. It's the medium in which we navigate and our job is to find ways of dealing with it. My three rules are a) always try to answer the question, b) try to rebut any false assumptions or if need be I will interrupt at the point of assumptions – that throws them – and c) most important of all, remain cool and courteous. You throw your audience away the minute you start getting angry with your interviewer just as they throw it away if they do the same with you.[25]

Politicians generally think that the motive for antagonistic questioning is to challenge government, rather than the right, though if you are a right-wing figure it is perhaps going to be hard to distinguish between the two. That should be seen as the background to Woodrow Wyatt's attack on the programme in 1990 – when he demanded to know how its presenters and producers voted – which followed the criticisms of 'Today' made by the Media Monitoring Unit. The Unit had been paid £1,500 by the *Daily Express* to listen to 'Today' over the course of a fortnight and concluded that it was guilty of numerous examples of left-wing bias. Time and again in researching this book I concluded that looking at 'Today' was a bit like looking at a stage production from the wings. If you stood on the right you would, quite literally, get a right-wing view of what was going on. If you go to the other side of the theatre you see things from a different perspective: you get a left-wing view. How you assess the programme therefore depends on where you position yourself. As Donald Dewar says about John Humphrys's interviewing, whether you like it or not depends on where you're looking from.

Virginia Bottomley, who talked of her irritation at not being able to get positive 'good news' stories about her department on the programme, does not however deduce from this that the programme is anti-Tory, only that it's anti-government, and, like so much of the media, prefers to stir the pot of national controversy rather than report things straightforwardly. She said, 'I would separate sharply between the frustrations of not being able to go on "Today" and set out what the department's achievements are and saying the programme is no good. I think the programme is great.'[26] Indeed, she thought it was so great that she chose it as her luxury on 'Desert Island Discs' in 1993, a choice, she admits, that made most people call her a 'creep'.

Anna Ford expressed similar views:

> I hope that if Peter Lilley thinks there is left-wing bias at the BBC at the moment that if Labour are elected they will think there is right-wing bias in the BBC, and feel equally got at. Any government ought to feel got at. Harold Wilson was paranoid about the press. Lady Thatcher became paranoid about the press.[27]

And so too did David Blunkett: 'Government ministers, and God willing we will be them, have to put up with being questioned about what they're doing because they are the ones making the decisions as opposed to the ones criticising the decisions that are being made.'[28]

John Birt tried to put all this into perspective when he said early in 1997:

> The government of the day will always figure large in the life of any political programme. They're governing, they're doing things, they're negotiating with foreign governments, they're creating a budget. So when some Conservative politicians switch on the programme and hear ministers being tested they start to form a view that the BBC is in some way opposed to them, just as some Labour politicians did when there were Labour governments. You understand it from a human point of view.[29]

He also said about political coverage on 'Today':

> I've never argued that broadcasting can ignore the day-by-day disputation. It's a fact of life in politics ... 'Today' melds well with the parliamentary tradition ... and in its generally good-humoured way is as testing an experience for those politicians in broadcasting terms as standing on the floor of the House is for them.[30]

Birt did admit past mistakes, however. He conceded that even though Labour had been in opposition and thus questioning it was not of the same importance as questioning the government, it had still not been interrogated with sufficient rigour:

In that long period when the Labour Party was weak in the polls and didn't look like it was near to forming a government, I think sometimes that our style of journalism has been less interested than it should have been in explaining what opposition policies were and testing them. I don't think that's been true in recent years. I think we've been very rigorous and that has brought equivalent complaints sometimes from Labour politicians.[31]

He added, however, that these complaints, from whatever quarter, were usually in the form of 'grumbles at parties'. 'They bend my ear at social occasions,' he said. 'Given the importance the programme has for politicians, and there is no doubt that for most politicians it is the most important programme the BBC makes, they very rarely make any kind of formal complaint.'[32]

There are other dangers in the way the programme has evolved. Legitimate questions can be asked, for example, about the relationship between presenters and those they quiz. Redhead did masses of paid work for the Department of Trade and Industry and various big companies, which may help to explain how he was able to leave such a substantial sum (£675,000) in his will. Timpson hobnobbed with the great and good including Sir Martin Gilliat, Private Secretary to the Queen Mother, who, as we have seen, sent him fan mail from time to time. He lunched at Chevening with Sir Geoffrey and Lady Howe, went to Christmas drinks with the Chancellor, and to receptions at both 10 Downing Street and Buckingham Palace. Brian Redhead and Virginia Bottomley had a mutual interest in the hospice movement and John Humphrys and Lord Archer worked together on fund-raising for Macmillan Nurses, their friendship cemented in the invitation Humphrys received to Archer's Christmas party in 1996. Humphrys told me that he was then on first-name terms with every member of the former Cabinet, with the exception of John Major, whom he addressed as 'Prime Minister'.[33]

Humphrys freely admits that he did a great deal of media training up to the point when the BBC stopped it, following a critical article in the *Independent* in 1995:

I have trained for British Telecom, British Gas, British Steel, BP, you name it, but never politicians, ever, under any circumstances whatever, never South African arms salesmen or tobacco sales-men. Charities I didn't charge for. It was always a grey area. Some of my colleagues felt very strongly about it but I didn't, as it happens. I was quite glad [that the BBC clamped down] because it cut back some of my work and I did too much of it. They stopped it after the *Independent* did a big thing on it which resulted in a leader written, I suppose, by Ian Hargreaves, who was fairly puritanical about things generally when he was running BBC News and Current Affairs.

The situation now is that we can chair conferences and talk to a group of people and say this is what we expect of you and this is what you can expect from us. What we cannot do is practise interviews. I was actually quite relieved [when the BBC banned presenters from doing it] because it means that when people ring me up I can say, 'No, I'm not doing it any more,' which is rather nice, actually. I'm glad I stopped doing it, in short.[34]

The BBC does, however, expect any such conferences to be non-partisan, which is why Humphrys was admonished for chairing a meeting at Westminster convened by the teaching unions and where the only MPs were from the opposition parties. Humphrys also made this point about tax:

It does have to be remembered that we are freelances. If the BBC were to say to us, 'You may not do any outside work,' a number of consequences would flow from that. One of which is that the Inland Revenue would be frightfully interested. 'What do you mean, you're not freelancing? I thought you were freelance . . .'[35]

Sue MacGregor gave media training to Angus Stirling, then Director-General of the National Trust, and also to its Chairman and some of its senior staff, just before the organisation's high-profile centenary year in 1995. 'I also did some stuff for British Gas and other organisations. Not very much and I rather enjoyed it because it made you think about what you do as well as how they react to being interviewed. After there was this clampdown we all stopped. It's frowned on more than anything else, I think.'[36] Hobday did a lot of media training, too. But Naughtie, with his strong Presbyterian conscience, does not and will not do it: 'I've never done any [media training] and I wouldn't. I feel slightly uncomfortable about helping people to perform in interviews which you yourself may some day be conducting.'[37]

Partly because so many interviewees have now been expensively media-trained by broadcasters, they know the tricks – and this, as

John Timpson says, has meant that the interviewers have had to be yet more aggressive. This in turn can lead to the sort of interruptions for which 'Today' has sometimes become notorious. Politicians do not always mind this, as Peter Lilley explained:

There's no doubt the audience out there sympathise when you are a victim of hostile and interruptive interviewing. So it's quite useful as long as you retain your cool and remain courteous yourself. I've benefited from that. I was on the morning after Lady Thatcher's Keith Joseph Lecture and I was put up to speak for the government. They [those on the programme] were trying to argue Mrs T was attacking the Party and being divisive, and they were ignoring her head-on criticism of Blair. So I kept on saying why are you putting that meaning on it and ignoring her attacks on Blair, and I started quoting them. Humphrys made the mistake of continually interrupting and tried to stop me quoting her attacks on Blair. There were hordes of letters and even he admits that the weight of letters indicated that the public were on my side and not his. There was a rumpus about it in their letters spot and some of the newspapers took it up as well. It was tremendously to my advantage. It happened to be the day I was up for re-selection in my constituency and everybody was overjoyed at the way I had handled it, so I have no complaints. But I think since then John Humphrys has been ultra-polite to me.[38]

Politicians may be able to turn interruptions to their advantage – it is all part of the game to them – but listeners can find it irritating. Tony Hall admits:

The half of, or slightly less than the half of, the programme which is politics is confrontational, and usually the confrontation is in the right measure for the audience at that time in the morning. Sometimes it goes to the point when you get the famous spats, a lot more heat than common sense, and that's the yah-boo nature of politicians across the floor of the Commons which occasionally 'Today' reflects. I never enjoy it very much and the audience doesn't either.[39]

A memorable example of one of those famous spats came in 1992 just before that year's General Election, when Sue MacGregor recalls having to referee a discussion between Michael Howard and Jack Cunningham:

> They were talking about local government plans, as I recall, and they just sank their teeth into each other's necks, like fighting terriers. I found it impossible verbally to separate them. I wanted to shout at them but all my radio training, doubtless terribly old-fashioned now, said that when two people are yelling on radio you can't hear what either of them is saying and when three people are it's a cacophony. Much was made of it at the time in the press, who said that possibly a male interlocutor would have inserted himself more forcibly and shut them up earlier. I spoke to John about it and he said he wasn't sure he could have handled it any differently, though I suspect he was just being nice. He probably would have shouted and with hindsight I probably should have done. I wouldn't let that happen again. At an earlier stage I would yell, 'Gentlemen please!' or, 'Nobody can hear anything you're saying, let's just behave like civilised human beings,' or something. After all the yelling they shared a taxi back to the House of Commons, as politicians do.[40]

Donald Dewar, one of many other politicians who has shared a taxi back to the Commons with an opponent, agreed with the 'confrontational' tag. 'If you're on with Michael Portillo or Michael Heseltine or whoever, that is a head-to-head by definition. That's what you call it. It's obviously meant to be confrontational.'[41]

Virginia Bottomley, who not only takes her jacket off when squaring up to Humphrys but also her ear-rings, echoed Tony Hall's description of the programme. In addition, she thought that its approach might have distorted the public perception of politicians in general:

> It is confrontational. I know that the public don't like, on the whole, women being strident and assertive, but it's almost impossible as a politician to do the 'Today' programme without being strident and assertive and so I'm aware that there came a moment when a lot of people thought I was becoming very forceful. That's because it's like being a boxer. If you're constantly punched you have to sort of put yourself in a mode where you can punch back, otherwise you'll get completely rolled over. Therefore

I think it does create a perception of politicians that is slightly distorted. The only way you can survive on the programme is to be determined, aggressive and pugnacious and that's the side of politicians that the public don't much like. The in-house audience probably knows this is the way to cope, but I suspect that for the wider audience it makes us all seem less emollient and reasonable.[42]

Roger Gale, former 'Today' producer and now chairman of the Tory backbench media committee, has serious reservations about his old programme:

What they try and get is a nice scrap – confrontation radio. That's what it's about. I don't believe it's a very good way of getting across people's points of view. I listen now to Radio 5 Live, which may be tabloid radio but you don't hear the sound of the axes grinding so much. I'm not suggesting that politicians or football managers or indeed anyone else on Radio 5 Live don't have their own forcefully put points of view, but because 5 Live is not yet, and please God never will be, seen as the agenda-setting political programme, perhaps people feel the ability to be more honest, to answer questions more fully and don't feel the need to try and score political points the whole time. It's axiomatic that if you're a senior politician and you're invited on to the 'Today' programme you go in with your hackles already raised prepared to do battle with John Humphrys in the certain knowledge that if you don't talk quickly you'll be interrupted, so you use the John Prescott blunt instrument technique of just carrying on talking. I don't think it elucidates anything.[43]

Gale also made a general point about this kind of broadcasting culture:

I began my BBC broadcasting career as a local radio journalist, learning from highly polished professionals such as Godfrey Talbot and Alistair Cooke and Gerry Priestland, intellectually streets ahead, incisive but courteous. Today's young journalists on local radio are learning their trade from a lot of very rude people who are broadcasting on the national networks. It isn't the only way it can be done or should be done.[44]

Robin Cook came up with an elegant description of how and why the aggressive style has emerged:

Inevitably, and naturally, programmes do change over decades, because the stories they cover, the audiences they broadcast to and the politicians they deal with also change. The culture of society changes. I would say that I find the 'Today' programme inclined to be more combative than it was, say, ten years ago and that interviewers, particularly the anchorman John Humphrys, regard themselves as people who are not there to give the interviewee the opportunity to express a point of view, or indeed a story, but as participants in a fight. And it becomes a test of skill between interviewer and interviewee as to who comes out on top. There's a place for that and politicians should not be too wimpish in demanding a deferential interview, but I have sometimes felt in recent times that it has got to the point where it is no longer possible for the politician to communicate either what is a legitimate political point or what is actually the news story that got him the invitation on to the programme in the first place. They're interrupted too much and you disappear down byways and avenues.[45]

Not surprisingly, John Humphrys had a rather different way of looking at his role on the programme and, in particular, the charge that he saw himself as a gladiator of the airwaves:

I think they [politicians] do regard it as a contest, as a fight that goes to a number of rounds, as indeed they have to because they have to be seen to win often. But we don't have to be seen to win. All we have to be seen to do, though I'm not quite sure if the boxing metaphor works, is defend ourselves if, as occasionally happens, they try to land a low blow. We are there to get information, to challenge them, to test their argument. They're there to prove that they are right, but we are not there to prove that they are wrong.[46]

Confrontational as many think 'Today' is, however, Lord Archer says it is not the worst offender: 'There is a programme I won't go on where I think the interviewer is ill-mannered, discourteous and just downright too clever and I won't go on it for that reason. John Humphrys does not fall into that category and neither does Jim

Naughtie.'[47] When I said I could only think of Jeremy Paxman, Archer replied:

> Exactly. I think he's an ill-mannered lout and I've told him to his face. Once by mistake I got to the wrong programme when he was doing breakfast in the old days. I said to the producer, I apologise, I was determined never to appear with this man again, he is one of the most ill-mannered louts I've ever dealt with.[48]

Robin Cook also mentioned the long-running BBC2 series:

> This gladiatorial style is by no means confined to the 'Today' programme. It has become even more marked on 'Newsnight', for instance, the hallmark of Jeremy Paxman, but not only Jeremy Paxman, all the 'Newsnight' presenters do it. And Nick Clarke on 'The World at One' can be just as aggressive and interventionist as John Humphrys, so one is actually talking about a change across what is apparently the job description rules.[49]

Combative interviewing is welcomed by many politicians. It's what they're used to in the Commons, it sharpens their claws, it forces them to think on their feet and it gets them noticed by their peers. As Robin Cook says, 'I like the programme, I appear on it I think as often as anybody else and will continue to do so, because it is a good opportunity to get to the key political opinion formers and set up a story to run through the day.'[50] He is right about appearing on 'Today' as often as anyone else: indeed, he appeared more frequently than any other politician in the year October 1994–September 1995, followed by Malcolm Rifkind, Paddy Ashdown and Michael Howard.

But this kind of combat is often near to being a charade, because interviewee and interviewer can be great friends away from the studio – just as politicians of all sides are in the Commons. Consider this account from Lord Archer, who sees every appearance on the programme in terms of a duel:

> I remember one particular programme when Anna Ford was sitting next to us [John Humphrys and Lord Archer] and we were having a row about the way he had treated something Tony Newton [Leader of the House] had said. Tony Newton had made some statement and John Humphrys had said, 'Surely, Minister,

what matters is what the people *think*, not what is actually happening?' and I went on the next day and said, 'I know about your character, John Humphrys, you're the sort of man who thinks it's more important what people think than what's actually happening. That's what you said yesterday, you said it on this programme.' And he went, 'Well, that's not what I'm asking you today, Jeffrey, I'm asking you . . .' And I said, 'Well first and foremost let's get it clear, do you or do you not think what is important is how it's put or what you actually achieve?' and he said, 'Obviously I made a mistake,' and I said, 'Yes you did, now ask your question.' And Anna is going like this [Archer starts punching the air like a boxer squaring up to his opponent]. And as I left the show, and that one I won – I don't win them all but that one I won – Anna looked at us to see what would happen and John went, 'Now what I want to discuss with you about this charity auction, Jeffrey, is whether you would be free . . .' and she realised straight away that we get on very well. We're both professionals and we don't give a damn a split second afterwards.[51]

Interviews on 'Today', in other words, can be a sort of three-minute pantomime. As in the Commons, it is often a sophisticated but essentially artificial debate, with more than a touch of theatricality. The duellists all belong to the same charmed circle and sometimes, as we have seen, the interviewees have actually been trained by the interviewers – though not, it should be emphasised, by Naughtie – for a handsome fee, of course, to negotiate their way round difficult questions. All this no doubt was in Archer's mind when, three times to me, he described 'Today' interviews as sometimes being a 'total charade'.[52] For him the point of doing them is simple: you score points off your opponents and build up your reputation in the Party.

The other day I was on the programme doing the abolition of the Lords with Wedgwood Benn. And Tony said, 'Well, those apparatchiks in the Conservative Party are just about to give you a knighthood, John.' That was a gift. You don't get those that often. So when he said to me, 'Well Lord Archer, do you want to abolish the Lords?' I replied, 'Before we start John, I want to make it clear, with all the authority at my command, that we will *never* give you a knighthood.' He burst out laughing and before he could reply, I went on, 'But now, on the other hand, Baroness MacGregor has got a real ring about it,' and she laughed. And I'd got them on the run then, you see. I'd got Wedgwood Benn on the run and I'd got the other two on the run. Now I'm in command. I know I've got two-and-a-half minutes only and I've got them on the run. Humphrys is as sharp as a bloody razor and very fast on his feet but it's hard for him to come back, it's hard to get back in if there's two guests, because he's got to go to the other man.

Humour is *always* effective in politics if you can use it with a knife and if it's relevant to what's just been said. It has to sell a political point and the political point was that we would never give you a knighthood. Why? Because you're so bloody anti-Tory. All my Tory listeners are saying, 'Quite right, Jeffrey, kick him in the balls!' All the others are laughing. So I won both ways.[53]

But, as his colleague William Waldegrave so sagely says about all the politicians' views on the 'Today' programme: 'It's no good politicians complaining about it ['Today'] because politicians have made it. If politicians didn't go on it, it wouldn't be what it was. And we *do* go on it.'[54]

There is also the charge that the agenda for interviews is very limited, that interviewees are not asked a wide range of questions. The most troubling aspect of this is that listeners are never told what behind-the-scenes arrangements have been made. Michael Howard, for example, once appeared only on condition that he would not be asked about allegations that, while a junior DTI minister in 1987, he was involved in the decision to set up an inquiry into the Al-Fayeds' takeover of Harrods without declaring what was arguably a family interest. And Paddy Ashdown, after the disclosure that he had had an affair with his secretary, started his rehabilitation by returning to the airwaves with an interview on 'Today', done on condition that he would be asked only about Bosnia and not about his private life.

Another example is Lord Archer, who has never been asked about the furore over his purchase of Anglia Television shares, although it was the subject of a lengthy Whitehall inquiry, occupied the headlines for weeks, and prevented his return to government. Archer instructed his stockbrokers to buy 50,000 shares in Anglia the day after his wife, Mary, a non-executive Anglia director, had attended a board meeting which agreed a secret takeover deal. Five days later the bid was made public and the Anglia share price rose sharply. That day, Archer gave instructions for the shares – which had been bought in the name of a friend – to be sold, yielding a profit for his friend of £80,000. After a five-month DTI inquiry into alleged insider dealing, Michael Heseltine, then Secretary of State, decided to take no action against Archer, who always denied any impropriety and pointed out that he had derived no benefit from the transaction. Later he did, however, apologise for what he agreed was his 'grave error' in embarrassing his wife, who early in 1995 resigned from the board of Anglia TV.

Perhaps BBC interviewers thought that Archer would simply walk out if they broached this subject. Indeed, some, such as Radio 2's Derek Jameson, were told that the subject was off-limits. But perhaps they ought at least to have *tried*, because Archer *is* prepared to talk about it – as his comments show:

> I may be kidding myself, but most interviewers knew it was a farce. Peter Snow said, 'I've read the details, it's a farce, how did it ever reach that stage?' and I said, 'Well, it was just a piece of bad luck and bad timing.' Most of them saw the clearance [the DTI press release exonerating him of fraud] and they wouldn't touch it. I earn £4 million a year. Would I really risk my whole career? It was a farce. If it had been for £20 million I could have understood, but I earn £10,000 a day sitting still chatting to you.[55]

Archer feels the Anglia affair prevented his return to government and deprived him of a place in the Cabinet:

> The DTI sent a letter of complete clearance but it was too late. I'd lost the chance. I was going to get Heritage and Dorrell suddenly got Heritage at the last moment. He never enjoyed it from the moment he was there to the moment he left. I would have loved it. He was doing theatre, arts and sport and he didn't even know the colours Manchester United play in. I know the colours Bristol Rovers play in. It would have been made for me.[56]

Now this may or may not satisfy those who thought Archer was guilty of insider dealing. But it *is* a response. It has never been heard on the 'Today' programme, however, or any other programme. Perhaps interviewers could at times be a bit more curious.

The most remarkable item about itself that the programme has broadcast in recent years concerned its role, unlikely as this may sound, in a nuclear holocaust. Peter Hennessy, a highly respected former Whitehall journalist with *The Times*, and the main presenter of Radio 4's 'Analysis' from 1986 to 1992, published a book,[57] in the preface of which he claimed that 'the final check the commander of a Royal Navy Polaris or Trident submarine would make deep under the waters of the North Atlantic to determine whether a United Kingdom still existed before opening his sealed orders on retaliation after a pre-emptive nuclear strike would be to tune in to the Radio Four "Today" programme.' Hennessy, now Professor of Contemporary History at Queen Mary and Westfield College, University of London, went on, 'If after a highly secret number of days there is no Jim Naughtie, John Humphrys, Anna Ford or Peter Hobday, those last instructions from a by now deceased Prime Minister will be opened – a final if macabre tribute to a broadcasting service *sans pareil.*'

So the absence of 'Today' from the airwaves is the final trigger of Armageddon? The programme could hardly fail to take an interest in this unexpected revelation of its key role in national survival. Hennessy appeared on the programme and told John Humphrys how this proved what a vital programme 'Today' really was, and so on. Humphrys seemed to have left his scepticism at home that morning, for he failed to ask if there was a shred of evidence for these startling claims. The temptation not to do so was presumably just too great: it was wonderful publicity for the programme. (And also for the book, on a programme not noted for giving books free plugs.)

When I contacted Hennessy to ask him what evidence he had for his completely unsupported assertion, he said he could not produce any and declined to say anything about those who had allegedly told him. 'I can't tell you who they are. But they are people that don't lie to me. I've been a journalist long enough to know when people are bullshitting me.'[58] He claimed that the submarine would release to the surface a buoy which would have on it an aerial capable of picking up very low frequency signals sent from a transmitter outside Rugby, 'near the main London railway line'. He said this was all very secret.

Tony Hall seemed faintly sceptical:

There were at some point all sorts of arrangements for broadcasting in times of emergency and there aren't such plans now. I've never heard of the 'Today' programme being the final thing we have to keep going because submarines would know all was well.

I've never heard that before. I thought it was quite a nice story but I assumed he had some sort of hard evidence for it.[59]

Kenneth Clarke seemed more than faintly sceptical:

If I was a nuclear submarine commander, realising the time had come to press the button, much as I love the 'Today' programme, the last thing I'd wish to know was whether the 'Today' programme was on or not. I have no idea what the last thing a submarine commander does before he presses the button. I've never been trained as one. I can't think what I would particularly wish to do if I was told to press the nuclear button. The 'Today' programme might make my top ten, I don't know, but I doubt it would be the first thing I'd think of. If the 'Today' programme is not on the air, this is calamity? The time has come to end it all? It's news to me.[60]

Now Hennessy's stature as a Whitehall analyst is considerable, and books such as *The Hidden Wiring* have done much to enhance his reputation as a constitutional pundit with a deep understanding of Britain's governmental machinery. But he would surely be the first to agree, as a historian, that it is unwise to believe something simply because one wise man says it is true. It is at least possible that his sources garnished the story for his amusement, knowing it would never be traced back to them. One final point about Hennessy's extraordinary claim is this: his preface is dated May 1996, more than a month after Hobday was last heard on 'Today'. It is just as well that those responsible for firing our nuclear missiles have not paid too much attention to his absence from the programme.

'Today' has the most upmarket audience of all the BBC's news and current affairs programmes on either radio or television: 46 per cent of its listeners are in the AB social grades, compared with 44 per cent for 'PM', 42 per cent for 'The World this Weekend', 41 per cent for 'The World at One', 39 per cent for 'The World Tonight', 24 per cent for BBC2's 'Newsnight', 23 per cent for BBC1's 'Breakfast News', 21 per cent for BBC1's 'Nine O'Clock News' and 20 per cent for BBC1's 'Six O'Clock News'. The age profile of the programme is slightly younger than Radio 4 as a whole, though even in the period when it attracts its youngest audience, which is from 7.30 to 8 am, only 29 per cent are 44 and under (compared with the Radio 4 average of 24 per cent) compared with 47 per cent who are 55 and above.[61]

The BBC itself calls 'Today' 'Radio 4's flagship programme'[62] and John Birt calls it 'a major landmark in broadcasting'.[63] Its traditional appeal and enduring ethos was nimbly expressed by Anna Ford:

> It appeals to busy, high-powered thinking people in a number of professions and walks of life. People who are doing all sorts of things, who want to be informed about what's going on and have got time to listen while they're doing other things. They can't be glued to the television set because they're moving around, they're in their car, they're going to work. It negates the necessity of reading all the newspapers because you have them read to you, and you have the major issues gutted and put to you in a different light, with people on either side arguing their point of view. So I think it's a wonderful way of summarising everything that's happening, and you feel bang up to date if you listen to the 'Today' programme, and one of the things about radio for me is that I remember what I hear on the radio far more than I remember what I see on television.[64]

Clearly this is a personal opinion, but I think most listeners would agree with the assessment of William Waldegrave, a former Fellow of All Souls, that 'it's a well-run programme, a good programme, subject to all the changes and difficulties of a programme prepared in the middle of the night . . . an alpha programme which occasionally lapses into beta.'[65] It is up to us as well as the BBC to ensure that it remains largely in the alpha category and that lapses into beta are as infrequent as possible. Listeners' letters are always noticed, and the Social Market Foundation report shows that outside arguments, cogently expressed, can also have an influence.

John Birt is a strong defender of the programme:

> It's great fun to wake up to. You look forward to switching on your radio in the morning, in part because of the character of the people that are there. They are jolly, they are spirited, they're cheerful, all the things that one isn't necessarily oneself when one wakes up. They are a group of people you are happy to spend time with, and I think that is an understated achievement of the programme. It is a friend to the listener.[66]

There is an echo here of a shrewd point made by Will Wyatt, Chief Executive of BBC Broadcast:

> The people who present the programmes do not just introduce them or carry out the function of saying the necessary words; in the audience's mind they assume ownership. They are not just identified with a programme, they are its identity.[67]

Though this final chapter has aired some of the criticisms made of the programme in recent years, and raised questions about it – and any national institution should be examined in this way, particularly at the time of an anniversary – this book is intended as a tribute to the presenters and all their behind-the-scenes colleagues on a programme which gives much pleasure. The cheerful dawn caucus deserves its birthday party. Over four decades they and their predecessors have sent countless millions off to work or launched them on the business of the day in the realisation that, to quote the mathematician Professor John Taylor, 'the world will not blow up today, even if it might tomorrow.'[68]

Notes

WAC stands for the BBC's Written Archives Centre, Caversham.

1   Nothing Too Long for People on the Move

1 Article in *Radio Times* (27 September 1957).
2 Robin Day, *Grand Inquisitor*, vol.2 (Weidenfeld & Nicolson, 1989), pp.72–7.
3 Interview with the author, 9 January 1997.
4 Interview with the author, 29 September 1996.
5 Letter to Alan's daughter Amanda Skempton, 26 March 1994.
6 Memo from Isa Benzie to Janet Quigley, 21 August 1957, WAC.
7 Memo from Benzie, 3 October 1957, WAC.
8 Memo from Benzie to Janet Quigley, 9 October 1957, WAC.
9 Headed 'Comments on Today', 28 October 1957, WAC.
10 For de Manio's own wry, contrite and funny account of this, see his memoirs, *To Auntie With Love* (Hutchinson, 1967).
11 28 July 1958, WAC.
12 13 August 1958, WAC.

2   Jolly Jack

1 Nigel Andrew, *Radio Times* (1987); later quoted by Asa Briggs in *The History of Broadcasting in the United Kingdom*, vol. v (Oxford University Press, 1995), p.223.
2 Robin Day, *Grand Inquisitor*, vol.2 (Weidenfeld & Nicolson, 1989), p.77.

3 8 April 1963, WAC.

4 Interview with the author, 24 October 1996.

5 *Sunday Times* (30 October 1988).

6 Letter to the author, 4 October 1996.

7 Interview with the author, 25 September 1996.

8 Unpublished memoir of Rees's radio days, made available to the author in September 1996.

9 File R51/1, 297/2, WAC.

10 Ibid.

11 Ibid.

12 From John Lade, Chief Assistant (Music) Gramophone Programmes to the editor of 'Today', 16 October 1967; held in File R51/1, 297/2, WAC.

13 Quoted in a memo from Gerard Mansell, Controller of Radio 4 (who had apparently received a letter of complaint) to Stephen Bonarjee, 7 August 1968; held in File R51/1, 297/1, WAC.

14 File R51/1, 297/1, WAC.

15 File R51/1, 297/3, WAC.

16 Interview with the author, 25 September 1996.

17 File R51/1, 297/1, WAC.

18 File RCONT12, Jack de Manio 1970–1, 29 January 1970, WAC.

19 File R51/1, 297/3, 7 August 1970, WAC.

20 File RCONT12, Jack de Manio 1970–1, 14 June 1971, WAC.

21 File RCONT12, Jack de Manio 1970–1, 15 June 1971, WAC.

22 File RCONT12, Jack de Manio 1970–1, 22 June 1971, WAC.

23 File RCONT12, Jack de Manio 1970–1, 1 December 1970, WAC.

24 File RCONT12, Jack de Manio 1970–1, 2 December 1970, WAC.

25 File R51/1,000/11, 3 September 1963, WAC.

26 File R51/1,000/11, 31 October 1963; the figures were worked out by Diana Greenhalgh in the 'Today' office.

27 File R51/1,297/2, 16 May 1967, WAC.

28 Ibid.

29 File R51/1,297/2, 8 August 1967, WAC.

30 File R51/1,297/1, 14 February 1968, WAC.

31 File R51/1,297/1, 10 December 1969, WAC.

32 *World's Press News* (15 May 1959).

33 *Smith's Trade News* (16 May 1959).

34 Ibid.

35 The results are similar for both bulletins, with one exception. The *Financial Times* is quoted twice as often as the *Daily Star* on the 6.40 am bulletin, but an hour later the roles are reversed and the *Daily Star*

is quoted twice as often as the *FT*. The BBC says this is simply fortuitous, and adds that the *FT* is mentioned much less than the other broadsheets because it is a specialist, financial organ and that the *Daily Star* is mentioned much less than the other tabloids because 'it is more of an entertainment paper than a news paper'. It is noticeable that the communist-allied *Morning Star* and the soft-porn *Daily Sport* are two national papers never mentioned at all: they are not considered to be mainstream publications.

36 Interview with the author, 13 November 1996.
37 Interview with the author, 21 November 1996.
38 Interview with the author, 24 February 1997.

3   The Man with a Chuckle in His Voice

1 File R51/1,000/11, 14 August 1964, WAC.
2 Interview with the author, 14 October 1996.
3 Letter to John Timpson, 29 February 1984.
4 Interview with the author, 20 January 1997.
5 File R51/1,000/11, 11 March 1963, WAC.
6 Interview with the author, 7 November 1996.
7 Interview with the author, 21 February 1997.
8 *News of the World* (21 March 1971).
9 File RCONT12, Jack de Manio 1970–1, 14 June 1971, WAC.
10 File R51/1,297/3, 17 June 1971, WAC.
11 File RCONT12, Jack de Manio 1970–1, 13 July 1971, WAC.
12 *Evening News* (8 September 1978).
13 Interview with the author, 19 January 1997.
14 In his book *Today and Yesterday* (Allen & Unwin, 1976), p.143.
15 Interview with the author, 19 January 1997.
16 Interview with the author, 25 September 1996.
17 Interview with the author, 2 December 1996.
18 Ibid.
19 Ibid.
20 Note to the author, 18 December 1996.
21 File R51/1,297/3, 30 December 1970, WAC.
22 Interview with the author, 14 October 1996.
23 File R51/1,297/3, 15 March 1973, WAC.
24 File R51/1,297/3, 15 August 1973, WAC.
25 File R51/1,297/3, 12 September 1973, WAC.
26 Letter to John Timpson, 26 October 1973.

27 Interview with the author, 19 January 1997.
28 File R51/1,297/3, 2 December 1974, WAC.

4 'This Perfect and Unbeatable Duo'

1 Interview with the author, 14 October 1996.
2 'Today', 24 January 1994.
3 Interview with the author, 25 September 1996.
4 Interview with the author, 14 October 1996.
5 Interview with the author, 25 September 1996.
6 Unpublished memoir about Rees's radio days, made available to the author in September 1996.
7 Interview with the author, 25 September 1996.
8 Ibid.
9 Interview with the author, 8 January 1997.
10 Ibid.
11 Ibid.
12 Speech to the Radio Festival, Birmingham, July 1993.
13 Interview with the author, 19 January 1997.
14 Interview with the author, 14 October 1996.
15 Ibid.
16 Interview with the author, 8 January 1997.
17 Interview with the author, 25 September 1996.
18 Ibid.
19 Interview with the author, 8 January 1997.
20 Ibid.
21 Interview with the author, 25 September 1996.
22 Speaking to Michael Parkinson on 'Desert Island Discs', 6 July 1986.
23 *Evening Standard* (3 July 1978).
24 *Evening Standard* (c. February 1983).
25 *The Times* (22 July 1978).
26 *Sunday Times* (13 August 1978).
27 *Northampton Mercury and Herald* (10 August 1978).
28 Interview with the author, 25 September 1996.
29 *Sun* (24 June 1982).
30 Interview with the author, 25 September 1996.
31 Interview with the author, 12 February 1997.
32 Letter from Monica Sims to John Timpson, 25 January 1983.
33 *Daily Telegraph* (1983).
34 Memo dated 9 May 1983.

35 *Evening Standard* (14 January 1983).
36 *Guardian* (c. February, 1983).
37 *Listener* (17 February 1983).
38 *Daily Express* (23 March 1983).
39 *Daily Express* (c. March, 1983).
40 *The Times* (c. March, 1983).
41 *The Times* (16 April 1983).
42 *The Times* obituary for Brian Redhead (24 January 1994).
43 Quoted by John Humphrys in Radio 4's obituary programme, broadcast on 23 January 1994.
44 In Brussels, 9 February 1989.
45 Interview with the author, 24 February 1997.
46 Interview with the author, 27 November 1996.
47 Interview with the author, 28 November 1996.
48 'Today', 24 January 1994.
49 Interview with the author, 27 November 1996.
50 Interview with the author, 28 November 1996.
51 Interview with the author, 14 October 1996.
52 Interview with the author, 13 December 1996.
53 *Birmingham Post* (24 March 1984).
54 *Radio Times* (5 July 1980).
55 BBC Broadcasting Research Listening Panel Report for the week of 28 May–1 June 1984.
56 *Daily Telegraph* (21 June 1986).
57 *The Times* (16 April 1983).
58 'Today', 24 January 1994.
59 Interview with the author, 20 January 1997.
60 Interview with the author, 14 October 1996.
61 John Timpson, *The Lighter Side of Today* (Allen & Unwin), 1983.
62 Interview with the author, 14 October 1996.
63 Ibid.
64 *Sunday Telegraph* (21 December 1986).
65 *Glasgow Herald* (17 December 1986).
66 Letter to John Timpson, 24 December 1986.
67 *Daily Mail* (28 December 1983).
68 *Sunday Times* (8 December 1991).
69 Interview with the author, 19 December 1996.
70 Ibid.
71 Ibid.
72 Interview with the author, 21 February 1997.
73 *Church Times* (27 December 1996).

5 Storms in the Studio

1 Interview with the author, 21 November 1996.
2 Ibid.
3 Interview with the author, 4 December 1996.
4 *Sunday Times* (29 May 1988).
5 Interview with the author, 4 December 1996.
6 Ibid.
7 Ibid.
8 Interview with the author, 13 December 1996.
9 Interview with the author, 21 November 1996.
10 Interview with the author, 26 November 1996.
11 Ibid.
12 Ibid.
13 Interview with the author, 12 February 1997.
14 *The Times* (25 January 1994).
15 *Sunday Times* (23 June 1985).
16 Interview with the author, 7 November 1996.
17 Interview with the author, 21 November 1996.
18 Interview with the author, 14 October 1996.
19 Interview with the author, 12 February 1997.
20 *Guardian* (1986).
21 Letter to the author, 20 October 1996.
22 Interview with the author, 20 January 1997.
23 *The Times* (28 December 1989).
24 Brussels, 9 February 1989.
25 Interview with the author, 28 November 1996.
26 Ibid.
27 Interview with the author, 13 December 1996.
28 Interview with the author, 14 October 1996.
29 Interview with the author, 24 October 1997.
30 Interview with the author, 7 November 1996.
31 Interview with the author, 4 November 1996.
32 Interview with the author, 28 November 1996.
33 From his posthumous anthology *Personal Perspectives* (André Deutsch, 1994).
34 Interview with the author, 26 November 1996.
35 Interview with the author, 31 October 1996.
36 Interview with the author, 17 October 1996.
37 Interview with the author, 21 November 1996.
38 Interview with the author, 13 December 1996.

39 Interview with the author, 4 November 1996.
40 Ibid.
41 Interview with the author, 2 December 1996.
42 Interview with the author, 4 December 1996.
43 *Sunday Times* (11 December 1988).
44 'Today', 24 January 1994.
45 *Kill the Messenger* (HarperCollins, 1991).
46 *Sunday Times* (7 March 1993).
47 Interview with the author, 20 January 1997.
48 *Sunday Times* (22 December 1991).
49 *Church Times* (27 December 1991).
50 Interview with the author, 16 October 1996.
51 Interview with the author, 13 December 1996.
52 Released on 24 January 1994.
53 Interview with the author, 28 November 1996.
54 Interview with the author, 13 December 1996.
55 Letter dated 25 January 1994.
56 *The Times* (24 January 1994).
57 Interview with the author, 5 February 1997.
58 *Independent on Sunday* (10 November 1996).
59 *Daily Telegraph* (9 November 1996).
60 Addressing the Radio Academy News and Speech Conference, 23 October 1996.
61 Interview with the author, 4 December 1996.
62 Interview with the author, 20 January 1997.
63 Interview with the author, 15 January 1997.
64 Ibid.
65 *Reader's Digest* (June 1986).
66 Interview with the author, 24 October 1996.
67 Interview with the author, 19 December 1996.
68 Ibid.

6   Hirings, Firings, Status and Journalism

1 Interview with the author, 7 November 1996.
2 Written in February 1993 and a summary shown to the author.
3 Ibid.
4 Interview with the author, 2 December 1996.
5 Letter from Tony Hall to the author, 11 December 1996.
6 Interview with the author, 4 December 1996.

7 *Sunday Times Magazine* (30 June 1996).
8 Interview with the author, 2 December 1996.
9 Interview with the author, 4 December 1996.
10 Interview with the author, 20 January 1997.
11 Interview with the author, 19 December 1996.
12 Interview with the author, 4 December 1996.
13 Interview with the author, 21 February 1997.
14 Interview with the author, 17 January 1997.
15 Ibid.
16 Ibid.
17 Interview with the author, 5 February 1997.
18 Interview with the author, 17 January 1997.
19 Interview with the author, 15 October 1996.
20 Interview with the author, 17 January 1997.
21 Ibid.
22 Interview with the author, 20 January 1997.
23 BBC Programme Complaints Bulletin, October 1996.
24 Interview with the author, 20 January 1997.
25 Ibid.
26 Interview with the author, 31 October 1996.
27 Letter to *Ariel*, the BBC's newspaper, 8 October 1996.
28 'Today', 1 April 1997. The report in *The Times* the next day was headlined: 'Archers villain prompts farmyard slip by Ford.'
29 Interview with the author, 17 January 1997.
30 Ibid.
31 Ibid.
32 Interview with the author, 24 October 1996.
33 Interview with the author, 5 February 1997.
34 Ibid.
35 Interview with the author, 15 October 1996.
36 Interview with the author, 31 October 1996.
37 Interview with the author, 20 January 1997.
38 Interview with the author, 11 December 1996.
39 Interview with the author, 28 November 1996.
40 *Sunday Telegraph* (29 September 1996).
41 Interview with the author, 14 October 1996.
42 Interview with the author, 13 November 1996.
43 Interview with the author, 7 November 1996.
44 Interview with the author, 2 December 1996.
45 Interview with the author, 16 October 1996.
46 Interview with the author, 18 November 1996.

47 Interview with the author, 21 February 1997.
48 Ibid.
49 Interview with the author, 20 January 1997.
50 Interview with the author, 21 February 1997.
51 Interview with the author, 11 December 1996.
52 Interview with the author, 26 November 1996.
53 Ibid.
54 Ibid.
55 *Evening Standard* (12 October 1995).
56 Ibid.
57 Interview with the author, 2 December 1996.
58 Interview with the author, 4 November 1996.
59 Interview with the author, 11 December 1996.
60 Interview with the author, 20 January 1997.
61 Interview with the author, 5 February 1997.
62 *Daily Telegraph* (2 March 1996).
63 *The Times* (2 March 1996).
64 Interview with the author, 21 November 1996.
65 Interview with the author, 2 December 1996.
66 Ibid.
67 Ibid.
68 Interview with the author, 14 October 1996.
69 Interview with the author, 12 February 1997.
70 Ibid.
71 Interview with the author, 23 January 1997.
72 Interview with the author, 2 December 1996.
73 Interview with the author, 21 February 1997.

7   The Breakfast Pulpit

1 Kenneth M. Wolfe, *The Churches and the British Broadcasting Corporation, 1922–56* (SCM Press, 1984), p.310.
2 *Church Times* (19 October 1990).
3 Interview with the author, 24 October 1996.
4 Interview with the author, 13 November 1996.
5 Interview with the author, 19 December 1996.
6 Interview with the author, 11 December 1996.
7 Interview with the author, 31 October 1996.
8 Interview with the author, 20 January 1997.

9 Rev. Ernest Rea, *Church Times* (19 October 1990); reiterated in letter to *The Times* (19 October 1996).

10 Rea, *Church Times* (19 October 1990).

11 Interview with the author, 27 November 1996.

12 Letter to the author, 20 October 1996.

13 Interview with the author, 6 December 1996.

14 Interview with the author, 27 November 1996.

15 Interview with the author, 6 December 1996.

16 Ibid.

17 Interview with the author, 27 November 1996.

18 Interview with the author, 6 December 1996.

19 Ibid.

20 Ibid.

21 Ibid.

22 Interview with the author, 28 November 1996.

23 Interview with the author, 27 November 1996.

24 Interview with the author, 25 October 1996.

25 Ibid.

26 Interview with the author, 6 December 1996.

27 Interview with the author, 7 November 1996.

28 Ibid.

29 Interview with the author, 6 December 1996.

30 Letter to the author, 20 October 1996.

31 Letter to the author, 1 November 1996.

32 Ibid.

33 *Religious Broadcasting* (BBC, 1975).

34 Interview with the author, 21 November 1996.

35 Interview with the author, 27 November 1996.

36 Ibid.

37 Ibid.

38 Ibid.

39 Interview with the author, 28 November 1996.

40 Ibid.

41 Interview with the author, 7 November 1996.

42 BBC Programme Complaints Bulletin, October 1996.

43 Rea, *Church Times* (19 October 1990).

44 Ibid.

45 Letter to *The Times* (11 May 1996).

46 Ibid.

47 Interview with the author, 27 November 1996.

48 Ibid.

49 Letter to the author, 20 October 1996.
50 *Daily Mail* (27 April 1996).
51 *Financial Times* (27 April 1996).
52 Interview with the author, 5 November 1996.
53 *Guardian* (23 December 1996).
54 *The Times* (12 October 1996).
55 Ibid.
56 Interview with the author, 27 November 1996.
57 *Evening Standard* (20 December 1996).
58 *Sunday Times* (29 December 1996).
59 *Independent* (28 December 1996).
60 *Daily Mail* (11 October 1996).
61 *Sunday Times* (22 December 1996).
62 *Evening Standard* (11 October 1996).
63 Letter to *The Times* (19 October 1996).
64 Letter to *The Times* (16 October 1996).
65 *Evening Standard* (17 October 1996).
66 Interview with the author, 5 November 1996.
67 Interview with the author, 6 December 1996.
68 Wolfe, *The Churches and the BBC*, p.467.
69 *Church Times* (30 December 1994).
70 Interview with the author, 9 December 1994.
71 *Sunday Times* (9 April 1995).
72 Letter to *The Times* (27 April 1996).
73 Interview with the author, 21 February 1997.

9   Morning Miscellany to Morning Macho

1 Interview with the author, 4 November 1996.
2 Interview with the author, 5 November 1996.
3 Interview with the author, 11 December 1996.
4 Interview with the author, 18 November 1996.
5 Interview with the author, 11 December 1996.
6 Interview with the author, 19 December 1996.
7 Ibid.
8 Ditchley Foundation Lecture, 12 July 1996.
9 Interview with the author, 31 October 1996.
10 Ibid.
11 Interview with the author, 13 November 1996.
12 Interview with the author, 15 October 1996.

13 Interview with the author, 24 October 1996.
14 Interview with the author, 7 November 1996.
15 Interview with the author, 2 October 1996.
16 Interview with the author, 16 October 1996.
17 Interview with the author, 4 November 1996.
18 Interview with the author, 11 December 1996.
19 *Independent* (24 April 1996).
20 Interview with the author, 4 November 1996.
21 Interview with the author, 16 October 1996.
22 Interview with the author, 4 November 1996.
23 Interview with the author, 5 February 1997.
24 Interview with the author, 2 December 1996.
25 Interview with the author, 4 November 1996.
26 Interview with the author, 31 October 1996.
27 Interview with the author, 17 January 1997.
28 Interview with the author, 15 October 1996.
29 Interview with the author, 21 February 1997.
30 Ibid.
31 Ibid.
32 Ibid.
33 Interview with the author, 26 November 1996.
34 Ibid.
35 Ibid.
36 Interview with the author, 4 December 1996.
37 Interview with the author, 5 February 1997.
38 Interview with the author, 4 November 1996.
39 Interview with the author, 2 December 1996.
40 Interview with the author, 4 December 1996.
41 Interview with the author, 18 November 1996.
42 Interview with the author, 31 October 1996.
43 Interview with the author, 4 November 1996.
44 Ibid.
45 Interview with the author, 19 December 1996.
46 Interview with the author, 26 November 1996.
47 Interview with the author, 24 October 1996.
48 Ibid.
49 Interview with the author, 19 December 1996.
50 Ibid.
51 Interview with the author, 24 October 1996.
52 Ibid.
53 Ibid.

54 Interview with the author, 11 December 1996.
55 Interview with the author, 24 October 1996.
56 Ibid.
57 Peter Hennessy, *Muddling Through* (Gollancz, 1996).
58 Interview with the author, 8 January 1997.
59 Interview with the author, 2 December 1996.
60 Interview with the author, 20 January 1997.
61 *Today*: demographic listening patterns and comparisons with other news programmes, BBC Network Radio Research and Analysis Team, November 1996.
62 In the public advertisement for its editor, 4 November 1996.
63 Interview with the author, 21 February 1997.
64 Interview with the author, 17 January 1997.
65 Interview with the author, 11 December 1996.
66 Interview with the author, 21 February 1997.
67 Royal Television Society Huw Wheldon Memorial Lecture, November 1996: he was talking about television presenters, but the comment applies equally to radio presenters, too.
68 *Listener* (1976).

Index

INDEX

MacGregor, Sue 201–2
Maxwell, Robert 159
May, Steve 114, 182, 187, 190
Mayer, Mrs 40–1
Media Monitoring Unit 204
Meyer, Sir Anthony 84
Michelmore, Cliff 82 Milligan,
    Spike 17
Mitchell, Austin 47, 96, 100, 117,
    133
New Statesman 199–201
Modlyn, Monty 29, 40
Monson, Jolyon 93–4, 150
Moore, Jo 200
Morley, John 8
Morley, Robert 17
'Morning Review' 2–6
Morris, Estelle 195
Mortimer, John 169
Morton, Andrew 113
Mosey, Roger 72, 85, 108–12,
    117–18, 122–3, 129, 138–44,
    146–8
    The Times 141
    'Thought for the Day' 168, 172
Mountbatten, Lord 17
Mullin, Chris 135–6
Muncaster, Claude 161
Muncaster, Martin 39
Murray, Jenni 91
Music Programme 38–9

National Pharmaceutical Union 17
National Secular Society 171
Naughtie, Humphrys, MacGregor
    relationship 118–21, 128
Naughtie, James (Jim) 47–8,
    117–18, 121, 131, 133, 138,
    144,181–2, 184–6, 188–90,
    197, 211
    Clarke, Kenneth 134, 184
    even-handedness 203
    foreign assignments 147
    Humphrys, John 118–21, 128,
    131–2
    MacGregor, Sue 118–21, 128
    media training 207, 213

Neil, Ron 93
Nelson, James 76
Nevin, Charles 79
New Statesman 199–200
Newbury, John 164
Newby, P.H. 7, 65
Newton, Tony 212
Nixon, Richard 53, 55
Norman, Barry 50, 61–2
North American Service 17
Nottingham Trent University 113
Nursing Times 183

Odone, Cristina 166
O'Neill, Hilary 180–3, 191
Osborne, Alistair 50, 55, 62
Oxford, Bishop of (Richard Harries)
    76–7, 84, 107, 152–4,157–8,
    162, 164–6, 169

Packe, Cathy 175, 177, 181
Parkinson, Michael 74
Paxman, Jeremy 133, 211–12
Pearce, Garth 75
Pearston, Anne 88
Pelletier, H. Rooney 12–14, 18–19
Pentecost, Professor Brian 188–9
Philip, Prince 88
Philpott, Trevor 32
Pienaar, Jon 186
Plomley, Roy 26, 49
Pope John Paul II 84
Portillo, Michael 180, 209
Potts, Lisa 87–8
Powell, Enoch 70, 204
Prescott, John 100, 135, 192–3, 210
père et fils 136–8
Press Association 196–7
Price, Andy 70
Priestland, Gerald (Gerry) 40–1,
    210
Private Eye 80, 155, 171
Profumo Affair 36, 41
Purves, Libby 25, 51, 58–62, 64–6,
    68, 93
    de Manio, Jack 31
    foreign assignments 68–70